Broken Rhapsody

Rüya 1

Neslihan Stamboli

CreateSpace
Charleston, SC

Copyright © 2015 Neslihan Stamboli

All rights reserved.

ISBN-13: 978-1514818220
ISBN-10: 1514818221

To the memory of my grandmother
Erzsébet de Kandó Egerfarmos Sztregova Marcali Bayındırlı
(4 April 1904 - 14 July 1966)

*Happiness is a moment's interval
between desire and sorrow.*
                    Gyula Krúdy

June 2004
Istanbul

"I've had far too much to eat," thought Rüya, with a weary sigh. This was what usually happened at family dinners. Her mother had overdone it, yet again, with her culinary skills and prepared enough food to feed an army. How many were they? Twenty-five? Thirty? Cousins, cousins once removed, cousins twice removed, aunts, sisters-in-law, the husband of the granddaughter of an aunt, the complete set. Sometimes she could hardly figure out who was who and how she should address them. There were those demanding that they be called by their first names despite their old age while others, ignoring their youth, insisted on respectful titles. Some firmly kept a formal distance, while others took excessive familiarity for amity. This eclectic group was only a modest part of her extended family, dispersed all over the world. Her mother, a meticulous organiser, more proficient than the best catering companies in town, had taken great pains to reach the farthest corners of the globe, from New York to Kabul, and invited almost every relative they had but, to her great disappointment, she could not realise the great family reunion she had been dreaming of for years. "Unfortunately," she kept complaining, "we're still missing a great number of people."

Rüya pushed her chair back, no longer able to persevere in her effort to finish the lamb chops getting cold on her plate. The guests had stuffed themselves from the buffet overflowing with known and not-so-very-well-known types of cold and hot appetisers, large and small bowls and platters of hot and even hotter dishes of all kinds, and were now slowly letting themselves drift into a sweetly satisfied after-dinner languor. Some had already reclined in deckchairs after opening a few of their buttons and discreetly lowering their zippers in the hope of relieving the gastronomic pressure they could no longer tolerate, while others paced the garden, assuming that exercise would bring a certain relief and open up some space for dessert. However, no lassitude of any kind could ever be powerful enough to stop this lot from chattering. Rüya slumped down on her chair, drained by their natter echoing in the quietness of the garden, an oasis among the pine trees despite the suffocating concrete apartment buildings around it. She felt the stickiness of the humid summer night gradually weighing down upon her.

She looked at her great-grandmother Alexandra, who, as always, was sitting with the young. Nobody called her Alexandra or Alex anymore, for she had long ago become Mami for everyone in the family, irrespective of their relation to her, as well as for those not related to her at all. She was sitting back on her chair, watching the guests, her hands peacefully resting on her lap and her soft lips gently curled in a warm smile, emanating an air of serenity. She had steadfastly refused to have the tables set on the veranda, although she knew that the nocturnal humidity would be unbearable without a cover over their heads. "I must see the night sky," she had insisted, so the tables had been set on the lawn. She was sitting at the long table, placed under the acacia tree near the wisteria-festooned garden wall as she had specifically requested. It might have seemed otherwise at times, but she was the one who held the reins in this house of Amazons, where she lived with her daughter Nili, granddaughter Aslı and her great-granddaughter Rüya.

Rüya turned her eyes up to the stars twinkling through the acacia leaves, restless even in a night as calm as this. Suddenly she saw a shooting star. "*Maradj velem,*" she whispered. Her sleepy eyes lingered on the sky for a little while longer as she gazed at the invisible track left by the long-gone star.

"What was that?" asked Attila from across the table.

Attila, her mother's cousin, was fifteen years older than Rüya, but she hardly felt the difference. He was one of her favourite relatives, although they did not get to see each other often enough. Always young at heart, with an insatiable desire for adventure, Attila had been spanning the globe as a journalist for years and currently worked in Kabul.

"That's what Mami says when she sees a shooting star. It's Hungarian."

"*Maradj velem,*" whispered Mami from her place at the head of the table, a subtle smile barely touching the edges of her lips as she gazed at the sky with her beautiful eyes, still a shimmering bluish-green like the transparent waters of a tropical sea, belying the ninety-four years they had left behind. For a brief moment she closed her eyes, took a deep breath as though she wished to take in all the stars, and then slowly opened them again. "Stay with me," she said under her breath.

"Rüya!"

Rüya snapped out of her involuntary torpor. Her grandmother Nili had unexpectedly stopped on her way to the kitchen with the plates she had cleared off the other two tables, set by the swimming pool giving on to the Bosphorus. "Rüya, dear! Stop watching the stars and finish up your food, please. It's getting really late now."

Rüya was a young woman of twenty-five, but her grandmother loved to treat her like a baby – when it suited her, that was. When it did not, she never hesitated to tell her off regularly with the same refrain: "Please do behave your age, darling. You're a young lady now."

"I've had enough, Grandma," Rüya retorted. "Please give me a break. Why don't you go and sit with the guests? We'll do all that later."

"Well, young lady, if we want to have some cake, we ought to clear the tables a bit, don't you think?"

The sarcastic tone her grandmother's voice took when she reproached her always irritated Rüya. Opening her long and skinny arms wide, she turned to Attila and, barely moving her tightened lips, hissed through her teeth. "Yes, but what's the hurry?" Her question was obviously addressed to her grandmother.

"What is the hurry? It's ten o'clock, for God's sake. People will be dozing off soon." Nili seemed determined to bring some order back to their house, which, from her point of view, must have looked in complete disarray. Scarlet and Chestnut, the Irish Setters, were circling around her, rubbing against her bright yellow dress, certain that they would have their share of what was left on the plates she was carrying so carefully. "Wait you naughty little girls! Wait a minute. Wait, I say!" Her voice had suddenly softened to a level of tenderness she never showed to people. She moved along with her beloved dogs towards the house, lightly hopping right and left, challenging the weight of her sixty-nine years.

Rüya turned to Attila and, hoping to start a conversation that would prevent the return of her disrupted after-dinner indolence, asked, "Well, my dearest birthday-boy Attila, how does it feel to be a forty-year old mature man?"

"Old."

"Are you planning to settle down in the near future?" she continued, knowing very well that she would be getting on his nerves, but perversely enjoying the tease.

"Are you?"

"I'm only twenty-five, for God's sake. And you ..." She raised her right eyebrow, no less arrogantly than her grandmother. "I should remind you yet again, in case you've forgotten, that you're forty years old today. Forty!" With a sweep of her arm, she guided his attention to the guests spread around the garden, as if to

3

remind him that all this commotion was a rite of passage leading to his adulthood.

"Nonetheless, I repeat my question, dearest Rüya: any hope of marriage within the next century? Sinan seems to be a very nice person. By the way, why isn't he here tonight?"

It must have been her grandmother who had told him to interrogate her on this subject. She had been pushing her too hard lately, continuously drumming into her that too much partying would only make her ill, and that it was high time she had found herself someone who might eventually prove to be a good husband.

"Why should he be here? This is only family. Can you see anyone around you who is not on our family tree?" Rüya's arm drew a half-circle that seemed to include not only the garden but the whole world.

"Do you know what your problem is, Rüya?"

"Do you think I have a problem?" she asked back, sensing that she was about to fall into her own trap and, without waiting for Attila's reply, continued, "I'd better go and help my mother prepare the cake."

As she walked towards the house, she tried to push Attila's question out of her mind. Various desserts had already been lined up on the buffet table set on the veranda. Her mother Aslı had embellished the menu, resolutely straining herself to make this night a perfect one with a sense of duty that allowed no room for pleasure. "How many different kinds of desserts can one eat?" she wondered, only to forget her qualms about stuffing herself, along with everything else that had been occupying her mind, when the *kadayif* bathed in syrup, accompanied by large dollops of clotted cream, caught her eye. She loved this infamous dessert affectionately prepared by Hatice, the good old cook, who humbly credited the recipe to Mami but nevertheless took great pride in her masterpiece, which was religiously worshipped by everyone including Mami herself – a rather surprising compliment since, being an excellent cook herself once, she had lately developed the habit of finding something wrong in every dish. Rüya extended her hand towards one of the towering piles of dessert plates, only to pull away the next second, cringing at the thought of her grandmother scolding her for indulging herself in a dessert before they cut the cake. She relented and reluctantly went inside.

"Hold it from the other side," she heard her mother giving orders in the kitchen. "You'll ruin it. Leave it. Leave it to me for Heaven's sake! I'll handle it much better by myself."

It sounded like a cake crisis at full blast. A lot of courage was required to go near her mother at a time like this. It was incredible how much energy she still had after having cooked with unremitting vigour for the last two days. Rüya detested her for being so ambitious. What was she trying to prove? And to whom? Everything should be perfect, she kept saying. What did perfect mean anyway? Perfect for whom?

She realised it would be wiser to return to the garden and hurried out to resume her seat at the table. Reluctant to go back to her conversation with Attila, she turned her attention to Mami, sitting hand in hand with Lila – her other daughter, who rarely came to Istanbul.

"I shall come, dear," Mami said, "I'll definitely visit you again in September. It isn't so easy for me to travel nowadays, but I will come. We ought to get together again in your house for Nili's birthday."

Rüya looked at her great-aunt, known to everyone as Lila *néni* – Aunt Lila. Despite the three-year age difference between them, Lila and Nili were like twins, and with age they now looked very much like Mami. For the last twenty years, Lila and her husband André had been living on the island of Simi, happily surrounded by the turquoise waters of the Aegean Sea. Last week they had come to Istanbul for the birthday of their beloved son Attila. Ever since their arrival, Lila had been displaying a permanent smile on her face, continually repeating how utterly happy she was to be with her son, whom she had not seen for a year, and with her daughter Giselle, freshly in from Paris, whom she always missed terribly, as they had been living far away from each other for years. She took every opportunity to spoil her grandchildren rotten and, to some degree, even her son-in-law. They were all happily settled in the rooms on the first floor, diligently reorganised for the occasion by Aslı in line with Nili's precise instructions.

"Giselle will be coming with the kids," said Lila, trying to encourage Mami. "They'll stay for a month. You must come."

Mami remained silent for a moment, as if at a loss for words, before she turned to Giselle and, out of the blue, asked, "Are you helping them to improve their creativity, *tatlım* – sweetie? It's already a bit late for Daphné, but your son is just about the right age."

Little Daphné, dozing off on her mother's lap, snapped her curious eyes open. "What am I getting late for, Mami?"

"I remember Rüya," Mami continued, almost talking to herself, "she was only eighteen months old."

"Here we go again," whispered Rüya, rolling her eyes towards Attila, slightly upset as she could guess where this conversation would eventually take them.

"You should teach them to be free, Giselle. That is the most important thing: to be free. You should teach them *now*. They must understand what it means to be free while they're still naturally and unconsciously free-spirited. This is how they can grow up into free individuals. Once their self-consciousness starts dominating their emotions, then it will be too late. They have to learn how to give free rein to their emotions before they even learn to talk. This must be ingrained in their souls. Don't ever intimidate them by limiting their means of self-expression. Pencils, papers, paints are not enough for them. Give them anything and everything. Anything that is edible, of course, because, rest assured, they'll put everything in their mouths first." She paused momentarily and looked at Daphné, who was not very keen on food. "Except for food, that is," she said, smiling cheekily before turning back to Giselle. "Let them be. Let them discover on their own that a pencil doesn't taste so good, and must therefore be good for something else. I remember Rüya, when she was only a tiny baby ..."

"Mami, this might not be an interesting topic for everyone," intervened Rüya, thinking that a late night sermon on child development would not appeal much to Attila, who had no kids, or to Giselle, who was finding it very hard to keep her sleepy eyes open.

"Rüya was much younger than you are now," Mami continued, bending over towards little Daphné and ignoring what Rüya had said, "when I first gave her some colouring pencils. Her initial reaction was to take one and taste it. I didn't stop her." She had changed the tone of her voice and was speaking like a little child. "She found it hard to suck on and most probably tasteless, so she tried poking herself with it. That hurt. Then she banged it on the floorboards. It didn't make much noise. She must have wondered what she could do with this peculiar thing. Oops! It just made a nice, coloured streak. Oh, there are others like this one, and they make different coloured streaks." She raised her eyes to Giselle again. "Let them get dirty, my dear," she said, her voice back to normal. "Let them express their emotions and thoughts freely in whatever manner they choose to do so."

"Mami believes," cut in Lila, "that sooner or later we'll have a great artist in our family and insists that this person be discovered at a very early age."

"*Another* great artist, Lila darling," said Mami, correcting her daughter. "We already had one. My brother Károly was an exceptional painter, albeit not very much appreciated during his lifetime, and you know that."

"Just *one* artist, you say?" interjected André, who was most probably bored but, being too polite not to listen, had focused all his attention on Mami. "Please madam, you're just being modest; your family is replete with great artists." Much as he usually preferred to reserve his words for the novels he wrote, he could not resist the opportunity to say, again, how proud he was of Lila's family – the exceptional family of his exceptionally adorable wife, his pride and joy, the source of his undying passion ever since the day they had met.

"And now we have you, *tatlım*," said Mami, addressing herself to Rüya before shifting her gaze back to André to explain. "She's impressively talented, and, please mark my words, she would become a great artist if she painted a bit more and remembered how she used to express her emotions." She paused as if to underline what she was going to say. "I should say, how *freely* she used to express her emotions." Then raising her eyebrows, she continued more mischievously. "Unfortunately, nowadays all she does is display her artistic identity by dropping paint on her pants and shoes and by dyeing a good bundle of her beautiful chestnut hair bright red." She gave a beguilingly innocent smile, much like that of an impish child who knew that she had said something wrong and hoped to be forgiven. Extending her hand towards Rüya, she mimed an imaginary pinch on her cheek. "I must admit, however, that bright red does bring out the beauty of your green eyes, sweetheart."

"Mami, you must be getting tired," Rüya interposed gently, not happy with where this conversation had taken them, but unable to be cross with her great grandmother, whom she loved dearly. "Why don't you go to the gazebo and relax for a while? It's very humid tonight. We wouldn't want you catching cold, would we? I'll let you know when we're ready to cut the cake."

Mami looked around for the ebony and ivory walking stick she always kept by her side and, more often than not, tapped on the floor to announce one of her silent interventions. André jumped to his feet to help her stand up and, pulling her chair back, handed over her walking stick. Mami draped her lilac shawl around her shoulders. She politely refused André's extended hand, as she usually did whenever someone attempted to help her walk; she detested being treated like a glass figurine that might shatter at any moment. They all watched her slowly walk to the gazebo.

"She's a tough cookie, isn't she?" remarked Attila.

"She certainly is," said Nili, back from the kitchen and busy clearing the remaining plates from the tables as fast as she could before Rüya interfered again.

She watched Mami climb the few steps to the gazebo and settle down in her wicker rocking chair.

The round gazebo stood at the far end of the garden, offering a panoramic view. It was open on all sides and had a ridiculously small roof. Mami, an avid sky-watcher, had initially opposed the idea of having anything over her head, but eventually acquiesced to a minimal structure as it would serve for watching the Bosphorus on rainy days. The velvety lawn stretched from the veranda to the gazebo, where it unexpectedly rolled down for a few yards before it came to a halt at the garden wall under the tall maritime pines. In tenebrous nights such as this, it looked almost as black as a raven's head; only the garden lights perforated the dark, giving it an emerald glow, emerald except for the small stubborn patches that remained tawny despite the impeccable care of Dursun, the gardener, and the relentless attention of Mami.

Rüya looked at Mami. As was her habit, she had turned her back to the house and cut herself off from everyone and everything, drifting into another world. Her solitude was complete.

"Happy birthday to you. Happy birthday to you." Nili and Lila had come out onto the veranda self-consciously singing the birthday song in various languages they spoke and did not properly speak. Aslı, not sure that Lila *néni* would manage to carry the cake to the table in one piece, followed her with her lean and long arms extended, ready to take control if need be. Rüya thought how embarrassed she would feel if she were in Attila's shoes. She hated spectacles like this. Attila, on the other hand, far from being embarrassed, seemed to enjoy every second of the masquerade, wearing a wide grin on his face and readying himself to accept the good wishes and receive his presents. He was such a big baby, he really was.

"I don't think we should disturb Mami. She might be sleeping."

"As you wish, Nili," said Lila curtly, without taking her adoring eyes off her son.

They all applauded and applauded. Attila blew at the candles, though not strongly enough. "Once again. Blow once again!" they hollered. "Oh no! The flash didn't go off. Light the candles again. Attila, please blow once again." Everybody kissed Attila. Then, God only knows why, they all kissed each other. And finally, presents, and more presents, and more and more presents. When this over-the-top ritual came to an end, everyone attacked the dessert buffet, somehow convinced that they had already digested the food they had consumed or, worse still, greedily thinking that they would not miss this exuberant finale whatever the physical cost.

Eating her *kadayif* with clotted cream (or rather the clotted cream with *kadayif*) Rüya, full to the point of bursting, once again thought how well Mami knew when to withdraw to her own world.

After their gluttonous endeavours, some guests complained about having eaten too much and having no room left even for coffee. Someone asked Aslı and Nili why they had gone to so much trouble. A group retired to the deckchairs by the pool to chat with their long-missed next of kin or, more importantly, to listen to the latest gossip. Rüya's cousins, unable to keep their eyes, jittery fingertips and minds off their mobile phones, were impatiently dreaming of the clubs they would be going to once this never-ending gathering was over. As soon as one of the guests made for the door, the rest would follow suit; it was something of a family custom.

"Mum! Stop clearing the tables, for God's sake," Aslı implored Nili, who was pirouetting around the tables. "It's all family here, and there are quite a lot of people who can help you do that later. They want to see you rather than a clean table. Why don't you go and relax by the pool next to Lila *néni?*"

"She's right, Grandma. Relax."

"All right, all right," Nili said sharply, raising her right eyebrow, obviously annoyed at her own helplessness under the crossfire of her daughter and granddaughter. "Why don't you two mind your own business? It's not like I'm going to change at this age, is it?" she continued, casting an intimidating look at each of her attackers. Then she shot a quick glance at Giselle. "Doesn't she have any intention of putting Daphné to sleep?" This in Hungarian so that Giselle would not understand her criticism.

"Leave her be, Grandma. Daphné is as curious as a cat. She won't go to bed before the guests leave even if it kills her. You know that," said Rüya.

"It's all her mother's fault. And Lila's. They're spoiling her rotten."

Rüya took Daphné from Giselle's lap. "I'll go and sit with Mami under the gazebo. It's rather quiet there; she might fall asleep."

"I'll come with you," said Aslı.

They walked to the gazebo and sat on the soft cushions of the wicker sofa where the mouldy odour of humidity subsided, and the air was pregnant with the sweet and balmy perfume emanating from the jasmine on the trellis behind the gazebo. Mami had fallen asleep with her head to one side, and was snoring heavily. She looked so peaceful: one of her hands resting on her walking stick and the other invisible amidst the soft white fur of Snow White, her cat from Van,

9

purring away on her lap. The free-spirited Carbon, on the other hand, had curled beside her feet, as was his custom, with his ears perking up at every little movement or sound in the garden. He was a warrior at heart. Once when Eros, their Sivas Kangal shepherd dog, was off-duty locked away in the doghouse, he had jumped to his feet before Scarlet and Chestnut could even make a move and chased off a stray dog that had had the misfortune of ending up in their garden.

Rüya started at the sound of Mami's walking stick hitting the ground. Her heart skipped a beat. Snow White jumped down. Mami had stopped snoring. Her head was hanging down over her chest.

I open the door. A dark and dense forest. A narrow path stretching out into the obscurity of the unknown, hardly visible under a carpet of fallen leaves soggy with humidity. The smell of putrefaction is so intense that it becomes threateningly scary. I can't imagine what might grab my leg from underneath that mugginess. Ambiguity is menacing. I can't get myself to step into it, but somehow I feel that I have to enter the forest. Absolute silence. Only the sound of my apprehensive footsteps on the soft, damp leaves. I'm frightened to look around. I must reach my destination as soon as possible, but I don't know where I need to go. I'm going into the unknown.

Worried, Rüya slowly got up, trying not to disturb Daphné, who was about to fall asleep in her arms. She walked over to Mami and, gently holding her chin, raised her head and leaned it against the back of the chair. To her great relief, she saw her mouth open and a thunderous sound come out as she took a deep breath. Everything seemed to be fine. She picked up her walking stick and placed it against her chair, then went back to sit beside her mother again.

"Lately, she's been sleeping too much – almost the whole day," complained Aslı. "She's very weak and, God bless her soul, still smokes like a chimney."

"Let her be, Mum. She has no other diversions, poor soul. She's lived this long, smoking a packet a day of the worst kind of cigarettes. What would be the point of her quitting now?"

"And you know what? Her memory seems to be getting weaker and weaker." Aslı's voice was bitter, with a sad, weary ring to it. "She's crystal clear on things that happened seventy years ago, but forgets what she's eaten for breakfast. She repeats what she said ten minutes ago; five minutes later she starts telling the same story all over again. I'm scared that she might be going senile."

"We ought to be grateful, you know. Don't forget that she's ninety-four years old," said Rüya gently. "I wish we could all be like her when we reach that age. She has everything. She has us. She's in perfect health. This morning she was telling me that she needed a little tan, even though people say it's unhealthy nowadays. Paleness did not suit her, she said; she wanted a bit of a golden glow." Rüya was briefly lost in thought. "I wish we could all be as perfect as she is. I wish we all had a life like hers."

Aslı was gazing at an invisible point in the dark of the night. "I don't think you would want that, Rüya."

"God help me if even Mami is not up to your standards of perfection."

Act One

Lassú, the first part of the rhapsody, begins unruffled and leisurely in the languor of a golden summer day.

A Hungarian Rhapsody
A Novel in Three Acts
Act One, Tableau One
1915 - 1932

Tableau One

1

It was an unexpectedly cool day for spring, casting a chill over the whole household. They had gathered in the high-ceilinged drawing room on the ground floor. Alex, Magda and Károly were sitting on their usual sofa, feeling rather edgy, not knowing what might have caused the change in their routine; they had been summoned at an hour when they were supposed to be playing in the garden. Throwing furtive glances at their nanny standing behind them, they tried to work out from her expression whether it was a reward or a punishment that they were to receive. At long last, their father Gusztáv rose from his desk at the far end of the room and, with a worried expression he hardly managed to hide, walked over to his tapestry armchair in front of the French windows. He puffed at his pipe as he sat down, his eyes fixed on his fiery red roses in the garden. After an excruciatingly tense moment of silence, he took a deep breath and announced that they had to leave Italy and move to Budapest.

The children were initially happy at the news. Although they had never lived in Hungary, they rather liked the idea of moving to Budapest, where they had always had a great time with their relatives and friends during the holidays. With every passing moment, however, a new question popped up in their minds, especially in Alex's. Eventually, no longer able to restrain herself, she darted off to her mother, who was perched on the edge of the other armchair next to the French windows.

"*Anyukám* – Mummy? Could we take Maria with us?"

Turning her back on the arresting red roses, Gizella hugged her daughter, making no effort to conceal her happiness. "That would be rather difficult, Alex."

"Why is that? She's my best friend."

"Because she has a family here, darling. Would you like it if you had to be separated from your family?"

"No, I wouldn't."

"Well, you can write to each other, now that you write so beautifully."

"Yes *Anyukám,* we will," she mumbled in disappointment. After a moment's silence, she tried a new request, emboldened by Magda, who had just joined her and was now holding her hand, "Could I please take Snow White? And could Magda take the Seven Dwarfs? And could we take their cottage?"

"Yes, my love, you can take Snow White and the Seven Dwarfs, but I'm afraid their cottage would have to stay behind."

"Why?"

"We can't carry everything, darling. But don't you worry, we'll get better ones once we're in Budapest."

"Why are we leaving?"

"Because of the war, Alex. They no longer want the Hungarians, in Italy."

"What does war mean?"

"It means fighting, dear, big fights – fights between countries."

"But fighting is bad," Alex declared, opening her eyes wisely. "You get very angry at Károly when he fights with his friends. Don't countries have parents who get angry when they fight?"

"We don't fight," remonstrated Károly. "We play games."

"Alex, you ask far too many questions, sweetheart," said Gizella as she stood up, stroking her daughters' heads. "Why don't we go and choose which other toys you might like to take with you?"

Gusztáv de Kurzón Egerlövö Szarvaskó Gadány, or Gusztáv de Kurzón for short, had been one of the most eligible and handsome bachelors in the aristocratic circles of Budapest, before eighteen-year-old Gizella captivated his heart at first sight. She was a legendary beauty; her coppery chestnut hair was usually pulled up in an elegant chignon, but she let it down to her hips when they were alone. Gusztáv's strong hands easily encircled her elegant waistline. Her deep blue eyes were almost as beautiful as her future husband's, though they lacked the greenish tint that gave Gusztáv's azure eyes the most attractive profundity. Although their marriage had been arranged by their families, they loved each other. A couple of months after their marriage, Gusztáv decided to take his wife, twelve years his junior, away from their pompous life in Budapest and move to Italy.

Gusztáv's brother Kelemen, the developer of the world's first electric train, had attracted the attention of the Italian Government after completing the project for the electrification of the Valtellina railway in northern Italy. Consequently, Gusztáv and Kelemen, both mechanical engineers, had been invited to work at the Westinghouse factory recently set up in Vado Ligure, a small town on the Ligurian coast of Italy near Savona. They were to manage the production of the locomotives to be used in a project for the electrification of another two thousand kilometres of railways in Italy. Although he was well aware of Gizella's unwillingness to leave Budapest, Gusztáv did not hesitate to accept the offer, not so much for the generous salary (since he came from an already comfortably wealthy family) as for the prestige the position offered and the success he was sure he would obtain.

One freezing Friday in February they left Budapest with Kelemen and his wife Etel. Their journey towards the warm shores of the Mediterranean was tiring, but the cold feeling that had been benumbing Gizella's heart showed signs of thawing upon their arrival at the Villa Marchese Gavotti in Albisola, a little town next to Vado Ligure. Their new home, which Gusztáv described as the only habitable house in the region, had a certain grandeur that slightly compensated for the dull life in this town Gizella preferred to call a village. Although not as attractive as their house in Budapest, it had a truly impressive garden with tall palm trees and maritime pines promising to give the mansion a unique sense of serenity on hot summer days, a garden that would make up for the disappointment created by the rather limited size of the property.

With an incurably ambitious and almost always absent husband in a town with a desperately lean social life, Gizella ached to get pregnant, and in January 1906 she gave birth to a baby boy. Under the influence of new Western trends, Gusztáv turned his back on hundreds of years of family tradition and – despite Gizella's objections – named their first son not Gusztáv but Károly. The baby boy was most lovable, although he drove everyone crazy with his inexhaustible energy and proved himself an unruly little rebel even before he was a toddler. Gizella, hoping for a calm and obedient little baby girl, resolved to get pregnant again as soon as possible. But she had to wait four years before she gave birth to not one but two baby girls, on the tenth day of the tenth month of the tenth year of the twentieth century. Alexandra was born attached to her twin sister Magdaléna by the top of her left ear. Gently separated from each other by the doctors, Alexandra was to lack the top curvature of her left ear – while her sister Magdaléna would have a

17

tiny little bit of an extra flesh on her right – for the rest of their lives, as if to remind them that they were the two halves of a whole.

Alexandra and Magdaléna, or Alex and Magda as everybody in the family preferred to call them, came like a breath of fresh air, brightening up the life in Villa Gavotti for Gizella, who was fatigued by her uncontrollable son Károly, and also for Etel, who would have died for a baby girl but, much to her disappointment, had been advised not to have any more children after the birth of her only son, Sándor. Alex and Magda were beautiful babies and grew up to be beautiful little girls. Their intolerance to being separated from each other was absolute. The one would neither eat nor sleep nor go anywhere nor accept any presents unless the other one did the same. They woke up and went to sleep at the same instant; the nightmare of one made the other cry; a cut on a finger hurt them both; the moment one got hungry or thirsty so did the other one. The resemblance they bore to each other was so strong that it gave them the ammunition to play the only naughty trick they knew, which was to fool their nanny Ildikó, and at times even their mother, by pretending to be each other. Gizella could never be cross with her daughters; she knew it was Károly who usually provoked them into being disorderly, and they always took their brother's word as law.

The Kurzóns' peaceful life in Italy came to an end when the war, triggered by the assassination of Franz Ferdinand, the Archduke of Austria, in June 1914, took the whole of Europe in its grip by the end of the summer. Finally, upon Italy's declaration of war on the Austro-Hungarian Empire towards the end of May 1915, Gusztáv and Kelemen decided that it would be wiser to go back home.

They left Italy with only a few trunks as they had to leave almost all their furniture behind. After a long railroad journey over and through the mountains of Switzerland, they arrived in Budapest, where their house in Rózsadomb, the beautiful hill of roses on the Buda side of the River Danube, was waiting for them with open arms. It was a stately mansion surrounded by spacious gardens with corners unknown even to their owners, in a green neighbourhood which had in recent years become the most prestigious residential area, a magnet for affluent families. Along with the identical house next to it where Kelemen moved in with his family, it stood on Vérhalom Street, conveniently situated in the middle section of a quiet thoroughfare, lined with huge chestnut trees, just before it became strenuously steep. From the garden gate at the end of the wrought-iron railings, the welcoming fragrance of the lilac trees extended a warm invitation that encouraged even the most timid visitors to come in. It was a three-storey building with a roof slanting at different angles to hold the various alcoves, bay windows, niches and overhangs together and, in some strange way, compensating for the formal air imposed by the sober rectangular windows giving on to the street. The land sloped slightly downhill, and the façade overlooking the back garden was more cheerful with its French windows, the conservatory and the veranda that ran the whole length of the drawing room on the ground floor. The River Danube and the Pest side of the city were visible in all their splendour from the upper floors and the back garden.

Alex, Magda and Károly had no difficulty in adapting themselves to their new lives in Hungary; there were no major changes in their routines except for the absence of Uncle Kelemen who, right after their arrival in Budapest, had been recruited to the Defence Ministry in Vienna to work as a Transportation Expert. The relentless care and attention of their mother was lightened by the presence of Aunt Etel, who had taken her son Sándor and moved in with them a few weeks after the departure of Uncle Kelemen. They continued to savour the reassuring love of their busy father though in fewer, smaller doses; Károly went on driving everyone mad by constantly teasing them; Alex and Magda never stopped adoring Károly despite all the jokes he played on them; and they all carried on having a good time with their growing circle of friends. Nothing marred their happy existence, not even the grown-ups continually talking about the difficulties of wartime, and Sándor repeating over and over again how much he hated the war and missed his father. They were a little resentful about their toys since their mother, blaming the war, had not kept her promise to buy new ones to replace those they had left behind in Italy, but all in all everything was fine – at least until the day when their father asked them to wait for him in the Green Salon after dinner.

Alex had a hunch that there was something important at stake. "One of us must have misbehaved," she thought. However, neither she nor Magda had done anything wrong so far that day. "It must have been Károly," she reasoned, "and he'd better get ready for a good dressing down." She had not told her mother how he had scared them that morning, so he must have committed some other mischief.

"Children," she heard her father say in a solemn tone. "I'm afraid I'll have to go away for a while to defend our country."

She felt a sudden pain grab her stomach and send tremors through her whole body. This was far worse than Károly being scolded. "For how many days *Apukám*

19

– Daddy?" she asked, with an acute sense of foreboding. "Will you come back tomorrow?" She had involuntarily started to pull at her skirt. I'd better stop it before Mummy gets cross, she thought in panic.

A bitter smile appeared on her father's face. "No, my little pumpkin, it might take a bit longer than that. But your brother Károly is here and Sanyi as well. They'll take care of you and Magda while I'm away."

Alex sneaked a fleeting glance at her cousin Sándor, who, being a total sissy, was scared to talk, let alone protect anyone. "Károly won't go with you to defend our country, will he?" she asked, alarmed. "Let him stay. Please?"

"I've already told you that he'll stay here with you. There's nothing to worry about."

"Are you going where Uncle Kelemen is?"

"No, my darling, I'll be going east – to the front."

"What does that mean?"

"You wouldn't understand," Károly broke in. "Our father is an honourable soldier. He'll fight the enemy bravely in close combat."

Alex suddenly burst into tears, knowing in her heart that this was something terrible. She flung her arms around his father, who took her onto his lap. "Please don't go," she pleaded, hugging him tightly, tears choking her words. "Couldn't others defend our country? You have to stay here to protect us."

"Come on, sweetheart. Look at Magda. She's not crying, is she?"

"Will you be back before our birthday?"

Magda had come over and put her head on their father's shoulder. "Don't worry, Alex," she said reassuringly. "Daddy will be back soon, right after he saves our country."

Although her sister's explanation left Alex unconvinced, she felt the pain in her stomach gradually subsiding; she hoped to stay on her father's lap as long as she wanted, enjoying that unequalled comfort till very late that evening. Pulling Magda by the hand, she made her squeeze in next to her. She so wished they could stay like this forever, side by side in their father's arms.

Gusztáv did not come back as quickly as Magda had predicted. For Alex, soon meant the next day. She would go to sleep that night and wake up in the morning to find everything the same as before. However, it did not quite work out that way. Their father did not return either for their fifth or their sixth birthdays.

2

Two days before the year 1916 came to a close, the Mátyás Cathedral, ruling over the city from the hills of Buda, was surrounded by flocks of people. The Kurzóns were there to watch the coronation of Emperor Karl I and Empress Zita of Austria as King Károly IV and Queen Zita of Hungary. This was to be the third coronation of the twentieth century in Europe, a continent devastated by the Great War for more than two years.

As the main doors opened, royalty, glamorous in their glittering diamond tiaras and brocade capes embroidered with pearls and embellished with furs and feathers, made their way into the cathedral alongside representatives of the world's nobility. Moving in slow, measured steps, they all took their seats. Clergy had lined up outside the cathedral waiting to receive the King and the Queen. A few minutes later the powerful sound of the organ echoed from the walls of the cathedral, announcing the imminent arrival of the royal carriage. A sudden and total silence fell over the crowd. Everybody stood up. Finally, the King and the Queen made their entrance. People held their breaths while they proudly watched their king, with his admirable wife Zita elegantly gliding beside him in her white satin dress and white lace veil cascading down to the floor. They moved towards the crown and the sceptre. The Crown of Saint István evoked reverence in people; not only because of its radiant enamels and hundreds of pearls and precious stones, warmly glowing even after a thousand years, but also because of its connection to a legendary past. Next to it stood the Royal Sceptre, shining in glory, its golden shaft carrying a crystal ball as big as a fist, covered in intricate golden filigree.

Following a long and magnificent mass, Károly IV was crowned under a ray of light that shone through a window above the altar, touching his shoulder as if to give a celestial blessing to his coronation, the ceremony consecrated by the sword of Saint Maurice. From outside came the sound of saluting cannons.

Alex was watching the ceremony in spellbound admiration, comfortably seated with her family in the places reserved for them in one of the upper galleries. Everything was like in the fairy tales her nanny often recounted. People were decked in an abundance of exquisite jewellery and garbed in formal attire, richly adorned with elaborate gold-work and a wide variety of furs. Her mother had decorated her neck, ears, wrists and fingers with jewels that she said were a very precious family heritage. Alex revelled in the pearl necklaces that she and Magda wore; they looked splendid on their identical red velvet dresses. Their nanny had prepared them with the utmost care, braiding their coppery chestnut hair with red ribbons and crowning the braids around their heads. Alex's black patent leather shoes were a little bit too tight, but she did not mind it so much since they looked gorgeous. She looked at Károly, who was the best-looking boy in the cathedral, more handsome than even Crown Prince Otto himself. Despite his defiant refusal, their mother had succeeded in convincing him to put on his dark blue suit. To the surprise of everyone, he had managed to leave the house without staining it. That suit beautifully accentuated his platinum blond hair, but he obviously did not fancy it much, finding it very uncomfortable, as one could tell from his constant fidgeting. Sándor, on the other hand, who was dressed exactly like Károly, seemed absolutely at ease, on his most decorous behaviour as always. Alex's eyes left her cousin and moved along the hand holding his mother's. She looked at Aunt Etel's chignon, wondering if her hair was as long as her mother Gizella's. She could not tell since she never let it down. Perhaps she was born like this, with a tiny brown chignon that looked like a bird's nest that grew as she got older. Conversely, her thin lips, too small for her face, seemed never to have grown, giving her face an odd expression. Her almost non-existent lower lip disappeared altogether as she smiled. She stood up. Alex looked at her mother, who was standing up as well. She held Magda's hand, and they also rose to their feet, arranging their dresses. This part of the ceremony seemed to be over.

They slowly descended the stairs along with the rest of the crowd. As they were about to go out, Alex saw some men coming into the cathedral through a side door. What were they doing in this fairy tale, she wondered, dressed in faded and patched grey uniforms, tattered leather belts and old boots? Some – with wooden legs, leaning on crutches – were limping along, knocking against each other, coughing and making painful sounds as they breathed; others were already seated at places provided for them, waiting in silence. Each had a row of medals on his chest.

"*Édes Anyukám* – Mummy dearest, who are these people?" she asked in a loud whisper, pulling her mother's hand.

"Soldiers, my darling. Our King will declare them Knights of the Golden Spur. They are heroes, our wounded heroes."

"How were they wounded?"

"In the war."

"Did they fall down?"

"Come on, Alex, watch your step please. We have to hurry now."

"Why isn't Daddy back? You said he would come back soon. It's been more than a year since he left, hasn't it?"

"Why? Why? You ask too many questions. He'll be back soon. Now do be quiet please. We ought to make a move and take our places outside for the Swearing of the Oath ceremony."

Following the ceremony, the King and the Queen, with little Crown Prince Otto in his mother's arms, saluted the crowd from one of the windows on the upper storey of the cathedral. The celebrations continued with a banquet given in honour of the coronation, followed by the presentation of the aristocracy to the royal couple; and ended as Károly IV and Zita boarded the train that was to take them to Vienna. All that remained was the gossip of the day.

"Did you notice how his crown stood crooked on his head? They couldn't straighten it up. This is not a good sign."

"What about the King stumbling over every word as he repeated the oath?"

"During the preparations a glass plate as thick as my finger cracked and dropped like a guillotine on the altar. These are ill-omens."

3

The final days of September. Alex and Magda were drawing pictures on the veranda, warmly dressed against the chill in the air under the feeble autumn sun.

"Sanyi said that Uncle Kelemen will be coming back soon. He told us that he's fine – that he's not injured," muttered Alex, almost to herself, without raising her head from her sketchbook. "Will Daddy be back? Will he be here for our seventh birthday?" she continued with apprehension as she turned her questioning eyes to her mother.

"No, sweetheart, he's not finished yet. But he should be back soon."

Magda stopped drawing and looked at Aunt Etel. "Has Uncle finished what he had to do? Has he saved our country?"

"He hasn't finished either, dear. He'll be carrying on here in Budapest. Your uncle is making trains for the soldiers to travel more comfortably."

"All right, children," Gizella said sharply. "You've had enough fresh air for today. Stop asking questions and go inside and make us some nice train pictures, would you?"

A couple of days later Kelemen returned to Budapest to start working as the general manager of the Ganz Engine and Wagon Factory, located at the foot of Rózsadomb. Although a hard worker with rarely any time for his family, he nevertheless went to great lengths to satisfy every whim not only of his son Sándor but also of Alex, Magda and Károly, striving to make up for the absence of their father and to ensure they wanted for nothing. They hardly had any time to feel lonely, with their mother continually inviting their friends over after school or sending them off for a visit, Nanny Ildikó constantly inventing new games for them, their French governess never leaving them without homework, and everyone including the servants showing them the utmost care and attention. However, nothing anyone ever did proved to be enough to ease the incurable yearning Alex felt for her father.

Their father did not come home for their seventh birthday either, after which Alex started to fear that he might never return and that the adults were most probably lying. Nevertheless, she did not give up dashing to her mother's bedroom on the upper floor first thing every morning, her heart racing with the hope that her father would have arrived in the middle of the night and that she would see his shoes beside the rosewood sofa with golden angels spreading their wings on its armrests. Although she went back to her room in heartbroken disappointment every morning, she never wearied of rushing to her mother's bedroom again the next day, her heart throbbing with hopeful anticipation. Another Christmas went by without their father, but she did not lose hope. Her optimism even endured the whispers that escaped from the boring conversation of the grown-ups and reached her ears one day in March, while they were painting at the table next to the lovebirds in the conservatory.

"Finally, the Russians have thrown in the towel. They've signed a ceasefire treaty in Brest-Litovsk. This means Gusztáv will soon be back."

"Gizi! They're remobilising some of the soldiers from the Eastern Front to the west. You know that. We haven't heard from Gusztáv for so long; it would be better if we didn't raise the children's hopes now that they are almost used to his absence."

Not allowing her hopes to fade, Alex never tired of running with her heart in her mouth to the garden gate of their summerhouse in Lake Balaton throughout the summer months whenever she heard the whistle of an arriving train, and waiting for her father with her eyes on the door until bedtime. After they moved back to

Budapest at the end of the summer, she resolutely kept darting to the drawing room as soon as she arrived from school, clinging to her illusion that her father would be sitting in his armchair, calling out, "My little squirrels!" Although she found nothing but his empty armchair, she persistently denied that it was a trick her imagination played on her and kept hearing the same voice day in and day out, her heart skipping a beat each time. And every single day, she held Magda's hand tightly to ease the pain of her broken heart as they followed their nanny to their room on the upper floor.

The same thing happened that day too. When they arrived from school, she thought she heard her father's voice, but she no longer took it to be real; it was slowly dawning upon her that he might never come back, now that he had not made it to their eighth birthday either, which was three weeks ago. They went up to their room, took their bath, changed their clothes and went down to the Green Salon. Tea was being served. Károly was not back from school yet. They sat down side by side on their usual sofa.

"We saw a lot of flowers on our way back from school. Everything was decorated with flowers. Nanny Ildikó said they were ... I've forgotten. What were they, Magda? They were really pretty."

"Asters! The whole city is smothered in asters," said Kelemen as he came in.

Etel, opening her big brown eyes wide in surprise, turned to her husband. "Is something wrong, Kelemen? You're home early."

Alex was happy to see her uncle back early from work. She sprinted towards him and jumped into his arms, extending her cheek for a kiss. His beard, covering half of his face, did hurt her a little bit, but she never refused a kiss from him.

"Finally, Count Mihály Károlyi gave his long-awaited speech at the Hotel Astoria. They proclaimed the Hungarian National Council." With a forced smile, which failed to hide his deep preoccupation, he continued, "Let's hope for the best. That's all I can say."

"This wasn't unexpected," snapped Gizella. "Budapest has been chaotic lately. Soldiers, workers ... there's no end to their demands. What I can't understand is how Mihály Károlyi could possibly do such a thing. How can somebody from such an aristocratic background, so well off, so highly regarded and so extremely conservatively Catholic, be so radically liberal with such leftist inclinations? It's truly incredible. The leader of the Independence Party! How absurd! A Red Count. And what about his wife? How does she let him do all this, considering the size of her estate, the breadth of her esteem and the length of her family name – Countess

Katalin Andrássy de Csik-Szent-Király Kraszna-Horka? Don't they have anything better to do?"

Kelemen put Alex down, took the porcelain teacup Etel handed over and walked pensively towards the window. "There are asters in everyone's hands, on every balcony, at every street corner. They call it the Aster Revolution, a democratic revolution."

"The grown-ups are into one of their tedious conversations again," thought Alex, turning to Magda, who seemed to be bored as well. "We should finish our apple *rétes* quickly and go upstairs," she whispered almost inaudibly.

"What's going to happen now?" asked Etel.

"Our King will declare our Red Count prime minister; that's certain. Even if he's not very sympathetic towards the Habsburgs, Károlyi wants the monarchy to survive. I'm sure about that. It's impossible that he would want to break all ties with Austria. The Empire could still be saved, you know. They'd never allow Hungary to break from the Habsburgs."

Ten days later, at the eleventh hour of the eleventh day of the eleventh month of 1918, the Great War came to an end, exactly four years, fifteen weeks and one day after it had started.

Budapest, 12th November 1918

It's a tough job keeping a diary. I can't find anything to write. I'm also a bit lazy. I'd rather draw or paint than write. But today is an important day. We had lots of visitors. Aunt Irén and Uncle Filip came over as well. Everybody hugged and kissed us. They say the war is over. I think this is a good thing because it means that Daddy will come back. He hasn't been to our last four birthdays. He's a very good person.

The end of the war saw the disintegration of the Austro-Hungarian Empire, which Gusztáv de Kurzón had so honourably sought to defend. The whole continent was awash with great joy, while Hungary harboured mixed feelings. The end of the Austro-Hungarian Dual Monarchy meant independence for their country, but it also meant the end of Hungary's territorial integrity. On the one hand, people were happy that they had survived to see the end of the war, yet on the other, they were mournful for having lost it.

Budapest, 13th November 1918

I hate the war. Today Mummy said that Daddy is a hero. I asked if he's like the wounded heroes we saw at the Cathedral. She said no. She said that he might not come back. What kind of a hero is he? Will he always stay at war? Will he never come back? I don't want my Daddy to be a hero. I want him to stay with me. Always! Mummy says he'll always be by our side. What does that mean? I don't understand anything. I want my Daddy. Magda does too. We can't stop crying. I'm crying now, and my diary is getting all wet. I know that he'll be back. He's not a hero. I told Magda and Károly to go and wait by the window. Now I'll go as well, and we'll wait together. He will come back, I know. Mummy doesn't know anything, or else she's lying. I won't ask Mummy anything about Daddy anymore. I won't ask anybody anything anymore. Daddy will come back.

"I can't believe he surrendered his powers as king of Hungary. How can he abandon us like this?" Gizella appeared more distressed than ever.

"He might have surrendered his title, but he didn't abdicate his throne," said Kelemen, somewhat more optimistic.

"What's that supposed to mean? He left for Switzerland, didn't he? What's going to happen to us without him? I'm terribly worried, Kelemen."

"He left the door open for his return to the throne."

"Moreover, I don't like this riffraff of a republic. What is this Hungarian Democratic Republic anyway? I'll tell you what it is: nothing but sheer nonsense. Our country is a kingdom that is part of an empire, and we have a king. Who the hell is Károlyi to declare himself the president of the republic, even if only provisionally? How dare he!"

"Calm down, Gizi. The situation isn't so gloomy. At the end of the day Mihály Károlyi is an aristocrat, and this is an indication that the political reins in Hungary are still in the hands of the nobility, even if elsewhere in Europe the political power of the aristocrats have receded. Let's not despair. Please."

4

The Red Count, Mihály Károlyi was so adamant about a democratic land reform that in February, to the anguish and indignation of many, he began distributing the lands of his estate in Kál-Kápolna.

"He said, 'This land which was mine until today is now yours.' The kings of the old times bestowed upon their generals and soldiers lands from conquered regions. Now Hungary has lost the war and driven out its king, and they're distributing land to everyone. Could someone please explain to me what this unprecedented gambit means?" Gizella fumed, regarding the new system as utterly unnecessary and inappropriate.

There were others, however, who found the measures taken by the Red Count insufficient. Consequently, Mihály Károlyi, the founder of the new system (a system allowing the election of as few representatives as possible from ethnic minorities and tolerating discrimination against parties that represented the workforce), failed to win the support of the social democrats in the National Council. His cabinet had to resign four months after he had declared himself the provisional president of the republic and two months after the National Council had officially declared him the president. The political reins passed into the hands of a Bolshevik government consisting of People's Commissars under the leadership of Béla Kun. In March 1919 they announced the establishment of the Hungarian Soviet Republic.

That Sunday, like every other Sunday, Gusztáv and Kelemen's sister Irén, her husband Filip and Gizella's unmarried cousins Judit and Anna were invited to Rózsadomb for lunch. At the table, Kelemen was talking to Filip about the problems at work.

"Ganz is financially very unstable. The Italians want me to work on a new three-phase locomotive."

"Is it Westinghouse?"

"This time, it's Emilio Romeo."

"Are we going back to Italy, *Apukám?*"

"No, Sanyi, this time we don't need to move," said Kelemen before turning back to Filip. "People don't realise how critical the situation is in our country. It's as if they were hypnotised. There's nothing in the papers. There are no more newspapers worth reading anyhow. We're forced to read this." Filled with much abhorrence, he pointed at the *Népszava* newspaper the butler had placed on the mantelpiece over the fireplace to let it warm up, thinking that the cold of the street would disturb his master's hands. "They closed them down one by one on the pretext of a paper shortage. I wonder why they don't just admit it's censorship."

Gizella was lost in thought, holding her cheeks and shaking her head in objection to all that was going on. "What's happening for God's sake? What will befall us?" she kept repeating as if talking to herself.

"*Anyukám*, aren't we going to have some chocolate *palacsinta?*" complained Alex.

"You shouldn't interrupt when grown-ups are talking. We're not going to have any chocolate *palacsinta*, and you know it."

"Why? We used to, every Sunday."

"Stop whining," cut in Magda. "We should be quiet."

"No more talking now! Finish up your food please. Károly! Take your elbow off the table. And don't forget that you must go straight to your room to do your homework as soon as lunch is over. You must set a good example for your sisters."

"Calm down, Gizi," said Etel, holding Gizella's hand. "Everything will be fine. Don't worry so much."

"How can I not worry? They're ruining our country."

"Have you seen the front-page headline in today's paper?" asked Kelemen. "*Proletarian children will be able to swim.*"

"What does that mean?" asked Gizella with weariness.

"It means that we shall have to accommodate poor children in our summerhouse this year. The order is right from the very top. The People's Commissars have decided it."

"Look at us! We've jumped out of the frying pan into the fire. I could never have imagined that I'd be yearning for the return of our Red Count. The Democratic Republic was bliss, and we didn't know it. This wretched Béla Kun will destroy us."

"Rumour has it that the People's Commissars are mostly Jewish," said Anna, in her trembling voice.

"Béla Kun is no different, is he? We all know that the Jews are behind all this communism hullabaloo." Gizella's veins, swollen with anger, were visible through the high lace collar tightly embracing her neck.

Judit, knowing her cousin Gizella well, cast a disapproving glance at Anna as if to say, "Look what you've done now!"

Gizella, who for the last few minutes had been tapping the tip of her dessert knife on the back of the silver swan that served as a knife-rest, suddenly put the knife on the snow-white tablecloth, staining it red, took the silver swan and, after fidgeting with it for a few seconds, let it drop onto her empty coffee cup, which shattered under the falling swan. Gazing at the broken pieces with blank eyes, she continued as though nothing had happened. "They draped the colonnades in Hősök Square in red. They even have a slogan: *Proletarians of all countries, unite!* I can't believe that they put a statue of Marx right in the middle of the square."

"They've commissioned all the artists in the country to paint our city red for May Day celebrations. They're terribly excited about it all, saying it's to be the first free Labour Day in Hungary," said Filip, perturbed.

"The artists are at the forefront of these preparations. There are revolutionary placards everywhere." Gizella raised both her hands and furiously banged them on the table. "It drives me insane to see those Cézanne-inspired figures under slogans like 'Forward Red Soldiers!'"

Kelemen put his napkin on the table, a gesture that announced the end of lunch. "Equality, they claim. The masters of favouritism wanting equality – or, should I say, in want of equality? By the way, guess who was appointed to the head of the Budapest Theatres? Who else but Her Royal Highness, Madame Béla Kun!" He stood up and, throwing up his arms, announced with a flourish, "And curtain." He then gave a slight bow of the head to each one around the table and concluded in a sarcastic tone, "*Bon appétit.*"

"As a matter of fact, there's one thing I find quite delightful amid this craze of appropriations and confiscations," said Gizella, rising from her chair, her lips slightly curved in irony. "The theatres! It's great to know that, at long last, they also belong to the people. I believe it to be an important step in their education that anyone will be able to go to the theatre from now on. However, they say that one shouldn't applaud too loudly at the curtain so as not to wake them up."

"I'll never go to the theatre again. It would be awfully crowded," put in Etel irritably before swallowing the last few sips of her coffee with a gulp. "We can no longer go to the movie theatre either. There's nothing but propaganda films." She pushed her chair back and stood up.

"What does propaganda mean, Aunt Etel?"

"It's none of your concern, Károly. You should have been upstairs by now doing your homework," stormed Gizella. She swished her head towards the door to the service stairs. "Mademoiselle Ildikó," she called out irritatedly, reaching out to the silver bell on the table. "Where on earth is she?"

Alex smiled at Károly, trying to encourage him to keep his spirits up. Recently, all she had been hearing from him was that he was thirteen years old and, being an adult now, needed to make his voice heard in the grown-up world. Apparently determined to do just that, he blurted out, "This week," and continued in an exaggeratedly solemn tone, "a new teacher started and taught us a lot of new things – about the life of farm workers, for instance."

"You already know these things, Károly. Don't you know how the peasants in

Kengyel live?"

"Then they took us to a factory in Csepel," Károly carried on with resolve as he ran after his mother towards the Green Salon. "We joined a workers' class there given by our math teacher."

"I'll take him away from that school," hissed Gizella, addressing Kelemen. "What, in God's name, are they doing in Red Csepel?"

"Teacher Lajos says that very soon the world will be turned upside down," persevered Károly, ignoring his mother's wrath.

"Don't you concern yourself with these things, son. Mathematics is what you should be thinking of. Look at Sanyi and try to be like him."

The adults settled down on the sofas. Nanny Ildikó was waiting at the door, with Sándor docilely standing next to her. Károly went up to his mother and, holding himself bolt upright, declared self-confidently, "I don't like maths. All of my teachers say that I'm artistically talented. They say I should go to the Academy of Fine Arts."

"That's true, Gizi. His creative imagination has no limits," chimed in Aunt Irén in her crystal clear voice, sweet as honey. She had always been Károly's greatest supporter when it came to arts. "His inexhaustible energy must be channelled wisely. Haven't you noticed how he becomes another person while he paints, how the naughty boy in him turns into a keen-eyed artist fully absorbed in his work? He has everything that an artist should have, Gizi. He wants to experiment and enjoys discoveries, courageously trying novelties. It's quite remarkable, really." She turned to her husband sitting next to her. "Filip, we must show Károly's paintings to your father, don't you think?" she asked softly, arranging his dishevelled hair with her extraordinarily long and slender fingers – a trait considered by many to be a sign that she should have been an artist.

"I totally agree with you, darling."

"Irén," interjected Gizella firmly.

The glow in Károly's eyes vanished at his mother's caustic tone of voice.

"There are two aspiring artists in this household, whom Monsieur Patrik Merse has already approved of. That's more than enough, I think." Gizella smiled at her daughters. Momentarily, her anger seemed to have melted away, only to return precipitately as she continued in sharp contrast to her brief lapse into tenderness. "He should use his creativity, energy and curiosity to invent things; follow his uncle's example. Please stop putting ideas in his head. He's very good at mathematics. He'll become an engineer just like his father and his uncle. Look at his paintings carefully. They're full of geometrical shapes."

"You should try and understand the emotions hidden behind his eccentric nature, Gizi."

Károly threw his arms around his aunt. "Only you can understand me," he whispered softly in her ear.

5

Every summer in June the Kurzóns went to their summerhouse in Balatonfüred on the northern shore of Lake Balaton, and stayed there for three months. Despite the economic difficulties and shortages, they did not change their routine and, packing up trunks of clothes, moved to Balatonfüred before the unbearable heat started to melt the asphalt on the roads in the capital. As was their habit every late afternoon, they were relaxing in the deckchairs spread out in the shade under the thick canopy of trees, trying to cool down and regain the energy they had expended during the day. After scorching the lakeside all day, the sun was gradually losing its vigour as it approached the horizon, relinquishing its rule to a gently bracing breeze. The children were on the veranda. Magda was drawing, and Sándor was as usual reading a book, sunk into a rocking chair. There was no sign of Károly. Alex was concentrated on the letter she was writing.

Balatonfüred, 27th June 1919

My dearest Maria,

It was very hot today. In the morning we went to the Golden Beach on the other side of the lake. There's a very high springboard, and we – Magda and I – are learning how to dive. Károly is teaching us. He's excellent at it and can even do a somersault. I often fall flat on my tummy trying the head-first dive, but I really enjoy it. At least, it's not as boring as rowing. But Magda loves rowing, so every day I go on the canoe with her for a short while even though it's not much fun. Sanyi always wants us to get on the sailing boat. Between you and me, I suspect he's a little bit scared of diving.

I do miss you a lot. I wish your parents would let you come here for a couple of weeks this summer. We'd have so much fun. There are so many things we can do together. We can go to the beach every day and stay up really late at night. I have loads of friends in the neighbourhood. They always come around, and we play for hours. You'll also meet our new dog, Cerise. (It sounds like "Soereez.") Magda and I chose this name for her. It means cherry in French. She's as sweet as a cherry, and her fur is almost as red as one. She takes part in all our games. Do please come. But come before August, if you can, because we'll be having some poor orphans staying over at our house then, and it will be too crowded.

How are things with you? How are your friends? Do you do any sports?

Magda and I will be starting the *gimnázium* this year. *Gimnázium* is the school that we go to after we finish elementary school. We want to go to the school Károly goes to. Uncle Kelemen graduated from there as well. But Fasori is a boys' school. My mother says ...

She jumped to her feet with a start. Károly had silently approached her and done the most annoying thing: he had grabbed her on both sides of her waist and startled her. "*Öcsi!* – Brother!" she shouted. "Look what you've done! You've ruined my letter."

Károly hugged her and planted a kiss on her cheek, something that always made her forgive and forget everything. She could never be angry with her brother because no matter what he did he always knew how to make up for it straight away.

"You can write your letter later. Come along now. I've set up a game in my room." He quickly turned around and slapped one of Magda's braids. "Come on! Don't be so boring." He took Sándor's book and threw it on the table. "You're coming as well, Sanyi. This game requires a lot of players."

"Shall we call Margit then?" asked Sándor, enthusiastically looking towards the villa next door.

"I've already asked her to come over. She won't be long."

Alex continued in haste to finish her letter.

... My dearest Maria, please forgive me. Károly startled me and ruined my letter. My mother says that they'll be sending us to another *gimnázium* that is for girls.

That'll have to be all for now. I'm sorry that it's such a short letter. My brother calls me to play. I shall write again soon. And please do write to me.

With love and longing,
   Your friend,
      Alex

She folded the letter and put it inside an envelope. "I'll write the address later," she thought, and pulled Magda by the hand. "You can finish your drawing later. Let's go."

Sándor had already gone. They dashed upstairs.

Károly had taken all the pillows from his bed and the cushions from the sofa and put them on the floor. "Now I'll be Danton. Sanyi, you'll be Robespierre. Magda, you'll act as Desmoulins, which means that you'll have to pretend to be a man. And Alex, you'll play Lucile. Is everything clear? Margit will be Louise. Where is she?" He rushed to the window and looked out. "She's coming." He came back and started piling up the pillows on top of each other. "These are the barricades. Sanyi, why don't you bring all the pillows from your room? Girls! You go on and bring a red, a blue and a white dress. Come on. Get going. Quick! Quick!"

"Why?"

"Because these are the colours of the French flag, my sweet ignorant sister."

"Is this a French game?"

Their mother appeared at the door. "What sort of a game is this?"

"We're playing Danton, *Anyukám*," said Alex joyfully.

"Károly! Is it you who started this game?"

"Yes, Mother. On May 1, my classmate János gave a speech about Danton. Do you know who Danton is? He's a very important personality, one of the leaders of the French Revolution."

"I know, son, I know. You should all go and take your baths now. Your uncle will be arriving shortly with Aunt Irén and Uncle Filip." She looked around. "Where is Mademoiselle Ildikó?" She then turned to Margit, who had just come through the door. "Margit darling, go home and get ready. You'll be joining us for dinner this evening."

"But we've just started," whimpered Sándor.

"Yes, Mummy, please let us play at least for a short while," insisted Alex, bouncing up and down on her knees.

"You can play later. Don't object to everything I say. You should do as you're told."

Upset that their game had been interrupted, Alex reluctantly went to her room to change. As she dressed, the excitement of her uncle's imminent arrival took over, and she was ready before anyone else. She went down to the veranda and sat down to wait for the guests.

Finally, they heard the whistle of the train. A short while later the horse carriage that had gone to the station to fetch the guests entered through the garden gate. Too excited to wait for the carriage to stop, Alex leapt to her feet and made a head start so as to hug her uncle before the others. They all ran towards the new arrivals. Alex jumped into her uncle's arms, although she was too tall now to do that; Károly, as always, threw his arms around his aunt; and Magda hugged Uncle Filip.

"Calm down, children. Calm down now." Kelemen's face showed signs of great distress. "I have some bad news."

"What's wrong? What happened, Kelemen?"

Everybody looked anxiously at Kelemen and then at the others.

"Béla Kun finally declared the dictatorship of the proletariat," said Filip, his voice ice-cold.

"*Anyukám*, may I sit next to my uncle at dinner this evening? We'll eat in the garden, won't we? May I, please?" Alex had come down from Kelemen's arms and was eagerly jumping up and down, trying to hug her mother. She stopped abruptly when Gizella stumbled a few paces.

"Now it's really the end," Gizella stammered, her voice hardly above a whisper, showing no signs of anger but only hopeless weariness. She had gone as white as a sheet, holding on to the wheel of the carriage to prevent herself from collapsing to the ground.

Alex could not work out why her mother was so upset but was reassured that neither she nor Magda nor Károly was responsible for her terrible mood, since they had been allowed to sit with the grown-ups at dinner. She loved the summer holidays in Balaton especially because they could stay up late, a privilege that made her feel like a big girl, although she was bored listening to the conversation of the adults.

Dinner was being served in the garden, and, much to Alex's delight, their table was rather crowded this evening. She loved having guests around. "The more the merrier," she always thought. Margit was there with her parents, sitting next to Sanyi, right opposite Alex. Her huge blue eyes moved right and left as she tried to follow the conversation. Alex had a lot to tell her, but grown-ups who never stopped talking would not, for some unfathomable reason, allow the children to say even a single word. Whatever we say is held to be an interruption, she thought. They're all edgy this evening anyway, so it would be best if I kept quiet and finished my food sooner than later. She glanced at Magda, who had already cleared her plate. "It's the end," she heard her mother say in a drained voice from where she was sitting at the other end of the table.

"It's the end," Gizella repeated, as she had been doing for the last few hours.

Alex looked at her uncle Kelemen, who seemed rather thoughtful tonight, unlike his usual self, not telling any jokes that would make them laugh. She did not quite like the grim look on his face, an expression that somehow frightened her, so she hastily turned her eyes to Károly, attentively listening to what Uncle Kelemen was saying – as if he understood anything. Alex decided to listen as well.

"It won't make any difference, I tell you. They're confiscating all landholdings one by one, sparing nothing – well, except for those that are smaller than forty hectares. Kun nationalised each and every private enterprise, be it industrial or commercial, every bank, every hospital, everything. They've socialised housing, transportation, cultural institutions, you name it. Every single thing!"

Alex was so full that she felt she would not be able to finish her fish. Her mother would be furious if she didn't. "Do dogs eat fish?" she asked herself. When she couldn't finish her meat, she secretly gave it to Cerise, who gluttonously waited underneath the table throughout dinner, but she guessed she shouldn't be giving her fish. It must be because of the bones, she reasoned as she took another forkful and washed it down with water, for she swallowed it much more easily that way.

"There's only a small minority that supports Kun for the social reforms he has promised." Now it was Uncle Filip talking. His disciplined but nevertheless loving blue eyes tucked under his bushy eyebrows had lost their tender streak tonight. Károly was carefully listening to him as well.

Alex wondered why Aunt Irén and Uncle Filip did not have any children. She wished they did because that would have meant having another cousin. She studied her aunt, who was beautiful in her own way, with a very long and slender neck reminding Alex of the swans swimming in the lake. At that very moment, she saw her aunt looking at her with a smile unexpectedly impish for her age. Resting her chin on her thin thumb, she was gazing at Alex with her green eyes, which looked as if they were going to pop out of their sockets. Could she have read Alex's thoughts? Was she cross because Alex thought she looked like an animal? But swans were beautiful animals.

"There aren't more than a handful of communists in this country," Uncle Filip continued heatedly. "The majority of his supporters are tricked into believing the promises he made to restore our borders."

Uncle Filip was the same height as Aunt Irén. Is my aunt too tall or is Uncle Filip too short, mused Alex? She decided it was her uncle who was too short because when he stood up, his eyes reached as far as Uncle Kelemen's chin. Or perhaps he was not short at all but only seemed that way next to Uncle Kelemen; Uncle Kelemen was really a very big man. Everybody seemed little next to him.

"He's doing everything he can, really, to take our lost territories back."

Alex looked at Uncle Kelemen who had started speaking again. Does he look like my father, she pondered? As far as she could see from the photographs, their faces were similar. She wondered if her father had the same voice as Uncle Kelemen and tried to remember if he used to talk like him. She forced herself to summon up her memories, but the picture she had of her father was extremely hazy. She tried to examine her uncle's green eyes, partly concealed behind his wire-rimmed spectacles. Did her father look as lovingly as he did? No, his eyes were far more affectionate – that was something she recalled vividly. They sometimes looked blue, sometimes green, but they always looked most lovingly.

"He did march the Hungarian Red Army northward to occupy part of Slovakia, didn't he? However, they don't leave him alone. He didn't have much choice but to withdraw his troops when the French threatened to intervene."

"Don't tell me that you approve of what these communists are doing."

Alex was surprised to hear Aunt Etel raise her voice like that. She had never before in her life witnessed her do that. Everybody was really touchy tonight, but she was certain that it was not their fault since neither she nor Magda nor Károly had done anything wrong. They had been behaving themselves very well, in fact. Something else must have happened. She reached out and touched Uncle Kelemen's hand. "Uncle? Are you angry at something? We haven't done anything to upset you, have we?"

"No, my love. Nothing of the sort." Her uncle looked at her with tenderness in his eyes, peering over the glasses perched on his nose. He stroked her hair. Everything must be all right, thought Alex. "Of course, I don't approve of them," she heard him hurl at Aunt Etel in a fuming tone of voice. "Kun is nothing but a coward."

At long last, the dessert was being served. Alex studied the red flowers adorning the dessert plate placed in front of her and wondered when they would be able to eat from the golden-rimmed plates like the grown-ups.

"Like all other Jews," her mother exclaimed condescendingly.

Rétes with sour cherries! Hoorah! She loved this dessert. It was the best thing their cook did. She enthusiastically set upon the contents of her generously filled plate, flashing a smile at Magda, who smiled back.

"He's hoping for an intervention by the Soviets."

"While he's doing that, by the way, he does everything he can to secure his rule," joined in Margit's father in a voice harsher than usual. "They say that the revolutionary tribunals have ordered hundreds of executions, most of them based on crimes against the revolution."

"They are expropriating grain from the peasants."

"What about the violence they commit against the clergy?"

"The rumour has it that they've been using the mauve-coloured velvet upholstery of the railway seats in first class compartments to make trousers for the children of the working class."

"There's no middle way," Gizella barged in, her voice rising above the clamour at the table, stifling all others and sending echoes into Alex's ears. "People strive to be absolute masters or absolute servants. Look at what they're doing, those who talk about equality. Roles might change, but there will always be masters and there will always be servants. The most ruthless oppressor is the former oppressed who is given unprecedented power."

Alex was truly bored and wished they could go and play. She leaned back on her chair and looked up at the sky. There were so many stars tonight. Before long, she saw a shooting star. "I should make a wish," she thought in haste. "*Maradj velem!* Stay with me!" she said, grabbing Károly's hand. Her brother clasped her hand tightly with both his hands. Unable to reach for Magda's hand, Alex stood up in panic and extended her other hand towards her sister, who was sitting next to Károly. She looked into her eyes and repeated her wish to make sure she heard it. "Stay with me! Both of you, stay with me forever."

6

The first days of August brought an unbearable wave of heat. Despite the blazing sun sucking up everyone's energy, the Kurzóns left the cooling waters of the lake and the leisurely summer torpor to hurry back to Budapest. Gizella wanted to be at home in Rózsadomb, having heard the news that the Romanians were moving towards the capital and Béla Kun had fled to Vienna. Upon her arrival, she invited Irén and Filip to dinner to celebrate the defeat of the Reds. With revengeful delight, she had allocated a special place in her drawing room for the latest issue of *Vörös Újság*, the daily newspaper of the Communists, an unprecedented exception since she had banned it from the house a long time ago.

"*The Proletariat in Danger!*" she chimed, letting out an expansive laugh as she read the headline again. "Hungary could tolerate Communism no longer than five months, not even five months but only one hundred and thirty-three days. Exactly one hundred and thirty-three dark days."

They opened yet another bottle of champagne; corks had been popping since the arrival of the guests. Gizella was in excellent spirits. "They say he fled by plane. He was flying the aircraft himself and flew so low over the hills of Buda that they could see his wretched face. They couldn't see his pockets, but they were apparently filled with his favourite chocolates and, more importantly, with jewels and precious stones. Golden chains were dangling from his wrists and arms. One such fine chain fell down onto the Vérmező Gardens, they say." She laughed mirthfully. "Just like a seesaw. As one side goes up, the other side comes down. You could create perfect masters from lower classes, but the process would require a couple of centuries. First of all, they would have to be fed till they burst – I should say for generations. Then it wouldn't be easy for them to learn how to walk with their backs straight, while the masters would need to learn how to stoop. In that case, what's the point of changing the system? The fact is, things don't change easily." She raised her glass, inviting everyone to drink yet again in honour of this excellent piece of news.

"The Romanian army is expected to occupy Budapest tonight," said Kelemen apprehensively.

"The Great Powers would never allow it. The Italians, the French and the British will never leave this honour to the Romanians," burst in Filip, ostensibly more optimistic than the others.

The following day the Romanian troops were marching along the streets of the capital, continuously blowing their deafening trumpets under the incredulous gaze of the Hungarians, who were mortified beyond description at what was happening to their beloved city. This could be nothing but an unbearably preposterous incubus for the Hungarians and a far-fetched dream for the Romanians, who found the whole episode no less unbelievable.

The Romanians revelled in the beauty of the Pearl of the Danube – in contrast to its inhabitants who suffered in humiliation – until one rainy Sunday in mid-November when Miklós Horthy, a former admiral of the Austro-Hungarian navy, entered Budapest, proudly sitting on a white horse. The dark clouds over the capital somewhat dispersed with the departure of the Romanians, and the Hungarians entered 1920 with warm hopes despite the freezing cold, the incessant snowfall, an omnipresent frost and a blinding fog. Their spirits rose even more in January, when men and women cast the first secret ballots in the history of their country. Everyone watched in delightful amazement the shortened skirts and loosened dresses – a symbol of female independence – as women put away their corsets to enjoy the possibilities offered by their newly gained rights. The parliament, dominated by the right-wingers, decided to restore the monarchy in March, but the king's return was postponed until civil disorder subsided. Miklós Horthy was elected as the provisional head of state.

In June all hopes and high spirits gave way to a profound sense of despondency. The news from France was cataclysmic. The peace treaty signed at the Grand Trianon Castle at Versailles had divested Hungary of two-thirds of its territory, which had to be turned over to the newly formed states of Czechoslovakia and Yugoslavia, and to an enlarged Romania. Half of the country's population lived in these territories, and they had unexpectedly found themselves outside their homeland. The bad news left the streets of Budapest in a deadly silence. Black flags flew; church bells rang; trams stopped running; shops were closed. The whole nation was in mourning.

The Kurzóns did not go to Balatonfüred that summer. The end of July was drawing closer, and like all other Hungarians they were still mourning; their hearts, frozen stiff in the icy clutches of the Trianon disaster, needed a lot more than the summer heat to thaw them. That evening, after finishing their dinner on the veranda, the grown-ups moved to the Green Salon as the children bid them goodnight and retired to their rooms.

A few minutes after going to bed, Alex heard quiet footsteps outside her room. She jumped to her feet and opened the door a crack. Károly had just passed the Gallery, the landing that overlooked the large entrance hall downstairs, and was now creeping down the stairs. She darted a cursory glance at Magda, who seemed to be fast asleep. Thinking that she had better not waste time waking her up, she ran on tiptoe across the Gallery to the head of the stairs, quietly went down and then ran across the hall to the foot of the statue next to the door of the Green Salon, where she crouched down behind her brother.

"What are you doing here?" Károly whispered angrily through his teeth. "Go back to bed. Right now!"

"Please let me stay, *Öcsi*. I'm a big girl now."

"You must keep dead quiet then."

They heard Gizella's fuming voice. "Well, ever since March we've been calling ourselves a kingdom. However, there is one minor detail I find rather difficult to grasp, and that is the type of monarchy we have. A king in exile without a kingdom, a kingdom without a king and with an empty throne, and an admiral without a fleet as our regent. What, in God's name, would you call such nonsense?"

"We must be patient, Gizi. They say they're leaving the path open to the restoration of the monarchy when the time is ripe." That was Aunt Irén's voice.

Károly stood up. "The men must be in the smoking room," he whispered. "Come with me. And do be quiet."

They glided softly along the hall and sneaked past the door to the servants' staircase. They could hear the mumbled voice of the cook from the kitchen down in the basement. They skulked into the dining room and hid behind the open door of the smoking room, pressing their backs against the wall.

"I must admit that after what happened at Trianon I have my doubts about the capability – and intentions – of Horthy."

"It's bad enough to lose so much land, Filip, but worse still is that all our natural resources are now outside our borders."

"We're lucky that most of our industry is concentrated around Budapest."

"What's the use of factories when they're cut off from their supply of raw materials? Even if we had the raw materials to produce, people don't have the purchasing power to buy the products. Apart from all that, we've lost almost all our coalmines. They're opening up new ones, but their quality is pathetically low. The only solution to our energy problem is the electrification of the railways, and that's what I'm trying to convince the government to do."

"What's more to the point at this moment, Kelemen, is that we don't have enough food. Half of our arable land is gone. Look at us, the granary of the vast Austro-Hungarian Empire. Now we don't have enough grain to feed ourselves."

Alex held her breath and pulled closer to Károly as she heard the voices approaching the doorway. They watched their uncles stroll to the dining room and then into the adjoining Green Salon, carrying on with their conversation. After waiting for a few seconds, they silently slid along the wall until they came to a halt next to the doorframe and knelt down.

"It's as if the whole population from the lost territories had poured into Budapest. How can this poor city tolerate so many people? There's bound to be poverty; there's bound to be unrest. They hold protest marches almost every day. People are helpless."

"They're destitute," joined in Gizella. "They say there are people living in railway wagons, people who are genuine Hungarians, pure Magyars, homeless and unemployed. They should be able to find work, shouldn't they? But they can't. And why is that? Because of the Jews. They're everywhere, grabbing every single position available, especially those in the civil service. There's one major cause at the root of all our misery: the Jews."

Alex gasped, feeling a sudden shortness of breath as she listened to her mother, who sounded as if someone were strangling her. She always wore dresses that were too tight, preventing her from breathing comfortably.

"There's talk of a land reform, meaning that they will be appropriating hundreds of thousands of hectares of land from the large landowners, divide them into smallholdings and distribute them to the people."

"What about our estates in Kengyel and Eger?" interjected Gizella, in a tone of voice that showed fury rather than worry. "I don't believe Horthy could possibly take such drastic action. Even the Communists didn't dare do it. I do hope we don't end up longing for those horrific days under Communism."

"Come, come, Gizi. You know that Horthy's all talk and no action. He's only soft-soaping the masses. I don't think such a reform could ever be put into practice."

"I so much yearn for peace; I'd give everything to go back to where we were before 1914."

"Stop daydreaming, Etel," grunted Gizella. "We should focus on what can be done now and be grateful that we have someone like Teleki as our prime minister; at least he had the decency to set that quota limiting the admission of Jews to universities. Six per cent of the total number of students seems an appropriate measure, I think."

"I do fear that they've gone a little bit too far in their measures," said Kelemen. Alex could hear his uncle's voice gradually rising in accord with the sound of his footsteps getting stronger as he paced up and down the wooden floor. "They jailed tens of thousands of people, claiming that they were a threat to the traditional order the military is trying to establish. Communists, socialists, Jews, leftist intellectuals, sympathisers of Mihály Károlyi and Béla Kun, you name it. Thousands are being executed without trial, Gizi. There are rumours of torture."

"Do you really believe these things?"

"In rural areas, there appears to be a wave of terror against the Communists and anyone who has any connection with them. They talk about beatings, even lynchings. The situation is very grave indeed. There is anti-Jewish sentiment spreading rapidly because of Béla Kun being a Jew. It goes without saying that it's extremely dangerous for the government to set such a limit at a time like this; it's like adding oil to the flames. People complain that what we're going through is not much different from what happened during the Red Terror, except for the colour; they call this the White Terror. All the leftists, intellectuals, and middle-class Jews are being forced to leave the country. And those who can't are converting to Christianity – tens of thousands of them."

"Please, Kelemen, that's enough. You make it sound so ghastly."

Alex could not understand why her mother was so cross. What did she have against the Jews? Were they bad people? János, Károly's best friend at school, was Jewish, and he was very kind and very clever.

A year before János was born, his parents had left their home in Nyíregyháza at the very northern tip of the Great Hungarian Plain and moved to Budapest to a flat on the second floor of a five-storey apartment building on Király Street north of the Dohány Street Synagogue in the Jewish Quarter, an area predominantly but not exclusively Jewish. Károly often talked about this little quarter, which he found very amusing. "It's an animated neighbourhood," he kept saying, "with its street vendors, tailors, barber shops, kosher shops, the mouldy odour emanating from its second-hand clothes dealers, bookstalls crammed with books, a miniature of a dark publishing house and several soup kitchens sending out mouth-watering smells." János's family was a real crowd. He had aunts, an uncle and numerous cousins, most of whom lived in this neighbourhood. Károly said that their table was always crowded, particularly on religious holidays when his father invited total strangers he met at the synagogue, people who were less fortunate than them. They always had plenty of good food accompanied by a good amount of prayers at meal times. János said he did not understand a single word of those prayers and had no intention of learning them. His parents Monsieur Fodor and Madame Fodor – or Rebeka *néni* as all of János's friends preferred to call her – were very warm-hearted people.

Károly's favourite among János's relatives, however, was his uncle – Sámuel *bácsi* – who often went to the countryside and returned with plenty of interesting stories, laughing at them himself more than anybody else did. Károly loved these anecdotes and recounted all he had heard from him to Alex and Magda in the most exhilarating manner. Alex, however, preferred to hear about the adventures of Károly and János, listening avidly to how they played in the small backyard of János's apartment building with other children from the neighbourhood, or raced their bicycles up and down the street. Once, provoked by János's cousin Dávid, they had sneaked out of the neighbourhood on their bicycles – something strictly forbidden by their parents – and gone to the train station, where they played cowboys, climbing on top of the railway carriages. Károly always said it was one of the most entertaining days of his life. Unfortunately, their fun had been cut short when the stationmaster, whom they had dubbed the Chief of the Indians, caught them and threatened far worse than flaying the skin on their heads. "I shall immediately report this to your parents," he growled, not giving in to the supplication of Dávid, who usually had no trouble convincing people of his innocence, with his huge glasses extending beyond his face and with his hair, even curlier and darker than János's, ingenuously dangling past his temples. In the end, the stationmaster had delivered each one of them to his doorstep. After this unfortunate incident, Gizella forbade Károly to see János outside school hours except for birthdays. "There might be only a few hundred metres between Andrássy Boulevard and that rotten neighbourhood," she often repeated, "but in social scale, there are kilometres."

"What are you doing here? Why aren't you in bed?"

Hearing their nanny's voice, they both jumped to their feet with fright, for they were doing something forbidden and had been caught red-handed.

"We've come down for some milk, Nanny Ildikó," said Károly guiltily. He was not convincing at all. "Please don't say anything to Mother."

"Go to bed now. I'll bring up your milk."

It was a very narrow escape. Luckily, Nanny Ildikó had shown some mercy this time. Their mother was so nervous today that she would have given them a good thrashing had she learned of their mischief.

7

As soon as Irén and Filip walked through the main door, Gizella ran to her sister-in-law and flung her arms around her.

"What we've heard is true, Irén. He's back. He has attended the christening of one of Count József Cziráky's children in Sopron. And today he's coming to Budapest."

"Who, *Anyukám?* Who is back? Is it Daddy?"

"Our king, Alex. King Károly. With Queen Zita. He's back. He's here. He's in Hungary. The king of the Hungarians is back."

Alex had not seen her mother so happy for a very long time. She had been continually hugging and kissing everyone since that morning.

"Children! You should put on your best clothes after lunch. We shall be going to the Pest side in the afternoon to welcome our king," said Gizella as they all walked towards the Green Salon, rejoicing and laughing.

"Will the Crown Prince be coming?"

Gizella seemed not to have heard Alex's question, for the grown-ups had already started talking among themselves. The children compliantly sat at their usual places on the sofa.

"Shall we put on our red dresses, the ones we wore in Easter?" Alex whispered, leaning towards Magda. "No, no, no. They're a bit worn out now. We'd better put on the new dresses we got for our birthday."

"Only our king could save us from this poverty."

"Don't put your hopes up too much, Gizi. This is nothing but an improbable fantasy. What happened when he came at Easter? Nothing. Horthy sent him right back to Switzerland. His arrival served only one purpose, and that was to divide the right wing into two."

"Which dresses do you think we should wear, Magda?"

"Whichever you like."

"Be quiet," said Károly firmly from where he was sitting between his sisters, trying to listen to the conversation.

Alex leaned back and over towards Magda behind Károly. "Shall we put on the white lacy ones, then?" she said in a barely audible voice.

"All right, but we'd better ask Mother first."

"You're eleven years old for goodness' sake!" Károly broke in. "Do you still have to ask Mother's permission for everything? Wear whatever you like. It's not so important, is it? And do please shut up now."

Alex waited impatiently for a suitable break in the conversation to say what she had in mind.

"Filip is absolutely right, Gizi. We shouldn't be too optimistic. They would never allow our king to take the throne again."

"Who, if I may ask, dear Kelemen, wouldn't allow it? Do you mean Horthy, that make-believe regent of ours?"

"I meant our neighbours before anyone else. Czechs and Serbs are waiting with their rifles in their hands. Yesterday they handed over an ultimatum declaring that if the king remained, it would mean armed intervention. England, France and Italy are also showing their teeth, implying, 'If you can't take care of your internal affairs, we shall willingly give you a hand.'"

"*Anyukám*, could we put on our white lacy dresses, please?"

"Of course, dear. Of course, you can."

After long hours of waiting, the morbid news that came to Budapest weighed oppressively on the house in Rózsadomb like a dark cloud. King Károly had attended the baptism ceremony in Sopron, going through every detail of the Habsburg royal protocol in all its glory and then, accompanied by his new ministers, his court and three thousand armed gendarmes and some artillery officers, had set off towards Budapest, where he had planned to claim back his throne. After stopping at almost every station to make addresses to the people, the royal couple had spent the night at the palace of Count Esterházy in Tata. In the meantime the gendarmes, who had been led to believe that they were going to Budapest to fight the Bolshevist revolution, learned the truth and, abiding by Horthy's orders, took the King and the Queen to a monastery in Tihany near Lake Balaton, from where they escorted them out of Hungary on a British vessel on the Danube "for their own safety."

Gizella was left with no other choice than to be content with a kingdom without a king.

8

The 1920s saw Budapest, the capital of the king-less Hungarian Kingdom, gradually return to its glorious days, despite all the difficulties of the post-war years. Fashionable in Paris-inspired styles, elegant ladies and gentlemen sparkled in the drawing rooms and filled the theatres, ballrooms and shops. Refinement was more than in attire; it glowed through the letters, journals, operettas and the new mansions designed and built by Hungarian architects on both sides of the last section of Andrássy Boulevard leading up to the Város Gardens. Looking south from the Margit Bridge in the evenings, the glitter of the countless electric lights in the apartment buildings along the embankment and the white headlights of the few automobiles slowly moving on other bridges raised people's spirits. Bethlen's government had stopped the White Terror and managed to secure a foreign loan, fuelling industrial growth. It gave priority to the further development of the electrical train system, which increased the workload of the Ganz Factory and therefore of Kelemen. The patents he obtained for the machines he developed soon reached seventy. He spent most of his time either at the factory or at the Parliament, where he had recently become a member.

Gizella, on the other hand, focused most of her time and energy on shaping the future of her daughters. By 1927 Budapest had become an attractive place for Europeans, and Gizella thought it would be an excellent place for her seventeen-year-old daughters, who were not only beautiful but also blue-blooded and well educated. Not only the Hungarian aristocracy graced the capital; everybody from the Prince of Wales to the King of Italy flocked in to see the Pearl of the Danube. Gizella often took her daughters to receptions attended by the French and the English nobility. The Kurzón twins, Alexandra and Magdaléna, alluring with their tall and slender frames, coppery chestnut hair and impressive sea-green eyes, soon drew the attention of Budapest society. Gizella was determined to choose the best husbands for her daughters. The *ancien régime* might have been destroyed, but her children were never to forget who they were and where they came from.

"You must never, ever forget who you are and where you come from."

"Here we go again," murmured Károly, as he nudged Alex's leg underneath the table and winked at Magda sitting opposite him.

"Today, you're living comfortably in this country only because some thousand years ago Könd and other chieftains led by the great Árpád conquered these lands. You should be grateful to them and to Kurszán, the son of Könd, from whom our family descends."

"We know, *Anyukám*. We've already listened to all this so many times. He did very well, indeed. However, if we go back long enough, everybody descends from a very important person: Adam! We're all relatives, aren't we?" Károly did not hesitate to use his sense of humour pungently, especially when it came to teasing his mother.

"Being born with a silver spoon in your mouth, it's very easy for you to take everything so lightly, son. These people died for our country. You're indebted to them for being here. Every single soul in this country is indebted to them for being here."

"I don't think being their descendent is anything to be proud of. After all, they were, if I understand correctly, a bunch of barbarians who burned and destroyed, raped and pillaged."

"We're talking about another time, about one thousand years ago when the world was quite different than it is today."

"I still find it hard to comprehend what raping has got to do with gaining control over a territory."

Ignoring her son's sarcastic remarks, Gizella continued, her eyes strolling over the portraits on the walls. "Your father's family has been part of the ruling class of the country for years. Like your father, they were all heroes who defended our country. And the land bestowed upon our family for their bravery and conquests increased with each generation. At one time our estates included villages and towns, but today what we're left with is unfortunately not too grand – only our estates in Eger and Kengyel."

She would soon start talking about the painting hanging over the fireplace, thought Alex, the portrait of our heroic great-great-great-grandfather or someone or other who had lived in the fourteenth century, and about the castle that King Lajos had bestowed upon him, and then about the large estates King István had bestowed upon the Könd Duchy long before that, back in the eleventh century. She would then go into the details of how their father Gusztáv had gone to America for a few months in 1910 to work for Henry Ford in Detroit, and how, upon his return to Budapest, he was swept by Westernisation and had anglicised their family name from Kurszán to Kurzón. How utterly boring it all was! She thought of a way to make her mother stop, as she had no intention of spending her Saturday afternoon listening to her. She was supposed to go out with Károly and Magda.

"And don't you ever forget that your family name is actually Kurzón Egerlövö Szarvaskó Gadány, a name that will serve as a reminder of the estates your family once owned and, most importantly, of the fact that your ancestors were heroes."

Kelemen, who had been listening in silence so far, cleared his throat, a gesture that demanded the attention of everyone present, signalling the start of a long and serious lecture. He adjusted his eyeglasses and, raising one of his eyebrows, looked first at Károly and then at Sándor, Alex and Magda.

"You should never boast about your privileges because, as a matter of fact, you have nothing to boast about. However, you do have a great responsibility: to look after your land." His eyes moved from one youth to the other, keeping their attention. "Nobility requires you to protect your land as well as the people living on it, to take care of them, to help them produce and make a living. You might obtain the most prestigious and important posts, because such posts are naturally offered to those like yourselves whose ample financial resources and wide connections would help them run their offices efficiently. These positions and the privileges, power and respect you might obtain should never delude you. If you use your position not to fulfil your responsibilities but to puff up your pride, you'll not only be preposterous but also fool yourselves into believing that you're really superior, and thus bring disaster upon yourselves as well as upon those around you.

"Nobility does not just mean having certain privileges, power and prestige. You have to shoulder the responsibilities that your noble blood imposes on you. Nobility means assuming your duties. Being noble carries the obligation to act nobly. As members of the aristocracy, you have no choice but be noble in your actions. You should never forget that the true meaning of nobility is to act in a way worthy of your lineage and do as your obligations dictate. You do not have the luxury of free time. You're obliged to set a good example to those less fortunate than you are, lead them, help them, show them the way and protect them. And most importantly, remember that a noble person never expects recognition or gratitude in return for the favour or help he has given. He helps because that is what is right and what his noble blood dictates. *Noblesse oblige, mes enfants.*

"No matter what happens to the noble class in the future, no matter what condition you may find yourselves in, you should never forget your duties. This is something you owe to your ancestors. You should always act in a way worthy of the blood that runs through your veins. This is the most important legacy that you will be inheriting from Gusztáv and from me."

Gizella was stroking the family coat of arms engraved on the silver knife lying by her plate. "Your father Gusztáv," she started, "would never accept a favour or help from anyone but his closest friends. He would respond to the favours he received in an equally substantial way, and, if the provider of such favour were socially inferior to him, his response would be all the more generous. It was one of his principles that he never be indebted to anyone in any manner whatsoever, be it financial or moral. He carried out the duties imposed upon him by his nobility until the very end, even if it cost him his life." Gizella's usual harsh expression disappeared for a few seconds before she abruptly turned to Károly and fixed her eyes on him. "Instead of traipsing up and down Andrássy Boulevard, you should go to the University Library and read the diaries of your ancestors," she said curtly, raising her voice.

Károly jumped to his feet. "Yes. What a splendid idea. Off we go, girls! Sanyi, you too. Come on, come on, let's make a move."

It was obvious that Gizella did not believe her son. She must have guessed that they would not be going to the library, but her dominance over Károly, who was now twenty-one years old, was wavering. "We all know where you'll be going," she grunted to herself.

Kelemen was silent again, sitting back with his hands clasped on his lap and a touch of a wise smile on his lips.

"I'm staying," said Magda. "I ought to work on my portfolio."

"Alex!" cried Gizella. "That's what you ought to be doing too instead of going out so much. And if you do not intend to go the Academy, then remember that you'll have to get married sooner than later."

"Come on Károly, come on," hissed Alex between her teeth. "I'm suffocating."

As they went out, Károly said, "We'll be meeting József in the lobby of the Hotel Hungáriá."

"Who else will be there?"

"Do we always have to be in a crowd? Don't you ever have enough of your friends? Sometimes I do agree with Mother, you know. Her comments might be surprisingly to the point every now and then. It really would be better if you stayed home like Magda. You only have a few months left – if you want to enter the Academy, that is."

"Enough, Károly. Please. My portfolio is ready. The problem is the entrance exam. I'm really nervous about it." She felt her mood darkening. She had to focus on more amusing subjects. "Who else was coming, did you say?"

9

Finally, the day Alex dreaded arrived. In May she and Magda had presented their portfolios to the Hungarian Royal Academy of Arts and were found worthy of taking the entrance exam. At breakfast that morning Alex could not stop the shaking of her hand holding the coffee cup.

"Magda, I'm so nervous. I won't be able to do it. I really won't."

"Don't be such a fool. We'll be accepted even if we draw a single line in the exam. Aren't you aware of your talent, you silly girl? Relax."

Károly, who took every opportunity to tease his sisters, was dead serious this morning, knowing how important a day this was for Alex and Magda and what it meant for the rest of their lives. He took Alex's hands into his and closed his eyes. "Now listen to me, Alex," he said, slightly raising his chin. "Once in the exam room, before doing anything, close your eyes for a moment and try to imagine yourself under the trees next to our lake in Kengyel. Breathe in the sweet fragrance of the spring flowers lingering in the air. Watch the sunlight dancing on the water. Stroke the velvety lawn. Listen to the song of the birds. And then take a deep breath and let all of those sensations penetrate your soul."

Upon entering the high-ceilinged, menacingly huge exam room of the Academy and sitting at the desk reserved for her, Alex tried to recollect the mental image Károly had conjured up for her that morning. The white lily on her desk momentarily evoked the fragrances in their garden by the lake. Next to the lily stood a large sheet of white watercolour paper and a sable watercolour brush, but there was no sign of any paint or water. They had been informed not to bring anything to the exam room, so she was lost as what to do. Looking around with questioning eyes, she thought of calling the professor sitting at the far end of the room, submerged in her book, to tell her that they had forgotten to give her paint and water. Then she noticed that there were different materials on each desk, tubes of paint on some but no brushes, palette knives and oil paints on others but no turpentine. They had not forgotten to give her paint or water; they had done it on purpose. She envied the girl sitting at the desk next to her. She was so lucky in that she had an excellent charcoal pencil and a huge piece of drawing paper to work with, and all she had to do was to draw the nude model sitting in front of her. She looked at Magda, who was already engrossed in shaping the clay on her desk. A sharp pain clenched her stomach, a pain that would soon bring about a disastrously depressive mood. How was she supposed to paint a white lily on a white piece of paper without any paint, water or pencil but with only one brush? At that instant she heard the birds twittering outside. Recalling Károly's words, she turned her gaze out the window and tried to visualise the sunshine glittering on the lake. Closing her eyes, she took a deep breath to smell the spring flowers. Kengyel ... She was there by the lake, its coolness soothing her soul. Her eyes opened. She picked up the brush, noticing how dusty the desk was. And it was not only dust. In one corner, there was some graphite powder probably left by the previous occupant, who must have had a lot of pencils to sharpen. She licked the hair of her brush, gave the dust on the desk a brisk sweep and began shading in the outlines of a flower on the paper. A few minutes later a lily started to appear. She was soon lost in the exuberance of her creativity, cutting herself off from the world around her. She rubbed her finger into the graphite powder and made darker shadows. When the dust on the desk was finished, she picked up the dust on the floor with her brush. Her fingers, her brush, her hand, her soul were dancing. She surrendered herself to the rhythm of her inner world.

When she finished her lily, she leaned back, feeling a great sense of fulfilment, and glanced at Magda, who had almost transformed the piece of clay into a nude female figure. She looked at her sister's lips which she intermittently wetted with her tongue, at her perfect nose and at her long fingers shaping the clay. She was so beautiful. "Am I as beautiful as her?" she asked herself. I must be since we look exactly the same. She took a deep breath and waited for Magda to finish her exam, spending her time gazing at the portraits hanging on the walls.

10

It was a beautiful day, reminiscent of the early summer days of the Mediterranean Alex vaguely remembered from her childhood. Pansies had long given way to lilac blossoms, followed by a wealth of blooming wisteria and acacia, all of which were now enveloped in the delicious perfume emanating from the apricot trees. They had had a most amusing game at the Budapest Lawn Tennis Club, and Alex was feeling utterly satisfied and proud of herself for having beaten Károly for the first time in her life.

"Let's go and get something to drink, *Öcsi*. I'm really thirsty."

"You go ahead. I'll join you later. I want to go to the centre court. Rudi is playing there."

"Who is Rudi?"

"What do you mean, who is Rudi? Rudolf – Rudolf Takács. He's trying to get on the national team. I strongly advise you to watch him. You'll learn a lot and improve your tennis a little bit."

They started to walk towards the centre court.

Alex had no intention of being undervalued. "If there is someone around here who needs to play better tennis, it isn't me, dearest Károly."

"You must have a very short memory span, I'm afraid," snapped Károly, putting his arm around her shoulders. "Winning one match shouldn't make you forget how many times you've lost – and will lose." He planted a kiss on Alex's cheek, slightly damp with sweat. "So enjoy it while you can because it won't last long."

They sat down on the chairs along the side of the court.

"Which one is Rudolf?"

"Can't you tell? The one on the right, of course."

Alex should have guessed, not because of how well he was playing but because of how good-looking he was. She had actually heard his name many times before, often mentioned in bitter praise accompanied by several adjectives denoting pain. The infamous Rudolf, a distraction for the hearts, souls and minds of almost all the young girls in Budapest looking for a suitable husband, as well as of many a young lady who had already found one; a confirmed bachelor adored by all but never seen with anyone whom he introduced as his girlfriend, although he was known to have a lot of discreetly managed relationships; the only son of György Takács, probably the most renowned lawyer in Hungary, and Terézia Takács, one of the three daughters of the Vastag family, known for their boundless wealth. They lived in one of the superb mansions on the spectacular Andrássy Boulevard. Rudolf had graduated from law school that year and was ready to take over his father's law firm. He was said to be very ambitious and very successful. A bright future awaited him and the wife he would choose, something that opened doors into young hearts all over Budapest. Rudolf, however, loved to enjoy life and had nothing but tennis on his mind. Everybody knew that girls meant no more than a fleeting pastime for him. Despite his notoriety, this was the first time Alex had seen him, and she had no difficulty in understanding why they all adored him so much.

"Károly!" she whispered excitedly into her brother's ear. "Why don't you introduce us?"

"Are you sure you want to meet him?"

"Of course I'm sure."

"Well, I'm not so sure if I want to introduce you."

"What makes you say that?"

"You aren't deaf, are you? Or aren't you living in Budapest? Listen, darling. I don't want you to get hurt. Come on, let's get going."

"Come off it, Károly. I'm not a baby anymore. Don't forget that I'm seventeen years old; stop protecting me. You wouldn't want me to become an old spinster and pester you for the rest of my life, would you now? Besides, what is in an introduction? It's not like I would fall head over heels in love with him at first sight, and he'd make my life miserable forever after. You should start writing novels. I'm sure you'll be great in melodramatic fiction."

"Just a word of warning. Don't say I didn't tell you, all right? Please be careful."

"All right, all right."

He held out his hand as he stood up. "Let's go then."

Alex practically jumped to her feet. She could feel her heart's thunderous hammering as they walked hand in hand along the court towards Rudolf, who had finished playing and was wiping the sweat off his face with a towel. As they approached him, he wrapped the towel around his neck, leaned his head slightly to one side and fixed his eyes on Alex. His arrogant and perhaps somewhat ironic gaze, which nevertheless failed to hide his admiration, set butterflies flying in her stomach. His piercing deep blue eyes were so captivating that they threatened to draw her in where she felt she would be unconditionally lost. When their eyes met, her thundering heart skipped a beat, her knees went weak, and she held on tightly to Károly's hand. It was as if she had suddenly turned blind to the world around her, bewitched by Rudolf's eyes, which, despite their intimidating harshness, had a compelling attraction to them. When in the end she managed to tear her eyes away from his, she noticed his bony nose, irresistibly potent and dangerously overpowering in contrast to the soft curls of his short brown hair. A hesitant but sweet excitement grabbed her. His self-confident demeanour, fuelled by his raw power, made her twinge; her whole body was enwrapped by a consuming desire. Forget it, Alex, she said to herself, forget it! She tightened her hold on Károly's hand. And then Rudolf smiled. It was a smile that changed everything. His entire face lit up, and his features melted into a soft expression. He was smiling with his eyes. He had such a perfect set of teeth. Not knowing what to do, Alex looked away and turned to Károly, hoping that he would say something.

"Hi there, Rudi." Károly let go of Alex's hand to shake Rudolf's.

"Why, hello," he greeted Károly and swiftly turned to Alex. "Hi. I'm Rudolf."

"Rudi, this is my sister Alexandra," barged in Károly before Alex could open her mouth.

Rudolf had taken Alex's hand into his and was gently raising it to his lips. "It's a great pleasure to have met you at long last, Mademoiselle de Kurzón."

Alex wished that these few seconds would last forever, with Rudi's lips touching her hand and his eyes penetrating hers. "It's a pleasure for me too," she said faintly.

Károly grabbed Alex by her waist in an effort to control the situation. "Now then. Shall we go and have a drink?"

The three of them walked towards the clubhouse.

11

Two weeks later Alex, leaving her mind and heart in Budapest, moved to the summerhouse in Balatonfüred with her family. Not even a week had passed when she lost her patience and, finding a moment when her mother seemed to be in a good mood, reminded her that they had not yet celebrated their acceptance into the Academy, giving a strong hint of their wish to invite their friends over for the occasion. Together with Magda, they begged her, insisting like little girls, bouncing on their knees. "We wouldn't even think of celebrating such an important event on our own, *Anyukám*. And besides, we're already missing our friends in Budapest." Their mother, hesitant at first, finally gave in, since she could not tolerate seeing her daughters suffer from even a trace of loneliness. The reason behind her leniency, however, might well have been her intention to keep the upper hand, knowing very well that her daughters, hand in hand with Károly, would do as they pleased as soon as she left with Kelemen and Etel for Frankfurt for the premiere of Béla Bartok's *Piano Concerto No.1* in two days. Eventually, she gave her permission for a picnic in their garden the following Sunday. Alex and Magda called all their friends. Alex did everything she could to ensure that Károly invited most of his friends as well, especially Rudi.

Finally, Sunday came. Almost everybody had arrived except for the person who was the reason behind all Alex's efforts to organise this picnic. She checked the cars parked on the road; the white Bentley was still nowhere to be seen.

"Magda. He's still not here. I don't think he'll be coming."

"Of course, he will. If you don't wait so anxiously, he'll come sooner," Magda reassured her, draping her arm over Alex's shoulders.

"How do you mean?"

"If you keep your mind on other things, time will pass faster. That's what I mean. Come now, let's join Károly and the others."

Loud laughter rose from a group spread out on the lawn under the trees. Károly was on his feet, heatedly engrossed in what he was relating while everyone around him listened attentively, riveted by the magnetism that never failed to make him the focus of any group. He was a true gentleman, an entertainer with an indefatigable sense of humour, putting everyone in good spirits with his jokes, which he never exaggerated except when he teased his sisters; a gallant man when it came to girls and an adventurer when it came to his male friends. He held an allure, a sort of childishly innocent charm that went beyond masculine attractiveness. His straight hair, which had been almost platinum-white when he was a baby, had slowly turned into light brown as he grew up, but still shone in blond streaks under the sun. It often fell across his forehead, accentuating the tenderly loving look in his hazel-tinted green eyes, touching the soul. His aquiline nose, however, although much finer than the aggressive predatory noses of the Kurzón men, reflected, in stark contrast with the tenderness in his eyes, his uncontrollably rebellious spirit, ready to erupt at the slightest provocation. This was probably the only feature he had inherited from his mother. He moved with the agility of a deer, something quite unexpected from someone with such a tall frame. He had endless energy; he never stopped moving. When he spoke, he expressed himself with his whole body, especially with his hands, which, despite their size, reflected the refinement of his creative disposition, perhaps because of his long fingers – a trademark of his father's side of the family. Alex often felt tired as she watched him talk. There were times, however, when he suddenly cooled down, saying that it was time he poured all his energy into his creative and mental faculties. During such periods, which never lasted too long, he evoked a sense of compassion in others with his slim body, elegant posture and, if it happened to be wintertime, with his pallid skin. Then quite unexpectedly, as if he were determined to prove everyone wrong, he would snap out of his reverie and, with a big smile on his thin lips, show his perfectly white teeth, dazzling everyone. As in everything he did, there was an inborn refinement in the way he spoke and laughed. He was so polite that when he was with some of his male friends who were less courteous than him, he would try to be less mannerly as though he did not want to make them feel self-conscious. He never could, however, manage to be uncouth and therefore turned everything into a joke. Alex found it hard to understand what Károly found in some of his friends – in János, for instance.

János and Károly had known each other ever since they were ten years old. They had met in the *gimnázium* and their friendship went from strength to strength in their university years. They were vastly different from each other in their physical appearance, attitudes and the way they had been brought up. János was the very antithesis of Károly, not only because of his curly black hair, slanting dark brown eyes and dark skin but also because of his serious nature, sober disposition and angry expression, exaggerated by his eyebrows being too close to his eyes, all of which made him look much older than his age. Although unnoticeable at first sight, his attire, contrary to Károly's, hung askew on him, for they had been selected not by desire but by obligation. He was much shorter than Károly, but his frame was considerably larger. It seemed to Alex that János was what Károly strove to become but never dared to be. He was like the bastion of how his rebellious nature, which he was forced to suppress, might surface. Following his graduation from the *gimnázium*, Károly had decided to study mechanical engineering at the Royal József University, despite not being in the least interested in the subject matter. The driving force behind this unlikely choice had not been his mother's constant drumming into him that he had to go to the university where his father and uncle had studied, but his desire to be at the same school as János. Alex witnessed, more often than not, how he forced himself to read the books János read, probably because he did not want to break his heart or, most likely, because he sought to be like him. She would not be surprised if he became a Communist soon. A few months ago János had joined KIMSZ, the youth organisation of the illegal Hungarian Communist Party. Alex did not take János to be a Communist at heart and was certain that he had become one out of spite, in reaction to his father who, although somewhat relaxed under the influence of János's mother, was still fanatically pious.

Alex's thoughts scattered as she heard Károly call out, "József! Finally. What an honour to have you with us at long last. You're late, old boy."

Alex adored József. He was a true gentleman. He explained, in that economical yet unmistakably polite way that only a gentleman like him could adopt with success, how his car had broken down the day before, obliging them to take the morning train; how, thanks to the slowness of the staff at the Anna Grand Hotel, it had taken them ages to unpack; how terribly sorry he was to be so late and why his brother Ákos could not make it. He spoke with a lisp, most probably not inborn, giving a supercilious tone to his voice, unexpectedly deep and full coming from such a thin frame as his. As he spoke, the gentleness in his black velvety eyes immediately arrested the attention of those around him. He parted his straight dark-brown hair on one side and meticulously combed it back, indifferently revealing the receding hair on his temples. He was the image of his father, Count Almás, not only physically but also in his behaviour and attitude.

József and Ákos were the two sons of Count Almás, coming from a family of important diplomats, and, true to family traditions, both of them had studied first at the Fasori Gimnázium and then at the Royal József University. Their friendship with Károly went back to a time before their days in Fasori. The Almás family estate in Martfü was adjacent to the Kurzóns' estate in Kengyel.

Ákos, much better built than his elder brother, had thick and rebellious hair partly covering his face and harsh-looking blue eyes that bore an exact likeness to his mother's. Despite his rough looks, he was extremely timid. As always, he had devised an excuse not to come. Alex sometimes thought he loved his horses more than he loved human beings. József, on the other hand, enjoyed social life and was an indispensable part of every reception in town. He had come with Klára. Alex could not fathom what somebody like József could possibly find in this girl. She was definitely not his type and certainly not a suitable match for him. She was too light, so to speak, and it seemed as if she were trying to compensate for her lightness with an uncalled-for display of excessive jewellery. That brooch she had put on the belt surrounding her hips, for instance. More suitable for a ball than a picnic luncheon. Utterly kitsch, really. How old was she? She must have been older than József surely, or perhaps she looked that way because of her heavy make-up. Even Alex's mother's lips were not so prominently painted, like a bow. And her cheeks looked like Easter eggs. Was it true love that oozed out of her as she gazed at József with those ostentatiously amorous eyes from underneath her darkly coloured eyelids, or was it all part of the role she was hoping to play?

"That's enough, Alex," whispered Károly in her ear, grabbing her by the waist. "You're going to kill her with your stare."

She had probably overdone her scrutiny. Switching her attention to Fábián, she started listening to the artificially sweet compliments he was paying Klára, who displayed a smile that was no less artificial. Fábián was as sticky as his jet-black hair, which he always combed back with an excessive dose of brilliantine. Alex looked at his huge meaty hand, quite inelegantly resting on Klára's hips, and then at his tiny nose squeezed in between his fat cheeks. They hardly seemed to belong to the same person. How could Rozália, his poor wife, looking so fragile and helpless next to his oppressively wide shoulders, put up with that philanderer of a husband who constantly came on to anything female in sight? And Fábián? What on earth did he find in women that was worthy of so many compliments? His wife, with her blond hair and dreamy green eyes, was one of the most attractive women in that party, if not in all of Budapest. It seemed like a joke that he would talk about the beauty of others in Rozália's presence.

"The smile on your sweet lips is not convincing at all, gorgeous." This time it was János whispering in her other ear. He had finally given up his position on the lawn, where he had been sceptically watching others behind a veil of smoke rising from the cigarettes he had the habit of chain-smoking. Disregarding the fact that he would be leaving Ada – the girl he had come with – on her own, he had walked over to Alex and grabbed her waist from the other side. Károly pulled his arm away, at ease with the idea of entrusting his sister to the safe hands of János and, cutting short Fábián's pointlessly exaggerated compliments, started, no less needlessly, singing János's praises. He talked about how bright his dear friend was and how easily he had been admitted to the university despite *Numerus Clausus* – the quota limiting the number of Jews entering the university, permitting six Jews in every hundred students – as well as about many other details that made Alex lose all her interest in his discourse.

"If it were not for your uncle, it would have been rather difficult for me to enter the university," said János, interrupting Károly with his usual modesty and, most unfortunately for Alex, started to talk about even more boring details, presuming that Klára and Rozália had no idea about the quota.

Alex could hardly concentrate on what János was saying, for her mind and her eyes were glued to the garden gate. Why was he so late? Perhaps he would not be coming after all. If he did not, all this effort would have been in vain.

"Proving your 'loyalty to the nation' was more important than your grades, and that criterion was determined by the university leaders. In that respect, I'm much obliged to Monsieur Kelemen de Kurzón."

"He only voiced the truth. You and your family are among the most patriotic Hungarians I've ever met," said Károly, and he continued with his praises for a while longer, showing how proud he was of his friend. Then he went over to where Ada was and lay down next to her on the lawn.

Had Károly forgotten to invite Rudi? He probably had. Or it might have been that he did not even consider inviting him in the first place, turning a deaf ear to her entreaties. Should she ask him if he did eventually call him? Suddenly the smell of her perfume, which she had sprayed all over her several times since this morning, felt too strong. She had overdone it. "What sort of an impression would I make on Rudi," she thought, flinching, "garbed in Schiaparelli's shocking pink dress and soaked in Chanel No. 5?" She was no more than a brightly coloured flower sending out its heavy scent to attract the bees so as to ensure the reproduction of its species. It had been the wrong choice. She could have put on something simple like Magda's plain pair of trousers and comfortably casual top.

Margit had come over and, with admiration that overflowed from her blue eyes too big for her round face, was watching János, who had skilfully managed to bring the conversation to politics again.

"According to our Right Honourable Prime Minister Count István Bethlen, an anti-Semite is someone who detests the Jews more than necessary."

Alex was bored to tears. Even the searing heat could not dry up János's enthusiasm for politics. He rattled on about how Bethlen, knowing very well that the country needed foreign capital for its restructuring, protected the rich Jewish industrialists while having no objection to the elimination of the Jewish opposition, how he tolerated the expression of opposing ideas in Parliament while he demanded absolute silence on the streets; and how the government imposed many obligations on the people while it refused to accept any responsibility towards them. And thus speaking, he managed to bore everyone, except of course Margit. She clearly did not understand a word of what he was saying but was listening anyway since it was János who was speaking. "She's so naive, despite her sixteen years of age," thought Alex. Unable to put up with János's tirade any longer, she grabbed József's hands. "Come Józsi, let me introduce you to Ada," she implored. Holding Klára's hand too, not by choice but by social graces, she pulled them towards where Károly was.

Her brother had gathered a large group of friends around him including Ada who, for the first time since her arrival, had a smile on her face. All of János's friends were far too serious and pessimistic. Alex found a convenient pause in the conversation and asked József if there were any other of their friends staying at the hotel. He said he did not know; he had not seen anyone he knew. Alex's hopes were swiftly fading away. Rudi would definitely not come.

Suddenly, she gave a little shiver as a breeze flicked at her bare arms. Was it a breeze, a breeze so light that it had not even moved the leaves on the trees but had given her a chill?

She heard the girls behind her whispering eagerly.

"Zsazsa! He's arrived. Rudi is here."

Alex caught her breath as she turned her head towards the garden gate. At long last!

"He knows so well when to make an entrance – after all the other guests."

"My God, he's so handsome!"

"He has different girls with him again."

Why does he have to fill his car up with girls, thought Alex? Well, it's better than just one girl. I wonder which one has been his girlfriend. Or maybe he's had a relationship with each and every one of them! The giggling of the girls behind her was so annoying. She dashed towards János and took his arm.

"Are you still talking about politics? Please Jancsi, that's enough. We should teach you how to have a good time." She put her head against János's shoulder.

Rudi, glowing in his white flannel suit, had jumped out of his car before Álmos, the head butler, had had the time to open the door, and he was helping the girls to get out.

"Aren't I right, Margit?" Alex asked, her eyes fixed on Rudi.

"I'm having an awfully good time," she vaguely heard János say, "especially when you torment me with your nagging." He squeezed the tip of Alex's nose with his fingers.

Rudi left his car keys to Ádám, the driver, and started walking towards Alex with his arms wide open and his overflowing energy reaching out to everything and everybody around him. He strode confidently a few steps ahead of Álmos, who was carrying the box of French champagne Rudi had brought, and slightly in front of the three girls who carried nothing but the pride of having made it to the party in Rudi's car. "I must say something," thought Alex as she dragged her gaze away from Rudi. Come on Margit. Say something. Talk! She tightened her grip on János's arm, maybe a bit too much. He must be hearing my thundering heart, she panicked, hastily moving her arm away.

"Congratulations, Alex," Rudi called out as he approached her. Then he paused for a second, narrowing his eyes to focus his gaze. "Or should I say Magda?"

"Alex."

He grabbed Alex by her waist and pulled her towards him. "Congratulations," he repeated as he kissed her temple.

Does he take me for a child? Why doesn't he kiss me properly on the cheek? Or he could have at least kissed my hand.

Rudi took her hand and raised it to his lips as if he had read Alex's thoughts.

Keeping his eyes on hers, he said, "The men in Budapest are truly lucky. There isn't just one such beauty but two."

Alex knew that she was blushing. Rudi left her as fast as he had arrived and, starting with Magda and Károly, shared his attention, affection and attraction with almost everyone present, triggering a sense of utter frustration in Alex. She could not expect him to stay with her all the time, but she believed she deserved to be at the epicentre of his attention since this party was being given in her honour – and, of course, in Magda's – to celebrate their entry into the Academy. She tucked her empty champagne glass into the hand of Izabella who was walking by, and snatched her full one. Poor Izabella. How upset she must be that Ákos could not make it today. She hid her feelings rather well though, her big brown eyes showing no trace of disappointment. Or perhaps she was not as much in love as she said she was.

"Izabella, I'm so in love," she said below her breath.

Her friend had question marks in her eyes, obviously ignorant of whom Alex was talking about.

"Who do you think?" whispered Alex, glancing surreptitiously at Rudi talking to a group of girls.

"He's not for you, Alex. Besides, it's only been a month since you've met him. That's rather quick to decide you're in love, don't you think? How many times have you seen him so far? Three? Four?"

"Just once. And that was enough. It was love at first sight."

"You should be careful, my sweet sister," Károly barged in as he joined them, apparently guessing exactly what Alex was talking about. "Everybody knows what Rudi is like. He's a heartbreaker. And that means he'll take your heart in his hands in an instant and then break it in the next."

"If I remember correctly, you were very happy to be Rudi's friend, weren't you?"

"That's a different kettle of fish altogether. As a man, one could hardly find a better friend. He's adventurous, sportive, loves to have fun and is always surrounded by the most beautiful girls. However, such a man could only break your heart, sweetie. There are many suitors around you who could make you much happier. Open your eyes a little."

"Come on, Károly. Please don't ruin the day with your gloomy warnings."

"Don't depress our princess," cut in János, putting his arm around Alex's shoulders.

He had finally come up with something useful to say, thought Alex.

"There you go. Here's your prince coming to your rescue on his white horse," butted in Károly.

Yes, she had a prince on a white horse, but it was not János.

Adrian Rollini's voice filled the air, spreading from the portable gramophone they had taken out into the garden:

"I need lovin'
That's what I crave
I need lovin'
I can't behave ..."

The head butler signalled that lunch was ready to be served. Alex and Magda invited everyone to the tables set out on the lawn under the trees. Alex had placed herself at the same table as Rudi, giving him the seat right opposite her. As hosts, Magda, Sándor and Károly had to accompany other guests at different tables. Alex had made sure that Károly – as well as János – conveniently sat at the table farthest away from her. She was determined not to let anyone spoil her mood, at least during lunchtime. She had placed József, whom she knew would be her saviour in awkward moments, next to her – unfortunately, along with his tawdry girlfriend. Throughout lunch, she could hardly concentrate on the mumblings of Margit sitting on her right and constantly talking about János, neither could she relish the dishes that kept coming, nor could she enjoy the conversation among her friends, whom she used to find most diverting until a few weeks ago. Nobody, nothing aroused her interest more than Rudi did. Every time he opened his mouth or shifted his arresting eyes towards her, she felt thousands of butterflies in her stomach. She had so little appetite left that she managed to eat only a tiny bite out of her *Dobos* tart, a most delicious dessert, watering the mouths of even the most replete guests with its buttery cakes sandwiched with an abundance of mocha cream and topped with chopped hazelnuts under a hard caramel glaze.

József was watching the dessert wine poured into his glass. He stroked his beard, which marked him as a person of consequence, someone who had an important social status and kept to traditional values. Most keen on analysing different types of wine, he focused his discriminating gaze on the liquid swaying and swirling in the glass he delightfully moved in small circles on the table. A few lines appeared on his forehead as he raised his eyebrows and mused over his glass.

He put his aquiline nose almost entirely into the glass, closed his eyes and took several deep breaths. "I don't even need to taste it," he said confidently. "The grape is Tokaji Aszú. Château Szepsy. The best of Tokajhegyalja." He took a small sip. Keeping the wine in his mouth, he slightly opened his lips and drew in some air. After a short pause, he swallowed. "1923," he said proudly, "*Premier cru*, six *puttonyo*. *Vinum regum, rex vinerum.* The wine of the kings, the king of the wines." He raised his glass to Alex. "*Egészségédre!*" He turned to others and repeated the toast. "Cheers, everybody."

Rudi had preferred to continue with the wine they had been having with the fish. He raised his glass, trying to catch Alex's eyes. "For me, nothing can surpass the Szürkebarát grape, an unequalled treasure of exceptional strength despite its sweetly honey-scented taste. You can feel its power the moment it touches your lips, sending trickles down to your soul. A genuine Hungarian beauty. The only wine that can cope with our heart-burning hot dishes."

Alex felt his insistent gaze slowly sliding down to her heart as he sipped his wine. She was ready to surrender her whole being to his seductive eyes, still wandering all over her while he gently put his glass down. She sat up on her chair, trying to straighten up not only her posture but also her heart. Unable to look at him any longer, she lowered her eyes to the dessert on her plate, waiting to be consumed.

"Have you ever been to a grape harvest?"

Rudi's question, directed to no one in particular, was picked up by one of the covetous girls sitting at the other end of the table. "No, but I'd love to," she chirped eagerly.

Alex, pretending not to have heard Rudi's query, carried on struggling with her dessert. He was now talking about a friend of his who had a wine estate famous for its Szürkebarát grapes in Csopak, a small village very close to Balatonfüred. "Lajos Sonenberg. He's a very close friend of mine from law school. We've got to go to his chateau at harvest time in September. He'd be most happy to have us there."

A disturbingly long pause followed. Alex could feel him searching for her eyes, which were still fixed on her plate. She timidly looked up, unable to find anything to say more than a mere, "Thank you."

He rose from his chair to pour wine into Alex's empty glass. As he reached over the table, his thin shirt revealed the small movements of his strong muscles. How would it be to wake up in his arms every morning, she wondered, to know every single part of his body by heart, to be able to smell him as much as she liked, to be by his side all the time, to become Takács Rudolfné de Kurzón Alexandra – Alexandra de Kurzón, the wife of Rudolf Takács – and to go everywhere together, to be the woman everybody envied?

Margit had started to whine again. The wine seemed to have gone to her head a little. Alex listened to her laments, or rather tried to, but could not help picking up snatches of Rudi's conversation with the others.

"Nowadays girls are like fish," she heard Ferenc say. "They glitter in their sequined dresses and slip out of your hands."

"What could be more exciting," Rudi began, the tone of his deep voice mesmerising Alex, body and soul, "than running after a girl who slips from your hands and runs away in panic? Her resistance, in fact, reveals a secret. You see the suppressed desire covertly burning inside her, behind the veil of her objections. Resistance proves that you're about to win the game."

"Enough of this lethargic indulgence," snapped Alex, cutting short whatever Margit was muttering in her ear, and jumped to her feet. Raising her voice so that everyone could hear her, she went on, "All those who are in for some water-skiing, sailing or rowing! On your feet! Change into your swimsuits please." Then bending over towards Margit, she whispered, "A little bit of action will make you forget everything. You shouldn't brood so much."

As she hurried away from the table, she heard Rudi say, "It's impossible not to admire her energy after all that food." She quickened her pace, taking care not to step on Cerise scampering by her, and eventually broke into a run. She rushed up the stairs and into her bedroom, threw on her swimsuit, her new cream-coloured silk shorts, blouse and the matching beach coat, scrambled into her sandals and ran back down and out, all in an impossible rush as if she regretted every moment she spent away from Rudi. He was standing next to the steps of the veranda with his swimsuit in his hand, listening to Ferenc.

"Aren't you going to put on your swimsuit, Rudi?" she asked, walking towards them.

"I'd like to try Feri's motorcycle first."

Ferenc continued his animated discourse. "I really hesitated between a BMW R47 and this one. However, I believe Harley Davidson is the king of single-cylinder motorcycles."

"Feri," cut in Alex, stopping short, "you ought to teach me how to ride it one of these days. I'd love to be the first girl to do that in Budapest."

Rudi looked at Alex, his face lit up in a pleasant surprise. Then swiftly turning to Ferenc, he asked, "Could we borrow your motorcycle?"

A wave of excitement shot through Alex.

Rudi, without waiting for Ferenc's reply, had already taken off Alex's beach coat in one quick sweep of his hand and draped it over Ferenc's arm along with his own swimsuit. "Come with me," he ordered, holding Alex's hand.

She dreamily followed him as they walked towards the motorcycle parked close to the garden gate. I could walk like this till eternity, she thought, hand in hand with him. When he released her hand to push the motorcycle to the pathway that passed through the woods behind the house, she clenched her hand tightly to imprison the warmth of his skin. As they approached the pathway, he began telling her what she should be doing.

"It's very easy," he reassured her, turning on the engine.

Alex could hardly keep her mind on what he was saying; she was excited not because she was to ride a motorcycle for the first time but because it was the first time she had been alone with Rudi. Suddenly, for no reason in particular, she lost heart and was no longer sure if she wanted to ride. Her courage came back, however, as she felt Rudi's strong hands grab her by the waist to help her mount the motorcycle. When she finally settled down on the seat, her shorts slid up, leaving almost the length of her thighs exposed. In a futile move of her hand, she tried to cover at least the topmost part of her legs.

"Are you ready?" he asked, holding the seat from behind.

"Don't let me go, all right?"

"Don't worry. You'll see. It's easier than riding a bicycle."

She started to move at a very slow pace and eventually took her feet up from the ground. There you go, she thought. You're riding a motorcycle. The gentle breeze had pushed her shorts up almost to her hips again. She felt Rudi let go of the seat. Fearing that she might lose her balance, she dared not look behind. It was easy, after all. And so much fun. She took a deep breath, enjoying the wind caressing her face. This was freedom. An ecstatic laugh escaped her. "I want to go faster," she said to herself. The pathway was soon to join the main road. What should I do? I'd better not go onto the main road. Well, how on earth am I to turn this thing around? I'd better stop. No, no, I should continue. I'll go back to the house through the main road. At the crossroads, she turned slightly to the right and all of a sudden the motorcycle slid away from underneath her. I'm going to fall down. I *am* falling down! My leg! It'll fall on my leg. In panic, she tried to get off it, pulling away her leg just in time. The motorcycle was lying flat on the ground, its engine dead silent. She just managed to get it upright. How was she supposed to start it now? Flustered, her eyes searched the main road. There was no one in sight. She called out to Rudi at the top of her lungs, but she knew it would be rather difficult to make herself heard. She should turn back, for Rudi might have followed her. She started to walk, pushing the motorcycle. Yes, she was right; Rudi had followed her.

"What happened?" he asked, looking worried.

"I fell down."

"Are you all right?"

"Yes. Yes, I'm all right. But ... you shouldn't have left me."

"I didn't leave you. I'm right here, aren't I?" He pouted, imitating Alex's sulking face. Holding her chin, he pulled her closer. "I'm right here next to you," he repeated most tenderly. Then he took her in his arms as if trying to calm down a frightened little child. Alex felt her heart melt. God, he was so strong. She wished they could stay like that forever, for all eternity.

"Do you want to ride some more?"

"No, thank you. I think I've had enough for today."

Rudi started the engine and told Alex to get on behind him. Taking her hands, he put them around his waist. She could feel his muscles between her fingers. His shirt ballooning in the wind touched her lips, arousing in her an irrepressible desire to kiss him. She drew in the scent of his skin, feeling a sudden urge to embrace him really tight. I wish we could go away, she thought to herself, leave the guests and everything else behind and just go away ... as far as Budapest, as far as Vienna. She could go to the end of the world.

They left the motorcycle where they had found it. Magda was scurrying towards them.

"Where have you been? Everybody is waiting for you."

"I'm here, Magda."

Rudi went to one of the cabins by the beach to change into his swimsuit. Alex walked towards Károly, lounging in one of the deckchairs lined up under the trees where the lawn met the beach. He was in one of his quiet moods again. Just the right day for such a mood, thought Alex. With a dangerously dreamy gaze, he was watching Ada talking to János under the trees on the other side of the garden. She began watching her as well while she slipped out of her shorts and blouse. Couldn't she find anything better to put on, she thought, than a black dress in such hot weather? Is she in mourning, or what?

"A girl in a black dress," Károly said, reading Alex's mind, and continued without taking his eyes off Ada, "draws the attention to herself not to her dress. And like her dress, she might not be stunning, but she's discreetly essential. She's minimalist yet elegant, not mysterious perhaps, but impeccably refined and sophisticated."

She let out an expansive laugh. "I didn't know you read such magazines as the *Femina*. Your appreciation of Mademoiselle Chanel's idea of a little black dress, or rather your awareness of such an idea, comes as an utter surprise. Now, my dear *Öcsi*, I'll be going water-skiing, and I strongly advise that you stop lazing about daydreaming and start socialising." She stole a passing glance at Ada. "And don't let yourself get carried away too much." She whisked away towards her friends on the pier trying to figure out who wanted to do what.

Rudi, already in his swimsuit, walked towards Alex and, putting his arm around her shoulder, whispered into her ear what a gorgeous body she had. Suddenly self-conscious, she felt herself blushing. Leaving her, Rudi walked to the edge of the pier and, under Alex's admiring gaze, plunged into the water with an impeccable dive. As he put on the skis, Alex took Ferenc's hand and jumped onto the speedboat. The thunderous sound of the engine sent the swans waiting to be fed by the beach swimming away in fright.

12

Alex was sipping her ice-cold lemonade on the porch of the tennis club when she saw Rudi almost running towards them with a smile that melted her heart. A year had passed since they had met, twelve long months filled with moments of excitement, days and weeks of expectations, hopeful instants and hopeless hours. A whole year had gone by without a private moment together; they had never had a proper date, but only seen each other at parties, at the tennis club or at the opera, each an occasion where he had been extremely polite and paid her lots of compliments, each an occasion where Alex's heart surrendered more and more to his irresistible charm.

"I did it, Károly. I did it. I'm on the national team."

Károly stood up, opening his arms to greet his friend. "Bravo!" he shouted, grabbing him by his shoulders.

Hardly able to stand still, Rudi freed himself from Károly's hands, bent over to Alex, held her cheeks between his palms and planted a hurried kiss on her lips. "I'm so happy," he sang, his eyes shining.

"Congratulations," murmured Alex, bringing her fingertips to her lips to seal the unexpected sensation. Rudi seemed too excited to have realised that he had kissed her on the lips. He practically flew off to the next table and then to the next to spread the good news to his other friends, visiting almost every single table on the porch. Alex noticed, however, with joyous pride, that none of the kisses he distributed among the female population was planted on their lips. Her elated mood did not die away even when she heard Károly say, looking up in the air as if he were talking to a third person who was not there, "Trying to imprison an accidental kiss given at the wrong time, at the wrong place."

"You think you know everything so well, don't you?" she snapped crossly. "Do you really have to ruin the magic?"

Rudi was back. "I'm giving a dinner party at the Márkus Restaurant this evening. Please do come. János, József and Klára are also invited. Would you please tell Magda and Miklós? Is Sanyi still in Balatonfüred? Let Margit know that she's invited as well, would you? There'll be others too. I invited everyone. We must celebrate."

She could not make sense of Rudi's feelings. Was he simply being polite or was he really interested in her? If he was, however, why was he waiting before making a move? He was never seen alone with a girl. They said that he often went to Vienna. He definitely had a girlfriend there, Alex thought with pain. It was impossible for a man like him to be alone; girls would not let him alone even if that's what he wanted. He must have a lot of secret affairs. People did talk a lot about him, not knowing how much their petty gossip hurt her. And Károly. She did not understand why he had to dishearten her by informing her of Rudi's every move. He was simply being unbearably possessive of Alex. He had driven her mad when they were in Lech for skiing this winter, not leaving her alone even for a second as if she were a little baby. Rudi would not have been able to break through the wall Károly had built around her even if he tried. During those two weeks, she had no more than a few opportunities to ski with Rudi alone, and, on those rare occasions, she turned absolutely timid, unable to utter a single word since Károly's comments about Rudi constantly gnawed at her mind. He kept saying what a wrong match Rudi was for her, how he thought of nothing but his tennis and how he would never commit himself to a serious relationship. Rudi's tennis dreams, however, had come true now. Alex shooed away these unpleasant thoughts because, having been chosen for the national team, he would definitely be a bit more relaxed from now on. It would be better if she thought of what she should be wearing tonight. I must put on my creamy rose silk chiffon dress, she thought. Everybody said she looked beautiful in it.

13

They stepped out of the car in the middle section of the Margit Bridge, where the road turned towards the Margit Island on the River Danube. The jazz music coming from the island mingled with Viennese waltzes against a backdrop of cheerful chattering and the merry laughter of people enjoying themselves; an exhilarating *Csárdás* threatened to overpower all other sounds and voices. The lawn spread like an oasis under the shade of the gigantic two-hundred-year-old plane trees and the weave of colourful tulips; the alluring fragrances from the rose gardens, the serenity of the chestnut and the oak trees lining the pathway and the magical light of the setting sun conspired to enchant people away from the crowded city and into another realm. Alex and Magda were walking arm in arm in front of Károly towards the restaurant, their bird-like steps barely on the ground as they kept pace with the rhythm of a melody only they could hear. They moved comfortably in their loosely cut, sleeveless and collarless dresses which flew about them like the proud flags of their declaration of independence before sticking to their bodies in the breeze of their happy gait. The long narrow chiffon shawls around their slender necks, left bare by their bobbed haircuts, floated behind them, reaching down to their knees. They stopped a few times to fix each other's hair, giggling. Both of them were excited; both of them were in high spirits; both of them were head over heels in love. Károly said that it would be better if Alex forgot about Rudi, while he totally approved of Magda's relationship with Miklós. He believed that Magda had found a most suitable person for herself since she had, as always, used her brain rather than her heart and fallen in love with the right person. She had chosen someone who would not take her away from her passion for ceramics, but on the contrary would further her chances to enhance that passion. Miklós, who had succeeded in conquering Magda's heart in July, was not only handsome, polite and loving but also a very promising ceramic artist; he came from the Nerády family, which had produced many artists over several generations. Magda was discreet about her relationship, but Károly couldn't help teasing, saying, "I bet you met in front of a kiln, and your first kiss was rather a muddy one, beside a revolving piece of clay trying to become a vase."

Rudi was waiting for them at the entrance to the restaurant. The tables under the trees in the garden were already crowded with their friends, laughing and enjoying themselves. They walked among the vibrant-coloured flowers that surrounded the fountain and spread their fragrances into the garden. Rudi had reserved a place for Alex right opposite him. They settled down on their chairs. Everybody was there. Even Ákos had left his horses in Martfű to make it for tonight. Champagne, perfectly chilled in ice buckets, was generously poured into glasses. They drank to Rudi's admittance to the national tennis team.

The gipsy violin king Imre Magyari was playing a long and slow *Lassú*. Despite his excessive weight, he moved among the tables like a young Arabian stallion galloping on the Great Hungarian Plain. Other musicians did their best to follow him, and hoped for the moment when he would sit next to a client he knew and, narrowing his raven-black eyes, start whispering the latest gossip.

"What I meant was," said János, cutting the congratulations short, "that the policy of the Bethlen government might have straightened up the economy. However, we shouldn't be fooled by the glitter on the surface. Let us not forget that the only thing holding everything together is the foreign loans, which might precipitately be pulled out from under our feet. There is a huge wealth gap between different sections of society, and it's increasing all the time. The living standards of the working class are very low."

Next month János was to start his two-year military service as an officer; he was clearly proud to be the only one among his friends to have enlisted voluntarily. "It's the least I can do for my country," he kept saying, before adding enthusiastically, "for the moment, that is."

Ada was making calm and reasonable comments on János's heated discourse, but with a despondently serious air, rather unbecoming of a twenty-one-year-old girl. "The peasants are in a far worse situation. And the government is stubbornly ignoring calls for land reform."

Károly broke in, saying that Ada's serious words created an utterly attractive contrast with the femininity of her generous and full lips, making everyone laugh except for Ada.

For the last three months, Károly had been living in another world, completely lost in ecstasy. In May, following his graduation from the engineering school – a surprising outcome given that he had detested it all along – he had finally won Ada's heart. He'd been desperately in love with her for months, since the moment he had met her last summer at the picnic in Balatonfüred. He took every opportunity to praise her, especially her intelligence. Like János, she was a member of the youth organization of the illegal Communist Party. Her parents, ardent communists since the time of Béla Kun, had been exiled in 1919. On their return, they had continued to work as professors of mathematics at the Hungarian Royal University, where Ada had started to study mathematics. This summer, after three years of study, she had declared that she would drop out. "I've decided that I don't want to become a maths teacher," she had said. No one could change her mind, not even her parents who were furious about her change of heart.

Alex looked at Károly, who was kissing Ada's underarm, and at Ada, whose grave expression suddenly evaporated as she, tickled beyond her control, instinctively nestled in Károly's arms, only to pull herself away the next second. "Stop it, Károly! Stop this nonsense! Can't you please be serious just for once?"

"You, all of you, bear witness. She considers my love total nonsense."

Jaded by János's dismal discourse, everyone readily turned to Károly, who had adroitly changed the atmosphere at the table. Determined not to let the conversation go back to its sombre tones, he looked at everyone individually and continued, "Let us not despair, dear friends. The Trianon disaster of 1920 might have amputated our country's limbs, which had already become gangrenous after the Great War, and our people might have been impoverished. However," he paused briefly and, with a wave of his hand, beckoned the musicians before he carried on, "as long as there is *Csárdás* and as long as they can sing and dance their *joie de vivre* will never die." He rose from his chair, picking up his glass. "There's something I would like to drink to, or rather *we* would like to drink to," he beamed, looking at Ada. "We'll be starting *Műhely* in October."

Műhely, Sándor Bortnyik's new graphic school, known as the Workshop, was the only school in Budapest that followed the principles of Bauhaus, where artists such as Wassily Kandinsky and Paul Klee had taught.

"Finally, I'll be doing something that will make me happy."

They all looked at Károly, some exclaiming in surprise, some supporting his decision, while others mumbled a few words of no consequence. Alex proudly raised her glass, happy that the artists' front in their family was getting stronger.

She turned her eyes to Magda, who seemed to have melted in Miklós's arms. She had raised her glass as well, with a happy smile on her face and an expression – almost a dreamy look – in her eyes which Alex found rather unfamiliar. The way she shielded her eyes from Miklós, hiding her challenging stare, said a lot about her feelings. She probably did not want to expose the emotions that created havoc in her heart. Magda was in love, deeply in love. She had, after all, listened to her heart and not to her mind in making her choice.

"Will you be turning down the job offer at Ganz?" asked József in alarm. "You can't miss such an opportunity, Károly. You're being ridiculous. Have you thought this through?"

"I've been thinking for months," replied Károly, avoiding József's incriminating stare, but unable to escape the deprecating eyes of János, who had said nothing so far. "I've been thinking for years, actually," he went on with resolve. "My biggest mistake was to try and shape my life in a way that would please my mother and my uncle, surrendering my freedom by succumbing to choices they made." He raised his glass once again, while hugging Ada in his other arm. "We're living in a world that demands hierarchy and obedience, a world that obliges us to relinquish our true selves and unconditionally accept everything that is imposed on us. I have something burning deep inside me that resists such oppression." He raised his glass even higher. "Let's drink to a colourful future. Let's drink to freedom."

Alex noticed Rudi whispering something to the violinist, who listened with a twisted smile, curling his lip slightly upwards before turning to the other musicians and signalling them to start playing. Alex felt her heart lurch as she watched them walk around the table and stop right behind her. Rudi had followed them and was now standing next to the violinist, a gesture that meant only one thing: "I'm the one who asked for this serenade." Lost for what to do with herself, Alex put her fingers on her lips to hide a smile that might betray her proud satisfaction at this turn of events. Her hand slowly glided down her neck, and, with indistinct movements of her fingers, she started fidgeting with the skin surrounding the tiny hollows between her collarbones. Her mouth had suddenly dried up; she wetted her lips with the tip of her tongue. Uncomfortable at the attention of the table concentrating on her, she turned her head back a little and tried to focus on the music, her eyes mesmerised by the intense look in Rudi's eyes.

After the first song, her anxious excitement gradually gave way to a blissful sense of gratification. Towards the end of the second song, she turned back to the table and lit the candle that one of the musicians had left there. The flicker of a candle lit by a young girl and placed in front of the window of her bedroom was a sign that showed her acceptance of the serenade of her beloved waiting under her window, acceptance of his serenade and of his love. As soon as the candle was lit, the violinist broke into an enthusiastic *Csárdás*. *Csárdás!* The exhilarating *Csárdás,* the climax of the rhapsodies, the final explosion of soaring emotions before they died away into satisfaction. Not too many people knew about the ritual of a serenade anymore, but everyone at the table that night did. Alex and Rudi had declared their love to each other without uttering a single word. Alex suddenly noticed Károly staring at her. "Alex," he was saying with his eyes. "Be careful, my fragile little Alex, please be careful."

She lightly shrugged her shoulders with a smile and pouted her lips as if to say, "What else could I do, *Öcsi?*"

"You'd better change the expression on your face," said Ada, ironically rebuking Károly. "Why are you so worried? Alex can't stay under your wing forever. Leave her alone, for goodness' sake."

14

It was well past midnight when they came home. For the last couple of hours, Alex had not been able to control either her throbbing heart or her trembling hands. Her excitement had reached its peak as they climbed the hill towards Rózsadomb in Rudi's white Bentley after having left the Márkus Restaurant. Károly had invited everyone, including the gypsy musicians to come over, saying that, with the elderly household in Balatonfüred, he would not miss such an opportunity. Imre Magyari had taken out his violin, which he had carefully wrapped in a piece of silk cloth, and was trying to figure out the unintelligible off-key melody Károly, obviously far too drunk, was murmuring. And then with a brisk movement of his bow and much pride and enthusiasm in his expressive eyes, he started playing, shooting a hasty glance at the other musicians to make sure that they had understood what they were to play.

Everybody had had too much to drink and was still drinking. Some were conducting an imaginary orchestra with their hands, a few were swaying to and fro deluding themselves into thinking that they were dancing, while others were courageously trying to keep up a conversation in an effort to negate the effect of alcohol on their ability to reason; many of them were intermittently dozing, sunk into the comfortable sofas of the Green Salon.

"Play the *Red Sarafan!*" shouted Károly.

Rudi came over to where Alex was standing in front of the fireplace and offered one of the wine glasses he was carrying. Alex thought it would be better if she stopped drinking, as she was already tipsy and, more gravely, barely able to figure out how to comport herself. Cut off from the outside world altogether, Károly was dancing cheek-to-cheek and literally body-to-body with his Ada, while Magda was doing practically the same with her Miklós, their movements more in rhythm with their hearts than with the tempo of the music.

"Very handsome, indeed. That's your father, isn't it?" Rudi was looking at the faded photograph on the mantelpiece.

Yes, he was handsome, very handsome indeed. From the depths of that photograph of him sitting at his desk, he had been watching out for Alex with loving eyes for years. As she caressed her father's face, she realised, for the first time, that the pain inside her was slowly giving way to a sweet sense of nostalgia, brimming with pride.

"For Papa, it was a great honour to fight for the future of the Austro-Hungarian Empire. That was the tradition in our family. He could have gone to Vienna with Uncle Kelemen and worked at the Ministry of Defence, but apparently that was not honourable enough for him. He chose to fight as an officer at the Eastern Front." She pulled her hand away from the photograph and took a sip from her wine before she continued, "They say we lost one million souls during the Great War or maybe even two, some say three. My father didn't die right away." She carried on in a monotonous voice, narrating how in 1916 her father, after not even a year at the front, had fallen prisoner to the armed forces of Tsar Nikola in Galicia and had been sent to a prison camp on the Trans-Siberian railway, where he had nearly starved to death. After the war had come to an end, he had been stuck in a small Siberian village, east of the Ural Mountains. His Russian had become fluent by then, and he had been able to work as a teacher of mathematics in a primary school throughout the Russian Civil War. He had managed to survive a while longer, dreaming of the day he would return to Budapest, only to finally pass away in the middle of a frozen wasteland, thousands of kilometres away from his country.

Alex was twelve years old when she had learned all this. "A friend of his, someone he had met at the prison camp and remained friends with until the day he died ... I'll never forget him, his name was Szabo. Monsieur Szabo showed up at our door one day. It was 1922. He talked to my mother and my uncle for hours. Later that evening my mother related to us what he had said, probably cutting out most of the details." She stopped. There seemed to be one single thing left in her mind from all she had heard that evening. Still looking at her father's photograph, she went on, "My father was the representative of the prisoners at the camp. Once he was almost shot, to set a terrifying example to the others. It was a narrow escape. Monsieur Szabo said that being a representative was an honourable thing to be but definitely not the cleverest of choices. He said that being a hero, being a leader, being prominent in a totalitarian regime, was as good as committing suicide. One had to be invisible, remain unseen and unheard, avoid meddling in anything." She fell silent, finding it difficult to digest what she was saying, since it was the first time she had articulated the thoughts that had been filling her sleepless nights. "Deep down, I knew that he would never come back, but I waited. I waited for years. I was never convinced. I was unwilling to accept it. I missed him so much. I still miss him so terribly."

Rudi touched her bare shoulders with his lips in a long kiss, light as a feather, as though he were scared to hurt her. He gently held her by the waist and led her onto the veranda. They silently looked out over Pest, extending into the darkness of the night on the other side of the river. Alex's eyes wandered over the few remaining lights of the sleeping city.

15

Alex sat up in her bed with difficulty. She desperately needed to drink some water. How long had she been sleeping? Was it already morning? No, it couldn't be. It was still dark. What time was it? She remembered feeling very unwell on the veranda last night, overcome with a nauseating dizziness. She had unwillingly decided that it would be better if she went to bed and, asking Rudi to excuse her, had quietly gone upstairs to her bedroom without saying anything to the others. She still had her chiffon dress on, which was creased all over. She forced herself out of bed to get some water. Her head was no longer spinning, but there was a ghastly pain rising up from the back of her neck. She searched for her shawl in the dark, wrapped it around her shoulders and went out of her room. The party must be over, she thought, for it was dark downstairs except for some patches illuminated by the garden lights infiltrating through the windows. She dragged herself down the stairs and stopped in the hall to take a look at the drawing room. Károly had dozed off in one of the armchairs by the fireplace. She had better wake him up and send him to bed, or otherwise he would be stiff all over in the morning. As she made to move towards him, her sleepy eyes suddenly opened and she froze. It was not Károly but Rudi who was sleeping there. In panic, she whirled around and ran out of the drawing room. She was wide awake now, with no trace of her former headache. Dashing to the back of the hall towards the service door, she fled down the stairs to the basement and into the kitchen. She gulped down a glass of water, refilled her glass and hurried up the stairs to go back to her room.

In the hall she slowed down and, keeping her eyes on Rudi's silhouette, continued on tiptoe towards the stairs, only to stop impetuously, turn around and walk into the drawing room. She put her glass on one of the side tables and stripped her shawl off her shoulders as she noiselessly moved towards Rudi. He seemed sound asleep. His tie lay on the back of the armchair. The top buttons of his shirt were undone. She felt a tempting desire to touch his chest, visible through his white shirt. He looked as vulnerable as a child, defenceless against the dangers of the world, but somehow even his slumber could not completely veil his innate strength, the look of a predator. She gently draped her shawl over his chest. For a brief moment, she watched him. Then tentatively she bent down and lightly touched her lips to his cheek. As the sweetly tangy smell of his skin rose to meet her, she recoiled in panic. What am I doing? Am I crazy? I should go. Right now.

As she was about to turn around, he grabbed her arm and pulled her towards him. Firmly clasping her neck with his other hand, he passionately kissed her lips. In alarm, she tried to free herself from his grip, but, as his tongue entered her mouth, her body gave in, no longer able to resist his passionate onslaught. They kissed, in a strong embrace. She had been dreaming of this moment for so long that she could hardly believe it was really happening. "Perhaps it's only a dream," she thought in trepidation. When Rudi slightly bit her lip, she realised that it was not. She so much ached for this moment to last forever that she lost track of time. At one point, however, she knew it was time she put a stop to it. Károly would kill her if he could see her now. Reluctantly, she squeezed herself out of Rudi's embrace and, without looking back, whisked out into the hall and up the stairs into her room. She slammed the door shut and leaned her back on it. Out of breath with a thundering heart, she threw herself on the bed.

He had kissed her. Finally, Rudi had kissed her. On her lips! A long kiss. They had kissed like lovers. Lovers? Was she Rudi's beloved? And now what? What was going to happen now?

When she woke up the next morning, she found herself smiling. It was already eleven o'clock. She got up, threw on her silk dressing gown and went to see if Magda was awake. Her bed was empty. She walked across the Gallery to Károly's room, where she found him fast asleep. Going back to the Gallery and leaning over the railings, she tried to see inside the Green Salon downstairs. There seemed to be nobody there. She stumbled down the stairs and across the hall to have a look at the armchair by the fireplace. Her shawl was still there, but Rudi had gone. Where did he have to go at this hour? Why did he leave? When would she see him again? She thought of last night. It was incredible that he had actually kissed her. What did that kiss entail? Did it mean that she was to be his girlfriend? Was she already his girlfriend? Rudi's girlfriend! At this thought, a sudden pang of anguish seized her. She probably would become nothing more than one of the hundreds of girls blessed with his kiss. He would most likely ignore her, pretending to have been too drunk to remember what had happened. "Rudi must be mine!" she murmured vehemently as a covetous passion possessed her. "He must belong to me and nobody else!" she whispered to herself with firm resolve, only to ruefully rebuke herself a moment later. "You're already being possessive, Alex. What do you expect?" She tried to exercise some control over her thoughts, which seemed to have a mind of their own. When would she see him again? This evening? Suddenly, she remembered that they ought to be going to Balatonfüred that evening. I'd better wake Károly. Or perhaps I shouldn't. I don't want to go away from Budapest. I don't want to stay away from Rudi. "I shall return in a week, at the most," she promised herself.

16

They were having dinner under the trees in the garden of their summerhouse in Balatonfüred.

"Who was there last night?" asked Gizella, her forbidding stare focussed on her son.

"Friends," replied Károly with a similarly cold gaze, still very much hung-over from previous night.

Everybody at the table knew what was at the root of Gizella's inquisitive interest in her son's nocturnal activities: Ada. She must have been wondering if she was also present last night and how deep she had probed down into her much-prized son's heart.

"Yes, *Anyukám*," hissed Károly through his teeth in a barely audible voice. "Ada was there as well, and she has already conquered my heart. You'd better get used to it."

Alex's mind was still busy with what had happened last night.

"Alex? Alex in Wonderland!" Clearly determined to continue her interrogation, Gizella was now bracing herself to attack Alex.

"She's brooding over how to finish her fish," joined in Sándor, who, waking up from his reverie, saved the day for Alex.

"I'll be starting the graphic school of Sándor Bortnyik in October," declared Károly unexpectedly, his words dropping like a bomb on the table.

A short silence followed.

"Pardon me?" snapped Gizella, switching her stare to Károly, with one of her eyebrows raised high in consternation.

"I'll be starting the graphic school," Károly reiterated.

On the way to Balatonfüred, Károly had told Alex and Magda that he would announce his decision and was ready to face up to the havoc that he knew their mother and uncle would create. "No one can stop me from doing this," he had said, "Not even Mother. Whatever they say, I don't want to work at Ganz. Even the thought of spending my whole life behind a desk, doing something I detest, is enough to drive me up the wall."

"Would it not be difficult for you to work at Ganz and go to school at the same time, son?" Kelemen inquired with apprehension, narrowing his green eyes as he usually did when he tried to observe deep into the core of the matter at hand. He hardly showed his anger, but could be menacingly serious.

"I'll turn down the job offer at Ganz," Károly replied courageously without a moment's hesitation.

Nothing seemed strong enough to make Károly change his mind, neither his uncle's reasonable arguments throughout dinner nor his attacks when he eventually lost his patience and scolded Károly like a child, nor Gizella's condescending remarks followed by her emotional threats, fortified by her last resort ultimatum that she would deprive him of her financial support. As soon as Uncle Kelemen angrily left the table, Károly, knowing very well that he would be infuriating his mother further, but self-confident in his determination, started talking about the Workshop, about what he wanted to do and about the leftist views of Sándor Bortnyik.

"A school on Nagymező Street! In the middle of music halls and nightclubs!" Gizella scoffed.

"The Workshop is a laboratory of form following the principles of the Bauhaus," Károly continued, paying no heed to Gizella's relentless tirade of discouraging comments. "It embraces all the visual and plastic arts from architecture to painting, from weaving to manufacturing. It's a workshop of revolutionary experiments where teachers are not professors but masters of form, a guild without the class distinctions that raise an arrogant and insurmountable barrier between the craftsman and the artist. It focuses on applied graphic art and typographic design based on theories of rationalism and functionalism. Its main objective is to integrate art and craft with industrialisation. And most importantly, Bortnyik's teaching questions national identity."

"It seems to be the perfect place for those who question their own personal identities," Gizella fumed, and, after a simmering, turbulent pause, "This is all her doing," she erupted, trying to sound acerbic and ruthless, while panicking with the knowledge that she had, quite some time ago, lost her power over Károly. "Why doesn't she find a Jew like herself for a husband? Did you ever ask her that?"

"Come come, Mother," interrupted Magda. "Who said anything about marriage? They've only been seeing each other for three months."

"Yes, Mother," Alex added, encouraged by Magda's interruption. "Leave *Öcsi* alone, please."

"You mind your own business, young lady!" Gizella blurted out, turning imperiously to Alex. "And get your act together. I know what you have on your mind and in your heart. You'd better forget about him." Her face had gone red with rage.

"Calm down, Gizi. You're exhausting yourself," said Etel, who had not uttered a word all evening but intervened at the most inappropriate juncture, as usual.

"You mind your own business, Etel," growled Gizella, more infuriated than before.

"Listen, Alex. Mother is quite right on that issue. You must forget about Rudi."

"Hello, hello? I thought you liked Jewish people, Károly. Besides, you seem to have forgotten that Rudi was baptised as a Calvinist and his family converted to Christianity years ago. He's a Christian just like you are, just like I am, just like all of us are."

"Don't be ridiculous. You know perfectly well that I'm not talking about religion here. I don't care what his faith is. What's important is how happy he'll make you. He's not the man for you, Alex. How many times do I have to repeat myself?"

"Once a Jew, always a Jew, even if he converts to another religion," said Gizella icily, as if a bucket of cold water had been poured over her nerves.

"What is it that bothers you so much about Jewish people, Mother?" asked Alex.

"Nothing really," Gizella replied ironically. "Nothing bothers me about them except for the simple fact that they are to blame for the collapse of our Monarchy. It was their ridiculous ideas of liberalism that had weakened us. And of course that wretched Jew, Béla Kun, and all those communist Jews of the Hungarian Soviet Republic. It was those Bolsheviks that ruined us. You're too young to remember what the Red Terror did to our beautiful Budapest." She abruptly stopped shouting, and her anger thawed into bitter sorrow. "They're the reason why our heroes who had been captured by the Russians during the Great War could not return. The Russians held your father and all the other prisoners of war as hostages to use against those communists who were arrested after Kun escaped."

"I don't want to listen to this any longer," said Alex, irritably throwing her napkin on the table. "Otherwise, I shall have no respect left for you, Mother."

Károly followed Alex as she left the table. He took her arm, and they walked towards the house, their footsteps crunching on the pebbles of the pathway.

"You know what the real Red Terror was, don't you?" Károly asked, with a sweet tinge of revenge in his voice.

Alex turned to her brother, not knowing what he was talking about.

"Our father's fiery red-haired Jewish mistress when we were living in Italy. Her hatred of the Jews is justifiably well-founded in a way – by her broken heart."

17

"I'm certain that their house is decorated in Art Nouveau, a perfect style for the *nouveaux riches*. They have so much in common with the style, such as having no more than twenty or perhaps thirty years of history."

Alex no longer minded her mother's sarcastic remarks. Linking arms with Magda sitting next to her in the car, she cuddled up to her in the hope that their closeness would boost her strength. As they approached the final section of Andrássy Boulevard, lined with imposing mansions enveloped by expansive gardens and mostly populated by the aristocratic and diplomatic families of the capital, Alex reminisced about the night Rudi had kissed her for the first time.

Contrary to her initial foreboding, she had become not only one of the hundreds of girls he had blessed with his kiss, but also the one he introduced to everyone as his girlfriend. The ten months that followed went by in a dream. She was in seventh heaven as the love and attention she received from Rudi reached a level that was beyond her wildest dreams. At the parties and receptions they went to they were the couple everyone envied, although she could not care less about what she did or did not do so long as she was with him, enjoying the romantic victory of having succeeded in something nobody else could. Sports, parties, friends, everything gained a new meaning as they became accessories to her life. She could no longer imagine a life without him. In autumn they went to a pheasant shoot where she saw, for the first time in her life, the fun side of a sport that she used to hate and refused to refer to as a sportive activity. They went to Lech for the first fortnight of the new year, where everyone kept saying how happy she looked. Her feet hardly touched the ground whether on or off the slopes. Winter went by like a white dream. As spring breezed in and his tennis practices increased, she luxuriated in the exclusive pleasure of watching the perfectly built, athletic body of her boyfriend in all its glory.

Finally in June, after the victory of the Hungarian National Team led by Rudi against Holland in the quarter-finals of the International Lawn Tennis Challenge, he took Alex to the Márkus Restaurant where he gently put his lighter in her palm and pushed the unlit candle that he had had brought to the table, whispering that he wanted to spend the rest of his life with her. Alex, hardly able to hold back the tears of happiness welling up in her eyes, lit the candle as a sign of her acceptance of his marriage proposal. She made sure that Rudi did not see her gently touch the flame of the candle with the tip of her finger so as to prove to herself that all this was not a dream. She was the luckiest girl in the world; she was to be the only woman in Rudi's life until the day she died. All her dreams were coming true.

The following day, when she asked about the reaction of his family to their decision, Rudi looked straight into her eyes and said, "They were very happy that finally someone has conquered my heart and that someone is – I repeat the exact words of my mother – a lovely girl like you, coming from a perfect family despite being non-Jewish."

Alex, on the other hand, had to lie about her mother's reaction. The preceding evening, after Uncle Kelemen had come back from work, Alex, accompanied by Magda, Károly and Sándor for some moral support and encouragement, had announced Rudi's proposal. Her mother's first reaction had been a vigorous attack on Károly.

"You couldn't be a proper brother to Alex, Károly. Shame on you! If your father were alive, he would never have allowed such a thing."

"What thing, Mother?" interjected Magda. "Alex has received a marriage proposal from the man she's madly in love with. Could there be anything happier?"

Ignoring Magda, her mother continued to shout in rage. "They might presume that buying a house on Andrássy Boulevard has given them status in a society which has already lost many of its values anyhow, but this doesn't mean that they now belong to the nobility, or to the Christian faith. Once a Jew, always a Jew!" She turned to Alex and continued yelling. "I'll ask you the same question I asked Károly last year: why doesn't Rudolf consider marrying a Jew like himself?" Without waiting for an answer to her query, which was not meant as a real question in any case, she continued sardonically. "Oh, how did it slip my mind? There is no shorter and quicker way to be accepted into society than marrying a pure-bred Magyar aristocrat, is there?"

"Rudi loves me. Not everybody is like you, Mother. Some people are more open-minded, more humane."

"Enough! I forbid you to talk to me like that."

"Come now, Gizi," implored Kelemen. "It's well past the time to be a bit more moderate. Don't forget that Madame Takács's uncle Mór Vastag was a wealthy and powerful businessman who had the honour of being the first Jew to make it into Parliament. It's quite remarkable that he was one of the few Jewish people who turned down the noble title offered to him. Rudolf comes from a family held in high esteem for what they've done both for the business world and for the Jewish community. They acquired the position they deserve in society a long time ago."

Even Kelemen's efforts to soften Gizella proved futile, and she carried on, beside herself with fury, "They might have, but they have no roots. Nobody knows where they came from. We should never forget that until forty years ago they were living in Lipötváros."

"You should have been a secret agent, *Anyukám*," Károly interrupted, obviously taking pleasure in aggravating his mother even further. "You're rather well informed. What else have you learned? Have you investigated Ada as well? I hope it wouldn't be too disturbing for you to know that her parents are professors at the university, despite being Jewish. Or is there something else rooted well in the past that has been bothering you about the Jewish people, dear Mother?" he concluded, adding insult to injury.

"Both of you are completely out of line. Both of you. I shall not tolerate such behaviour. I cannot!" She stood up in fury and walked towards Kelemen. "Kelemen! Isn't there any way we can put some sense in these children? It's as if there were no one better than the Jews to marry." And she stormed out of the drawing room without waiting for Kelemen's response.

Károly wheeled around to face Alex and, ignoring his uncle, extended his finger towards Alex's nose and firmly said, "You shall not change your mind, Alex. Don't you give in to such nonsense. Don't you ever forget that you have every right to make your own decisions freely."

It was not the time to agonise about these unpleasant memories. She was the happiest girl in the world. She had not yielded and eventually had convinced her mother to consent to her marriage to Rudi. Finally, two days earlier, following the month-long preparations, they had been engaged at a low-key engagement dinner party given at their house in Rózsadomb for sixty selective guests. This evening, six hundred guests were invited to the Takácses' mansion on Andrássy Boulevard to celebrate the happy event. The boulevard in front of the two-storey mansion was lined with cars; there was no more parking space for them in the well-groomed, spacious front garden that extended the length of the mansion's façade, a most impressive façade adorned with marble statues of Greek goddesses that seemed to shoulder the weight of the building from where they stood on two ends of a wide balcony. One of the white-gloved butlers, waiting at the wide-open wrought-iron garden gate crowned by golden globes, ushered them along the stone-paved walkway decorated with red roses. At the main entrance, they were taken over by the head butler.

"I should have guessed," hissed Gizella as they entered the large hall, scrutinising her surroundings with a condescending gaze accentuated by her eyebrow raised even higher than it had been for the last hour. "Not even *Art Nouveau,*" she continued, slightly bending her head sideways towards Etel. "It had to be *Art Déco,* surely. That is definitely more fitting for those who only have a few years of family history."

Etel, noticing Kelemen's cold glare that told her to move away from Gizella, took Sándor's arm and hastened her pace. They followed the head butler into the drawing room. Bronze, wood and marble furnishings with elaborate floral and animal motifs dominated the room, making it look more crowded than it actually was. Golden and silver deer on black lacquered ebony panels, silk wall coverings, the mother-of-pearl engravings on heavily veneered screens, and piles of tasselled cushions on the sofas, on the armchairs and on the parquetry floor fashionably reflected the influence of the Far East. Alex thought how very modern it all was.

"The only furniture of any value in their house seems to be that rosewood corner cabinet over there – which can't be more than fifteen years old, mind you."

"Mother! Please. You're like a tax collector."

"Not bad. Not bad at all," she said, narrowing her eyes to see better. "The exotic ebony embellishments on it are truly impressive."

They walked towards the French windows giving on to the back garden.

"They seem to have bought everything from the 1925 Paris Exhibition. Isn't there one single item that belongs to their past?" Gizella knew no limits in her criticism.

Never mind, Alex thought, you have what you wanted. Let her talk as much as she pleased.

"Are they in mourning, for goodness' sake? What is the point of having so much black in your drawing room? And everything is so shiny. Magda darling, you should have brought some of those chunky ceramic wall lightings you've done. They would have gone very well with the decoration here." She smiled, an ironic twist on one end of her lips. "I can't understand this modern aesthetic. It's so crude."

"It isn't crude, Mother, it's simple," whispered Károly through his teeth as he leaned over Gizella's shoulder and continued in a slightly louder tone. "Such simplicity creates a delicious contrast with the richness of the materials used."

"I think it's nothing more than wasting beautiful fabrics and best quality wood. And what about those leather armchairs! This is a drawing room, not a library, is it not?"

Alex felt her nerves tightening. However, the moment she saw Rudi coming in through the French windows, all her apprehension instantly melted. She threw herself into his arms. Nobody could harm or upset her while she was under his wing. Her mother disappeared among the guests in the garden, leaving the decoration of the house – and Alex – alone.

Rudi held Alex's hand and dragged her towards the library at the far end of the drawing room. "There's something I'd like to give you before we join the guests," he said, beaming.

Once they were in the library, he went to the desk and took out a little box from one of the drawers. "I thought it would enhance those beautiful green eyes," he whispered affectionately as he gave it to her.

The box had Gaston Laffitte written on it and contained a brooch depicting a nude woman lying down, with her butterfly wings spread over the black velvet. A radiant pearl dangled from her feet at the end of her long enamelled legs – a rare example of *plique à jour* that made Alex remember her mother's ugly comments about Art Nouveau. Forget about them! Forget about her! Look how beautiful your brooch is. It had been chosen by someone with truly refined taste. She took out the pearl *sautoir* hanging from her neck to her waist, re-arranged her dark red dress and placed her brooch on her chest. She could see now why Rudi had insisted that she wore a red dress for the engagement party. The wings of the brooch were engraved with diamonds and blood-red rubies. In the mirror, she looked at her fiancé standing behind her. I'm so happy, she said to herself. I'm the happiest girl in Budapest. No, no, the happiest girl in the world. Rudi planted a gentle kiss on her, where her neck joined her back. She turned around and, not in the least worried about her dress becoming creased, put her arms around his neck. "Thank you ever so much, Rudi," she whispered. Thank you for everything.

They went out onto the terrace and stopped before the few steps leading down to the garden, which was lavishly decorated with red roses. The orchestra, on a slight hand gesture from their conductor, who had seen the newly engaged couple, paused for an instant before they started playing Tchaikovsky's *Serenade for Strings, Opus Forty-Eight*. Everyone in the garden stopped talking to watch them. Alex put her hand on her chest, hoping that it would calm her thundering heart.

"I'm the luckiest man in the world," she heard Rudi whisper as he tightened his grip on her hand.

At his comforting words, her heart somewhat quieted down and her anxiety disappeared. She drew in the perfume of the crimson roses as they slowly walked down the steps. An introduction ceremony, which promised to be rather long, commenced.

"Our neighbours Baron and Baroness Orbánstein and their daughter, my dearest friend, Éva."

"The British Ambassador, Sir and Lady Mahagan."

They were exchanging only a few words with most of the guests, while slowly moving into the depths of the crowd.

"Lajos Sonenberg, a most dear friend. He's a lawyer as well."

"Rudi often talks about you. We frequently enjoy your wines."

"What a pity not to have met you before," said Lajos, looking Alex in the eye and taking her hand to his lips. He looked like an English gentleman in his perfectly knotted bow tie and exquisite tuxedo, obviously made from English fabric by an English tailor. Although he had no beard or moustache, his bearing sufficed to indicate his prominent position within society. "Why haven't you introduced us before, Rudi?" he asked, without taking his eyes off Alex.

"Caution, old chap, caution. You never know, do you?"

"I'd love you to come to the grape harvest in September. Have you ever been to one?"

Another group of Rudi's friends, dominated by males, joined them to meet Alex. He had so many friends she did not know.

A round of applause rose from the guests. The crowded orchestra, consisting of a rich variety of instruments from oboe to saxophone, from violins to double bass, had finished the piece they had been playing to accompany the entrance of Alex and Rudi, and the famous Italian soprano Mafalda Salvatini had taken the stage. The guests turned their eyes away from Alex and Rudi to examine the ostrich plumes rising from Salvatini's golden-threaded turban and the eye-straining glitter of her caftan, reflecting the most ostentatious designs of Paul Poiret. The soprano, an attractive prima donna who had led Duke Adolf Friedrich VI to committing suicide by refusing his love, was known to enchant her spectators with her unique acting skills rather than by her voice.

The garden was teeming with guests, an animated concoction of self-assured married ladies of a certain age, bashful young girls unsure of where to turn their timid and tremulous eyes, young women liberated enough to powder their noses or to smoke in public, relishing the use of their enamelled powder compacts or bejewelled cigarette cases, and gentlemen – married or unmarried – constantly sweeping their hawk-like eyes over the entire female population. They moved from one group to another in coiling and uncoiling clusters, turning the garden into a wavy ocean. Beautiful and attractive women became the focus of one group and then, spoiled by their victory, glided away to another group, confidently swaying their bodies, resolved to increase the number of their admirers. As the sun set over the horizon and darkness fell, the light from the myriad of candles scattered around the garden and the lanterns hanging from the trees reflected more brightly from the diamond-studded brooches worn on shoulders, on belts embracing the hips and on glittering bands wrapped around the foreheads. The night was further illuminated by the sparkle from the precious stones embellishing the dangling earrings that touched elegant shoulders, from the long chains of pearls hanging from necks along the length of the lusciously exposed backs and from the platinum, gold and onyx bracelets and bangles adorned with diamonds and decorated with geometric designs, crowding up slender arms from wrists to elbows.

Champagne flowed like water at the bar set right next to the terrace, where barmen prepared colourful cocktails, and French and Hungarian red and white wines waited their turn to be served at dinner. Endless open buffets placed on three different corners of the garden were true works of art. Guests were already queuing up in front of colourful salads, delicious-looking pâtés made from the livers of fattened geese, traditional rice-filled cabbage rolls, plump ducks (not as glorious as they would be in October but nevertheless mouth-watering), the perfectly-roasted pork and French, German and Hungarian breads and baguettes, along with many other varieties of gorgeous-looking dishes Alex did not recognise.

Alex and Rudi were supposed to sit with their parents at the table set right at the centre of the garden, where the guests at other tables could see them. Everyone except for Károly had already settled down in their chairs. A few moments later, having delivered Ada to the table where she was to sit with János and a group of their friends, Károly came over, gave Alex a kiss on the cheek and reluctantly took his seat.

"At long last, young man! At long last!" hissed Gizella as she opened, with a brisk movement of her wrist, her antique swan's-feather fan, which she used exclusively on special occasions, and fixed her intimidating gaze on her son. As usual, she somehow gave the impression of sitting at the head of the table even if it was a round one.

The waiters were serving the tables for those who did not deign to queue up at the buffet or were tired after having stood for too long. Alex asked for liver pâté. Terézia Takács, sitting right across her, insisted that she taste the cabbage rolls and, without taking her eyes off the guests, gestured to one of the waiters to bring a few to the table. Magda agreed with Madame Takács as she momentarily took her eyes away from Miklós, who shared a nearby table with his family.

"I shouldn't be too upset about not having Ada invited to sit with us, given that even Miklós is not considered worthy of such an honour." It was Károly whispering in Alex's ear.

Alex remembered what her mother had said some time ago. "You should try and be like Magda. Both of you. Miklós might not have an aristocratic lineage, but at least he comes from a well-known family such as the Nerádys, a family that has produced generations and generations of valuable artists." Károly, of course, had taken no time to snap back. "He certainly does. His family is full of artists, but unfortunately they're all too far behind in time. An artist should be ahead of his time. He must be a leader not only with his works of art but also with his lifestyle, relationships, attire and, most importantly, with his ideas. Miklós does occasionally come up with genuine novelties, but they're far from being satisfactory. His father, in particular, is too classical for an artist in every aspect of his life. No wonder you find them so much to your taste, Mother."

Gizella, holding her chin up as if carrying a fragile glass figurine there that might easily fall down and break, was busy scrutinising the guests with that frigid stare of hers, giving the impression that she looked down upon everyone – even those much taller than her. From the disapproving glances she threw over her fan towards Rudi's father György Takács, it was clear what she thought of the way he ate his food – most excitedly and with great appetite but, according to Gizella, with no manners. "Refinement, just like wealth," she said almost inaudibly, thus obliging everyone at the table to listen to her even more attentively, "stands out if it doesn't have long established roots."

Monsieur Takács, an eminent lawyer and a highly successful financier, not only in Budapest but all over Europe, kept adding to the wealth of his already extremely rich wife. He was a good-looking man for his age, despite the thinning hair and the slightly fat belly camouflaged by his tall stature and his self-confident posture. He must have been a heartbreaker once. Apparently, Rudi had inherited his good looks from his father. As to the colour of his eyes, they were exactly like his mother's. Although not a beauty, Madame Takács was a well-groomed and elegant woman. Her nose was too long and her mouth was too small for her face, but every female in town envied her thick strawberry-blond hair cascading down in shiny waves, accentuating her exquisitely white skin, which proudly showed that, contrary to what the fashion dictated, she never exposed herself to the sun. What the ladies present that evening envied more than her hair, however, was the arresting diamond necklace covering almost all her décolleté, the earrings reaching down to her shoulders and the emerald and diamond rings too big for her tiny fingers. She was known to be a charitable person, who spent a considerable amount of her time and wealth for the benefit of philanthropic societies.

None of this, however, seemed enough to make the Takácses win Gizella's approval, Alex thought before diverting her gaze away from her mother and towards Uncle Kelemen. He looked quite cheerful, talking to his future in-law György Takács. "Once upon a time," he was saying, "traditions required that men of a certain age grow a beard. A judge without a beard, for instance, was unfathomable. Only actors and waiters used to shave. Nowadays, however, the modern youth, so to speak, love to shave, claiming that they look cleaner and cleverer. Having no moustache or beard is like a symbol among the Freemasons."

"Things can't stay the same forever, dear Uncle," Károly joined in enthusiastically. "If they did, they would be doomed to rot away. New generations come with new ideas and new concepts. They have dreams they want to realise. You can't blame them for striving to reach their ideals."

"All these new ideas will be the end of our country, you'll see."

Alex was surprised to notice, for the first time, that her uncle, who seemed gigantic to her when she was a child, was in fact a relatively small man. It might be that he had shrunk as he got older. He appeared to have diminished in size, in stark contrast to Aunt Etel, who had put on too much weight. He had lost most of his light brown hair, and what remained had become almost invisibly grey. His once bushy beard and moustache had thinned down, resembling an unhealthy shrub. His voice, however, was still as strong as his personality.

Aunt Irén let out a cheerful laugh, interrupting her conversation with Magda. Her voice rose above every sound, not only at their table but also at all the nearby tables, making everyone smile, even Sándor, who had long ago retired to his inner world. Alex thought how elegant her laugh was. She was not too striking in her looks but had that particular attractiveness – an attractiveness that Gizella lacked – enhanced by her elegance, underlining her special and distinguished personality. She had cut her hair very short right under her chin in the latest fashion, tinted it dark red and inevitably had been subjected to Gizella's ruthless scrutiny. "Short-sighted ladies would mistake you for a man, Irén. And unfortunately, at your age, most of your contemporaries do have a poor sight." Alex adored her modern aunt. Only matrons insisted on not cutting their hair nowadays – and the rigid conventionalists like her mother who resisted novelties of any kind.

"That's the Turkish Ambassador and his wife over there, isn't it?" asked Etel, fidgeting with the silver clip of her brocade handbag, carefully placed on the table. She was checking out the guests, making comments on their attire. Presuming that everybody was as eager as she was in criticising everybody else, she had put on an insipidly black evening gown that no one would remember the look of the moment she disappeared from sight.

Alex looked at the Turkish Ambassador and then at József sitting opposite him. His eyes were lost in Éva's as he listened to her at a distance far closer than that required by the rules of savoir-faire. She wondered what attracted him to this girl, searching for something noteworthy in her polite face that had nothing special other than two little dimples. She was utterly flat and boring, with her brown hair cut in the latest fashion just like all the other girls at the party, her neither too small nor too big well-shaped eyes, her neither too big nor too little nose and her temperate smile resembling that of a compassionate nun. József, however, must have found something in her. Alex thought how well her mother had directed Madame Takács regarding the seating arrangements.

Dinner dragged on in a heavy atmosphere that even Alex's happiness failed to lighten. Her patience slowly wore out until the whole thing finally became intolerably torturous, owing to Rudi hardly saying a word and to Uncle Kelemen surprisingly and boringly saying too many words, to her mother making the most upsetting comments and throwing her most murderous looks, to Madame Takács's endless questionings and constant insistence that Alex should eat some more, and to the absolute silence of Magda and Károly who – unable to take their minds and eyes off their beloveds unfortunately seated at other tables – were as eager as Alex to see the end of this dinner. Sanyi made no verbal contribution to the night but visually added some melancholy to the table as his dreamy eyes travelled back and forth between his inner world and Margit, perched on the edge of a chair at another table, except of course when he catatonically stared around the table from

91

under his flattened eyelids as if to show that he had no interest whatsoever in the conversation. Alex could hardly wait until they ate from the countless varieties of French cheese accompanied with sweet wine, finished their dessert and finally drank the strong coffee served with whipped cream, accompanied by delicious *petits fours* and exquisite chocolates. At long last, while her uncle was delightfully engrossed in choosing a cigar from among the wide selection offered, she, forgetting all her manners, jumped to her feet as if breaking free from her chains.

"Rudi! Shall we dance?" she chimed.

Rudi seemed more willing to leave the table than Alex did. Károly, always the pioneer, had already stood up and was dragging Magda to the dance floor. They swiftly moved away from the table as it gradually disappeared from their sight and minds under a thickening shroud of cigar smoke. Now they could finally have some fun. She let herself go in the embrace of her fiancé as they joined others on the dance floor. Couples, experts in the latest steps, were proudly trying to dominate the floor while experienced gentlemen span and twirled timid young girls around and free-spirited self-sufficient girls swayed on their own, drawing deprecatory stares from Gizella and the likes of her. After the first song, Károly readily handed Magda over to Miklós and, yearningly grabbing Ada from János's arms, reunited with his beloved. Thus were all the lovers happy.

Deep into the night, as the effect of alcohol, intensified by too much dancing, had removed all barriers, giggles gradually turned into laughter, conversations into meaningless compliments or sarcastic remarks, hatreds into animosities, and amities into love. Morning was drawing in. A slow *Csárdás* was playing. Alex and Rudi were seeing the last guests off.

"Congratulations."

"Thank you very much. It was a superb night."

"We wish you a life as happy and glamorous as tonight."

Alex's eyes caught János talking to Margit in a far corner of the garden. He looked even more serious in his officer's uniform, which he carried with great pride. He was resolutely talking underneath a cloud of smoke, and Margit was resolutely listening. There were still a few couples on the dance floor. Alex looked at Ákos, who never stayed at a party this late, and at Izabella, who had closed her eyes, most probably not from the numbing effect of an overdose of alcohol but rather from an unexpected feeling of happiness she felt in the long-awaited embrace of Ákos. The slow tempo of their entwined bodies revealed that Ákos was not talking about his horses. Finally, Alex looked at Károly – at Károly and

Ada. They were not dancing but standing in a close embrace in the middle of the dance floor, looking utterly tired after all the champagne and wine they had had. They seemed to have no intention of letting go of each other. Károly was trying to say something to Alex over Ada's head. She could read her brother's lips, saying, "I'm in love. Head over heels in love."

18

A week after the engagement party, Rudi went on a business trip to Vienna, Paris and London that was supposed to last for a month. He came back five weeks later. In October, in tandem with the decline in world markets, Alex gradually saw less and less of her fiancé and finally lost him altogether when a crisis broke out at the end of the month. The glitter in Alex's dreams started to fade away as the ruthless reality of adult life crept in, pushing her towards an incurably depressed mood. Everybody was talking about how hopeless the situation was. Hungary's grain exports – the mainstay of the country's economy – plummeted as grain prices hit the bottom following the crash of the New York Stock Exchange. Rudi kept saying that the situation was getting worse day by day and that his business was almost at a standstill. Desperately working day and night, looking for a way to pull out of this nightmare, he hardly had a free moment and whenever he did, he wanted to do nothing but play tennis, which, he said, was the only thing that helped him cool his overheated mind. At times, they only met once a week and sometimes could not even manage that. When they were together, Rudi always seemed far away, totally ignoring Alex, let alone showing her any attention. Having practically warded off the Christmas festivities, he did not take Alex to the wild boar shoot in February, claiming that it was too dangerous for her. He frequently went to Geneva, which made Alex suspicious of a clandestine affair there. Knowing Rudi, it was quite possible that he did have a lover. Alex could not get Károly's words out of her mind. "He's a heart-breaker," he had once said. "And that means he'll take your heart in his hands in an instant and then break it in the next." Even the thought of losing Rudi was enough to make her heart cringe with fear. She could not get rid of the thoughts devouring her brain during his absences, finding it extremely difficult to concentrate on her studies, so much so that she almost failed her exams in spring. Throughout the summer months, she restlessly shuttled between Balatonfüred and Budapest. When summer came to a close, and they returned to Rózsadomb, she felt relatively more relaxed, although still unable to wriggle completely free of all her suspicions about him.

It was during the last days of September. The temperature had already begun its autumnal decline. Alex was walking with Magda towards Centrál Kávéház where they were to meet up with their friends. Although she knew that she would be repeating herself, she could not help but lament, hoping to hear some consoling words from her sister. "He works like crazy," she began, in a protesting tone of voice. "Apparently, his father is delegating everything to him. Do you know how many times he went to Geneva and to London this year? Well, I don't. It's impossible to keep track of it. He doesn't leave his office till midnight during the weekdays and practically has no time to speak on the phone, let alone see me. And on the weekends, he either has a tennis match or he has to practice. Well, that's fine since we can at least be together on such occasions, but when it's not tennis it's either hunting with his male friends or any other sport you can think of – and, of course, all those dinners *en garçon*. He's been neglecting me so much since our engagement. Shouldn't it be otherwise? He says that we'll be together for a lifetime and that he doesn't understand why I worry so much about just a few days. He keeps talking about putting everything in order first. What order, for goodness' sake! He has everything. Sometimes I think he's fed up with me."

"Rudi has always been like this, Alex. He was like this when you met him. You can't expect him to change and sit by your side all the time."

"And all that gossip, Magda, it really upsets me. I know that people talk far too much, but sometimes I think that Mother may have been right. Lately I've been asking myself if he truly loves me or if he's after a social status that his wealth can't buy."

"Don't be ridiculous. You speak as if you didn't know him at all. He doesn't need to do such a thing. He's quite happy with his social status. Even if he were after such a thing, he could have chosen any one of the tens, maybe hundreds of girls among the nobility who were, and still are, ready to throw themselves at his feet. You know it as well as I do. He chose you because he loves you."

"I do agree with you, but there are times when he does things that make me think that if he loved me he wouldn't behave like that."

"Behave like what? He treats you like a princess, Alex. We must admit that both you and I are rather spoiled when it comes to love and attention. Our uncle and brother gave us rather too much of it."

"All right, he does treat me like a princess, but unfortunately it isn't only me that he treats so. He constantly pays compliments to every single female around him. And believe me, they're not just plain compliments; he openly flirts with them." She stumbled on the uneven pavement and grabbed Magda's arms for support. "He drives me up the wall with his flirtations. Moreover, all those nice things he says to me are full of platitudes. He says them from force of habit, without even realising what he's actually saying."

"Rudi is like that. You fell in love with him just for that reason, didn't you? How many times must I repeat myself? You can't change him. He might be a flirt, but it's not because he doesn't love you; it's the way he is."

"Well, if he loves me, then isn't it high time that he talked about marriage? It's been more than a year now since the engagement and not even a single mention of when we'll be getting married."

"Alex! You seem to forget that you have school to finish yet. We both do. Miklós and I have decided that we should wait until after my graduation. I hope you don't suffocate Rudi by rushing him into anything."

"You just said it, Magda: you have decided on a date. You should have seen his reaction when I asked him when we were supposed to get married."

"Come on, Alex. Stop nagging him before he's totally fed up with it all."

"I feel so utterly lonely, Magda."

They arrived at Central Kávéház. Seated in front of one of the windows, Károly was heatedly talking to Rudi. They both stood up when they saw Alex and Magda enter.

"How very chic you both are. A spectacular sight, fresh out of a fashion magazine."

Alex knew they were rather chic and was very proud of being the epitome of the latest trend in her tobacco-coloured tweed dress and *Agnès* cap with its elegant bow gently touching the back of her neck, drawing the attention of everyone.

Rudi helped her settle down on a chair and then sat next to her. Holding her hands, he turned to Károly. "She's getting more and more beautiful by the day," he said. "I love your sister so very much." As soon as he finished his sentence, he jumped to his feet and, letting go of Alex's hands, excused himself before drifting away from the table with his arms wide open towards a group of girls who had just entered the café. "How very enchanting to see you here. Your beauty sheds light into our souls."

Alex leaned over towards Magda and grunted irritably, "Do you get my drift now?"

"What of it? Stop being so jealous, Alex. It's not normal."

Alex was sinking deeper and deeper into a terrible mood. "Do all of these girls have to wear short caps? They look like nurses in uniform," she grumbled as she darted an indignant glance at Rudi, who had returned to the table. Then looking at her brother, "Károly," she said and continued with heavy sarcasm in her voice. "Could you please ask for some candles? It seems that the light at our table isn't enough to shed light into our souls." She noticed Rudi clench his fist as he sat down. A storm was in the making, but she could not care less. She had had enough of him coming on to every other female in town.

Károly, in an effort to change the subject, started flipping through the pages of the *Reklámélet* and *Magyar Grafika* magazines, excitedly showing Rudi the photographs of the advertisement graphics he had designed and the articles on the exhibition he was to open. "I'm talking about a conscious analysis of new forms with an open mind, emerging from the interplay of material, function and structure. Creation should be based on the principles of rationalism and functionalism; it must have spiritual as well as material elements at its heart."

"It's harder to unravel the language of your profession than that of the law, my friend."

"In brief," Károly continued, smiling, "a poster, for instance, should convey its message in the shortest way, with the simplest of devices if it is to have a durable effect. Our language might be complex, but what we create is very plain. I'd like you to come to the opening of the Art of Books and Advertisements Exhibition at the Museum of Applied Arts on Saturday. They accepted twelve of my designs."

Although he had not yet graduated from the Workshop, Károly's graphic designs, dominated by simplified decorative elements in line with Bortnyik's theories, had been used for the stage design of two plays, and he had designed one record jacket and several posters. He said that his visits to the seminars in sculptor Tibor Vilt's studio in Buda and the discussions with Ada's leftist friends at Simplon were widening his artistic horizon in directions surprising even to himself.

"How is Ada, by the way?" asked Rudi. "We hardly get to see her."

"She should be here soon. I too get to see her very little lately. She's very busy. Last week she spent one night at the police station. She's attending the communist rallies and won't listen to reason. It's an illegal party, she's playing with fire."

"Well, well. Everybody is already here," Miklós chimed in as he entered the café, followed by Ada and János.

János had finished his military service and returned to Budapest three days ago. They talked about his new job at the State Railways, about the complaints of the people in the rural areas and about the increased budget deficit created by Prime Minister Bethlen's successful efforts to inflate the bureaucracy to create job opportunities for the university graduates who, he believed, might threaten the civil order if left idle. Rudi seemed to have lost his good spirits. He sat with them for a while longer for politeness' sake before he excused himself saying that he had a business meeting to attend to and left the café.

A few minutes after Rudi's departure, Károly pulled Alex to one end of the table, away from the heated conversation. "We must talk, Alex," he said in a strong whisper. "You should be careful, sweetheart. Sometimes you're quite out of line."

Károly had been saying that he had gradually, over the past twelve months, changed his mind about Rudi's intentions, seeing true love in the way he looked at Alex. He said he really appreciated how surprisingly attentive and respectful he was towards her and was amazed at all the compliments and the flattering remarks he kept on inventing. Once, he had admitted that even he could not be as romantic as Rudi despite his creative thinking and passionate love for Ada.

"Leave me alone, *Öcsi*."

"Why are you so edgy?"

"I'm not edgy. I just don't want to share the man I love with others."

"Do you really love Rudi?"

"I can't believe you ask such a stupid question. Do I look like I don't love him? I'm totally in love with him, Károly. Body and soul."

"Don't confuse love with slavery, Alex. Make sure that what you take to be love is not a feeling of pure frustration created by your inability to possess him completely."

János's ascending voice raised above all the others at the table, dominating the conversation. "Foreign credit sources have dried up. We're now dependent on short-term loans. The loan sharks are having a ball."

"I'm scared, *Öcsi*. I'm so scared of losing him."

"The Alex I know is not a coward. Fear makes you over-possessive. I can't believe that you didn't come to Kengyel this winter, not even once. And what about summer? You spent three weeks at the most in Balatonfüred. You should get your act together, Alex."

"What should I have done? What do you think it means to leave Rudi alone in Budapest all summer?"

"Don't you have any self-confidence? You couldn't stop him if he wanted to leave you. Be careful not to tighten your grip on him too much, lest you eventually strangle him."

"It's me who is suffocating, *Öcsi*, me. I can't draw a single line."

"Pull yourself together, sweetheart. This is your final year. You can't ruin everything. And besides ..." Károly stopped short, abruptly turning to János, who was still talking.

"It's rather surprising that Rudi has moved out to live on his own, to live in a flat on Andrássy Boulevard," János said in a most ironic tone, "while people are tightening their belts. He and his family seem not in the least affected by the economic crisis. Industrial production is at a standstill, unemployment is soaring, businesses are going bankrupt one after the other, government sectors are suffering from severe pay cuts." He paused as if to stress what he was about to say and took a sip from his drink before he continued. "And some of us know very well how to exploit this situation. Some of us are not tightening our belts but loosening them instead."

Alex thought that, like many others, János must be envious of Rudi. It was not very nice, however, that he openly expressed his feelings like that, putting himself in a rather demeaning position. They should accept that Rudi was more resourceful than all of them. She turned to Károly who had not finished his sentence. "Besides what?" she asked him. His gaze was still fixed on János.

19

One bleak Sunday in January Kelemen de Kurzón, who was at the height of his career, did not wake up from his usual afternoon nap. The doctors said that he had died peacefully of a heart attack.

Alex was devastated. For weeks, she could not get over the shock of losing her uncle, a shock that ripped the fragile skin over the vulnerable wound in her heart that was ready to bleed at the slightest misfortune. It felt as though another carpet had been pulled away from under her feet, leaving her utterly lonely and unprotected. She was truly furious at Rudi for not sparing enough time for her even at such a distressing time and, unable to hold herself back, aggressively attacked him despite knowing very well that it was not the right thing to do. Soon after her verbal assaults, however, she often scolded herself, regretting what she had said. Intolerant of others' company, she ran away from people, isolating herself in her own world. The more she cut herself off from the outer world, the more she came face to face with the turbulence of her inner self – something that drove her almost insane, triggering an unbearable sense of panic and urging her to try and flee away from her self-imposed seclusion. As she distanced herself from her inner world, she drifted away from painting. She could hardly draw a line. This vicious circle dragged her into a state of artistic coma. She could not care less about her classes or about graduation, lacking the energy even to move a finger.

Eventually in May, she managed to pull herself together and graduate, thanks to Magda's insistence, encouragement and the optimistic pictures she drew about the future. However, when Károly, after his graduation from the Workshop, started talking about taking his beloved Ada and moving to Paris – to the haven of freedom and art, as he called it – Alex became increasingly more indignant about Rudi's procrastination of their marriage formalities. She bitterly realised that eventually Károly would leave her, and that she had no right to ask him to be a father to her forever. She should get married and have children, a family of her own, and could see no reason why Rudi still did not marry her, now that she had finished school.

Magda and Miklós married in July as planned and, as befitting two people in love, moved to their happy home in the small town of Verőce north of Budapest. Magda had a slimly built, highly emotional, perfectly artistic husband madly in love with her. Ever since the wedding ceremony, all eyes had been turned to Alex. "Now that Magda is happily married, it's your turn Alex," they kept saying. She had had enough of their comments. She knew that she should get married, and get married soon. They had always done everything together, she and Magda, and that was how it should be now. She was left all alone. Károly said more often than she was willing to hear that lately she had been behaving quite differently than the Alex he knew. "Where has our Alex gone, the high-spirited girl Rudi loved, the lovely and lively Alex that not only Rudi but everyone loved?" he kept reproaching her, continually repeating that her bouts of jealousy would inevitably scare Rudi away. He strongly advised her to stop blaming him and asking too many questions. "You must trust Rudi," he said on many an occasion. "Marriage is not an easy step for a man like him. It's up to you to help him stop delaying his decision. Be wise. I can't understand how someone as free-spirited as yourself tries to limit the freedom of another person. Relax, Alex."

She could not relax. A sense of uneasiness cramped her, body and soul. She felt the same uneasy feeling on that scorching August day as she lay down on the stone paving surrounding the pool in the garden of Magda's new home, intent on getting a tan on her unfashionably white skin. This was probably the tenth party Magda and Miklós had given in the past four weeks. Miklós was really an eccentric man. He was rather unique, not only because of his indigo eyes, thick straw-coloured hair and the unusual attractiveness his slurred "r"s gave him, but because of everything else about him – he was really one of a kind. Who would think of having a peacock as a pet instead of a cat or a dog? In fact, Magda was no different than her husband. She said that peacocks were friendlier than cats and much more self-sufficient than dogs and, therefore, easier to look after. She often took Mókus – one of their identical peacocks she surprisingly managed to distinguish from the other – on her lap and lovingly hugged it. She had found the perfect husband; she had married the man she loved. They would soon have kids running around their garden. Why couldn't Rudi be like Miklós? Why were they still not married?

Losing her patience, she had on one occasion swallowed her pride and said that she could not understand why they were not getting married. "There is a time for everything," Rudi had replied curtly. Alex had felt utterly ashamed and promised herself not to open her mouth ever again about their marriage, for she feared losing her self-respect. Who knew, perhaps they would never get married. Perhaps I will become a spinster, she thought. I'm already twenty-one years old. A lonely life and a lonely death. Perhaps I should marry one of the suitors Mother finds me, despite Rudi. Aranys' son István, for instance. She cringed at the idea. He was disgusting. A complete sissy! And arrogant, on top of it all. Or maybe she should try and consider János, who was desperately in love with her. She hurriedly waved her hand over her eyes as if to send her thoughts away. I must be out of my mind, she thought. What am I thinking? János belongs to Margit. He not only inhabits her dreams but since March colours her whole life as her boyfriend. Besides, I'm not so foolish as to leave Rudi to others. Never! Whatever the cost, Rudi is mine. Deep down, she felt something she could not define, something like being torn apart.

"It's not like Gyula Károlyi would do what Bethlen couldn't, is it? He thinks he can solve all our problems by tightening our belts. He's as incompetent as his cousin, the Red Count." Rudi, who had been trying to cool off in the pool, had come over to where Alex was lying down and was dropping icy water on her belly, hot under the sun, while he chatted with Károly, sitting by the pool with his feet dangling in the water. After Prime Minister Bethlen's resignation, Rudi had become no less boring than János in his political colloquies.

Alex watched the glittering waters of the Danube snaking away down at the skirts of the hill as she relished the idea of finally being able to spend the weekend with Rudi, the first in a very long time. When would he be hers, and hers alone? When would he always be with her, sharing everything with her? Everyone was getting married. Even Izabella. Poor Izabella. The thought of her dear friend made her heart ache. Last year she had finally torn herself away from Ákos and from their hopeless love affair, or rather they had torn her away from him. Count Almás must have considered Izabella, a teacher of literature, unworthy of being a vessel to contribute to the continuation of their noble blood. Alex could not fathom why Ákos was so scared of his father. He probably did not love Izabella because if he did, he would not have let her go. Two months ago Izabella, losing all hope, had married Oskar – an Austrian working as a teacher of the German language – without giving much thought to whether she loved him or not, more like running away from it all.

Suddenly her thoughts scattered. She was wet all over. Infuriated, she jumped to her feet. Károly had dived into the pool and was swimming in hurried strokes towards Ada, who was walking with Magda on their way back from the ceramic workshop in the far end of the garden. He was so much in love. Ada was so lucky.

Rudi grabbed Alex's legs. "Come here."

She let herself slide over the edge of the pool into the water into Rudi's arms. Firmly holding her legs with his strong hands and wrapping them around his waist, he took her lips between his. The passion of his embrace, the desire on his lips and the almost-forgotten tightness of his grip reminded her of their first kiss. When he released her lips, his eyes lingered on her face, then in her eyes, admiring her, loving her in a way that he had not done in a very long time. He was about to say something, but then stopped and kissed her again on her lips, on her neck and on her hair. She surely had been blowing everything out of proportion. Rudi was not fed up with her at all. He loved her, he truly did. Her rekindled self-confidence gave her the courage to ask, without giving it a second thought, whether it was their turn to get married.

"Please don't start again," he sighed as his arms on her waist loosened.

"I'm tired of missing you, Rudi."

"Alex, Alex. Please. Please look around you. Look at other people's relationships."

"I do. And when I do, I suffer even more. None of them remained engaged for so long. Look at Józsi and Éva."

József had fallen in love with Éva, the daughter of Baron and Baroness Orbánstein, the moment he had met her at Alex and Rudi's engagement party. They had been engaged six months later, and less than a year after that, in October last year, they had married.

"We've been engaged for almost two years, Rudi. Such a long ..."

Rudi dived in without waiting for Alex to finish what she was saying. He swam under the water to the other end of the pool, where he pulled himself out in one brisk movement of his arms and, drying himself, walked over to where Alex was left frozen in the pool. "I have to go now," he said curtly.

"You always have to go," murmured Alex.

"I've already told you that I'm invited to a dinner, Alex."

"Can't I come as well?"

"It's a men's night."

"As always. Who will be there?"

"You don't know them."

"We've been engaged for so long and I still don't know so many of your friends. I don't understand why. Where will you be going?"

"It's not decided yet."

"I want to go back to Budapest with you."

"Everybody is still here. Why don't you stay and enjoy yourself?"

He must be joking, she thought. He couldn't be serious.

She hurried out of the pool. As she dried herself, she bid farewell to her friends lazing around the garden, gave Magda and Miklós each a hurried kiss on the cheek and walked towards the house to change. There was no sign of Károly and Ada.

When they got into Rudi's convertible, she knew in her heart that what she was doing was wrong. Don't you have any self-respect Alex? Aren't you ashamed of obligingly waiting for someone who treats you so ignobly? She felt like a defenceless bird shot down – a silly old bird totally besotted and unable to go anywhere, while Rudi continued to shoot at the other birds flying around. She was not happy with herself at all. Being jealous, begging, questioning and running after him were all very humiliating for her, but she could not help it. He was driving her mad. She could not bear being left in the dark, not knowing, not being sure. A series of questions that she tried to push back into the depths of her mind, a series of questions Károly had asked her last year, popped up in her mind: Do you really love Rudi, Alex? Or is it your eagerness to get married that blurs your judgement in interpreting your true feelings for him? Could it be your hunger for happiness and your desire to be loved that leads you into believing that Rudi would make an excellent husband? "Am I turning a blind eye to his unreliability?" she thought, quailing. She did not dare inquire further into the truth behind his absences; she much preferred to believe the excuses he kept making.

"You're too quiet. What are you thinking?"

"Nothing."

In Rózsadomb, Rudi stopped the car in front of the house. "You exaggerate everything, Alex," he said smiling as if nothing had happened, and kissed her lips affectionately, melting her heart and almost restoring her good spirits. "Please don't pull that face. There's no reason for you to be so down. Life is beautiful."

Life was beautiful, very beautiful indeed – for Rudi, of course. He lived his life to his heart's content, something Alex would like to do as well. The life she dreamed of, however, was not a life apart from him. She got out of the car and walked towards the garden gate, where she kissed her fingers to return the kiss Rudi had sent her. Turning around and walking towards the house, she had already made up her mind. She wanted to see with her own eyes what he was up to. Ignorance was not bliss but torture.

She could hardly wait for the evening to come. Her mother and aunt were in Balatonfüred, so she asked Álmos, the head butler, to tell her mother, if she called, that she was invited to dinner at Rudi's house and beseeched him not to mention that she had taken the car.

On Andrássy Boulevard, she parked the car on the side street next to the Opera House, across from the apartment building where Rudi had moved last year. His car was parked on the street next to the building. She would wait and see where he was going, if he was going anywhere at all. The façade of the neo-Renaissance style building was decorated with a pair of stone sculptures of the Roman goddess Flora, standing on both sides of the main entrance as guardians of the building – Flora, the goddess of flowers and spring, a masterpiece by Alajos Stróbol. It was a spectacular building constructed for Rudi's grandfather fifty years ago. Rudi's mother had lived there with her family before she was married. Alex wondered when she would be moving here. "Will I be moving at all?" she could not help thinking with an insuperable misgiving.

An hour passed and Rudi was still nowhere to be seen. It was ten o'clock. She was certain that he had lied to her. He must be with someone in his flat. She flung herself out of the car and crossed the street, trying not to think too much about what she was doing. Arriving at the main door, she hesitated for a brief moment before gathering her courage and ringing the bell of the second-floor flat. The huge door opened. Inside the courtyard, the refreshing sound of the water jetting from the fountain and the sweet fragrance of flowers somewhat eased her restless mind. Climbing the staircase decorated with impressive frescoes, she remembered the nasty gossip that had reinforced what her mother kept saying: "Ownership of a property on Andrássy Boulevard is now sufficient to obtain a rank for those without any hope of entering the Magyar nobility." People unnecessarily and excessively gossiped. This flat had belonged to Rudi's family for half a century.

Vilmos, the butler, was waiting at the open door to the flat. "Good evening, Mademoiselle de Kurzón," he said with vaguely perceptible question marks in his polite eyes.

"Is Monsieur Takács home?"

"He has gone out, Mademoiselle."

How would that be possible? His car was still parked down in the street. He must have gone on foot, then, she thought. "Do you know where he's gone?"

"To the Kárpátia Restaurant, if I'm not mistaken, Mademoiselle. It has been quite a while now."

"Thank you very much."

Had he gone out the back door? Or perhaps he had used the front door, but Alex had missed him. She ran across the street, rushed to her car and drove off towards the restaurant. Whatever needed to happen should happen. She was sick and tired of his lies. As she turned the corner into Király Street, she braked to a halt. What on earth are you doing Alex? Are you crazy? Look at you! Can you recognise yourself? Are you so desperate as to make such a fool of yourself? Well, yes. She might be making a fool of herself but at least only for this once. It was much better than being made a fool of every day in front of everybody. She stepped on the accelerator. She had to learn whatever was happening – and she had to learn it sooner than later. She drove on quickly. Her heart was pounding. Another two minutes and she should be there.

After parking the car at Ferenciek Square, she walked in unwavering steps towards the Kárpátia. Nothing, neither her flurrying heart nor her stomach clenching in trepidation could make her change her mind. She saw no sign of Rudi at any of the tables as she peeped through the window of the restaurant. He must have lied to his butler as well, or he had come and gone. She wanted to be sure. She went in. "Has Monsieur Rudolf Takács arrived yet?" she asked the maître d'.

"Yes, Mademoiselle," he replied as he gestured with his eyes towards the oak doors further ahead. "They're in the private room."

A sudden burning rage erupted inside her. In the private room! God knows with whom! He had never invited Alex there. Jealousy consumed her. Then to her horror she saw the heavy oak doors open in their intimidating grandeur. Rudi came out with a crowded group of men whom Alex had never met before. There was not a single female among them. She flinched with a pang of embarrassment clutching at her heart and making her wish she could disappear from the face of the earth right there and then. Rooted to the spot, she pulled her cloche hat, already shadowing her eyes, down to her nose. She would, if only she could, have run away to the end of the world, but it was too late; Rudi had seen her. His eyes flashed with fury. His features twisted into a fearsome expression. Alex noticed Lajos among the group of men behind him and gave him a hesitant smile.

Rudi had come over and grabbed her arm. "What are you doing here?" he spat out between his teeth without moving his lips.

She could not utter a sound.

"Are you following me, Alex? Alex, are you out of your mind? Get out of here right now before you make a fool of yourself and of me." He brusquely let go of her arm.

She stumbled out of the restaurant to her car, opened the door with trembling hands and sank behind the wheel. She burst out crying in great sobs. What is happening to me? Am I really going insane? What am I doing? This must be a nightmare. The door opened. It was Rudi. He climbed in without a word. She could not get herself to face him.

"Alex, you must trust me," he said in a voice that had softened. He pulled her towards him and wrapped his arms around her. "You don't realise, do you, what an insult it is to me that you don't trust me? Please, I beg of you, please trust me."

Unbearably ashamed of herself, she was at a total loss as how to pull out of this horrendous mess. "Do whatever you like," she said meekly, choking back her tears, "but please don't hide anything from me. I want to know everything you do whatever it is or however bad it is. I can't tolerate to hear it from others."

"Alex, what do you think I'm doing? There's nothing I hide from you. It's just that I want some space. You suffocate me."

"All right, go! Go and have fun! Do whatever you like, but don't ever leave me. Never! Never! Please." She did not want to cry in front of him but, no longer able to control herself, broke down in tears. She was sinking deeper and deeper into a bottomless well of shame.

"I'm not going to leave you. I have no intention of leaving you. However, I do have a life, Alex. *You* have a life too. You can't expect me to be with you all the time."

"I'm so very lonely, Rudi. I need you. I need you, your attention, your love."

"You're not alone, my precious. I'm right here." Rudi's embrace became tighter. "I'm right here."

Yes, he was here, but only so very rarely. However much she tried, she could no longer tolerate him spending almost all his time and his energy with others. She felt like a tree patiently waiting by the side of a road where Rudi ran up and down, a tree providing shade for him to stop once in a while to catch his breath and cool off, a tree soon to dry out as her hopeless pining for him would gradually denude it of its foliage. Perhaps one day you will understand what it means to love someone desperately, she thought, to fall in love hopelessly and yet suppress all your feelings to be able to put up with the pain of setting your beloved free.

She ached inside with the premonition of an inevitably pessimistic mood approaching, slowly creeping up on her, soon to shroud her spirit within its gloom.

20

József came out to the garden with a bottle of red wine and a plate of thickly sliced salami made from the wild boar they had hunted last time they had been here, carrying them both with much pride, the wine as it was the ultimate proof of his connoisseurship and the salami as it was the trophy of one of his most challenging conquests. Alex put her pen down on her lap next to the letter she had been writing and, taking a deep breath, leaned her head back. The sun was shining brightly, but she could tell from the smell of the wet leaves in the woods behind the lodge that it had been raining shortly before their arrival. She breathed in the crisp autumn air. Nature was her getaway, the solution to all her problems. Her pessimism, after being dramatically more oppressive during the stifling Budapest summer, locking up her soul inside its impregnable walls for months, had started to dissipate, albeit rather timidly, and her Cimmerian mood had begun to give way to a tentatively reticent sense of joy the moment she had arrived here. They were in Italy at the hunting lodge of Maria, her childhood friend from Albisola, and of her husband Giuseppe.

The morning after her eighteenth birthday, Maria had married her childhood crush Giuseppe and, without wasting any time, had started mass production – as Giuseppe proudly put it. Their first offspring Paolo, born seven months after their wedding, was far too developed – a healthy nine pounds, taking after his hefty father – to convince anyone that he had been born prematurely as his parents claimed. Within a year, Maria gave birth to their second son, Mario. Now she was hoping to get pregnant again, saying that she wanted to get over with "the reproduction business" before she reached twenty-five, unknowingly dispiriting Alex.

Alex tried not to brood over such unpleasant thoughts and continued to write.

... I so very much wish that you were here with us, dearest Magda. We're practically in the middle of nowhere deep in the heart of Italy, and I'm enjoying every bit of it. The hunting lodge is nearly eight hundred metres up a mountain with a view that takes your breath away. I never realised that autumn could be so uplifting. All shades of green, yellow, sienna, burnt sienna in particular, umber and every tone of dark red you can imagine are revealing themselves in all their glory. You'll find it hard to believe it, but I can't wait to paint.

Our trip was not too bad. The train took us to Pianello. As you might imagine, throughout the train ride János hardly let anybody talk and bored us all with his political soliloquy. We all learned by heart the things they did and planned to do for his new-found love, the Social Democratic Party, and, of course, his dreams about his forbidden love, the Communist Party. Once in a while, we did have a brief opportunity to utter a word or two as well. In Pianello, we climbed onto a horse cart that took us up the mountain to this little village called Lanino. It was quite a bumpy ride that made even our easy-going and calm Éva revolt. Everybody complained all the way. Sanyi, however, remained absolutely silent. He can't bear watching Margit and János so much in love, poor soul. Margit, who was already on top of the world, is now over the moon, for this is her first trip with János as his girlfriend. She's as happy as a clam. Unfortunately, I can't say the same thing for myself, although I can still smile thanks to Károly's never-ending jokes.

I'm looking forward to a relaxing and creative time here, dear Magda, and I can assure you that I'm not sad at all that Rudi could not make it. I must admit that I'm getting a bit tired of his excuses to make himself scarce. I'm tired of being jealous. I'm tired of being made jealous. I'm tired of feeling so worthless. Well, anyway. These are the things you already know, and you must be fed up listening to them. I'm in a heavenly place now and don't want to think of any of that. *Öcsi*, God bless his heart, is doing everything he can to make sure that I'm having a good time.

The lodge is very cosy with a huge fireplace in the drawing room. Everything is very bucolic, with lots of woodwork. There are six guest bedrooms upstairs. Mine is right at the very beginning of the hall, with a window overlooking the woods and a balcony giving on to the hills rolling down towards the skirts of the hills on the other side of the valley – total isolation from everything and anything urban. Right now I'm out on the patio in front of the house, basking in the sun, which is extraordinarily hot for this season. I repeat, yet again, that I wish you were here with us. Rest assured that I'll be keeping you up to date as to our activities in coming days.

Lots of kisses for now. (*Öcsi* also sends his love.)

Your always loving sister,

Alex

21

When she woke up the next morning, it took her a few minutes before she could remember where she was. Yawning and stretching, she climbed out of bed with her eyes barely open and dragged herself out of the room into the hall, down the stairs and towards the kitchen. She desperately needed a cup of coffee to wake up. "Good morning, Sleeping Beauty," she heard Károly call out from the drawing room. "Morning, *Öcsi*," she mumbled as she stuck her head through the door and, from underneath her heavy eyelids, saw her brother blowing her a kiss. Suddenly the weight on her eyelids lifted when she spotted a young man sitting on the sofa opposite Károly with his back to Alex, looking at her over his shoulder. "Oh, God!" she murmured, embarrassed to the core and totally helpless, thinking how awful she must look as she usually did in the mornings, more like a witch with her dishevelled hair. In painful self-consciousness, she hid her face with her hands, wishing that she could evaporate into thin air. Knowing the impossibility of her wish, she rushed back up the stairs into her room, quickly changed into some proper clothes, tidied up her hair, put some rouge on her cheeks and went out again in a rush, as if she were afraid that the scene downstairs might change if she delayed her return. She paused at the head of the stairs, took a deep breath and slowly went down. She peeped into the drawing room. Károly was gone, but his friend was still there.

"A very good morning to you too," he said with a vaguely ironic smile concealed beneath the well-trimmed moustache that partly covered his upper lip.

"I'm so sorry. Good morning." She felt herself blushing. Brusquely turning around, she hurried across the hall and into the kitchen. After preparing herself a cup of coffee, although not exactly as she would have liked it to be, she returned to the drawing room and sat opposite him on the other sofa, hanging tightly on to her coffee cup. Try as she might to find something to say, nothing came to her mind. She put her cup on the coffee table and reached for the silver bracelet and onyx rings she had left there the night before.

"I was wondering what their owner might look like," the young man said, curiously raising his perfectly shaped eyebrows and frowning, his wide forehead accentuated by his dark brown hair, neatly combed back with just the right dose of brilliantine. "I would never have thought she'd be so beautiful."

At that very instant something, some long-forgotten sensation, stirred deep inside her. A dormant feeling awoke, reviving her tired soul, yet at the same time melting her heart. She could not even remember the last time a man had made her feel so good about herself with so few words. She felt a sort of adoring gratitude for his words.

"I'm Aziz."

"Alexandra. Alex."

"I see that you've already met," said Károly as he entered the drawing room. He gave Alex a kiss on her temple, put his coffee cup on the table and sat down beside her. "I met Aziz in Istanbul. You remember the Ottoman Electric Works, don't you? It's the subsidiary of Ganz in Turkey where Uncle Kelemen sent me for my internship. Aziz was working there. And he still does." He turned to Aziz. "Which year was I in Istanbul? It was '26, wasn't it?"

"Yes, it was." Aziz looked at Alex. "They had given me the honour of taking care of your brother, thanks to my knowledge of Hungarian."

"Aziz is a mechanical engineer. He went to university in Budapest and then in Vienna. His German is even better than his Hungarian."

"I take that as a compliment, Károly."

"Unfortunately, we were too young to have met him when he was in Budapest. Our roads crossed much later in Istanbul. I'm much obliged to him for his hospitality there. I didn't even realise how quickly those four weeks passed, which, I must admit, I had expected to be rather tedious. Aziz has an extraordinary family. They didn't let a single moment pass by without creating a diversion for me. Parties, hunts, friends ... Istanbul remains one of the most memorable episodes of my life. And, of course his sisters. Aziz has three sisters and a brother, each one more courteous and delightful than the other."

Károly had never talked about Istanbul to Alex, or perhaps he had, but she did not recall. As she listened to Károly, her attention wandered off towards Aziz, to his dark brown pupils, extraordinarily big for his small eyes. How would I depict the depth of such a dark gaze if I were to draw him, she mused? Suddenly she noticed Aziz staring at her unblinkingly, smiling. She hastily averted her eyes in embarrassment.

Károly was blabbering along. "And Ayla ... sweet, tender, beautiful Ayla." He broke off and then remained silent for a brief second, as if at a loss as to how to continue, before asking with unconcealed enthusiasm, "How is she, by the way? What is she doing with herself?"

"She's very well, thank you," Aziz replied, putting his empty cup on the side table with a movement that was unexpectedly gentle for such large hands. Alex noticed how neatly manicured his nails were. "After Necla, we're marrying her off as well. The wedding will be in January. She's awfully busy with the preparations. She sends you her love as always."

"Is she still painting?"

"She does some things whenever she finds the time."

"She promised to send me one of her aquarelles. How very emotional they were – just like her."

As Ada entered the drawing room, Károly jumped to his feet as though snapping out of a reverie. "Enough of lazing around," he blurted. "All the mushrooms in the woods are waiting for us. Everybody has already gone. We're supposed to meet them in an hour." He snatched three of the silver spoons Ada had brought and gave one each to Alex and Aziz, keeping one for himself. They were to use them to check if a mushroom was poisonous or not. "Come on, come on, come on. They must be mushrooming after the rain. I can smell them from here."

Aziz was on his feet, extending his hand towards Alex to help her get up. She timidly placed her fingers in his palm as she rose from the sofa. They remained hand in hand a little bit longer than the occasion called for. She thanked him with a vague smile, trying to avoid his eyes on an instinctively self-defensive impulse, but her effort proved futile and a ripple of excitement ran through her as she caught a furtive glimpse of the inconspicuous passion in his eyes and of the elusive way he bit his slightly fuller lower lip. Be careful, Alex, said her inner voice, be very careful.

22

Alex looked at the watch on her long chain necklace. It was well past midnight, but she had no desire to go to her cold bed. She sank further into the comforting embrace of the soft cushions on the sofa where she had been peacefully enjoying the crackling fire after a physically and emotionally tiring day. This must be the most comfortable sofa I've ever sat in, she thought, and, as she smelled the burning wood, the warmest fire I've ever seen. Everybody had turned in – the men, for they would be getting up at five in the morning to go hunting, and the girls, for they simply wanted to be sleeping by their beloveds. She reached out to her diary on the coffee table. "Lanino, 29th October 1931," she wrote but could go no further. She hesitated, somehow ashamed of what she was about to write. She could not lie to her diary. She closed it and put it back on the table. Easing herself down on the sofa, she went back to watching the flames dancing in short and long movements, relaxing her strained mind. She took the blanket from the back of the sofa and spread it over herself. Cerise, quite old now, jumped up next to her with great difficulty and curled up by her feet. Alex's eyes were getting heavier.

She started with a shiver and opened her eyes. She must have drifted off. The fire had almost gone out.

"You'd better go to your room."

She gave another start at Aziz's voice. He was watching her, relaxing back on the other sofa with his arms spread open over the back.

"You'll be cold here," he continued tenderly.

"What time is it?"

"Almost five." He rose and came around to sit on the edge of the coffee table. Leaning over, he took her face between his hands. "Your cheeks are freezing," he said in a tone surprisingly compassionate for someone with such wantonly penetrating dark eyes.

Alex was happy to stay where she was but figured she had best make a move. She sat up.

"It's quite hard to believe that a girl like you is all alone."

"I'm not alone."

"Yes, you are."

"I have a fiancé."

"Where is he, then?"

Yes, in fact, where was he? Aziz was right. She did feel all alone and unwanted most of the time.

"Come along. Let's take you to bed."

He held Alex by her hands to help her rise to her feet. Wrapping the blanket tightly around her shoulders and keeping his grip on her for a few seconds more, he kindled in Alex a long-lost sense of safety that warmed her heart, despite the chill in the drawing room. As they went out into the hall and slowly walked up the stairs, she could feel Aziz's hand right behind her back, barely touching her but ready to give her support if she stumbled. They stopped before the door to her bedroom, facing each other. He gently pushed a few strands of her hair back with his finger and, for a brief instant, touched the top of her left ear where there was supposed to be a curve, before sliding his hand down and subtly caressing her chin. She was trembling, but not because of the cold. "Good night," she said in panic as she felt Aziz's warm breath approaching her lips and, opening the door to her bedroom, took a few steps back. He held her hand in both of his and took it to his lips. A long and warm kiss lingered on her fingers.

"Good night, or rather good morning, Mademoiselle de Kurzón," he finally said in a soft whisper and, leaning his back on the wall, watched Alex go into her room. He seemed intent on spending the rest of the morning hours there waiting for Alex to wake up.

"Good morning," said Alex, smiling faintly. "And good hunting."

She went to bed, enveloped in an intense sense of gratification.

When she woke up, rays of sunlight were streaming through the shutters into the room, leaving luminous lines on the wooden floor – a visual feast that always filled Alex with joy. It must be noon already, she thought, for she never felt like this in the mornings. Like what, she asked herself? What was it that she felt exactly? Lightness perhaps? Yes, an unusual sense of lightness. She jumped out of bed and went to the window to let in the daylight. As she flung the shutters wide open, the bright autumn sun blinded her. Undeterred by the cold, she took a deep breath, drawing in the crisp fresh air, and then another one, as if she wanted to inhale the whole scene. "The huntsmen must have left already," she thought as she put on her dressing gown and went out of her room. She went down the stairs in indolent steps. There was no one in the drawing room. She crossed the entrance hall towards the dining room where the girls were having their breakfast.

"Good morning, everyone."

"Good morning, Alex. Did you sleep well?"

"Yes, very well, thank you. And you?" she said, pouring herself a cup of coffee.

The girls went back to their heated conversation. Alex walked through the archway opening to the drawing room and settled into an armchair, taking Cerise onto her lap, unable to resist the pleading in her eyes. They were all very nice and friendly but talked too much, and Alex needed some peace of mind to think and sort some things out – her feelings, to be exact, which were in complete disarray. A sense of guilt had gripped her for having been attracted to a man other than her fiancé, something that made her think about her love for Rudi. What was that feeling called love? How could one define it? Often times, she wondered if it was only the jealousy and frustration of not having him exclusively to herself that she took to be love. And what about her feelings towards Aziz? Was she falling in love with him? If she loved Rudi, then what she felt for Aziz could not be love. She tried to figure out the essence of her feelings for Aziz. It was something she had never experienced before, either with Rudi or with anyone else, a very strong emotion that she had been missing since she had lost her father.

"What are you musing over, Alex?" asked Maria, bringing in some more freshly brewed coffee from the kitchen.

"She's simply enjoying her artistic license, turning inwards and having to explain nothing about why she behaves the way she does," Éva remarked.

"I'm still very sleepy," apologised Alex.

"We're planning to take a walk in the woods after breakfast," twittered Margit joyfully. "And we thought we could have a game of bridge after lunch. What do you think?"

"I'd like to paint outside. When will they be back – our huntsmen?"

Ada, apparently bored of the endless morning chat, had left the table and sunk into a book in a corner. "God only knows when," she grumbled without raising her head.

23

It was well after the sun had set behind the hills when Alex, having painted all day out in the woods, returned to the lodge. She entered through the kitchen door at the back. The huntsmen must have returned, she thought, wincing at the sight of a bunch of birds lying lifelessly on the kitchen table. She knew that if she caught even a single glimpse of their lightless eyes, there would be no chance she could think of them as food anymore. She put her painting materials on the floor and, shielding her eyes with her hand, dashed to the sink to wash her brushes.

"*Ciao bella!*" intoned Giuseppe in his stentorian voice as he barged into the kitchen with long thunderous strides. "How did it go?"

"I found this amazing place, Beppe, a clearing in the woods. I've been there all day."

"Let's see what you've got," said Károly, darting in through the door, driven by his usual explosive energy.

"Sunset was so extraordinary that when you see my sketches, you'll say that they look unreal and no such colours would ever exist in nature."

"My sweet little baby, I so wish you could paint in a way that I'd think looked unreal. Your paintings are far too photographic, sweetheart. You do nothing but copy nature. Painters don't copy. There's photography for that; Ada does it. You're a painter. You need to put yourself in between what you see and what you put on paper. Photography has diminished the value of certain styles of painting that primarily aim at the depiction of reality exactly as it is. And these styles are condemned to disappear altogether sooner or later."

"But I do put myself in between what I see and what I put on paper. What I paint is what I feel. I can't paint like you or like those avant-garde friends of yours. You're completely out of line. I'm sorry to say it but the posters and advertisements you once designed were much more meaningful."

"Art that merely serves rational and practical purposes no longer satisfies me. There's a myriad of undiscovered possibilities of self-expression in art that we can unearth. You should seek these possibilities as well, Alex. You're too traditional. And you know what? I think you're scared to experiment, to change. Modernise your style a bit, my darling girl. Nobody paints like you anymore. It is *passé – déjà vu.*" Károly turned to Giuseppe, who was getting ready to pluck the birds lying on the table. "Patrik Merse, the father-in-law of our Aunt Irén, is a very well-known painter in Hungary. The fact that he was once a prominent figure in the Royal Academy didn't facilitate the entrance of Alex and Magda into the Academy, but quite on the contrary, it made it even harder for them. To prove that they didn't benefit from any kind of favouritism, they had to accomplish much more than what was required by the already difficult entrance criteria. Alex took the exam with almost no preparation. Her talent is so outstanding that even someone like Patrik Merse, who has the habit of ruthlessly criticising every artist, could not help but say, 'These hands deserve to be kissed.' The National Museum bought the white lily she had painted at the entrance exam – I repeat Beppe, at the entrance exam – meaning before she had any academic formation. Do you know what this means? Unfortunately, my dear sister prefers to shackle this unique talent of hers." He turned back to Alex. "Please stop fidgeting with the details and enjoy the freedom of doing whatever you feel like doing. You get lost in the details and miss the big picture. Don't be so scared of how it will look in the end. Experiment! Waste your precious paints and expensive paper. They're there to serve only one purpose, and that is to be used. Look at Magda. She's doing great things in ceramics."

"You mind your own painting. People can at least understand something when they look at my aquarelles. You paint all that crazy decorative stuff that nobody seems able to make heads or tails of. One gets exhausted looking at those bizarre colours that I could never imagine myself using. I think you're wasting your talent as well as a lot of paint, my dear *Öcsi*."

"You shouldn't underrate abstract art. Abstract art. What does it really mean? Abstract? Abstraction? It means to separate or withdraw something from something else. You take a visible object and abstract its elements to create much more simplified forms. Sometimes you depart from reality altogether and catch forms that have no immediately visible source in nature. These forms are mostly simplified down to geometric patterns. The highest form of beauty, as Plato says, lies not in the forms of the real world but in geometry. Art should be purely about the creation of beautiful objects. Art for art's sake. Creating an effect with pure patterns of form, colour and line. As a matter of fact, it isn't abstract at all but concrete. Concrete art, if you will. I can't think of anything more concrete, more tangible or more real than a line, a colour or a plane. It's the most concrete way to represent the abstract thoughts and moods in a sensuous way."

"Are you saying that my paintings don't represent my thoughts and moods?"

"They might do, but it's not enough, Alex. You ought to look away from nature and turn your eyes exclusively to your inner world. Abstract art is an internal questioning. Just as science reaches out towards the infinity of space, art should be reaching inwards towards the infinity within the individual."

"Here they go again," said Ada to Giuseppe, who was busy plucking the birds. She had come in to prepare some drinks.

"Anyway," said Károly as he clasped his arms around Alex, busy washing her brushes at the sink. "At least we have variety in our family. Opposites always stimulate each other."

Having finished cleaning her brushes, Alex picked up the materials she had left on the floor. "I'll go change now, but we'll continue from where we left off when I come back," she said threateningly.

"She's extremely inspired," said Ada. "She can't keep her hands off her pencils. She drew all morning before going out to the woods. She sketched the interior, the garden, us, Cerise snoozing in front of the fireplace, everything. Non-stop."

"Good for her," said Károly. "She has been in an artistic coma for months," he added, turning to Beppe. "She even risked not graduating from the Academy."

Alex left the kitchen, pretending not to have heard any of her brother's last comments. Glancing into the dining room, she heard Maria say, "I do wish I could understand why Ada raised the bid to Six No Trumps."

"Maria!" demanded Ada as she swished past Alex into the dining room. "If you can't make this contract either, I'd suggest you never play bridge again."

"Stop talking please," intervened Margit in her soft voice. "Declarations are over. It's playtime now."

Éva took a sip from her drink and leaned back, greatly amused at their prospective victory. "They'll lose so many tricks," she said, smiling at Margit sitting opposite her.

"Hello everyone," said Alex.

The table was covered with empty teacups, half-empty wine glasses and overfilled ashtrays scattered over the green baize.

"Hello Alex."

"Hello Alex. How was your day?"

"Great. See you all in a bit."

Aziz was nowhere to be seen. Neither were József, János or Sándor. The real huntsmen were apparently reposing.

24

After dinner and a lot of wine, they were sitting around the fireplace. József had manoeuvred the conversation back to hunting, his most passionate subject, though not with much difficulty, since he had managed to control the reins of their late night chat, never letting it deviate too far from hunting in the first place. Standing by the fireplace, he extended his arms towards Alex and Károly. "Their father was the master among the huntsmen. Gusztáv de Kurzón, the great Gusztáv de Kurzón, a virtuoso, a sight to watch as he moved like a dancer, calmly, taking aim, firing, turning back, changing his gun and holding it up to take aim again. He was elegant, he was strong, he was self-assured. It was him who instilled the passion for hunting in me. May his soul rest in peace."

Alex, hardly able to concentrate on József's soliloquy so far, was instantly interested upon hearing her father's name.

"He used to come from Italy at least two or three times a year to organise a shoot in Kengyel," József continued. "My father always said that hunting was a pleasure for him and that he had never allowed it to become a competition, a challenge or an ambition. He was known to spare no expenses and employ hundreds of people during the long preparations and the shoot to ensure that everything went smoothly to the satisfaction of his guests. Everybody talked about the shooting parties in Kengyel and waited to be invited. He, however, invited only six guns to each shoot, saying that, with him and his brother Kelemen, there would be eight guns and any more than that would make the hunt unpleasant. He was very choosy as to whom to invite. They had to be good shots as well as true gentlemen. He took great care not to exhaust his guests, and made sure that the hunt started early and didn't last too long, always ending close to the manor house. He thought of every little detail." József had gone over to the window and was now looking out into the darkness of the night. He took a deep puff of his cigar before he continued. "I recall one shooting party he organised in particular. It was the first one I attended. I was nine years old then – back in 1913. It was the second day of a three-day hare shoot. I was there with my parents. I remember how proud I felt as we waited in front of the Erzsébet Manor and then climbed onto one of the carriages, drawn by strong and beautiful horses, which were to take us along the country road to the hunting lodge. Every single detail was nothing but pure elegance – the exquisite woodwork of the carriages shining to a high veneer, the impeccable black leather seats, the disciplined way the horses trotted, the coachmen in their meticulously ironed livery and black top hats, everything was in great style. Eight carriages slowly moved ahead one after another, keeping the distance between them exactly the same. In each carriage, there was one gentleman, who was the gun, and one or more ladies. I was the only child and I can't tell you what a privilege that was." He looked around as he puffed his cigar again. "I'm boring everyone with these reminiscences, I'm afraid."

"No, no. Please do go on, Józsi," said Sándor and Giuseppe simultaneously from where they were sitting side by side on one of the sofas.

József took a sip from his brandy, the expression on his face displaying the great pleasure he took out of it. "When we reached where the hunt was to begin, we found the bale of straw with the number that had been allocated to us and stopped our carriage right in front of it. Number eight was one of the two most prestigious positions on each end of the line. My father said that his neighbour Gusztáv de Kurzón always honoured him with one of these positions. Three people were waiting behind each of the eight bales, separated by more than a hundred metres. One of them carried the cartridges and was to load the guns. The other two were the game collectors carrying long poles on their shoulders to hang the hunted hares. There were five or six beaters with each huntsman, who would stamp their feet on the ground, follow the hare and direct the huntsman by shouting, 'Hare on the right!' 'Straight ahead!' 'On the left!' Young girls standing close to each other spread their colourful skirts wide and made up two walls, so to speak, to prevent the hares from escaping. These human walls started at each end of the kilometre-long line created by the eight guns and extended towards the manor house, eventually joining each other. My father, like all the other huntsmen, climbed down from the carriage. I had to stay behind with my mother and watch him from a distance. When everybody was ready, the horns sounded, first on one end of the line and then on the other. Then someone shouted, 'Forward!' and the shoot began. The young girls were thumping their feet on the ground. One of the estate's foresters, mounted on his horse, was giving orders to the young girls. 'Slowly!' 'Faster now!' 'To the left!' Hares of all sizes and shades were running along the line of the colourful skirts, either with the hope of finding an escape route or with the expectation that they wouldn't be shot there. The chase went on for about an hour. Finally losing all hope, the hares threw themselves in front of one of the two best huntsmen on each end of the line."

József carried on talking as he walked towards Éva and settled on the armrest of her chair. Alex had lost her concentration again, for she could sense Aziz watching her from where he was sitting on the floor in front of the fireplace. Throughout dinner, she had noticed him staring at her, but could barely bring herself to look in his eyes. She felt that, at this point in her life, she would be most vulnerable to reassuring eyes. What on earth was she thinking? How could someone she could trust be dangerous? She must have had too much to drink. She took another sip from her brandy. Yes, his eyes did look fierce and intimidating at times, but they could hardly conceal the reliable warmth deep down in his heart.

"Well Alex, what do *you* think?" she heard János ask.

"Sorry? About what, Jancsi?"

"Stop thinking about him. You'll make yourself ill," burst in Károly, briefly taking a break from kissing Ada's arm. He was sitting on the other sofa with Ada nestled on his lap, as if there were not enough room for her to sit in the huge drawing room.

"Whom are you talking about?"

"How do you mean whom am I talking about? Rudi, of course."

"I wasn't thinking about him."

"That's good, very good. Excellent."

Károly stood up holding Ada in his arms. Seating her back on the sofa next to János and Margit, who had their arms and legs intertwined, he walked to the gramophone in one corner of the drawing room, put a record on and started dancing on his own.

Alex watched her brother. He was in such a good mood these days. His plan to move to Paris was no longer a dream. He was seriously thinking of living there for a while with Ada. She would miss him terribly, she could not even imagine being away from him.

"Alex, would you like another glass of brandy?" asked Giuseppe.

"Yes, please," she said and then added with haste. "Actually, that would be great."

"Tell me, Aziz," said Ada, "I've never been to Istanbul and would very much like to go there to take some photographs. How much freedom would a lady have going around with a camera in her hand?"

Alex did try to listen to what Aziz was saying but lost her focus when she felt him lightly touching one of her fingertips as he talked with Ada. He was still sitting on the floor, but was much closer to Alex now. She pulled away her hand when his touch turned into a caress, and leaned back on the sofa. She seized hold of Maria's arm, waking her up from her snooze. They smiled at each other before Maria closed her eyes again. "What are you doing, Alex?" she asked herself. What was she doing? Or was she doing anything? She should stop it. She should be thinking of Rudi and stay away from Aziz.

"Come dance with me, would you please?" Aziz was up on his feet. He took Alex's hand to his lips without taking his eyes off hers. Dancing is off limits, Alex. It might be dangerously seductive. Aziz, however, had an attraction that she could not resist. She was not going to resist.

As they slowly moved around the limited space between the furniture, she felt his hand on her waist, slightly moving over her sweater. She tried, although to no avail, to control her trembling hand, tightly clenched in his. When he tightened his grip, the shivering stopped. Unable to look into his eyes, she started watching others. Károly had finally convinced Ada to dance. She smiled at her brother, who blew her a kiss. Behind them, Margit was dancing with János, almost invisible in his embrace. Everybody was so much in love. Despite her thick sweater, she could feel the warmth of Aziz's hand penetrating into her skin. Her body vibrated to the gentle but determined movement of his fingers as he pulled her closer. Now she could feel the warmth of his whole body against hers.

"Your hair has an incredible smell," he whispered in her ear, taking a deep breath.

His cheek brushed against her temple every now and then. For a split second, her lips touched his strong and thick neck. She drew back in panic.

"We shouldn't be doing this, Aziz."

"What makes you say that?"

"The sense of smell has the strongest memory, you know."

Why did I say that for God's sake! Wine and brandy. Bad combination.

Aziz moved his hand up her back to her neck and gently pulled her head towards his shoulder. "Let go, Alex. Let go. Trust me. Please."

She did not know how long they danced, but, when they finished, the music had already stopped. There was only Károly left in the drawing room, sitting on one of the sofas and probably daydreaming. When had everybody gone? Alex felt as if she had woken up from a dream. She went over to sit by her brother's side and cuddled him, planting a kiss on his cheek.

"Károly," Aziz said as he sat across from them. "What about welcoming 1932 in Istanbul? I'll be organising a party. You could stay a bit longer for Ayla's wedding as well. It would be such a great honour for us if you came."

"Why not? Ada would be delighted. She's never been there. I loved it. Such an amazing city."

"It would be more amazing if we had somebody as extraordinary as Alex there," said Aziz.

Alex felt her face blushing. She snuggled her head on Károly's chest, trying to hide her cheeks, probably already reddened. She hoped that the darkness of the drawing room would make it go unnoticed or the heat of the fireplace would allow it to be misinterpreted, but she was mistaken.

"Yes, Alex," said Aziz in a caressing voice. "You're truly exceptional."

Alex did not know what to say. "I should be going to bed," she mumbled. "I'm really exhausted. It must be the fresh air up here. Goodnight to you both." She kissed Károly on the cheek and stood up.

Aziz was already on his feet. He held both her hands and kissed them individually, softly pressing his lips to her fingers while looking straight into her eyes.

Alex felt once again, yet this time a bit more strongly, how hard and cold it was to go to bed all alone.

25

"Good morning, sunshine," sang Károly as he stormed into Alex's bedroom and jumped onto her bed before she could even open her eyes. He started tickling her, which was something she detested, and continued to do so until she had tears in her eyes.

"Wake up, you lazy bones. It's almost lunchtime."

Her laughter left no room for her to get annoyed with her brother. "Don't be so childish, for goodness' sake!" she said, giggling. "Stop it, *Öcsi!* Stop it, I said. Enough! I'll make you regret it. Enough now."

When she saw Aziz leaning against the doorframe, watching her with what she hoped to be admiring eyes, she pushed Károly aside and tried to pull herself together.

"How would Milady take her coffee this morning?" Aziz asked as Károly went to open the window to let in some fresh air.

Alex wanted to get up but did not dare make a show of herself in her unsightly pyjamas and sank deeper into the bed, pulling the eiderdown further up to her nose. "White, please. No sugar," she said faintly.

Károly warned Aziz about heating the milk and making the coffee boiling hot or otherwise risk his sister's pestering him all day about it. As soon as Aziz left, he came over and sat down on the bed. He was suddenly dead serious.

"I hope you know what you're doing, Alex. Your attitude is bordering on the flirtatious."

"I can't say I do, but he somehow makes me feel so very happy. I'm sick and tired of being treated like an unwanted, good-for-nothing, desperate-to-marry spinster of a girl, Öcsi. That's all I've been getting from Rudi lately. I can no longer figure out how much I love him. Marrying Rudi is a dream for most of the girls in Budapest, and I'm about to realise that dream. Sometimes, however, I wonder if what I take to be love is nothing but a compulsive desire to possess him, a covetous ambition not to lose him. I give too much to get a little drop of what he might offer. I want to be loved, Károly. I'm hungry for love."

"But what makes you think Aziz loves you? It's only been two days, Alex."

"I don't know. The thing is that he makes me question my feelings for Rudi and our relationship, that's all."

"Be careful."

Károly stormed out of the room just as fast as he had come in.

A few minutes later Aziz showed up, carrying a tray with a cup of coffee and some biscuits on it. "Your coffee, Your Highness." He put the tray on the side table by the bed and walked over to the armchair by the window. "If you would be so kind as to allow me to stay with you for a while," he said as he sat down.

She took a sip from her coffee. It was perfect. "Thank you, Aziz."

"You're most welcome, young lady," he said, watching Alex with a steady gaze.

She wondered what he might be thinking. Looking at his eyes, she felt a sudden urge to draw them. "Would you allow me to draw you?" she asked without a second thought. Before he could answer, she put her cup on the tray, took her drawing pad and pencil from the bedside table and started drawing with great enthusiasm.

She drew for hours, as if inebriated, the strength of her creativity exponentially enflamed by Aziz's compliments, his attention adding colour to her inner world. Too excited to eat anything at all during the long late lunch, she could hardly wait for it to end and, as soon as it was over, rushed to the clearing in the woods again, no longer able to resist the call of her creativity – something that even she herself found surprising. She drew a few sketches for the aquarelle she was planning to paint later on. Then, wanting to share all this beauty with Magda, she took a sheet from her drawing pad and started a letter.

Lanino, 31st October 1931

My dearest Magda,

I'm writing to you from this amazing place I discovered yesterday. It's a clearing in the woods where I've been painting. There is a wealth of different moods here that I want to capture and engrave in my mind, in my heart or on my paper. I don't want to let anything go unrecorded. The clouds and the light change so swiftly; emotions emerge, develop and grow faster than I can give expression to them. I'm impatient even as I write to you. I want to write about all my feelings quickly before they lose their intensity because I know that they will as soon as I discover a different colour.

The day before yesterday, Károly's friend Aziz arrived from Istanbul. I can't say he's very good-looking, but he's a true gentleman. As to the first impression I must have made on him ... well, I think it would be quite sufficient for you to get an idea if I simply said that he had the misfortune of seeing me two minutes after I had woken up. I acted so – how shall I put it? – so much like myself in the mornings that he must have thought I was a complete twit. At best, that is. He nevertheless seems determined to get the best out of me, practically hovering over me. The amount of attention I get from him makes me doubt his sincerity, really. Now don't get ideas and think that I'm falling in love. I'm in love with one person only, and you know who that is: Rudi. It's just that so much attention flatters me. Some feelings that I thought had died a long time ago are stirred up, I suppose, such as self-confidence, such as feeling good about myself. Little things, Magda, it's the little details that really impress me. His subtle words and hardly perceptible gestures send hundreds of butterflies fluttering in my stomach. The touch of his fingers, for instance, when he pushes away a hair from my lips or his hand on the small of my back gently leading me to the table ... and the looks he gives me. There is something about his eyes. They're very narrow but impossibly captivating, even sinister, I should say. Then, from one second to the next, that expression, which might even take on a cruel streak at times, changes and conveys a warmth that I find impossible to resist. He talks with his eyes; I shall not be able to write what they say. Now, writing about it all, I'm thinking if it's my imagination that is blowing things out of proportion. Is it my broken and tired heart desperately in need of some reassurance of its existence? I don't know. All I know is that I want to enjoy his attention.

I'm so full of inspiration that I can't stop drawing. This morning, or rather at midday, I drew Aziz, who posed for me – rather restlessly, although they were only a few ten-minute sketches. (I must admit that I might have made him sit for twenty of them in twenty different locations in and around the lodge.) I found it very difficult to get his expression down on paper. In fact, I ought to say that I found it difficult to concentrate on what I was drawing because of the way he watched me, somehow making me feel totally naked even in the presence of so many others around us. When I told him to stop looking at me that way, he asked, in faked innocence, "In what way?" before saying how much delight he took in watching me give all my attention to him.

Now I'm waiting for the sunset. Everything is so beautiful, and the only thing we miss is you, my darling sister.

Well, your selfish sister is only talking about herself. I hope everything is well with you.

I embrace you and Miklós with all my heart.

Your loving sister,

Alex

She lit a cigarette and leaned back onto a tree to relish the delicate details on the rolling hills. She could almost see the trees changing colour from one minute to the next as they lay bathed in the sun's rays that penetrated through the clouds. There were so many clouds, puffy and white, gradually darkening to a deep Payne's grey towards the edges and ending in a strong, almost shimmering silver lining. Another layer of even darker clouds stretched beneath all the others, letting the blue sky peep through and wink an occasional eye. The colours were getting warmer and warmer as the sun sank towards the horizon. Greys became bluer; whites became increasingly yellowish. Looking towards where the sun was about to set, she saw pale pinks. It was so peacefully quiet. She listened to the sound of silence. This was a different type of silence – not the lifeless, colourless muteness of the indoors but the silence of life, the animated silence of nature. Suddenly she heard the sound of footsteps in the woods behind her.

"*Öcsi?*"

It was Aziz, holding a red rose he must have cut from the garden, and carrying a bottle of red wine and two glasses. "You've been up here all afternoon. I don't mean to interrupt but thought you might be thirsty," he said, laying the rose on her lap.

"You're not interrupting at all. I'm waiting for the sunset. Autumn skies are so entrancing."

He sat beside her on the blanket, poured the wine and handed one of the glasses to her.

"To your happiness, Alex."

"To the happiness of us all."

They sat silently, watching the sun setting over the hills and listening to the subtle sounds in the woods. All the silver linings were slowly turning into an orangey dark pink brushstroke. At some point, Alex felt him watching her.

"Sunsets seem so dull next to your beauty, Alex."

Slightly embarrassed, she turned to him and, unable to raise her eyes to his, fixed her gaze on the barely visible dimple on his chin.

"The deep love in your eyes when you watch nature is so alluring." He held her hand and brought it to his lips. Without taking his eyes off hers, he gently stroked her hair and then her cheek. His hand slowly moved down to her neck, and his lips touched hers. A shock of alarm paralysed her when she realised how longingly she had been waiting for this moment to happen. She had wanted it badly but knew that she should stop. She pulled herself back. He held her neck firmly and, pulling her towards him with some force, kissed her lips again. This time his invigorating passion made her forget everything, and she kissed him back. Her mind had gone blank; she could not think. She did not want to think.

At that very instant she thought she heard something behind them in the woods. It sounded like footsteps again. She drew herself away from Aziz's embrace and hurried up to her feet. "We've got to go back. It's getting rather late," she said firmly, picking up her painting materials.

"I'm sorry, Alex. I'm really sorry. The last thing I wanted to do was to offend you."

"Please. It's not important. I just got carried away."

As they walked down the path towards the lodge, the multi-coloured evening sun was slowly giving way to a monotonously grey sky, announcing the imminent arrival of a dark night. Alex felt a chill of foreboding down her spine. She hastened her steps. From among the leaves still hanging on to the branches of the trees by the side of the winding path, she caught a glimpse of the patio in front of the lodge and froze where she was as she saw Rudi. He was sitting on one of the chairs, leaning back, with his legs spread wide and one of his arms thrown over the back of the chair. His head was slightly tilted to one side, his gaze threateningly fixed on Alex.

She stumbled down the pathway, leaving Aziz behind with her painting materials. "Rudi! What on earth are you doing here?" she called out. "What a surprise," she continued, trying to control her trembling voice.

"Nice to see you too."

At his icy tone, she stopped as if she had hit an invisible wall. Her knees gave way. Had he seen them? He could not have. It was only a brief kiss, lasting no longer than a few seconds. She carried on walking towards him with apprehensive steps. Rudi's smile was far from being warm or tender, and it definitely did not bear any good intentions. He was simply showing his cold white teeth through his lips, which were set in a severe straight line. She found it horribly difficult to look at his narrowed eyes, where all his strength seemed to have concentrated.

"Nice to see you here, Rudi." A dreadful surge of anxiety grabbed her. She did not want to lose him. "I thought you had to travel to Vienna for the tournament."

"It was cancelled; I thought I might surprise you, although I'm no longer sure if it was a good idea."

"What do you mean?"

Instead of answering her question, he turned to Aziz, extending his hand. "Hello. I'm Rudolf Takács. Alex's fiancé."

"How do you do? I'm Aziz. Halimzade Aziz. A friend of Károly's."

At the end of an unnecessarily long handshake, both Rudi and Aziz had expressions on their faces Alex could not quite make out. There was something in the way they looked at each other that betrayed more than any of the reactions to be expected from two people who had suddenly found themselves in an unforeseen situation – an instantaneous bewilderment, perhaps a moment of hesitation, something awkward.

"Help me unpack, Alex, would you?" Rudi's was not a request but an order.

26

They were all out on the patio to watch the stars. Alex went into the kitchen to prepare herself another cup of coffee. Maria had already refilled the espresso maker and placed it on the stove. The milk left in the milk pot was still warm. She poured some into her cup and started to wait for the coffee to brew.

"I beg you to forgive me, Alex. I'm really sorry." Aziz had followed her into the kitchen and was standing by the door.

"Please don't be," she said, her eyes fixed on her coffee cup. "It was my fault as well as yours."

"I can't bear to see even a trace of sorrow in those beautiful eyes. You deserve all the happiness in the world, and I do hope that one day you'll realise where you can find it. Alex ..." He broke off, and then remained silent, as though he was trying to choose his words carefully. "I want you to know that, no matter what happens, I'll be by your side; until the day I die, if you choose it to be so."

Something told her that she could trust and love Aziz, even if she could not work out exactly why. The coffee had started to gurgle. She turned off the cooker, poured some coffee into her cup and hastened past Aziz to join the others on the patio.

It was pitch black, and the sky was illuminated by the stars. Warmly wrapped up in blankets, everybody was sitting around the fire Giuseppe had made. József was engrossed in another one of his heated monologues. Rudi waved his hand to summon Alex to his side. The menacingly fake smile on his lips gave his face a most frightening expression. His eyes, although Alex could not see them clearly, somehow looked ominous as they reflected the vicious dance of the flames. She looked around her; her heart ached with a strong sense of panic. She desperately searched for the reassuring eyes of her brother, who was sitting with Ada, locked in an embrace, their backs to the fire. Ada was so lucky. She had a perfect boyfriend, who perpetually kept his attention as well as his eyes and hands on her, forgetting about everything – including Alex, his beloved sister. She walked timorously towards Rudi and perched on the chair he had drawn up closer to his. His eyes were bloodshot. Was it because of the drinks he had had? It must be, she thought with desperate optimism. Her uneasy heart filled with trepidation as he lifted his arm from where it had been resting on the back of her chair and clasped her shoulders, harshly pulling her towards him. Grabbing her neck, he planted a rough kiss on her lips, intending to hurt her more than anything else.

Aziz had also come out and sat on one the chairs on the other side of the fire.

"You're shivering," said Rudi sharply, picking up the blanket, which had fallen behind the chair. He wrapped it around Alex and, this time, almost clenched her shoulders. "I agree with Józsi," he said, disrupting József's monologue. "Hunting is a passion, a passion stealthily burning deep inside you, a passion to kill. Killing is in human nature. It's instinctive, just like in the animal kingdom. We might kill to protect our loved ones or to defend ourselves, or we might kill to prove our strength and power over the others. Human beings kill within legally justifiable limits, overtly aiming to protect the social order, or covertly seeking to realise their ideals."

Relaxed under the mesmerising spell of the flames and the wine, nobody had the energy to join the dialogue between József and Rudi. Alex looked timidly at

Aziz, who was gazing at the invisible view of the tenebrous night.

"Hunting is like a sacred ritual," Rudi went on fervently, "a ritual where one proves his power, a ritual of sacrifice, a special rite from the moment you wake up before dawn until the moment you pull the trigger. Everything about it is special. Your clothes are impregnated with the smell of the woods, of the fallen leaves putrefying on the ground, of the oily metal of the guns, of blood. You feel on your own despite the presence of the other huntsmen. There's nothing but you and nature. Silence gradually becomes oppressive. You hold your breath and wait with unwavering concentration. You notice everything. Even the faintest sound, the slightest movement, the tiniest sign of anything extraordinary catches your attention. For a huntsman, everything depends on how perceptive he is – sometimes even his life. And finally the instant you spot your prey, a shiver of excitement runs through your whole body. You freeze. The thrill brought by the imminence of satisfying your forbidden passion paralyses you, though only for a split second. You focus, with the unequalled satisfaction of knowing that you will soon prove that you are more powerful and able than your adversary. The ritual ends when you pull the trigger and watch your prey fall to the ground."

Alex could not stop trembling. She leaned back and looked up at the sky. Before long, a shooting star shot. "*Maradj velem,*" she murmured to herself, not quite knowing whom she meant.

27

It started to snow again. In winter it became clearer why they called the Great Hungarian Plain *Puszta* – emptiness. The snow fell incessantly, in lulling quietness, covering everything, sequestering the fields, the woods, the swamps, the marshes and the houses under an endless white shroud until springtime. Everything surrendered to its fate, as if enchanted by a singular mirage.

The train rumbled through the silence along the rails buried under the snow. Alex was dreamily watching the telegraph poles, barely able to support the wires bent under the heavy burden of the snow, as they swiftly passed by the misty windows of the warm compartment. Staggering through the confusion created by her turbulent mind and emotions ever since she had been back from Italy in early November, she had finally decided to get away from Budapest, taking advantage of Rudi leaving on another business trip right after New Year's Eve. In half an hour she would arrive at Kengyel, a small village of twenty households on the seemingly endless fertile lands of the monotonous *Puszta,* a village which was a small part of the lands bestowed upon the Kurzóns for their bravery in war.

When the train arrived at the station, Alex saw Tibor waiting for her in his lapelled overcoat and hat. Just like his father, grandfather and great-grandfather, he was the stableman and the coachman of the estate, among his many other duties. Like the estate manager, the butler and the gamekeeper, he lived here all year round, Erzsébet Manor being their home more than anybody else's.

The horses drawing the landau extended their heads towards Alex, their smiling eyes showing that they had not forgotten her. She hugged them longingly. Nothing ever changed in Kengyel; nothing unsettling or unbalancing ever happened here as the monotony of *Puszta* permeated through everything. The snow fell the same way each year. Springtime saw the same flowers invariably blossoming. Even Tibor was exactly the same as his father. Erzsébet Manor did not change either. Standing upright in all its glory at the further end of the snow-covered, muddy country road winding northwards from Kengyel, it diligently kept an attentive eye on the village and its surrounding fields. Facing the endless plain, it leaned against the woods that harboured a lake and a small stream among its trees, planted by Alex's family generations ago. It was waiting for Alex with open arms, like a prince on a white horse ready to help her get over her depressed mood, much worsened by the dismally dark winter in the capital.

They drove through the high wrought-iron gates. The stone building, protecting its inhabitants from the menacing desolation and the freezing cold of the outside, had a two-storey middle section with a ledge separating its two floors – a ledge where stood a series of stone-carved lions guarding the building day and night as vigilantly as they had been doing for more than a century, their cold stance discouraging any unwanted visitors. Alex felt a warm sense of safety as she entered through the main doors under the lions. They had opened the doors to the Yellow Salon on two sides of the large staircase across the hall leading up to the first floor. She smelt the wood burning in the fireplaces. The grandfather clock standing next to the door greeted Alex, its chime reverberating around the hall. Welcome home, little Alex.

Head butler Csaba, his wife Edit and estate manager Ernő had lined up by the wall under the family's coat of arms, waiting for their orders.

"Welcome home, my Lady."

"Please, Csaba. Just call me Alex. Please."

"If you would be so kind as to allow me, I would suggest that we do not open the North Wing. I took the liberty of presuming that you might dine in the Yellow Salon in the Middle Section. As to the South Wing, might I assume that you would not require your mother's bedchamber to be prepared?"

"That's fine, just fine. It would be quite sufficient if you prepared my bedroom and bathroom." After a moment's thought, she added, "And our playroom. I mean, our study."

She continued along the hall and entered the Yellow Salon. They had put the fire on in the fireplaces and in the porcelain stoves. It was pleasantly warm despite the seven-metre high ceilings and the spacious mezzanine floor. The sparkling crystal chandeliers reflected their light on the silk wall coverings, which, upon Alex's grandmother's special order from Paris, had been fabricated in muted green patterns separated with golden streaks, enhancing the sensation of light. The door to the dining room in the North Wing was closed.

"I understand that since you have not brought any maidservants or a cook from Budapest you might want Edit to take care of your needs."

Alex asked Edit to run a bath for her and went out of the Yellow Salon through the doors opening to the South Wing. She entered the wide corridor, the walls of which were filled with oil paintings in golden rococo frames. They were portraits of her family and of her ancestors, who almost looked identical with their aquiline noses and blue eyes. For years they had been staring questioningly at the inhabitants of the manor as the silent witnesses of a myriad of promises, broken friendships, budding romances, destructive arguments and devastating separations. The first room on the left was Magda's. Alex peeked through the door. The furniture was overwintering under white covers. Next was Alex's bedroom. They had already brought in her luggage. A delightful warmth emanated from the porcelain stove in the corner. They had lit a fire in the fireplace as well, knowing that it pleased her. She went straight to the window and opened the curtains wide. She needed light. Watching the snow-covered garden, the frozen lake and the woods behind it, she thought how much she had missed it all. She took a deep breath in as if she could, if she tried hard, inhale the serenity of this winter scene. The tranquillity of the woods penetrated her soul, relaxing her mind. She did not want to think of anything. Sometimes, being alone felt so surprisingly good. She was sick and tired of everything, especially of all the gossip; she was weary of the struggle.

In the hope of some oneiric relief, she lay down on her bed, which had always promised her sweet dreams. The scent of lavender radiating from the pillows pacified her inner turmoil, but only briefly, before her thoughts returned to storm her brain again. Ultimately she had been convinced that Rudi took excessive pleasure in torturing her. She could no longer tolerate him continually insulting her in front of the others, veiling his stinging sarcasm behind polite remarks. According to Magda, she was being too emotional and exaggerated everything. "You should be a bit more rational and try to understand Rudi," she kept saying. "Businesswise, he's going through a very difficult time." What had all this got to do with his business? Why did he need to exclude Alex from his life? Why did he have to make himself so scarce? Why did he have to drive her mad by openly flirting with every girl that came around, when he knew only too well how jealous it would make Alex? He was being totally unfair. And she, like an idiot, was putting up with all this. Why did she love him so much? What did she love about him? His absences? She thought of Aziz who, despite being kilometres away, made his presence felt as if he were right next to her through his letters.

"Your bath is ready, my Lady."

When she woke up the next morning, the raw and limpid winter sun had already brightened her room. It had to be freezing cold outside, but it was delightfully warm inside. They had lit the stove. Like in every other room in the manor, there was an opening at the back of the stove leading to a hole in the wall on the other side, covered with an elaborate panel, through which servants could feed the stove without disturbing their masters. She pulled the bell cord to let those downstairs know that she was awake. Edit, who knew her well, would soon bring her coffee exactly as she liked it, along with the Danish pastries fresh out of the oven. Edit's pastries, like everything else in Kengyel, never changed. She sat up, took her shawl from the headboard and draped it over her shoulders. Arranging her pillow, she leaned back comfortably and fell to gazing out of the window. Before long, a better idea occurred to her. She got up and walked to her desk to take her fountain pen and a few sheets of writing paper, before going out of the room and dashing to the end of the corridor to the playroom. It was still the playroom for her, even though it contained only a few of their toys after having been rechristened as their study a long time ago, when they had reached the age to leave their childhoods behind. Everything in the room was shipshape thanks to the immaculate care of Edit. Károly's tin soldiers had not moved an inch from where they were carefully lined up on the shelf. Snow White and the Seven Dwarfs, comfortably nestled in their cottage, were loyally waiting for Alex as they always did. She touched the roof of the cottage, smiling bitterly at the memory of her disappointment upon seeing this new cottage their mother had had made upon their arrival in Budapest; it was not nearly as beautiful as the one they had left behind in Italy. She pulled the cord of the wall-clock, something she used to do as a child upon entering the playroom. There was no sign of the toads that used to leap out and start fighting. She recalled how they used to laugh watching them. The paintings and the drawings they had done when they were children decorated the walls. She ran her fingers over the one next to the clock. She was six years old when she had made it. It was a picture of a frail wild duck with its green head peeking through the reeds as it vacillated between dipping its foot into the water and keeping it hanging in the air.

She sat at the desk in front of the window. Nature looked so calm and peaceful under the snow. The mature and respectable century-old plane tree, intimidatingly virile in its hardness, stood erect on its robust trunk with its roots well settled deep in the earth, guarding its post by the lake in all its majestic serenity and staidness. Rather gloomy at times, it stoically kept all its troubles to itself. For years, neither the snow nor the rain nor the thunder of the cold winter months nor the scorching summer heat had managed to move it an inch. Alex's eyes travelled down to the weeping willow tree standing right next to it. A strange feeling of envy embraced her as she watched how listlessly relaxed it was, protected against all calamities under the expansive canopy of the plane tree. "Why does it so bend to one side?" she wondered. Is it more comfortable like that, giving in to the weight of its branches?

She started writing in that impeccable calligraphic handwriting diligently taught to the girls of the upper classes.

Kengyel, 11th January 1932

My dear Izabella,

I received your letter of December 23 and do ask your forgiveness for my belated reply. I've been in a terrible mood lately and finally decided it would be best if I came to Kengyel.

I might agree with you that putting up with Rudi's capricious behaviour is rather masochistic on my part. However, he's like a bad habit I can't give up. I don't know what to do, really. Aziz is a very kind person with a heart of gold and, most importantly, understands me better than anyone else does. I truly feel very close to him. He expresses his feelings so beautifully, and genuinely treasures me, treating me like a valuable piece of fine crystal that might shatter into shards if mishandled. No one has made me feel so valuable since my father's death. And I can assure you that I've never before trusted a man as much as I trust him, for he has a very strong personality. Thinking about it all, I often think that I ought to take you as an example. You gave up so many things but gained a lot in return. Perhaps that is what is best for me too. I do hope that I would one day love Aziz although it may never be as much as he loves me. For the moment I deeply respect him and somehow feel grateful to him.

You keep praising Istanbul ...

Her eyes slowly drifted away from her letter and stopped on the little island encircled by the frozen lake. She put down her pen and started watching the twin girls skating hand in hand on the lake, under the snow-laden branches of the stooped trees that almost touched the ice along the shore of the island. I must be daydreaming, she thought, rubbing her eyes. But they were still there. A boy, as blond as a baby, showed up behind the two girls. He swished past them on his skates, his hair flying in the wind. Taken aback, the girls lost their balance and screamed; the boy let out an expansive laugh and started to skate backwards, watching the girls.

"Would you like me to bring your coffee here, my Lady?"

The children disappeared.

"Yes, please, Edit."

And she continued to write.

... However, I do have my doubts. What about the women in Istanbul? Can you go about the town freely or is your liberty cooped up within the confines of the school's garden walls? What about the theatres, the opera, art galleries? How do you dress when you go out? I'm aware that Aziz has a modern and westernised family, but I nevertheless beseech you to write me every little detail with no censoring whatsoever.

I'm really glad that Oskar is happy with his post. I do find it rather strange that he works at an American College in Turkey as a teacher of the German language, but I'm led to believe that it has proved to be a good mixture for you. I understand that your lodgings are in a heavenly place. What do you have in your garden? Have you planted any lilac trees? Probably not, for I remember you being rather keen on camellia. Please do send me some photographs of your house and garden. And please don't forget to include some shots of the Bosphorus, which you speak so highly of.

You ask about Károly. Well, he says he has made up his mind and will be moving to Paris in April with Ada. I don't know if this is good or bad. It would be impossibly difficult for me to survive his absence. They plan to stay there for quite some time.

133

Please give my warmest greetings to Oskar and accept my longing kisses for you.
Your devoted friend,
Alex

Edit brought in her steaming-hot coffee and the fat Danish pastries generously filled with apricot jam.

"Thank you very much, Edit," she said as she folded her letter and took a new sheet of paper. "Dear Aziz," she wrote, hesitant as to how to continue. How should she reply to his gallant letters brimming with compliments, where he openly declared his love for her and sometimes subtly expressed his passion, a passion he could no longer bridle? However she started, she eventually brought the subject to Rudi and how unfairly he had been treating her. By the end, not content with what she had written, she had ripped up three unfinished letters.

The snow had started to fall again. It was so silent that she could almost hear the snowflakes falling. The trees, the frozen lake, the earth beneath the snow, the invisible stars yearning for the darkness of the night, everything was waiting, holding its breath. Suddenly she felt an urge to paint. Right there and then! She took a sheet from her writing pad and started to draw. The plane tree, the weeping willow, the lake – she not only wanted to put them on paper but also to ingrain them into her soul. When she looked closer, she distinguished the colours of the earth underneath the disguise of its white blanket, which betrayed shadows of muted umber. She dashed out of the playroom and into her bedroom. Her watercolour tubes, sable brushes and palette lay on her desk, offended at having been neglected since when she had last used them in Italy. She grabbed them, along with the water jug and the glass from her bedside table, and returned to the playroom.

By the end of the week she spent in Kengyel, the icy coldness of the *Puszta* had cooled down her mind much overheated by turbulent thoughts, and her trembling soul had calmed down under the lulling effect of the falling snow flakes. She hoped that perhaps she would be able to face life with a more serene mind-set from now on. She would be returning to Budapest in the afternoon.

She handed Csaba the list of the wines and the champagnes Károly had asked her to bring back to Budapest and followed him to the narrow stairs at the far end of the entrance hall leading down to the cellar. The dark, mysterious and pungent cellar, with its walls covered in undulating layers of mould that thickened each year, was the nightmare of her childhood; she used to believe that every evil emanated from either the dark cellar or the coal shed. Watching Csaba easily spot what he was looking for among the lines and lines of bottles buried under a thick cloak of dust, she felt quite useless there, apart from making him uncomfortable.

"I'd better go upstairs," she said, making for the service stairs that led up to the closed North Wing. Her footsteps echoed on the walls as she climbed up. She timidly opened the door to the dining room a crack before she hesitantly pushed it further. Inside, the milky landscape seeped in through the heavy silk velvet curtains hemming in the French windows in a dark crimson frame; the furniture, hibernating under the white covers, recited the refrains to the verses outside. She walked on tiptoe across the dining room, scared to disturb this isolated dormancy, and quietly turned the knob of the door opening to the Crimson Salon, which yielded with a moan. Gliding into the formal drawing room equally shrouded in white, she felt a quiver of unease. Shivering, she trod her way towards the music room. Somebody was playing Chopin's *Nocturne, Number Twenty* on the white grand piano. A sweetly warm feeling embraced her wavering heart, as her father turned his head and smiled at her before fading away along with the music. With a sinking heart, she quickened her pace. As she walked past the piano, her nostrils burned with the smell of camphor, evoking childhood memories. She recalled watching the servants carefully place pieces of camphor in the piano to protect the felts before they moved to their summerhouse in Balatonfüred. Suddenly breaking into a run, she found herself in the smoking room. She hastily averted her eyes from the leather armchair where she knew she would find her father smoking his cigar. She knew that he would still be sitting there in front of the oak-panelled wall between the bookcases reaching up to the ceiling. She knew it, because she could smell the smoke of his cigar. She wanted no more of her childhood reminiscences. Memories hurt. She should get out of there. Hurrying through the door into the dining room, she flung herself out into the entrance hall. She almost bumped into Csaba exiting the Yellow Salon.

"Are you all right, my Lady?"

"Yes. Yes, I'm quite all right, thank you. Please tell Tibor that I'll be leaving early. I'd like to go to the hunting lodge."

"The lodge is not prepared, my Lady. It would be rather cold there."

"I shan't stay long. Only a few minutes."

Csaba swiftly disappeared. Alex felt her breath shortening. She leaned back on the doorframe, holding on to the bronze statue by the door. Her fingers stroked its

135

polished surface. It might be better if she did not go to the lodge after all; it would be full of memories of her father. No, she wanted to go. She wanted to see it one last time. What was she thinking, for God's sake? Why one last time? Why would it be the last time? Had she made up her mind? No, she did not know yet. She was not sure what she wanted to do. How could she leave all this behind? How could she leave her childhood, her past, her home, her homeland? She was desperately scared of being left all alone. I'm alone anyway, she thought. How long am I going to run after someone who doesn't love me?

"The carriage is ready, my Lady," announced Csaba, with Alex's fur and gloves draped over his arm. "Would there be anything else we might do for you?"

"I'd like to walk to the acacia-lined road," she said, putting on her fur and gloves.

The water in the fishpond was frozen. She wondered what they had done with the fish – the fish she used to love watching as a child. As she trudged towards the country road leading to the hunting lodge, under a canopy of leafless and lifeless snow-laden branches of the acacia trees, she recalled the day she had started to learn how to ride.

"Welcome home, my Lady," said the village postmaster as he hurried past her with his heavy bag slung across his shoulder, dutifully carrying expected and unexpected letters despite the sub-zero temperatures.

God, it was cold! Her breath was burning her lungs. She would not be able to walk anymore. She climbed into the landau, which had been following her. Taking the fur spread on the seat, she wrapped herself in it. It smelled of her father.

As they travelled on the country road her uneasiness built, and reached its peak when she caught sight of the hunting lodge. Tamás, the gamekeeper, was waiting on the patio with his hunting dogs barking joyfully.

"Tibor! Let's go back," she blurted out, suddenly changing her mind.

28

Alex nervously drew in another puff from her cigarette. Parties were so boring without Károly. If he were here, he would not leave her alone, not even for a minute, and he would do everything he could to cheer her up. She looked at Rudi standing at the far end of the drawing room. He was talking heatedly to some girls perched on the canoe-like sofa, constantly giggling like twittering birds trapped amidst the arresting pattern of the zebra-skin upholstery, blissfully ignorant of the fact that they would soon be shot down. Alex could no longer tolerate his comportment, which had become nothing more than sheer rudeness lately. There should be a limit to how far a host should go in entertaining his guests. Besides, Alex was a guest as well, and he should be showing her some hospitality too. What did he expect her to do – stand behind him, smiling and nodding her approval as he paid one compliment after another to girls who were obviously fresh out of the Eighth District?

The spacious drawing room was packed with people and, to Alex's frustration, they were all couples who sat or moved together, looking after each other, so to speak, while they socialised. Rudi, however, was looking after everybody but Alex. She once again thought of Károly and how cross she was with him for having left her. It had been more than a month since he had gone away, but they had received nothing more than a cold telegram from him informing them of his safe arrival in Paris. She was really worried and heartbroken. Finally last week, no longer able to bear it anymore, she had sent him a telegram full of reproach. There still was no reply from her neglectful brother.

"Alex, dear. It's so unbecoming of you to sulk like this."

She started at Éva's voice. The long ash at the tip of her cigarette fell on the silk cushion of the sofa. She hastily flicked it.

"Come on, princess. Give us a smile," chimed in József, offering her one of the two brandy glasses he was holding.

"Please, Alex," said Éva with an accommodating smile. "You are the hostess after all. It's rather rude of you to isolate yourself like this."

That is easy to say, Alex thought as her friends left her. Éva was really lucky. József did not leave her alone even for a second. He worshipped his wife. Éva was in her fourth month of pregnancy. She would be a mother soon. No wonder she constantly smiled. Envious of her self-assured, reserved and understanding smile, Alex tried to imitate her, getting no further than tightening her lips. I must look like an idiot, she thought. She could not do it. Anyone could see that the forced smile on her face was not sincere. Then why should she even try? Sulk as much as you please, Alex. She felt totally helpless. Her eyes caught the birds supporting the bronze coffee table. When will I sip my morning coffee, she asked herself, as I sit on this sofa? When will I be the lady of this household? She stroked the silk cushions of the sofa and then ran her fingers along the shiny curves of the rosewood frame of the armrest. Rudi must have thought of the large family he would have with Alex when he had left his family home and moved in to this five-bedroom flat. It had been almost two years since he had moved here and Alex found it hard to understand what they were still waiting for. Everything was ready. He had thought of every little detail, from the *Lalique* vases to the silver *objets d'art* when decorating this flat. She looked at the long mahogany dining table, imagining her blue-eyed children shouting while having their breakfast and their father Rudi peering from behind his newspaper and telling them to be quiet. When breakfast was over Rudi would stand up. They would walk arm in arm to the door where he would kiss her on the lips. The children would hug their father and bid him goodbye.

Suddenly the children vanished. Rudi was holding her hand. At long last, he had remembered that Alex was there as well and, managing to drag himself away from the girls he had enchanted, found the decency in himself to offer the first dance to his fiancée.

"Alex! You seem as if you were in mourning. What's wrong with you? You are the hostess. Would you please act like one?"

Once upset, she could hardly control her emotions. She knew she was unattractively sulky but could not change it. Smile, Alex, she said to herself. Force yourself! Look at Éva. Imitate her. She could not get herself to smile; she was furious. And Rudi was not helping her either. He could do something to lift her spirits, to make her forgive him, but he did not. Instead, he kept on openly insulting her. He obviously did not care. She looked at him for some encouragement. The harsh expression on his face, which she used to find thrilling once, seemed frighteningly serious now. Then he smiled, but only at another couple on the dance floor. He was more interested in others even when they were dancing. Perhaps she should just leave.

"Monsieur Takács. I'm really sorry, sir. It's London." It was Vilmos, the butler, whispering in Rudi's ear. He said something else Alex could not hear.

Rudi excused himself, saying that he had to attend to an urgent business matter. Alex returned to her rosewood sofa and watched her fiancé politely squeeze through the guests and out of the drawing room. Would there be a day when, while she sat here, Vilmos would come and say, "Madame Takács. It's Paris, my Lady"? Would she ever become Madame Takács? She rose from the sofa and, gliding on the shining parquetry, forced her way through the guests towards the door leading to the corridor. Reaching the library, she made to turn the doorknob, but before she did, the door opened a crack. She saw Rudi put down the telephone and then swiftly walk towards the young woman sitting on the black leather sofa in front of the desk, hold her hands and start an animated conversation. Her heart sank, her knees buckled and her world darkened. Stars started dancing in front of her eyes. Moving away from the door, she leaned her back against the wall for support. Go away, Alex. Get out of here, right now.

She hurried back into the drawing room, passed through the couples trying to keep pace with the accelerated tempo of the music, and stopped in front of a window. Her gaze hung listlessly on the happy crowd on the terrace of the Opera House, sipping their champagne through the interval. With trembling hands, she took out her cigarette case. The damn thing was stuck. I should buy a new one, she thought in frustration as she forced it open. It suddenly yielded; the cigarettes fell on the floor. She knelt down and nervously started picking them up. Was it really her or was she mistaken? Of course, it was her. It was the girl she had seen at lunchtime today. She was right after all. She had every reason to be jealous. What was she doing here? What on earth was Rudi doing with her?

This morning Magda had come to town and taken Alex first to Margit Island for a stroll and then to New York Kávéház for a bite to eat. However, as soon as they had entered through the doorway, they saw Rudi sitting at a table tête-à-tête with a girl – with this girl! – whereupon Alex practically threw herself out of the café. Despite Magda's insistently saying that she was being ridiculous, she could not get herself to go back in. Rudi had not told her anything about this clandestine rendezvous, and she could not find the courage to face his lies. She would not degrade herself in front of a worthless girl. In the end, they went to Gerbeaud. The crystal chandeliers, the heavy velvet curtains and the richly gilded chairs – an atmosphere she actually adored – oppressed her. She wanted to leave, unable to put anything in her mouth, even refusing the *Konyakos Meggy* that she had the habit of buying every time she went there, for she needed a lot more than chocolates with cognac-soaked sour cherries to cheer her up. She wanted to go back home, but Magda, always seeing the sunny side of life, said that she was exaggerating and dragged her to Váci Street for some shopping. She could not care less about shopping, about the drastically reduced prices of the beautiful fur coats, about the fresh spring air, or about the lilac trees she loved. All afternoon she had tried to work out what she was going to say to Rudi in the evening. Finally, Magda had convinced her not to ask him anything.

However, after what she had seen just now, she had every right to question

Rudi. She would ask him who the hell this girl was and why he had not introduced her to Alex so far, and what she was doing here. Everything was crystal clear now. For weeks, every time she had called him, he had hardly spoken to her, saying that he was busy and would call her as soon as he could. What was it that kept him so busy when he was at home – so busy that he could not spare a moment to talk to his fiancée? Now she knew what had been occupying him and why he could not give any proper answers to her questions. He could not, because he would have had to lie. How could she not have seen it all? How naive she had been! Had she not come across him at New York Kávéház on that Saturday when he had lied to her saying that he had had tennis practice? He was alone, but he had lied to her nevertheless. She remembered what Rozália had told her last week. She had seen him with two girls ambling in Város Park. Alex thought that it was quite normal as she too went on promenades with her male friends and decided that Rózsi was only being jealous. How stupid she was to think so! As Károly had once said, her optimism, triggered by her yearning for happiness, blinded her. Rudi had actually been behaving very strangely for months now, and there was no justification for such cruel behaviour towards one's beloved.

"What is wrong with you, gorgeous?" Miklós had arrived, politely extending his lighter.

"Nothing. Nothing is wrong."

Everything was wrong. She had nothing left. Nothing! Rudi must still be in the library. She could not wait any longer. What were they doing? She moved her head closer to Miklós's lighter, hardly able to hold her cigarette between her trembling lips.

"Alex. Please don't do anything that you might regret later on," said Magda, knowing what was going through her sister's head, sometimes even better than Alex herself. "Why don't you two dance?" she said, turning to Miklós.

Alex stuck her cigarette between Miklós's fingers, which he had extended to ask her for a dance, excused herself and walked away. She should go and see what Rudi and that spiteful girl were doing. She marched through the drawing room with determined steps, into the corridor and then towards the library. She peeped in through the open door. Rudi was pacing up and down the room with his hands in his trouser pockets, still talking heatedly. She barged right in. They had not noticed her.

"Rudi?"

He stopped abruptly and swiftly turned towards Alex standing by the door. His raised eyebrows and cold stare were asking her what she was doing there.

"Could we talk in private, Rudi?"

"I shan't be a moment."

"I ought to leave you two alone," the young woman said, looking pathetic in her insipid grey suit, more fitting for a jailor. She faintly smiled at Alex as she left on tiptoe.

Rudi had not even bothered to introduce them.

"Who is she? Why didn't you introduce us?" She knew that his answer would not be the truth and, turning her head away to avoid the lie she was sure to see in his eyes, fixed her gaze on her silver-framed photograph on the desk. "You seem to be forgetting your manners, Rudi."

"She's a friend of Lajos from London. She works for the British government. She's here on business. Lajos, although he is in Egypt, had the courtesy to arrange a meeting with her. She'll be helping me in a most crucial deal."

"That miserable creature? Helping you to do business? At this hour!"

"You shouldn't worry yourself about my business. What was it you wanted to talk to me about? Can't it wait? We shouldn't be leaving our guests alone too long."

"You were with her at lunchtime."

"Yes, I was. What of it?" His tone of voice had suddenly taken a harsh turn. "How do you know that?"

"Couldn't I have joined you?"

"You couldn't have."

"Why, Rudi? Why?"

"Because it was a business lunch, because it is impossible to guess how you would behave, because I was afraid that you would make a scene with one of your jealousy trips. That's why." Rudi had not raised his voice, but Alex could feel his anger brewing. "I've had enough, Alex!" he hissed through his teeth. "You're suffocating me."

"You're not behaving like my fiancé, Rudi. It's been three years, and I'm tired of running after you."

"How should I behave? Like your slave? Grow up, Alex. Try to be a little bit more mature, for Heaven's sake! What happened to the Alex I fell in love with? Where has she gone, the self-confident, free-spirited girl who wanted to live her life?"

He was right. Where has the high-spirited, cheerful Alex, whom everybody loved, gone?

141

"You don't understand me at all, Alex. You're so selfish that you're not aware of anything other than your own emotions. You seem to be living in a dream – in a fantasy. Please open your eyes a little and try to see my efforts, my worries, the things I want to achieve, the things going on in the world."

"You don't love me as much as I love you, Rudi," she murmured, offended. "I love you so very much that it makes me your slave."

"You want to make me your slave by enslaving yourself to me, Alex. Don't be a slave to your emotions. Please. Don't use your love to purchase my freedom."

Alex hated herself more than she hated anybody else. Furiously taking off her engagement ring, she threw it on his desk, turned around and dashed to the door, not daring to look Rudi in the face, for fear of a surge of remorse.

Rudi ran after her and grabbed her arm. "What do you think you're doing?"

Tears were streaming down her face.

"Alex." Rudi's expression had softened. "Are you leaving me?"

Was there a trace of irony in his voice?

"It's not me who is leaving, Rudi. You left me a long time ago. You've left me all alone." She hated herself even more for crying.

"Alex, please. You're being ridiculous."

Pulling herself away from his grip, she went out of the library and ran straight to Magda to tell her that she wanted to go home. Magda did not ask her anything. She was looking at Rudi, who was standing at the doorway opening to the corridor.

29

Alex opened her eyes. Seized by a dull, persistent pain, her body refused to wake up after an atrociously oppressive night full of nightmares. She should try to sleep some more. As soon as she closed her eyes, however, thoughts rushed in. What had she done? It was sheer madness, an incredibly idiotic and grave error that she had broken up with Rudi, that she herself had left him to others. She ought to have been more patient. No! No, that was not possible. How much more patient could she have been? She did not know. She did not know anything. She had no strength left to reason anymore. Frustrated that a peaceful repose was no longer a possibility, she opened her eyes again and reached for her watch on the bedside table. It was already midday. Lying there next to her watch was a letter with Károly's handwriting on the envelope. A sudden surge of relief eased all her pain. She grabbed the letter, ripped the envelope open and started reading it. He begged Alex to forgive him for having been so negligent, saying that she was right in everything she had said and that Paris, the enchanting city of his dreams, bewitched him into forgetfulness. His letter brimmed with the details of his bohemian lifestyle and with his pleas for her to come and visit him.

There was a knock on the door, and, before she could answer, her mother charged in.

"You should be getting up, Alex. It's lunchtime," she said. And then she stopped short. "What happened, dear? Is there something wrong?"

She was surprised that her mother could read her thoughts, only to realise that it was her tears flowing from her eyes that betrayed her emotions.

"Is it bad news? Is Károly all right?"

"Yes, Mother, he's all right," she mumbled, wiping away her tears, "but I'm not." She was not all right at all. She wanted to go away, run away from it all. She should go to Paris, to Károly. Right away. Tomorrow. "I ... I broke up with Rudi," she stammered and burst out crying in huge gulps as the pain of what she had just said slapped her in the face. She turned her head so as not to see the happiness she was sure to see in her mother's face. "Are you happy?" she muttered with difficulty. "We finally broke up."

Her mother sat on the bed. "I warned you, dear," she said in that most annoying tone of hers as she stroked Alex's cheek. "I warned you so many times. He's not worthy of you, sweetheart. But you never listen, do you?"

"I'd never have thought it would be me to break up our relationship."

"Don't worry, darling. He's not worth it. I'm sure ..."

She could no longer bear her mother's offending remarks and had no desire to listen to her. Pushing away her hand, she got out of bed and threw on her dressing gown. As she darted out of the room, words gushed out of her mouth. "I can't be as strong as you, or, ... I don't know ... as desperate as you. I can't share him with another woman."

Beethoven's *Fifth Symphony* was playing somewhere downstairs, its ominous rumblings assaulting her ears. *C Minor, Opus Sixty-seven*, she murmured faintly. "*Fate!*" She ignored her mother running after her, still grumbling something she no longer cared to hear.

* * *

Three weeks later Károly called.

"Rudi called me. He said you had a fight."

"We didn't have a fight, *Öcsi*. We broke up."

"Apparently, you haven't been answering his calls for the last three weeks. He said he would be leaving for Vienna tomorrow for a tournament. He wants to talk to you before he leaves. He must be really upset to have called me long distance."

"We have nothing more to talk about."

"Don't be such a child, Alex. There's no point in avoiding him. If you're going to break up, you should talk to him like a civilised person."

"I did talk to him, Károly. And we split up. Don't you get it? We split up. I've had enough. I'm sick and tired of feeling like a piece of rag that he thrashes about. You were right indeed in what you once told me. I'm no longer sure of my feelings for him. It's nothing but an unhealthy desire to possess him, a sickly craving that consumes me."

"We have to talk about this, and we shall do that when I see you next week in Italy."

They were invited to a ball organised by the Ganz Factory on the shores of Lake Como in northern Italy during the last week of June. It was given in honour of the memory of their uncle Kelemen, who had been the man behind the electrification of the Valtellina railroad extending from Sondrio to Lecco, the first railroad in the world to operate on a high-voltage three-phase electric current system. Hundreds of people from all over Europe and America were invited to the event. For Alex, the most pleasing aspect of it was that she would be seeing her brother, who was left with no choice but to join them since their mother had categorically refused to take no for an answer and even agreed to pay for all his expenses, including those of Ada.

"There's nothing to talk about, Károly. I wouldn't want to waste the precious time we'll be having together on such trivial matters. I miss you so much, *Öcsi*. These two months have been hell, but this last week seems like eternity. I can hardly wait."

"Don't exaggerate, Alex. You can come and see us whenever you like. Actually, you must. You should stay with us for a while. It's not such a big deal, is it? Only a few days' travelling, that's all."

30

A week later Alex, along with her mother, Aunt Etel, Magda, Miklós and Sándor, arrived at Villa d'Este, one of the famous hotels on the shores of Lake Como in Italy. She was to find not only Károly and Ada, who had arrived from Paris the day before, but also someone else sitting with them at one of the tables under the linden trees by the lake, sipping his tea. Aziz had told neither Alex nor Károly that he had been invited to this ball, but he was there as one of the Turkish engineers who had worked with Kelemen de Kurzón during the tramway project realised by the Ganz Factory in Istanbul. "I hope my surprise appearance was not inappropriate," he said in a tone of voice much more self-assured and with a look in his eyes much more courageous than they had been eight months ago in Italy. Alex was not convinced at all when Károly pretended to know nothing about this surprise, a surprise that inevitably pampered Alex. She was almost certain that her brother had dropped Aziz a hint or two about her separation from Rudi. This was something rather unexpected of Károly, for he had been siding with Rudi, so to speak, constantly drumming into Alex's head that she was being unfair to him and that she should stop being over-possessively jealous and try to be a little bit more understanding.

It was not long before Alex was carried into another world, a peaceful world where her tense body and tortured soul relaxed in a sweetly embracing languor under the persistently admiring gaze and enchanting compliments of Aziz, a world of solace where the balmy weather, the courting songs of the chirping crickets, the magnolia trees ablaze with white blossoms and the perfume emanating from the gardenias had an amazingly soothing effect on her broken heart. She was further enraptured as she listened to the cheerful monologues of her high-spirited brother, whom she had been yearning to see for two long months. This was an occasion of ecstatic bliss for her; they were all together again – Magda, Alex and Károly, just like in the old days, a perfect occasion to try and get Rudi out of her mind.

The next evening the ball commenced with cocktails on the lakeside, followed by dinner under the century-old magnolia and plane trees in the renowned garden of the hotel, by which time Alex had finally been able to distance herself from Budapest not only geographically but also emotionally. Between the starter and the main course, the general manager of the Ganz Factory gave a speech about how the crisis of 1929 had shaken the industrial sector in Hungary and how, in the past three years, production in their country had halved. Only large enterprises such as Ganz, he noted, that succeeded in bringing innovative changes to their products, had managed to strengthen their positions in foreign markets. "We survived this dire period thanks to the three-phased traction system Kelemen de Kurzón developed, initiating a new era in the history of the railways," he said as he concluded his speech, to which Aunt Etel had listened with a proud smile on her lips, and her lace handkerchief on the edges of her tear-dimmed eyes.

The main course was served as soon as he finished delivering his long eulogy.

"You must be very proud of being the son of such a valuable engineer. There aren't many inventors in the world of his calibre," said İskender, Aziz's friend, who was an engineer as well.

Sándor listened to İskender's tributes with a blank smile and, after a few clumsy smirks of forced politeness, returned to his own world.

İskender rose from his chair. Pushing up his eyeglasses, as thick as the bottom of a bottle, he said that he wanted to propose a toast to the memory of Kelemen de Kurzón. Alex reached for her glass, thinking how ugly İskender was. His chin seemed to suffer from some sort of malformation, something that gave his face a crooked and unpleasant expression when he spoke. He did not stand a chance with women, especially next to a man as charismatic as Aziz. However, he was obviously no less intelligent than Aziz.

"You're not cold, are you? A breeze has got up."

Aziz's light touch on her back and his breath in her ear made her remember Italy. She smiled, shaking her head, and raised her glass to take another sip from her wine. She was already feeling tipsy, probably because of the fresh air or most likely because of the numerous glasses of champagne she had drunk during cocktails, or perhaps because of the admiring looks, overwhelming compliments and relentless attention Aziz had been lavishing on her ever since her arrival.

"We can change the wine if it isn't to your liking."

"No, no. Everything is perfect," she said, relaxing her forehead, which she had involuntarily furrowed.

"It was your uncle who had made me love my profession, Mademoiselle de Kurzón," said İskender. "May his soul rest in peace."

"İskender is my closest friend, Alex," said Aziz, placing his hand on his friend's shoulder, a gesture meant to accentuate their proximity. "He's almost a brother to me. He comes from a distinguished family of Cretan origin. It's rather unfortunate that we've been seeing very little of each other lately; he's been living in Egypt for almost a year now, shouldering an important assignment in the project for the alleviation of the Aswan Dam. We do miss him terribly in Istanbul. I do hope that he'll be back sooner than later."

"A Cretan like you, then?" asked Gizella, suddenly interested in the conversation. Obviously she had asked Károly a question too many to brief herself on Aziz.

"We actually have no roots in Crete, madam. My mother's grandfather was the governor of Crete once, and that was why he came to be known as *Giritli* – the Cretan." Smiling, he added, "He even attempted to establish a principality in Crete at one point."

Throughout the main course, Alex listened to İskender, who spoke very highly of Aziz, saying that he was an invaluable friend. She enjoyed hearing what Ganz's head engineer, who had come to their table to ask if everything was to their satisfaction, had to say about Halimzade Aziz *Bey*, showering him with praises. All these compliments made Alex admire Aziz even more and feel proud for being loved so much by a man who invoked such respect.

Károly was still talking, even more animatedly now, about Paris and its neighbourhoods of narrow, cobbled streets that reminded him of Budapest. They were living on the Left Bank, close to the Montparnasse Railroad Station. "It's a *quartier* where artists live and hang out, artists in search of freedom and inspiration. Viktor, our friend from Bortnyik's Workshop, and his wife Karla helped us find a studio in La Ruche. They've been living in Paris for two years now, so they often give us a hand. Viktor and I, we share the same destiny; he also studied something he hated. He's a doctor of medicine but refuses to even talk about it."

"You have ample means," Gizella interjected from across the table, "but you choose to live in that miserable building called La Ruche side by side with penniless artists. And on top of that, I can't quite grasp the meaning of not buying any furniture – proper furniture, I mean. You're impossible. Still a child, despite your twenty-six years of age."

"It's such a privilege to live in this building, a shrine that once housed Modigliani and Chagall occupying adjacent studios, and, more significantly, a temple that was frequented by Dalí and Miró. You won't believe it, but Montparnasse is a neighbourhood that was blessed by the presence of an artist like Picasso only twenty years ago. This alone is more than enough to give us the inspiration we lacked in Budapest. As Wilhelm Uhde said, Paris is the empire of artists." Károly went on with great enthusiasm, telling them how La Ruche was home not only to artists but also to many with dire means in need of a roof over their heads, since the rent for the workshops was really cheap, and no one was evicted for non-payment. They had their meals in the soup kitchen across the street almost for nothing.

This last piece of information was the final drop that spilled the glass for Gizella. "These artists and their meaningless eccentricities. Do they have to suffer to be able to create?" she butted in with indignation, casting another disparaging look at Károly and Ada.

Alex found her mother's comments genuinely irritating. Poor Ada, she could not help thinking. She did, however, seem to be managing rather well despite the scrutiny of Gizella's icy and intimidating stare.

Magda leaned towards her mother as though she wanted to say something but then stopped short as Miklós, sitting between them, put his arm around her shoulders and whispered something in her ear, which probably made her forget what she was about to say. She turned her attention back to Károly's sketch of his happy life in the City of Lights.

"I've been painting continually for the last two months," he was saying. "There's such an intense bombardment of inspiration that sometimes I line up four or five canvases and paint them simultaneously. Unfortunately, my paintings are not, as yet, valuable enough to pay for a living, and, therefore, I do need to earn some money. Viktor helps me get some graphic work. He works for a well-known advertising agency as a creative consultant and a graphic artist. They offered me a job as well, but for the moment I can think of nothing but painting." He could hardly sit still, moving his hands and arms about and occasionally even standing up, thus breaking every rule of table manners in spite of his mother. "Last week we were at the opening of Picasso's latest exhibition. He's a genius. We should look at Picasso, I say. His approach to nature is so simple and so objective, and the vivid colours he reflects onto his canvas depict his rapport with reality in such a profound way that it's impossible not to worship his art. This approach of his doesn't change even when it's not a representation but the most abstract, the most spiritual subject. All of his works – even his least valuable sketches – glow with life. His works make me feel that I should bring more into my paintings." He leaned back on his chair. His expression, his whole body, everything about him emanated his high spirits and overflowing happiness. "Ada, on the other hand," he continued, obviously proud of what he would be saying, "is on a mad spree of taking amazing photographs. She says that images she hasn't been able catch for years are revealing themselves one after another. She sometimes goes out before dawn and returns after sunset." He abruptly turned to Alex. "You ought to come and visit us. Paris is a unique city, an enchanted dreamland." He then turned to Magda and Miklós. "You should all come."

When they reached the end of their dessert, Alex noticed, with much relief, that her long-lost good mood had returned and that she was readily bursting into frequent gales of laughter. With a sudden urge to smoke, she excused herself and rose from her chair, hoping that her mother would assume she was going to powder her nose. Aziz, as would be expected from a gentleman like him, accompanied her to the lobby. Once inside, she told him her true motive for leaving the table, upon which they went out into the front garden and wordlessly walked towards the iron railings by the lake. The moon had just appeared over the hills rising like a steep wall on the other shore, its light about to dominate a sky filled with stars doomed to fade away at any moment. The sailing boats, tired of cruising all day long, were tethered to a safe harbour where they gently rocked. Through their masts swinging like the pendulum of a long clock, Alex gazed at the twinkling lights of the mansions lined up on the shore. She smelled the sweet perfume of the linden trees. How peaceful it was. How very reassuringly peaceful. She relished the cigarette Aziz had offered. Tonight, it felt as though a great weight she had been carrying on her shoulders for years had been lifted. Károly was right. She ought to get away from Budapest more often.

"When will you be coming to Istanbul?"

"We were supposed to come for New Year's Eve, weren't we? It's all Károly's fault; he couldn't organise it."

The truth of the matter was that Rudi could not leave Budapest at the time, and Alex could not leave Rudi. Even the thought of him enjoying himself with others in her absence had been enough to send an unbearable torrent of panic into her heart. Now, however, there was no Rudi in her life. They had split up. She no longer belonged to Rudi; neither did Rudi belong to her. That thought repeated itself ominously: Rudi did not belong to her. A freezing hand clenched her heart. She had lost him. She had abandoned him. She had offered him to others on a silver plate. Her heart sank as she thought of him marrying someone else and becoming the father of the children someone else would bear. A sudden fury possessed her in the face of the error she had committed. She had acted too impulsively, too temperamentally if not foolishly. A scene from years later flashed in front of her eyes. She saw Rudi and his family passing by her on Andrássy Boulevard. She looked at his wife, at his children and then at herself – a beautiful but nevertheless unmarried woman, a middle-aged spinster.

Her cigarette fell into the water. She unclenched her fingers from the iron railing and took out her cigarette case. Aziz was ready with his lighter.

"I'd like everyone to come this year for New Year's Eve."

What was he talking about? New Year's Eve? Istanbul? Yes, Istanbul.

"Why not?" she said with unexpected resolve. She was free now; she could do whatever she wanted whenever she wanted. She should enjoy her freedom. She wouldn't become a middle-aged spinster. She just could not. She would not!

"I broke up with Rudi," she blurted out.

Why did she say that? She was sure Aziz already knew, for Károly must have told him, surely.

Her eyes travelled over the reflections of the lights from the lakeside mansions on the water, resembling diamonds scattered on black velvet. Aziz held her hand and gently caressed it. Not knowing what to do, she drew another breath from her cigarette. I should pull away my hand, she thought. Do I want to respond to his courtship? Do I really want to get Rudi out of my life?

"I would like everyone to come. And I would like you to be the hostess, Alex."

What did he mean? Did she not have to become the hostess of the house in Istanbul before she could act as one? And to become the hostess ... This was a marriage proposal! Yes, Aziz was proposing to her. He wanted to marry her. No, Alex. No! Stop dreaming your time away.

"I want you to be my wife, Alex."

Yes, it was a marriage proposal. She tried to avoid Aziz's eyes because she did not know what her own would be saying. What emotions would they be betraying? Did she want him? Or didn't she? She did not know. Rudi ... his wife ... his children. Beautiful Alex, a middle-aged spinster. She turned diffidently to Aziz. His expression told her that he was not asking a question. He was demanding. The self-assured look in his determined eyes triggered an unexpected sense of trepidation in her. She looked away in panic, without uttering a word. Aziz's warm breath caressed her fingers. He had brought her hand to his lips in a gentle but firm grip and was kissing it. Then he gently held her chin and turned her head towards him. Their eyes met.

"Would you grant me the honour of becoming your husband?"

Alex's head was spinning. Marriage ... a family of her own ... her own children. Yes, she thought. Yes, she repeated to herself. Yes, yes, yes! She wanted to get married. She wanted to be loved. She wanted to be loved madly ... to be loved till eternity. She could not get herself to articulate her thoughts, unable to erase from her mind's eye the image of Rudi walking down Andrássy Boulevard with his wife and children. This time, however, it was herself walking by his side. For an instant, she wondered if all this was just a dream.

"I want to be by your side till the day I die, Alex," she heard Aziz say.

She felt a burning sensation in her finger. Whatever had remained of her almost finished cigarette fell into the water. No, it was not a dream. Everything was really happening. Her dreams might come true. She might after all have a family, a loving husband and beautiful children.

31

They were having breakfast by the lake, comfortably seated at one of the tables set under the cool shade of the expansive umbrellas. Alex had had a terrible night; she had been far too excited to sleep. Waking up shortly after sunrise, she had gone down to breakfast much earlier than her usual hour, surprising everyone. Her mother was nowhere to be seen. She had apparently finished her breakfast long ago and gone for a stroll with Aunt Etel, disappearing into the depths of the garden. Károly, taking advantage of his mother's absence, was complaining that he had had enough of this sojourn and that he could hardly wait for the day when they would be returning to Paris. It drove him mad that here – in this respectable familial atmosphere, as his mother put it – he could not share a room with Ada, whom he shared his life with in Paris.

"I can't believe that I yielded to her demand to send Ada to a week-long exile in Alex's room. And yours truly is confined to endless nights perforated by lengthy periods of insomnia, listening to the sound of turning pages of the countless number of books our dear wakeful Sanyi reads all night under the constant illumination of his bedside lamp."

"That was rather poetic, Károly," chuckled Sándor as he sucked at his cigarette before he took another sip from his coffee, which was as close as he came to having breakfast. Seemingly no less unhappy than his cousin, he obviously looked forward to returning to Budapest; he did not enjoy such events, even those given in honour of his father. He often talked about moving to Kengyel next year, causing his mother great distress. She knew that her son's insistence on taking matters into his own hands at their estate there was only a pretext to hide his desire to live alone.

"Come on, Károly," cut in Miklós. "While your mother is away, let's hear what you have to tell us about the details of your life in Paris that you have so far censored."

"*Le Bal de Quat'z'Arts!*" exclaimed Károly with exaggerated elation, unwilling to waste even a second before grabbing the reins of the conversation when it came to Paris. "Ball of the Four Arts! More outrageous than rumoured."

He was referring to the infamous costume ball thrown by the students of the four arts – architecture, painting, sculpture and engraving – taught at the Paris School of Fine Arts, a masquerade attended exclusively by students, who paraded in the streets in elaborately designed costumes.

"The students gathered in front of the school in the Latin Quarter and then set off for the streets of the capital. It went on for hours. At some point well into the night, several students invaded La Coupole, snatching the glasses from the tables and draining them, fingering the food on the plates, you name it. Their favourite victims were the best dressed, the most 'respectable' people. Everyone, however, was extremely understanding, not saying anything since they knew about the ball and expected all sorts of outrageous behaviour from the students. You should have seen the costumes. They were truly spectacular. On the invitations, it said, 'Black or any other colour suits, evening gowns, black ties and bathing costumes are not allowed.' They were required to wear a historical costume. Each year they had a different theme. This year it was the *Death of War*. There were those who masqueraded as Ancient Greek warriors carrying shields, some as Spartans wearing helmets, others as Japanese samurais, palace guards of the Renaissance periods, Assyrians on chariots, anything you could think of, really. They sought to portray love replacing war. Different ateliers competed fiercely with each other as to which one would be more interesting, more eye-catching or more shocking. As a matter of fact, the obligation to wear a costume was utterly meaningless because, after a short while, almost all of them slipped out of their clothes. At La Coupole, one student undressed right in front of us. And two others stripped in the huge vase in the middle of the café. They took off everything until they were stark naked. And then they left, just like that. The streets were swarming with nude people. It really was bizarre. Finally, they lost it altogether. *C'est vraiment une grande fête païenne.* Can you imagine anything like this in Budapest? Magda parading completely naked on Miklós's shoulders! On Andrássy Boulevard!"

"Come off it, Károly. You are surely exaggerating."

"No, I'm not, Magda. Paris is another realm. It casts a spell, particularly on artists, enchanting them with the freedom it offers. I don't think there could possibly be any other place in the world that makes you feel so free – free to live without being a slave to the rules or to the traditions."

"I should think that such freedom would only lead the youth to commit silly mistakes."

"I totally disagree with you, Magda. It allows them to find their equilibrium and discover what the right values are. They teach themselves right from wrong instead of blindly accepting the rules imposed on them by others. And during this process, new setups are created, novelties are born. This is how it should be, not only in art but in life itself." He turned to Alex and put his arm around her shoulders. "I want you to come to Paris, Alex. I think it would be best if you stayed away from Budapest for a while. You're choking there. And you're suffocating others along with you. You must get out of that stifling atmosphere for a while." He looked back at Magda. "We must convince Mother to send both of you to Paris."

Alex took a sip from her coffee, the third one this morning. She held the cup in her hand before putting it down, her eyes carefully scrutinising it in search of an imaginary secret code written in it. "There's something else we must convince Mother about," she mumbled. She took another sip before raising her eyes, first towards Magda sitting opposite her, then towards Károly. "Last night Aziz asked me to marry him."

Károly's face suddenly darkened, and his brow furrowed. Alex was surprised at his reaction to such happy news, unable to understand why he had that apprehensive look in his eyes. Was he not supposed to be happy for her? His sister was about to get married. And her future husband was someone he truly valued. Then it suddenly dawned upon her why he was frowning. At this point, he must be thinking that one of his close friends would inevitably be heartbroken. Alex's choice would hurt either Aziz or Rudi. Károly might be right, but she was not going to change her mind. She seized his arm. "Károly," she pleaded, looking into his eyes. "Please say something."

"That wasn't what I'd bargained for," murmured Károly. "I'd never have thought Aziz would take things to such a level."

"I've made up my mind, *Öcsi.*"

"Get your act together, Alex. You can't do this to Rudi," he retorted. Then he paused, looking straight into her eyes. "Don't tell me you've already accepted. And without even asking Mother."

"Well, well? Wasn't it you who always said, 'You're a mature young lady now. Do you have to ask Mother's permission for everything?' What do you reckon I should have said? 'Hang on Aziz, I'd better ask my mother first before accepting your proposal.' Mother doesn't know, *Öcsi*, and when she learns about it, I want all of you to be there to help me out. Please. All of you." She turned to Sándor, who was watching the lake with a meaningless smile on his face. "You too, Sanyi," she said, grabbing his hand. "Please. Say something, would you?"

"Perhaps she's made the right decision, Károly," said Sándor in an insipid, monotonous voice. "Perhaps she should marry Aziz. Perhaps she's right. Perhaps Rudi does procrastinate. Perhaps she'll be much happier with Aziz."

"Perhaps, perhaps, perhaps! Am I going to marry my sister off on ambiguous expectations? It's absolutely ridiculous and utterly wrong that she makes such a rushed decision." He looked at Alex. His stare was oppressively dark. "You have accepted, haven't you? You shouldn't have, Alex. Aziz is a fine man, a gentleman, but you're in love with Rudi. What on earth do you think you're doing? You shouldn't forget that you're engaged to marry Rudi. You've made him a promise that you must keep."

"It isn't me who has forgotten to keep his promise. Rudi has gone back on his word. Besides, as I've already told you, we split up. There's no promise anymore, no engagement, nothing. I can't wait for him forever."

"Well, well, well. Look who is here. What happened to you, dear? You're up early. Did you fall out of bed?" Gizella was back from her promenade.

Yes, Alex thought, something would soon be falling to pieces. "Fresh air of the lake," she said dismally.

"It's different than the air around Lake Balaton, I suppose."

"The air of an Italian lake, *Anya.*"

Gizella and Etel made to resume their seats at the table they had left an hour ago. The waiter respectfully pulled their chairs to help them sit down. They asked him to change the position of the umbrella, since their chairs were no longer in the shade, and ordered their lemonades, insisting that they be ice-cold, an unnecessary request and an insult to the impeccable service of the hotel.

"It seems that it will be a rather hot day today. The sun is already blazing."

"*Anyukám*, Aziz has proposed."

This short sentence, which Alex picked up all her courage to utter, seemed not to have had any effect on Gizella.

"Proposed what?" asked Etel, busy wiping the sweat off her neck with her snow-white handkerchief. She was either being too naive or intending to give Alex another chance to say something to avoid Gizella's wrath.

Like everyone else, Gizella knew the answer to Etel's question. "I'm really sorry," she said. "It's obvious that he's very much in love with you. It would be rather difficult for someone as proud as him to accept rejection."

"I did not turn him down, Mother. I want to marry him." She had not refused Aziz's proposal, but she had not accepted it either. She could not. The idea to cut Rudi out of her life so definitely and so instantaneously with a simple "yes" had scared her. Now, however, she was determined. After a long night of brooding over it, she had made up her mind that the right thing to do was to marry Aziz, and nobody could change her mind now.

"Yes, Alex, I want you to marry too. However, I want you to marry someone who is right for you, dear."

Was there a barely perceptible trembling in her mother's hand as she put her coffee cup down? Was it a hint of worry that she had noticed in her eyes, which should have been fuming in the face of this new turn of events? Why? Why did her mother not want to understand her? Why should everything be as she wanted? Was she the only one who knew right from wrong? Alex courageously persevered, "I was hoping that he would have been up to your standards, Mother, being the great-grandson of one of the last prime ministers of the Ottoman Empire. I thought that his family would be noble enough for you." Her voice had acquired an extremely ironic tone. "However," she said, opening her mouth and putting her hand on her forehead in feigned revelation. "There's a problem," she continued, pursing her lips. "He is not a Christian," she hissed, as her feigned surprise gave way to indignation. "It's not important how much he loves me, how much he makes me feel protected, how ready he is to give me everything in the world. The only important thing is that he has to be 'one of us,' isn't it?"

"Get your act together, Alex. Please God, when will this girl be able to make the right decision?" Gizella turned to Károly for some help. "Say something to your sister. She's jumping out of the frying pan into the fire, and she's not even aware of it."

Alex looked at Károly with hope. He was stone silent. Come on *Öcsi*. Only you can handle Mother. Please say something. Was it not you who introduced Aziz to me? Why are you siding with Rudi now?

"You might be their mother, Gizi," butted in Etel, " but you can't decide whom they are going to fall in love with."

Alex wanted to give her aunt a warm hug. Surprisingly she had said the right thing at the right time for a change.

"Can't you see, Etel?" snapped Gizella, furiously turning towards her sister-in-law. "Can't you see what is behind her desire to marry, for goodness' sake? It isn't love. She simply wants to get married, and it's not important to whom. Currently there's someone who wants to marry her and she will marry him, and that's it." She turned to Alex and continued in a condescending tone, but full of rage. "What happened to your one and only love Rudi?"

"You must talk to Rudi before making your final decision, Alex. What you're doing is not right."

"Of course, I'll talk to him, Magda, but I'm certain it'll change nothing."

"Have you thought about how you would survive in Istanbul?" asked Gizella, with a grain of unexpected supplication in her voice. "You've never been there. It's a Moslem country. How would you manage away from us all, away from all your friends?"

"I'm sure everything will be much better. I'm sick and tired of Budapest and those living in it." She angrily pushed her chair back and stood up. "I've made up my mind. And you'd better get used to it. I want no engagement, no engagement party, nothing. I want to marry right away before the summer is over."

As she walked away from the table, she could hear her mother shouting at Károly at the top of her voice, apparently too helplessly furious to remember that she was in a public place. "You've left your sister all alone. You didn't take care of her properly. You failed to be a father to her."

Alex's heart sank as she heard Károly mumble, "I know *Anya*, I know."

32

The day after they came back to Budapest, the head butler Álmos informed Alex that Monsieur Takács had called a couple of times and asked if she might call him back as soon as she returned. Panic-stricken, she tried to figure out a way to tell Rudi about her decision. She dared not talk to him face to face, with the well-founded knowledge that she would change her mind and yield to his compellingly seductive charm the moment she looked him in the eye. It would be best if she called him on the phone.

The phone rang.

"Hello?"

"At long last! It would be easier to reach the king of England. I called you so many times, before I left for Vienna. Why didn't you answer my calls, Alex?"

What should she say? She was lost for words. "Somebody else did what you could not do. Someone else asked me to marry him. And right away." Was that what she should say?

"I'll be there to pick you up in half an hour," he said without waiting for Alex's reply and hung up before she could say anything.

"What am I to do?" she thought, her mind numb with trepidation. How am I supposed to tell him? She could think of nothing. Her mind had gone completely blank.

They did not exchange a single word in the car. Alex still did not know where to start or what to say. All she could do was to try to control her tremulous heart. Where was he taking her? They were on Andrássy Boulevard, driving past number twenty-three. So much the better that they did not stop there; she would never be able to talk about it in his house. Finally, they got out of the car in front of Lukács Cukraszda, opposite the Academy of Fine Arts.

It was not very crowded inside. Both in need of a strong drink, they ordered two glasses of *pálinka*, although it was not even noontime.

"Alex," said Rudi after finishing up his drink, "I know that I've been neglecting you a little lately."

"A little?"

He was holding Alex's hands now, his eyes looking straight into hers.

Don't look at his eyes, Alex. You don't want to change your mind. Pull away your hands.

She withdrew her hands.

Rudi grabbed them again. "Alex," he said, tightening his grip. "Alex, please try to understand me. Infidelity is very hard to digest. Sometimes your vanity makes you blow insignificant details out of proportion, and you burn with an irresistible desire to take revenge. Your pride prevents you from overcoming this destructive emotion. Consciously or subconsciously, you crave for it. You want to see the other person get hurt, suffer in agony just like you do."

He was now clutching at her hands so forcefully that he almost hurt her. Why was he telling her these things? To hurt her even more? To trample on her pride, which he had been tearing to pieces for months – for years actually? She already knew that Rudi had been and was still being unfaithful to her. She had no doubt about it. Why was he adding fuel to the flames? Had he not tortured her enough?

"Unfortunately, you realise that you've been a slave to your vanity when something shocking hits you right in the face."

She felt so low, so torn apart ... like a piece of rag thrashed about on the floor.

"Alex ... I realised that I want to spend the ..."

She had had enough of his infidelities. She had no self-esteem left. She could not tolerate such excruciating pain any longer. "Aziz asked my hand in marriage," she blurted out.

Rudi suddenly let go of her hands. "To win the heart of someone you saw months ago and only for two days," he scoffed, in a tone precipitously filled with anger before he continued ironically, "and to win it so very seriously can only be possible for someone as beautiful as you. Or is this the way in the East? Is it their habit to seek to marry someone they hardly know, especially if that someone is engaged to marry someone else?" He waved at the waiter to replenish their drinks.

"Especially if that someone is fed up with her fiancé failing to fulfil his promise to marry," she thought. "I accepted his proposal, Rudi. I'm going to marry him," she said, trying to sound resolved. She was lying. She had not yet accepted, but she would. She had told Aziz that she wanted to think, but now she no longer had to think about it.

"I beg your pardon?" Rudi's face cringed, betraying his surprise and disgust. "You're *my* fiancée, Alex. Or has it slipped your mind?"

"I was," she said, showing the empty ring finger on her right hand.

"And you still are." He took Alex's engagement ring out of his pocket and held it between his fingers, squeezing it as if he wanted to break it. He was waving his hand back and forth in front of her eyes. "Do you think that taking a stupid ring off your finger signifies the end of our relationship?"

"I need to be loved, Rudi. And you don't love me. Maybe you never did."

"You're being ridiculous, Alex. Do come to your senses, please. You don't know what you're doing or what you're saying." He picked up one of the glasses the waiter had brought and drained it. He did the same with the other glass.

Alex was sitting there, saying nothing.

"How dare he!" Rudi continued as if talking to himself. "It's incredible how blind he can be! How can he even consider that you'd be throwing yourself into the arms of someone you hardly know to go and live in a country you don't know at all?" He grabbed Alex by her chin and turned her head towards him.

Alex tried not to take her eyes off the empty glasses on the table. Rudi's gaze, however, was too magnetically strong to resist.

"Pull yourself together, Alex! You're mine!"

Alex felt tears welling up in her eyes. He still did not say the words she had been waiting for. He still did not utter the words "Marry me." He could not! Why? Why for God's sake? Why? Please, Rudi. Say it! Tell me that we'll be getting married tomorrow. Say that you won't keep me waiting any longer. Save me from this lonely existence. Please ... Tears gushed out of her eyes. She jumped to her feet and stumbled to the door. She threw herself out. She needed to find a cab. Rudi called after her. She did not stop. Her mind was made up. Dashing across the street, she flung herself into a cab and ran away from it all.

June 2004
Istanbul

Rüya was tossing and turning in her bed in the guest room upstairs. It was well past midnight when the last guest had left, and almost one in the morning when she had finally made it to bed. Although very tired, she was still wide-awake, probably because she was not used to sleeping in this room. Upon her mother's instructions, her bedroom, which gave on to the stupendous view of the Bosphorus, was allocated to Giselle and her husband Alain; it had been decided that, with their six-month-old son, they would be much more comfortable in a larger room. Amazing how much space a tiny baby needed, Rüya thought, as she turned uncomfortably in her bed again.

Feeling a sudden surge of heat, she restlessly kicked off the bed sheet clinging to her legs. Her neck was burning. She turned over the pillow and pulled her hair up in a bun. She knew she would not be able to sleep. Hoping not to wake up little Daphné, who seemed to be sound asleep in the bed next to her, she turned on her bedside lamp. Her eyes snapped shut at the light, which felt too strong after being in the dark for so long. After a few seconds, she tentatively opened them again, trying to get used to the brightness in the room. She might fall asleep if she read for a while, she hoped.

She had read only a couple of pages when she heard Mami's weak voice penetrating the silence of the night.

"Rüya! Rüya!"

She jumped out of bed, dashed down the stairs, ran through the entrance hall and barged into Mami's bedroom. She was sitting on the edge of her bed, holding on to her walking stick with one hand and stroking her forehead with the other.

"What's wrong? Are you all right, Mami? Why did you get up?"

"I have to say I'm not feeling too well, dear. Could you please bring me a glass of water?"

She kissed Mami's forehead. It was burning. She must be running a very high fever. "Please lie down. I'll fetch you some water."

She rushed out of the room and across the hall, almost slipping on the parquetry floor, and went into the kitchen. After pouring some water into a glass with trembling hands, she hurried back to Mami's room, gave her the glass and waited impatiently while she sipped at it. When she was finally finished, she helped her lie down and flung herself out of the room again, climbed the stairs and stormed into her mother's bedroom. "Mum? Mum, wake up! Mami is very ill." Suddenly she remembered that Lila *néni* and Uncle André were sleeping in her mother's room. "Excuse me," she whispered, darting back towards the door.

"What's wrong?" asked Lila.

"Nothing. Please go back to sleep," Rüya whispered, banging the door shut. She ran along the corridor and went into her grandmother's room, where her mother was sleeping as well. She walked straight to the bed and, grabbing her mother's arm, started shaking her. "Mum! Wake up! Wake up!"

Aslı jumped out of bed. "What? What's wrong?" she asked groggily.

"Mami is not feeling too well," said Lila, who had followed Rüya into the room.

"Calm down. Don't panic. Please ... What's wrong with her?"

"She's running a very high fever, Mum. We must call the doctor. Right away!"

Nili was up as well, putting on her dressing gown. "She must have caught a cold."

"Don't worry so much. I'll talk to Doctor Nesim," said Aslı, trying to stay in control of the situation although her calmness was obviously feigned.

Rüya hastened down the stairs before everyone else and ran to the door of Mami's room, where she had to wait impatiently for the others. Finally, her mother appeared at the head of the stairs. "Come on, Mother. Hurry up," she whispered through her teeth, waving at Aslı to quicken her pace.

They all went into Mami's room. Aslı put her hand on Mami's forehead. "She does have a fever. Rüya, go and get the thermometer, and I'll call Doctor Nesim straightaway."

The doctor prescribed a medication to reduce the fever and promised to call on her first thing in the morning. Eventually when Mami fell into a vaguely peaceful sleep, the others returned to their rooms. Rüya, on the other hand, unwilling to leave, curled up on the sofa at the foot of Mami's bed.

She had a wreath of pain in her stomach, which she seemed unable to untangle no matter how many deep breaths she took. Wishing that the morning would come sooner than later and everything would go back to normal, she tried to console herself with the thought that it could not be anything serious or otherwise she would not be sleeping so peacefully. It can't be anything grave, she thought to herself. I'm sure it's a simple cold. Her fever is already down. Is it? She wanted to be sure. She got up, went to the bed and gently put her hand on Mami's forehead. She was not burning anymore. Somewhat relieved, she returned to her place on the sofa and lay down.

> *As I move forward, my eyes get used to the intimidating darkness of the forest, my nose to the smell of decay, and my ears to the sounds of the forest that I've taken to be silence. I can now hear the crackling sound of an insect, the faraway chirping of a bird. The sound of silence starts to change everything. A ray of sunlight squeezing in through the high branches of the trees, shines on the leaves decomposing on the ground. I notice their coppery golden colour suddenly warming my heart. I look up with hope. The leaves still hanging on the branches reflect a sporadic shower of sunlight. They seem eager to tell me something. I kneel down and touch the earth, the leaves. I see life expiring. Raising my head again, I look at the leaves up there and hear them whisper something. They say that there will come a time when new lives will appear. I'm filled with joy. I stand up and move on.*
>
> *Slowly the forest loses its dark density, letting in more sunlight that partly illuminates the path. I notice a chink of blue sky ahead of me. Impatiently, I break into a run. A clearing. Suddenly, as if out of nowhere, a white beach comes into view, with a white house serenely leaning its back onto the woods behind it. A few steps separate its long veranda from the garden stretching down to the beach. The house glitters in the sun, but its veranda looks cool in the shade. A deckchair. Next to it, a small table with some chairs. Everything is snow-white. Everything gives on to the sea. The water is a luminous turquoise, almost green. The sun flickers on its surface.*

Rüya opened her eyes. She rose from the sofa, walked over to the bed and kissed Mami on the cheek. She looked fine. There were a couple of more hours till morning, but she knew that she would not be able to sleep. She went out into the garden. Eros, the imposing Sivas Kangal shepherd dog from the depths of Anatolia, enjoying his reign after a day-long sequestration in the doghouse, got up from where he was dozing off at a far corner of the garden and, swaying his huge body from side to side, came to greet Rüya, who apparently added some colour to his otherwise tedious watch. He accompanied her to the gazebo and watched her as she sat in Mami's rocking chair. After staying with her for a few minutes more to make sure that everything was fine, he turned around and went back to his post under the trees where he could keep an eye on everything.

Rüya could almost hear the Bosphorus rushing past down below. The beautiful Bosphorus. It looked so black now, so pitch black, so dark, so scary, so ruthless. She leaned back, anxiously averting her eyes from the turbulent waters and raising them up towards the hills on the Oriental side of the Bosphorus, towards the sky crowded with stars. She was filled with an unwelcome feeling of foreboding. A few minutes later she saw a shooting star. "*Maradj velem*, Mami," she murmured. She did not want to lose Mami. You can't leave me, she begged. You can't leave me, Mami. Another shooting star appeared. There were so many falling stars tonight.

A Hungarian Rhapsody
A Novel in Three Acts
Act One, Tableau Two
1932 - 1933

Tableau Two

33

Her wedding would be everything she had dreamed of and more. Sitting in front of the crystal mirror in the Royal Suite of the Pera Palace Hotel in Istanbul, while they refreshed her make-up, ruined with the tears she could no longer hold back at the sight of herself in a wedding gown, Alex found herself worrying if it was not the exceptional artifice of her fertile imagination contriving to fabricate fantasies again. Magda, always faithfully by her side, tirelessly checked every little detail and, when necessary, held their mother at bay to make sure that nothing happened to upset Alex. She had already told off Károly and Sándor, who had been in and out of the suite a couple of times talking about the preparations downstairs and adding to Alex's anxiety. She practically ordered them not to come upstairs anymore, asking Károly, below her breath, to take along Aziz's sisters Necla and Sema – Necla because she interfered with everything, and Sema because she talked too much. Aziz's third sister, Ayla, was already more than willing to follow Károly wherever he went as she was obviously enchanted by him, probably because she was emotionally more sensitive than she usually was due to her pregnancy, or simply because Károly not only aroused in her some old memories but also stimulated all her senses. When finally Maria, Margit and Izabella left the suite, after having helped Alex with her last-minute preparations, Aziz's mother Mehpare *Hanım* proudly placed her wedding present on Alex's chest. It was a crescent-shaped platinum and diamond brooch, which had been purchased by Mehpare *Hanım*'s grandfather, a prime minister during the reign of Sultan Abdülmecit, and given to her as a wedding present by her father, Haldun Pasha.

Mehpare *Hanım* was a graceful and stylish lady with a self-confident gait; as she walked she swayed coyly, her body surprisingly slender for someone who had borne five children. She was wearing a plain but elegant night-blue evening gown in harmony with the sapphires embellishing the two combs on her chignon, which surrounded the lower back of her head like a halo. Despite being only fifty-two years old, her hair had gone completely white. She said it had whitened in one night after her husband's death. She always kept her reserve, even on a day as exciting as this, never raising her voice, with the self-assurance that the quiet orders she confidently gave out would be carried out to the letter.

Aziz patiently waited his turn, standing behind his mother. When she was finished, he moved forward to give Alex the modern *Art Déco* style Lacloche Frères necklace and earrings; he had chosen them carefully, allowing their sparkling novelty to lighten the heavy weight of his family's heritage. Alex, looking at her mother's reflection in the mirror, inconspicuously raised her eyebrows and pursed her lips, as if to say that there was nothing she could do and she was really sorry that she would not be able to put on the emerald earrings Gizella had given her this morning as a wedding present. They were the earrings from a set, which Gusztáv, following the birth of Alex and Magda, had given Gizella who, in turn, had given the necklace to Magda last year as her wedding present. Gizella's slightly raised chin, which rendered her condescending gaze utterly intolerable, revealed a lot more about what was going through her mind than words could do. She must have been thinking that Aziz's modern present – with long and short little tubes of coral and a large pearl dangling from a bell embellished with diamonds – created quite a hideous combination when worn together with Mehpare *Hanım*'s classic present. Alex hated her mother's rigid rules, written in stone. Suddenly feeling Aziz hold her cheeks and kiss her forehead, she forgot about her mother and her air of haughtiness. Everything, every little thing was so beautiful.

"I'm grateful to you, Alex, for having bestowed upon me this happiness."

In a few hours this self-assured, loving and extremely polite man would be her husband. Her life would soon be changing radically. Allowing a sense of lightness that she had been missing for a very long time to envelope her, she surrendered herself to the trustworthy hands of Aziz.

"And I'm infinitely grateful to you for having raised such a priceless gem," Aziz continued, turning to his future mother-in-law and taking her hand to his lips.

Alex noticed, with much gratitude, a slight softening in her mother's expression.

"I do hope that you will be satisfied with our humble celebration although it is, I assure you, far from being worthy of you, Madame de Kurzón."

During the wedding preparations, Gizella had persistently found details to criticise, even making an issue of the fact that they would not be getting married in church although, being a Calvinist, she was hardly a religious person; Alex had never seen her so much as cross herself. She had taken every opportunity to nag Alex about how difficult she would be making her life and continued to talk about her suitors until the very last moment – until, in fact, they were about to board the Orient Express on their way to Istanbul. She had run after Alex, who was rushing towards the train ahead of everyone else, and, as her final trump card, had praised Rudi, despite her deep hatred for him. Finally grabbing Alex by the arm on the steps to their compartment, she had said her final words, "I've done everything I could to make you change your mind, dear, to make you give up this pursuit, which I know you've taken on out of pure spite. From now on, it's your call."

They had left Budapest with almost a trainload of friends and, of course, all their relatives. Károly and Ada had also joined them on this journey, having arrived from Paris a few days beforehand with Alex's wedding gown – an elegantly simple gown in dreamily floating chiffon that Alex had chosen from among the models of Madeleine Vionnet in the *Femina* magazine. Her anxious journey to the unknown proved to be most entertaining, and passed quickly thanks to her brother lightening up the heavy atmosphere rendered ever more repressive by her mother's comments. Finally, upon their arrival at Sirkeci Train Station in Istanbul, her anxiety subsided altogether when she threw herself into Aziz's arms. Relaxing in his reliable embrace, she decided that all her worries enflamed by her mother were, in fact, out of place. Aziz helped them settle in the Pera Palace Hotel, and the following evening they attended a reception given in their honour at the Giritli Mansion, their summerhouse on the Bosphorus in Baltalimanı where they met all the members, young and old, of Aziz's extensive family. Although the one-year-long mourning for Uncle Kelemen had ended eight months ago, Gizella and Aunt Etel – probably forced by Gizella – had preferred to be garbed in black for that reception.

They were wearing black tonight as well.

"We should be going down now. The guests will be arriving soon," said Mehpare *Hanım* before she followed the others out of the suite. She stopped at the door to turn around one last time and smiled proudly, her eyes lingering adoringly on her eldest son, who, at the ripe age of thirty-five, was finally getting married.

She had lost her husband six years ago. Halim *Bey*, whom Aziz always talked about with much pride, was an athletically-built, strong man who killed himself with a single shot to his heart when he learned that he had cancer, as he was too proud to become sick and dependent on others. The household woke up to the sound of a gun shot at dawn, and, while they were trying to work out what had happened, Aziz ran straight to his father's study to be the first one to find his father's dead body lying on the floor, and to read the farewell note on his desk, carefully placed on the pages of an encyclopaedia on wild birds. "No one is responsible for my death," said the note.

Alex loved Aziz now, and no longer wished to question her feelings for him or to make comparisons. What she felt for him was not the passionately obsessive love that secretly crept into the depths of her entire existence like a fatal ailment, sentencing her soul to death, but a calm and peaceful love towards someone who truly loved her and was sure to hold her hand if she tripped.

Aziz had finished his grooming and was now standing in front of her. He looked so smart, standing up straight, with his wide shoulders pulled back, making him look taller than he already was. After getting Alex's approval on the condition of his tailcoat, he carefully hung it and set about shining his shoes, which had already been shined to perfection. He did not sit down so as not to crease his pants and shortly started to pace up and down the room. It had been less than half-an-hour since the others had gone downstairs, but it seemed to Alex like hours had gone by. How much longer would she have to wait? She so wished her much-awaited wedding would start and end soon. Nothing could calm her anxiety, not even Aziz's jokes or the stories about how, as a child – and still as a fully-grown man – he teased his sisters, or the anecdotes about his brother Haldun's womanising. At long last, they heard an impatient knock on the door. Necla peeked in to announce that all the guests had arrived before she hastily closed the door again.

"It's time to go," said Aziz, holding Alex's trembling hand.

How could he be so calm? Alex's whole body was shaking.

"I'm right here by your side, *ma petite*. And I'll always be ... until death do us part." He was looking straight into her eyes. "And I shall never ever allow anyone or anything to hurt you. There's nothing to be scared of. Please take my arm and let me guide you. You're now part of our large and well-rooted family. A very happy life awaits us, a life that everyone downstairs, every soul in this city, envies. I'll do everything I can to make you happy, Alex. Trust me."

The rest of the wedding went by as if in a dream. Alex watched it roll like a movie before her eyes: her entrance into the ballroom on Aziz's arm to the sound of Liszt's *Hungarian Fantasy;* the words "I do" she uttered in Turkish as Aziz had taught her, without understanding a word of what the marriage celebrant was saying; everybody, including her mother, applauding them with smiling faces; walking around the tables hand in hand with Aziz, accepting congratulations and best wishes for a time that seemed like hours; the magical decoration of the Pera Palace Hotel; Aziz, who outshone everyone present with his elegant and sophisticated style, introducing his friends and relatives from the elite class of Istanbul, as he whispered a few words in Alex's ear to explain their status and importance in society; Ada continually dancing with Haldun, probably out of spite more than any other motive, for she was apparently jealous of the close attention Károly showed Ayla or, most likely, of Ayla's adoring eyes glued on Károly; Magda, who, despite being a married woman, captured the heart of each and every young Istanbulite present, albeit remaining blind to it all as her eyes saw no one but her husband Miklós; Aunt Irén's jocular laughter dominating the crowded ballroom as it echoed on its walls, driving Gizella mad; seven-month pregnant Éva's right hand constantly stroking her belly and her left permanently fondling József's arm; József's politeness impressing every member of Istanbul's high-society; Rózsi's blond hair and generously displayed full breasts attracting every male soul in the ball and evoking the jealousy of every female; Fábián showing, perhaps for the first time in his life and rather roughly, how jealous he was of his wife; Izabella's feigned happiness in the arms of Oskar – her husband of twelve months – and her efforts to hide her disappointment upon learning that Ákos had not come, probably unaware that the true motive behind his absence was to avoid seeing Izabella as the wife of another man – something he would not have been able tolerate; János's dreary seriousness giving his face that most angry expression, which even Margit's love had failed to brighten up during the eighteen months that they had been together; and finally the passionate white night Alex and Aziz had in defiance of their tired bodies in the indulgent and magnificently all-embracing royal suite of the Pera Palace Hotel.

34

Next day as they set off in one of the first class compartments of the Orient Express for Paris, where they would be spending their honeymoon, Alex, sitting in her husband's embrace, was watching the view glide by in front of the window and thinking how very happy she was. She had had a dream of a wedding. The fine details, which she, being so very excited, had missed, gradually revealed themselves.

The ballroom had been adorned with coral-coloured roses. Aziz said that he had sent word to all the flower shops in Istanbul to find roses that would match the corals on Alex's necklace and earrings. He had wanted everything to be a surprise to her and, therefore, had not asked her anything about the decorations, the menu or the music except for the piece of music she wanted for their entry into the ballroom, and the list of the guests who would be coming over from Hungary. He personally had taken care of every single detail to make their wedding a perfect one. The orchestra, as strictly instructed by Aziz in line with the briefing he had received from Károly, played Alex's favourite classical music pieces during the service of the rich dinner menu, abundant in delicious dishes, which neither Alex nor Aziz had a chance even to taste. The classical Turkish music chosen to accompany the desserts came to an abrupt end when Alex found them too sorrowful on a day like this, and, following the wedding cake ceremony, the orchestra started to play jazz, enticing everyone to the dance floor, where they stayed until the early hours of the morning.

The train took a sharp turn. She ensconced herself in her husband's arms. Her husband! She was Halimzade Azizné de Kurzón Egerlövö Szarvaskó Gadány Alexandra. Halimzade Azizné. The wife of Halimzade Aziz.

Alex and Aziz stayed in the City of Lights for a whole week, a dreamlike week that promised to remain in her memory forever, an unforgettably happy beginning to her new life, so happy that she did not even mind meeting Károly and Ada only once for dinner on their last night. They walked for hours in the romantic streets of the capital until her feet ached, visited the museums where Aziz watched Alex rather than the paintings and sculptures of the great masters, had exquisite dinners in restaurants diligently chosen by Aziz, who had a refined palate that allowed no room for mediocre cuisine, chatted until late at night sipping the best vintage wines, and spent more time than any of this in their hotel room where Alex relished the infinitely luscious sensations Aziz offered her.

Upon their return to Istanbul, it was time for her to come down from the clouds back to the real world. Aziz's family, except for Sema who lived in Adana with her husband Zeki *Bey*, lived in the Haldun Pasha Mansion in Nişantaşı. Alex was unwilling to live there and wanted a home of their own. Aziz initially rejected this idea, finding it meaningless and unnecessary, but eventually agreed to rent a flat in the Maçka Apartments two hundred metres down the road from Haldun Pasha Mansion, despite Mehpare *Hanım*'s emphatic objections. In making this decision, he was partly encouraged by Necla and her husband Nezih *Bey*, who were planning to move out of the family mansion into a flat in Nişantaşı, but the main reason was most likely that he wholeheartedly agreed with Alex who insisted that they should not be limiting their sex life to their bedroom.

Maçka Apartments was a modern building built by Vincenzo Caivano, a close friend of Alex's uncle Kelemen, with whom he had worked during the railway project in Italy. Their impressive flat, which gave on to the beautiful view of the Bosphorus and the Sea of Marmara, had everything Alex wanted including a lot of rooms for their future children, a large balcony, a back garden full of linden trees, a tennis court and, more importantly, freedom. Mehpare *Hanım* was much warmer and more loving than Gizella, but could be a little bit too intrusive at times, so it was better to keep a little distance between them.

They decorated their flat according to Alex's taste. Aziz objected to the colour she had chosen for the walls, saying that it would make them look like packaging paper, but Alex insisted that it was the best background colour for her paintings, and finally managed to have all the walls, except for Aziz's study and the bedrooms of their future children, painted in a mustard colour.

Although the classic furniture they had taken from the overfilled Haldun Pasha Mansion were enough to meet all their needs, Alex could not help but go on a shopping spree in the flea market, following Ayla's recommendations. She spent days and weeks there finding beautiful pieces for a penny. She bought a corner bookcase with golden angels on its corners spreading their wings, a piece for which she paid an exorbitant price without bargaining at all and with many tears in her eyes; it touched her heart as it reminded her of the sofa in her mother's bedroom in Rózsadomb. Necla recommended Varujyan *Usta*, the most well-known master in the art of *gomme a lacque* in town, who revived the rosewood chest of drawers and the marquetry coffee tables – pieces that won everyone's admiration, including Mehpare *Hanım*'s, who usually turned her nose up at anything that came out of a flea market. Alex did not interfere with the selection of the two leather Chesterfields, the desk and the gun cabinet Aziz chose for his study. She only insisted that he put in a couple of the ceramic sculptures of Miklós and Magda, saying, "They'll be food for your soul, Aziz." She had the silk tassels for her curtains and lampshades custom-made by Yovanaki *Efendi* in Beyoğlu. Her meticulous attention to detail sometimes pushed Aziz's limits of tolerance, but she eventually made him accept everything she wanted and finally had a house she truly loved. All they needed now were children who would bring their home to life.

By the end of her first few weeks in Istanbul, Alex had already decided that both Károly and Izabella had been absolutely right. Except for some minor peculiarities, there was almost nothing that made her feel ill at ease in this most interesting city, which even gave her back the motivation she had lost in Budapest. Károly, during their brief encounter in Paris, had told her that Istanbul was a magical city, full of inspiration, which embraced the modern and the traditional. He had talked about the drawings he had made during their short stay following Alex's wedding, and had concluded, "You'll see, your art will reach another level." He was right indeed. She had been painting ever since their return from Paris. Everything inspired her; she wanted to put every single detail on paper. Her enthusiasm was not limited to her art but pervaded all other aspects of her life, filling her with a *joie de vivre* she thought she had lost a long time ago. She was determined to expand her social circle in Istanbul and have at least as many friends as she had had in Budapest – an effort that soon turned into reality with a little help from Aziz's extended family and from Izabella and her husband Oskar, a teacher at the Istanbul American College for Girls. In a matter of weeks she started meeting new people, and the pace of her life promised to reach its former tempo.

Istanbul, 15th October 1932

My darling Magda,

It's well past midnight, Aziz is fast asleep, and I'm dead tired, but I know I won't be able to sleep before I write to you. I already miss you all so much that I don't know how I'm going to survive without you. The most difficult part of my marriage is being away from you all, and especially from you.

My life in Istanbul goes ahead full steam. This morning I played tennis with one of our neighbours in the building, Matilde *Hanım*, who, despite being fifty years old, is as fit as a fiddle. "*Hanım*" means Madame. Please take note of the "i" without the dot. It's an impossible sound, but I'm trying. As you can see, I'm learning Turkish as fast as I can.

At noontime Matilde *Hanım*, Izabella and Izabella's friend Anastasia came over for lunch. Anastasia – a very polite girl, much too mature for her nineteen years of age – is a *Rum*, which means that she belongs to the Greek Orthodox minority who have been living in Anatolia and Istanbul for generations. She says that they're not Greek and have nothing to do with Greece, since they have been living in Asia Minor for thousands of years.

Now get ready for a surprise: I cooked them Hungarian dishes. They really liked them. In fact, Anastasia immediately asked for the recipe of *rétes*. She's very keen on cooking and cooks much better than would be expected from such a young girl. She studied at a finishing school after graduating from Zappeion, the *Rum* College for Girls here in Istanbul. She's sure to become an excellent housewife, an excellent wife and an excellent mother, but all she dreams of is to become an excellent dressmaker. She promised to make me an evening gown – a lilac evening gown.

After lunch, we sat down to bridge and played all afternoon, or, to be more honest, we chatted all afternoon and bridge turned out to be, as Aziz sarcastically puts it, an accessory to our conversation. We had so much fun that we hardly noticed the passage of time, and, before we knew it, Aziz was back from the office. My dear husband, who gets really grumpy if dinner is not ready within half an hour following his arrival, had a few flames of anger in his eyes, which were swiftly extinguished as he started to converse with Anastasia in Greek. They immediately liked each other. (Anastasia says that the Greek spoken by the *Rums* is slightly different than the Greek spoken by the Greeks.)

I have another surprise for you that might even bring a few tears of happiness: I'm continually painting. And I'm so very sorry to have wasted so much time away from my art – or perhaps I should say that I'm so very furious at those who made me waste that time. By the way, Maria says that rumour has it – even in Italy! – that His Highness has fully immersed himself in his business and is interested in nothing other than tennis. As to his relationships, they apparently last for a shorter time than his tennis matches. All I can say is, "Let us forget about him."

I'm truly so happy to be Aziz's wife and to be living in Istanbul that I don't want to remember anything from the past but sweet memories. Aziz has taken me under his protective wing and really appreciates my efforts to adapt to my new life and to new customs. It's not like there is much that I find strange in this country anyhow except, for instance, the muezzin of the mosque across the street from us suddenly starting his call to prayer (which is five times a day, by the way!) with a loud "*Allahüekber*" – something that still makes my heart skip a beat although I must admit that even that has lost its novelty. I no longer wake up with a start when he chants his call to the morning prayer at dawn. I can happily say that Mother's fears and worries about me living in a Moslem country were absolutely unfounded. Aziz's family has long ago turned their back on religion for the sake of modernism, limiting their religious practice to family visits during the festive seasons and ignoring their obligation as Moslems to circumcise their male children. Next to them, even our Calvinist family might be considered fanatically religious.

We bought another Irish Setter. Goya joined our small family as Pepa's husband. Portakal (meaning Orange), although quite young yet, has already proven what a noble cat she is by accepting Goya into her dominion as well. They're all living happily together, determined to prove wrong the Turkish saying of "fighting like cats and dogs." The other day Portakal, after cleaning herself, went to Goya and started to lick his nose. I was almost in tears. Human beings have a lot to learn from animals.

As I've already mentioned in my previous letter, I'm fully absorbed in the details of my bedroom. At long last, I found the burgundy silk fabric I wanted for my bedcover and also had the green Marquise chair refurbished. Currently I'm busy with the table lamps in search of antique lamp bases.

My dearest sister, I do want to go on and on writing to you, but I need to scribble a few lines to Mother as well and I'm truly very tired.

    With much longing and love,
        Your sister,
        Alex

Aziz, whom she had taken to be fast asleep, was behind her fondling her hair.

"I'm so tired," she said, leaning her head back.

"You'd better stop playing tennis. They say too much activity might make it difficult for you to conceive. Besides, you might catch cold, half naked in such cold weather ..."

"What makes you say that? That's absolute nonsense, Aziz." She paused. "Half naked, you said?" She felt a sudden sense of being trapped. "How do you mean? If I can't wear shorts in my own garden, where on earth am I going to wear them?"

"Don't get fired up, Alex. It's for your own good."

Who was putting all these ideas into his head? It must have been that know-it-all Necla.

Aziz had knelt down in front of her and was sliding his hands under her dressing gown. Gently pushing her silk chemise up, he started stroking her legs. "These are mine!" he said jokingly. Alex threw her head back, forgetting about her tennis, her tiredness and her intention to write to her mother, as her husband firmly pushed her legs apart and his lips started wandering around between her thighs.

35

Alex took another piece of cotton wool, stretched it and placed it on one of the branches of the Christmas tree. That should be enough snow, she thought. It was Christmas Eve tomorrow – her first Christmas away from her family, her first Christmas with her new family and definitely a test tougher than the entrance exam of the Academy. Aziz and Haldun had found a tree to Alex's exact specifications, and for a whole week Ayla and Necla helped her with its decoration. Mehpare *Hanım* had sent her cook over to help with the preparations, assuming that Asiye *Hanım*, who had started working as a housekeeper for Alex and Aziz a month ago, would be insufficient. It took Erol, the driver, two full days to carry the groceries required for the rich menu; and still Aziz diligently interfered with everything, going through every detail with the competence of an experienced housewife who had prepared Christmas dinners all her life. Everyone was excited about tomorrow evening, including Pepa, Goya and Portakal, who could sense from the increased traffic in the house that a celebration was in the offing.

Alex mused over what they would be doing in Rózsadomb right now, how they would be preparing for tomorrow. Her mother, Aunt Etel and Sanyi were left all alone in that huge house. She wondered where Magda and Miklós would be celebrating Christmas. They would probably come to Rózsadomb along with Miklós's family, she thought, as a sense of longing choked her. This was going to be her first Christmas without Magda, without Károly. Károly? What would he be doing in Paris, away from everyone? They were scattered around the world. Her heart sank at the thought. Then suddenly Aunt Irén and Uncle Filip came to her mind. How did they live without any children all those years? She now realised better how much they must have loved each other.

She could not imagine a life without children. She put her hand on her belly. She was supposed to have had her period twenty days ago, but she had missed it. This meant only one thing: she was pregnant. She definitely was. She felt it in her heart. She was going to be a mother. A mother! She could hardly believe it. When her period had stopped, she had felt as if she had stopped bleeding her life away and everything suddenly became meaningful. A life was being created inside her. A warm and happy sensation embraced her heart, a sensation she had never had before. Perhaps I'll have twins, she hoped. Just like me and Magda. God, I do wish

I have twins. Please God. I want my children to taste the same happiness we did.

Christmas dinner started off in an atmosphere unexpectedly pleasant for Alex, despite Mehpare *Hanım*'s cynical remarks, which proved to be rather disturbing at times. The dishes she had cooked were almost as delicious as those prepared by the cook in Rózsadomb. She herself was astounded at her success. Everybody paid her compliments, including her mother-in-law. "I do hope that you cook as well as this for Aziz too." Sometimes Mehpare *Hanım* switched from French to Turkish, and Alex, although her Turkish was improving at a speed that amazed everyone, could not figure out whether she was praising or criticising her. She managed to ignore most of it with a little help from Aziz's endless love and attention, but was utterly irritated when Necla and Mehpare *Hanım* went on and on talking to Aziz in Greek. "*Den epitrepetai na kani voltes stin poli me ta pinela sto heri.*" Every time, Aziz cut them short, angrily saying the same thing. "*Endaxi, endaxi.*" And Ayla, turning away her big almond-shaped eyes, the trademark of all the female members of her family, tried to translate what they were talking about, stumbling over each word and ending up saying, "Nothing important really but a lot of trivia."

Before dinner was over, her mother-in-law used all her manoeuvring skills and successfully brought the conversation to Alex's expected pregnancy, finally managing to ruin the night for her. Alex did not want to talk to anyone about it except to her husband, because she knew that they would interfere with her life, telling her what to do and what not to do. She was no longer playing tennis anyway, given the cold weather. What would it be this time?

"You'll stop smoking once you're pregnant, won't you?"

She felt a cage closing in around her.

"As a matter of fact, you should stop now. What if you're already pregnant?" intervened Necla, pursing her full lips and lowering her eyelids half over her eyes.

It's none of your business, she felt like saying. "I've already stopped," she said instead.

"Well done!" It was not easy to hear Mehpare *Hanım* utter these words.

I wish they were gone, she thought to herself.

"Leave her alone," Haldun barged in, doing what Aziz should have done long ago. She felt like hugging him in gratitude. Not only his light brown, almost blond, hair but everything about him was very different from the rest of his family. He turned to Alex and continued in his joyfully carefree voice. "There are far too many females in this family, and they all have an opinion to impose. God help you, my dear sister."

It was past midnight when everybody had gone, leaving behind an army of glasses and a variety of empty wine and champagne bottles in the dining room, ribbons of every colour of the rainbow and shiny wrapping papers ripped off the presents and scattered around on the armchairs and coffee tables, a few surviving candles still burning on the branches of the Christmas tree, and a very tired Alex. Leaving everything as it was, she followed Aziz to their bedroom.

"Why don't you go to our summerhouse on the Bosphorus in Baltalimanı to paint?" asked Aziz out of the blue.

"I might eventually do that too. For the moment, I'm busy discovering Istanbul. Every little corner, every little detail gives me so much inspiration, Aziz."

"That's all very well, but Istanbul is not Budapest. As a woman, you can't just roam the city on your own with your brushes in your hand. You'll get yourself into trouble."

"I have the driver with me."

"That's another problem. Don't forget that Istanbul is far worse than Budapest when it comes to gossipmongers."

"Come off it, Aziz. Please."

"It's for your own good, Alex."

"Who decides what is good for me? Your mother or your sisters? Why do you always have to listen to them?" As soon as she uttered the last words, she knew that she had said the wrong thing, but it was too late.

"Now you listen to me! And listen very well!" Aziz said severely, articulating each word in a tone of voice Alex had never heard before. He was not shouting, but the harshness in his eyes was much more frightening than a raised voice. He walked towards her, wagging his finger. "You're part of my family, and they all love you dearly just as I do. However, in our family, there's a limit to being a rebel, and you must respect these limits. That's the way we learned from our parents. And believe me, it's all for your own good before anybody else's. You should listen to your elders. You can't wander around Istanbul with your paints and brushes."

Alex felt the doors of a gilded cage slowly locking her in.

"Get out!" she heard Aziz roar at the top of his voice at Pepa, who had just entered their bedroom. His voice, echoing from the walls, hit Alex's ears. He went on shouting as he banged his fist on the bedside table. "You must adapt yourself to the society you're living in. Stop acting like a rebellious artist! It's about time you learned how to become a proper mother and a proper wife, young lady."

She felt like a little girl, a very lonely little girl. Her first Christmas away from home should not have ended like this. Tears started rolling down her cheeks. She shrivelled up underneath the eiderdown as she felt her heart sinking. Please, Aziz, she begged mutely, please don't shout. Please. For Alex, who had almost never witnessed the grown-ups in her family raise their voices against each other, Aziz's anger meant the end of it all. Their marriage must have come to an end, and only four months after it had started. She wanted to sleep. Aziz had left the room. She could hear the sound of ice cubes being dropped into a glass in the kitchen. Sleep Alex. Just go to sleep. Everything will be all right in the morning. This is only a terrible nightmare.

When she woke up the next morning, she saw Aziz sitting by the bed, watching her. She averted her eyes in fright.

"I'm terribly sorry, Alex. I beg you to forgive me. Please forget what I said last night. Please, I beg you." He was stroking her hair. "I simply don't want you to get hurt, that's all. You're too precious to me."

She timidly turned to Aziz. Were there tears glistening beneath his eyelids?

"Come on, give us a smile now."

Alex tried to force a smile.

"I'll do anything for that smile."

"Don't shout at me, Aziz. Please don't shout at me ever again."

"Forgive me, *ma petite*," he pleaded, holding her shoulders and then folding her in his embrace. "You're my everything."

Alex hugged him tightly, burying her head in his chest. "I think I'm pregnant," she mumbled. "My period is twenty days late."

Suddenly Aziz released her to look at her in the face. His eyes shone with tears, and without saying anything, he started crying. A few seconds later he let out a loud laugh and then another one. He kissed Alex all over her face, her eyes, her whole body, stopping only to let out bursts of excited laughter. Pepa and Goya were trying to jump onto the bed in excitement.

"Stop! Stop it, Aziz! I'm not sure yet."

36

She had a terrible pain in her shoulder. She should ask Asiye *Hanım* to give her another massage.

"Asiye *Hanım*," she called out.

Asiye *Hanım* entered the drawing room, wiping her hands on a towel, and said that tea would be ready soon.

"Would you please give me a massage? It's my left shoulder again."

Asiye *Hanım*'s strong hands alleviated her pain straight away. She started reading Károly's letter, fresh from Paris. He said that they were happy about her pregnancy and could hardly wait for the arrival of their nephew Attila or niece Nili.

A month ago, Doctor Manara had confirmed Alex's pregnancy and estimated that she could look forward to becoming a mother in early September. That very evening, they had gone to Haldun Pasha Mansion and announced the good news to the whole family, as bottles of champagne were popped one after the other. Mehpare *Hanım*, when she could finally control her sobbing and her tears, asked Aziz what the name of their baby would be. "We want it to be Attila if it's a boy, or Nili, I mean Nilüfer, if it's a girl," jumped in Alex before Aziz could even open his mouth. "It won't be Halim then, will it?" said Mehpare *Hanım*, her eyes refilled with tears, this time of disappointment.

Lately Alex had started to question her relationship with Mehpare *Hanım*. She could never be sure, for instance, if her mother-in-law really enjoyed talking to her or simply wanted to satisfy her desire to speak French, for she loved squeezing in a lot of French expressions in her conversations in Turkish and switched to French altogether when she believed in the other person's capacity in this language. She genuinely looked interested in what Alex had to say, but their hearts spoke different languages. A small movement of an eyebrow, a passing scowl on her face, a short remark would be enough to remind Alex that she was an outsider. Although close enough to interfere with their life, she put a strange and oppressive distance between her and Alex that weighed quite heavily on her. There seemed to be an obstacle between them that she could not describe, a door, so to speak, which she felt was held open out of obligation and might be shut any minute.

That evening they had left early, and, just as they were going out the door, Mehpare *Hanım* had found something to say, yet again, to upset Alex. "I presume you'll be sending the dogs and the cat to the hunting lodge now that you're pregnant, dear. It's extremely dangerous for a pregnant woman and a new born baby to have animals in the house."

Alex remembered how, gathering all her courage together as they walked home that evening, she had said, not taking her eyes off the wet pavement stones drifting away under her feet, "I shall not send Pepa or Goya or Portakal anywhere!"

"You can't take care of them all. You've got to look after yourself, Alex."

"You grew up with dogs, and so did I. They won't be going anywhere."

"Neither you nor I grew up in a flat though."

"Our children will. They will grow up in a flat with dogs and cats."

She had managed to silence Aziz that evening. She would not give in. She was strong. Her baby was giving her the strength she needed. And nothing else mattered. I won't give up the things I love just to make Aziz's family happy. And Aziz will have to get used to my rebellious nature.

She continued reading Károly's letter.

... This summer, the Fourth World Scout Jamboree will be held in Hungary between August 2 and 13 in the park around the Royal Palace in Gödöllő. Twenty-six thousand boy scouts will be attending from forty-six countries. József is so very proud. In his last letter he says that the Hungarian Air Scouts led by his cousin László will be represented for the first time. It seems that we'll be listening to his bragging for quite a while now.

You ask about my paintings. The answer is: I'm painting like crazy. I enclose a review that came out the other day. They really interpreted my work well. If you cut the embellishments, what they say is, simply, "Even though highly influenced by the West, he seeks his Hungarian roots."

> *"On one hand, he paints surfaces melting almost into transparency in his post-impressionist still lifes, where nature serves only as a starting point; and on the other hand, he tries to find himself by using the clichés of cubism in his still life paintings accompanied by portraits. The landscapes he uses in his expressive self-portraits have a certain level of chilling objectivity and remind us of the classical works of the Hungarian Nagybánya Group. We see that what inspires him in his work is not what he has seen in Paris, but rather his search for his ancestors through expressions on his Hungarian palette."*

It's all well and nice, but doesn't bring any money. Viktor started to work at the Havas advertising agency, and, thanks to him, I get quite a lot of graphic work.

However, they pay so poorly that it's impossible to live solely on that in a city like Paris. We wouldn't be able to survive here if we didn't have the income from our estates in Kengyel and Eger, which, as a matter of fact, has gone down rather drastically. We all know that our dear estate manager Ernő is not doing much, especially concerning the management of the forests. Luckily, ...

She felt a sudden cramp paralyse the left side of her belly. She folded in half.

"What's wrong, madam? Did I hurt you?" Asiye *Hanım* asked in panic, and instantly stopped massaging Alex's shoulders.

"My belly! I have a terrible pain in my belly." The pain was slowly spreading, grabbing her insides. "It's not important. It shouldn't be. I'll lie down a little until teatime and it'll go away."

She had had pains earlier on but had not thought much of it since they had not been so strong. She had other complaints as well, a few drops of blood every now and then, though very light in colour, morning sickness and tiredness, but they said that these were all quite normal during any pregnancy. Perhaps she should not wait till the end of the month for her next check-up. The pain seemed to have subsided a little. She returned to Károly's letter.

... Luckily, Sanyi decided to take care of our estates. In her last letter, Mother says that he has moved to Kengyel. Now they're all alone in Rózsadomb and I'm rather worried about them. I do hope that our cousin might soon return to Budapest, although that prospect is rather unlikely as he seems to be very happy in Kengyel.

Asiye *Hanım* came back with the tea. Alex put the letter down and stood up with difficulty. She felt so tired.

"You should rest, madam. Tell me what you want and let me do it."

She wanted to listen to Tchaikovsky's *Violin Concerto in D Major, Opus 35*. Would Asiye *Hanım* learn how to put a record on the gramophone? Next time, she should teach her how. As she took one step, an excruciating pain grabbed her in the belly and she collapsed on her knees.

"Madam!"

She was suddenly bathed in cold sweat.

"You've gone all white. I'm calling Aziz *Bey*."

Asiye *Hanım* dashed out of the drawing room. Alex pushed away Pepa and Goya, who had run to her in panic and were licking her hands and face. What was happening? God, what's happening to me? She pressed her hands to her belly. She had to keep her baby! She wrapped her arms around her and folded in half. I must not move. I must stay put. I must hold on to my baby. I shall not let her go! She started stroking her belly. "Stay with me! Please don't leave me. Please. Please don't go." She suddenly felt a warmth between her legs. She was bleeding. No! She pressed her hands in between her legs as strongly as she could. I must stop the bleeding! I'm losing my baby! Everything went dark. Her head was spinning. She felt her head hit the floor.

June 2004
Istanbul

Rüya entered Mami's room again, probably for the tenth time since sunrise. Doctor Nesim should be here soon, she thought. It was almost eight. Mami had woken up. She looked so frail, with her head limply turned to one side and her silky white hair flaccidly lying on the pillow as she watched her roses through the French windows, which, with their white wooden panes, framed the spectacle of her colourful rose garden like a painting, a masterpiece that she had been working on for years. Each morning as soon as she woke up, she opened the windows, pushed the shutters aside and drew in the perfume of her roses as if it were her first breath of the day. She said that she preferred this room to those upstairs, although they had a better view overlooking the Bosphorus, because of her desire to be closer to her roses.

"Come closer, *tatlım*. I'm not sleeping. Come and stay with me for a while."

Rüya perched on the edge of the bed. "How do you feel this morning?" she asked, stroking her hand.

"I'm still here, and that means I ought to be fine." Holding Rüya's cheeks between her hands, she continued, "You look tired. Didn't you sleep well? You should look after yourself, sweetheart." She looked much livelier than she did last night.

"I'm fine, Mami, just fine." In fact, she had a terrible headache. Last night, she had fallen asleep in the gazebo and woken up with the first light of the day.

"Why don't you have some dried apricots?"

Mami had the habit of treating her visitors, especially the younger members of her family, to the dried apricots, dried figs and walnuts she stocked away in her lilac wardrobe by her bed. One of the most challenging tricks that entertained the children was trying to sneak into her room while she snoozed to steal some of these treats, a rather testing task since the key to her treasure was securely tucked under her pillow.

Rüya watched her sit up with difficulty, take the key from underneath her pillow and, reaching for her walking stick, try to stand up.

"I'll get it, Mami. You shouldn't tire yourself."

"I'm not dead yet, am I?" she said in feigned anger as she made towards the wardrobe. She took a piece of dried fruit from the open packet on top of a pile and handed it over to Rüya.

"Thank you."

"I'd better lie down again." She was back by the bed, looking exhausted.

"I'll bring in your breakfast," Rüya said as she helped her lie down, pretending that she was not helping.

"Would you please put some music on before you go?" After a brief hesitation, she added, "Liszt's *Hungarian Rhapsody, Number Thirteen*."

Rüya walked to the far end of the room, towards the over-filled bookcase behind the large table where Mami painted in front of a window overlooking her rose garden. She found Liszt's *Hungarian Rhapsodies* from among the CDs squeezed in a crowd of painting materials and photographs stacked up on one of the shelves slightly bent under the weight of tens or perhaps hundreds of objects, laden with memories.

"Rhapsody is the braiding of songs," said Mami as if talking to herself, her absent eyes gazing out the window, "an intricate plait of melodies and rhythms that sometimes take you to the endless Great Hungarian Plain on an oppressively hot summer day. You sweat under the ruthlessly scorching sun until suddenly an oasis comes into view, an oasis far away which you know is only an image of waves on the horizon, a mirage created by the hot air rising from the ground. It nevertheless cools you down. Yet at other times, you listen with a chill running through your body as its notes bring in the sound of an icy wind whistling over the steppes buried under the snow. The sensations that enrapture you gradually intensify like a mare steadily coming into full gallop.

"*Lassú,* the first part of the rhapsody, begins unruffled and leisurely, with the languor of a golden summer day. Initially, you listen with a sweet sense of joy, an irresponsible smile on your lips and a youthful thrill in your heart. Eventually, bliss leaves its place to melancholy and despair. You slow down; you turn inwards.

"The second part *Friss* marches in like an army. It roars! It's destructive. It mercilessly burns down everything. Your heart sinks. You hurt. Suffering, however, is accompanied by a certain sense of pride that alleviates your heart as you listen to the courageous deeds of dauntless heroes, epics of colossal proportions.

"And then *Csárdás!* The third and the final movement, the *Csárdás* is another realm where emotions soar to their climax. Everything depends on *Csárdás*, everything."

Rüya silently left the room, unwilling to wake Mami up from her reverie. As she walked towards the kitchen to prepare her breakfast, she heard the scrunch of pebbles in the garden under the weight of a car. She went back to Mami's room.

"Mami, Doctor Nesim has arrived. I'll bring your breakfast later."

"All right, dear."

Rüya could hear her mother and grandmother talking in the hall. A few minutes later they all entered the room. Nili went to the CD player and turned down the volume.

"How are you?" asked Doctor Nesim, sitting on the edge of Mami's bed and holding her hand.

"I'm rather unwell, I guess. I feel so very tired."

Doctor Nesim commenced his examination. As he listened to her chest, his face betrayed nothing of what he was finding out. "How is it going with the cigarettes?" he finally asked.

"Very well, thank you," Mami replied, smiling cheekily.

"I can see that." He turned to Nili. "How is her appetite?"

"Lately she's been refusing to put anything in her mouth other than coffee and cigarettes."

They all waited anxiously for the doctor to finish his examination, after which he stood up and, holding Nili by the arm, led her towards the door. "We'd better have an X-ray taken," he whispered. "There might be a build-up of fluid in her lungs."

"Which means?"

They stopped once they were in the hall.

"I'm afraid it might be pneumonia."

"What shall we do?"

"It would be best if you took her to the hospital. It might be necessary to drain out some of the fluid that has accumulated in her lungs. Take a few of her things with you; she might need to stay under observation for a couple of days."

"If I'm going to die, I want to do so in my own bed."

"What on earth makes you say that, Mami? It'll be nothing but a minor intervention."

"You can't make me go anywhere."

I make my way towards the house and slowly climb the steps to the veranda. I'm somewhat timid, uneasy somehow. I sit on one of the chairs by the table. White sheets of paper, a white pen, a glass of lemonade. Ice-cold. Half a slice of lemon sits on the rim. I reach out and hold the frosty glass. A cool sensation tickles my hand, then trickles into my soul. A sip. A sudden surge of energy. My eyes open up; my mind clears. An unforeseen urge to turn my head and look over the railing. A young tree, almost in bloom, sways dreamily as the gentle breeze kisses its flower buds. I can't see their true colour as the young tree is in the shade.

My eyes detach themselves from the young tree and stretch out towards the beach. They stop at the sight of a young woman sauntering towards the house. Almost an illusion in her transparent robe. Colourless. She moves closer. Now an illusion dressed in violet. Light as a feather. I can't see her face, for her eyes are cast down following her gliding steps. She quietly ascends the stairs and sits in the deckchair, slowly raising her head. Her green eyes reflect the colour of the sea. Virtually translucent. I see my twin sister for the first time in years.

She takes my hands into hers. A warm embrace enfolds my whole being. I wish she would never let go. A sweet dream. I'm scared to wake up. She reads my mind.

"You'll wake up one day," she says, "and on that day I may not be with you. But don't fear because you will no longer be needing me."

It took the whole family a couple of hours to talk Mami into going to the hospital, and it was almost noontime when she finally yielded. "There's nothing wrong with me," she grumbled as she climbed into the front seat of the car, refusing everyone's help despite her obvious difficulty. "Look at me. I can't even put on my own safety belt anymore," she complained bitterly, trying to reach for it before she grudgingly accepted Aslı's help. "Let's take the road along the Bosphorus, shall we?" she finally grunted, turning to Bedri, the driver.

"As you wish, madam."

The car had moved only a few metres when she beckoned Bedri to stop and, pressing the automatic button to lower the window, she called out, "Dursun Efendi!" hardly waiting for the window to open fully.

The old gardener was next to a pear tree, busy placing wooden sticks to support its branches, which were almost touching the ground under the weight of the ripening fruit. He dropped the stick he was fixing to a branch and rushed towards the car. "Yes, ma'am?"

"The sour cherries have already ripened. Pick me some, would you? A kilo would do. When we come back, I'll make *rétes* with sour cherries. Or better still, pick a lot more. We ought to make some marmalade as well."

"Poor soul," Nili murmured, shaking her head from where she was sitting next to Rüya in the back seat of the car. The pitying tone of her voice betrayed much more solicitude toward her mother than she was willing to display.

Lila, André and Attila had already settled in Aslı's car, ignoring Mami's objections, who, generously and ironically, scolded everyone, "What's all this fuss about? Are we all moving to the hospital or what?" The convoy slowly moved as Daphné, standing between her parents, reluctantly waved them goodbye, convinced that everyone was going for an outing.

As they drove down the hill to Bebek, Rüya, who had not uttered a word for the last hour, kept her silence with her gaze fixed on the rushing waters of the Bosphorus glittering under the sun, which, at this time of the year, was perfidious and might readily deprive the city of its fickly warmth, for it was prone to shy away behind a veil of clouds that might unexpectedly charge in at the slightest promise of a northerly wind.

"It's very difficult to live in a city where you can't smell the iodine the wind brings in from the sea," said Nili to no one in particular.

Rüya did not like the smell of iodine. She actually detested it. But the seagulls were different. Through the window of the moving car, she caught a few glimpses of the seagulls brazenly flying about the embankment. She loved their croaking voices. They might be a cacophony of insolent sounds to many, or a crude intermezzo to the inspiring panorama, but to her they were an indispensable part of life. She recalled how difficult it had been for her when she was forced to live in a city that lacked the sound of the seagulls, a city bereft of the jingle of the crickets singing gingerly under the scorching summer sun, a city where she longed for the generous snowfall of the freezing winter months, the Judas trees painting the rolling hills pink in springtime and the crisp light from a tired autumn sun. It would still be very difficult – almost impossible – for her to live in such a city.

"You'll never find the happiness you've lost somewhere deep in your heart if you keep searching for it elsewhere," Mami murmured without turning back. She seemed to have been snoozing, but was apparently wakeful enough to read Rüya's thoughts. "Every place, every city, every summer, every winter, every person has a certain beauty and, if you can manage to see it, even a certain ugliness that might show you a way out. Open your eyes, Nili, and try to see. Don't just look, but see. Seek to really see everything as it is. Don't fear, dear."

She had not read Rüya's mind, of course; she was talking to Nili.

"Mami, please don't exhaust yourself," said Nili apprehensively.

It took them forty-five minutes to reach the hospital, immured by the tall concrete apartment buildings on one of the side streets of Nişantaşı; a journey that would take no more than four minutes without the traffic – an unlikely occurrence other than at four o'clock in the morning. Rüya hated hospitals, the sickly smell of the corridors, the impersonal waiting rooms, the waiting itself, the unknown, her know-it-all mother constantly running about talking to the doctors, her grandmother's callousness, everything! Everything bothered her. She could not take it. She could take none of it.

"I'm not happy with this room either," Aslı said as the head nurse walked away. "I asked for another room on the fourth floor."

"Stop fussing about it, Mum. We're not going to buy the room. She won't be staying for long anyway."

They had taken about a litre of fluid from Mami's lungs. She was very weak and not well at all. The doctors could not tell how long she would need to stay in intensive care.

"Would you please stop sticking your little nose into everything, Rüya? If it were up to you, everything would be done your way, wouldn't it? No, dear, it won't be."

"But you're draining us all."

"Oh, I'm terribly sorry, my Lady. I've forgotten that I'm supposed to take care of everything without disturbing your noble self. It's you – all of you – who are draining *me*."

"Stop arguing," intervened Nili. "It's been a nerve-wracking day for all of us. Nothing is going to happen to Mami. She's a strong woman and will be up and about in no time."

"You're so insensitive, Grandma. She is dying!"

"Don't you worry, Rüya. She'll be fine, just fine."

When Aslı was finished with arranging a new room, instructing the cleaners how to clean it once again with particular care to the bathroom, and teaching the nurses and the doctors in the intensive care what they should be doing, they were informed that they would not be able to see Mami until the following morning, after which they reluctantly left the hospital.

A Hungarian Rhapsody
A Novel in Three Acts
Act One, Tableau Two
1933 - 1936

37

She tried to open her eyes. She could not. Her eyelids were sealed. She was in the garden of their house in Albisola in Italy. She had been running for a long time. It was so hot that her pink dress was soaked in sweat. It was her favourite outfit but she did not care, for she was in a rush. She had to find Magda. She knew that her sister was there behind the trees. She made to break into a run but was unable to move her feet. She looked down. Her legs were stuck in knee-deep mud. She was sweating all over. Her thighs were all wet. To her horror, she noticed that it was not sweat but blood that had bathed her legs. She had to run. She had to find Magda. "Magda!" she cried out. Looking around, she realised she was no longer in Albisola. With no warning, she had come to Erzsébet Manor in Kengyel. The house was empty. Everybody had left. They had taken her here to die. She was dying. Death! Mortality! Her dreams of immortality had bled away and deserted her. The house disappeared. She was now lying face up on the frozen lake. It was freezing cold. She started shuddering as she watched her spirit leave her debilitated and useless body and ascend towards the clear winter sky. She was among the clouds now. All her sufferings were no more. Free at last. Magda was by her side, stroking her cheek. "Magda!" she cried out again. Her sister slowly faded away. Don't go away, Magda! Don't leave me. "Magda!" she wailed. "*Maradj velem!* Stay with me!" She was leaving. She could no longer see her.

"Magda ... Magda ..."

She opened her eyes. Where was she? "Magda!" she bellowed. The ceiling was not the ceiling of their drawing room. She saw Aziz's bloodshot eyes approaching.

"Alex ..." he said between sobs. "My love ... my one and only love. Thank God. Thank you, God."

"What happened? Where am I?"

"We're in Manara Clinic, *ma petite*."

She suddenly recovered her consciousness. Her baby! "My baby!" she howled in agony, anxiously hugging her belly. Panic-stricken, she raised her feeble arms and grabbed Aziz by the neck. "My baby?" she screamed, pulling his collar. "Nothing is wrong with my baby, is it?" she begged, almost tearing his shirt.

Aziz held her tightly in his arms. A painful sense of fear clasped her heart. She had to check. She had to see if her bleeding had stopped. She pushed Aziz away with her frail arms. He did not let go. "Let me go!" she growled, violently throwing aside the bed sheet. She had to see if everything was all right.

Aziz would not let go of her arms. "Calm down, my love. Calm down. What's important is that nothing happened to you. You almost died."

She wanted to scream, cry out loud at the top of her voice. She opened her mouth. Nothing but a stifled sob came out. Somebody was wringing her throat. She was suffocating. This must be a nightmare. She pinched her arms, her legs and slapped her cheeks. She would not wake up. The nightmare continued. "Wake up Alex. Wake up. It's only a nightmare." She would not wake up. She started rocking back and forth. Her body was shaking in great sobs. "I must get pregnant again. Right away. Right now. Now! Aziz! Let's get out of here. Let's go home. Please. I beg you, please." She held on to Aziz's arm to raise herself from bed.

Aziz was stroking her wet cheeks and lips. "Alex, you must lie down. Please don't wear yourself out. You must rest."

She grabbed the hand of the nurse who was fiddling with something by her bed. "I can get pregnant right away, can't I?"

"Please lie down, madam. Everything will be fine. Don't you worry."

She held Aziz's hands. "Don't let me go, Aziz. I'm so scared of being left all alone. Don't ever leave me. Please."

"I'm right here, *ma petite*. I'll always be here."

"My baby died because of me. I couldn't keep it. I couldn't take care of it."

"It's not your fault, my love. It was an ectopic pregnancy due to a malformation in your fallopian tubes. You almost died, my love. You almost died."

She felt her head getting heavier and heavier. She could not keep her eyes open any longer. I'll never be happy. Never! I'm doomed to lose all my loved ones. "Magda?" she murmured. "Where is Magda? Please call her. Please. Magda ..."

38

Her mother had arrived the day before, exactly ten months after she was supposed to have come. Even Alex's condition, which might have proved fatal, had not been sufficient to bring her to Istanbul any earlier. Finally, and God only knows why, she had decided to honour them with a visit. As a matter of fact, it might have been better if she did not come at all, since she would probably make her life more miserable than it already was. Aziz kept saying that another pregnancy would mean taking a lethal risk and did not let her even speak about it. He almost shunned making love to her, saying, "How can you expect me to sacrifice you for a child? You must be out of your mind." Yes, she was out of her mind. She had to have children, whatever the cost. She could not think of her life being any other way. She did everything she could to get their sex life back on its track, trying to hide her depressing moods and worries and looking her best to seduce Aziz. She had to get pregnant and she would. She would do everything until she did.

"Where are you taking your mother today?" asked Aziz. "Do you have any plans? The driver will be at your sole disposal for the next three weeks."

"Thank you, Aziz. We're planning to go to Beyoğlu in the morning, and I'll be having some friends over for tea. I want them all to meet Mother." Alex had invited all her friends in an effort to prove both to her mother and to herself that she was not alone in this foreign country. "And tomorrow, we'll probably go and see the Topkapı Palace."

Even Gizella could not help but show her surprise at the richness of the breakfast table, which lacked for nothing. It was a spectacular display of carefully sliced tomatoes, cucumbers and green peppers, shiny black olives sprinkled with oregano, a wide variety of cheeses including feta cheese, cheddar and goat's cheese, fried eggs with spicy sausages, salami, anchovies and five different types of jams and marmalades proudly made by Asiye *Hanım*. Gizella tasted from almost all of them with great interest and appetite, forgetting about her figure. Her waistline, which, in her youth, her husband could encircle with his hands, had somewhat widened, but despite her forty-seven years she still had a body that would be the envy of even those who were much younger than her.

"One wouldn't be able to eat anything all day after such a filling breakfast."

"We don't always eat as much at breakfast but nibble on some toast, feta cheese, olives and tomatoes. This is all in your honour, *Anyukám*."

"It's I who nibble on toast, feta cheese, olives and tomatoes," interrupted Aziz. "Alex doesn't touch anything other than coffee and a few biscuits. It's impossible to make your daughter put on weight."

"We mustn't underestimate the importance of coffee; it does have quite a significant place in my life," said Alex, holding Aziz's hand. "He no longer prepares my morning coffee, but it was the first of a series of attacks that conquered my heart."

"I hope you had a good time at the reception last night," said Aziz to Gizella.

"Yes, indeed. However, Alex needs to inform your friends a little bit more about Hungary and the Hungarian people. All they know about our country is goulash and gypsy music. They presume that all Hungarians are goulash-eating gypsies, and that really upsets me."

She actually means that it drives her mad, thought Alex.

"I can't remember how many times I had to repeat last night," Gizella continued, turning her eyes to the ceiling and carrying on loudly as if she wanted the whole world to hear what she was about to say, "that the gypsies are only a small minority in Hungary and that we – or rather some of us – only appreciate their musicians and their music."

"Please don't be unfair, Madame de Kurzón," said Aziz, raising his eyebrows in feigned naivety, a gesture that indicated he was getting ready to make a humorous remark. "Some of us are more worldly in that we do know that Hungarians are as fiery as hot paprika, Hungarian men are excellent horsemen and Hungarian women are fatally beautiful." He turned to Alex and held her hand. "Nobody can deny that."

"How is Sanyi, by the way?" asked Alex, anxious to find a subject that would not provoke Gizella's wrath.

"I'm really worried about him. You know that he still lives in Kengyel. It's undoubtedly good that someone is running our estate there since things went haywire after your grandfather's death. No one knows exactly what Ernő is up to." She turned to Aziz. "Our estate manager," she explained. "I always had question marks about his trustworthiness. Well, anyway, Sanyi really does take care of everything. Recently he took our estate in Eger in hand as well and employed an agricultural engineer to manage the vineyards there. He himself is taking care of the management of the forests in Kengyel. Expenses have already halved." She looked at Alex with genuine worry in her eyes. "However, your cousin is far too lonely. He turns down all our efforts to marry him off. He's alone in that huge house. Nobody lives like that anymore. He's become a total recluse. He says he's very happy there with his horses, dogs, hunting and books. He must have read every single book in the library. We insisted that he sleep in Etel's bedroom upstairs, but apparently he's content with his little room downstairs. He says it's closer to the earth and talks about what a great godsend it is to be able to feel the earth close by and smell it while dreaming away. I'm scared he might eventually lose his mind in that godforsaken place."

"Don't say that, Mother. Kengyel is a paradise. Not everyone is a city-lover like you. Some people prefer being alone in nature to being alone among their so-called friends."

"Well, well, well! What a philosophical daughter I've got here. As if you're any different, dear. I wonder how many days *you* would be able to stay on your own in Kengyel." She turned to Aziz. "You know what a bright engineer Sanyi is, Aziz *Bey*. Everybody was convinced that he'd be no less successful than his father was, but he chose this simple country life. I feel so sorry for him. He took his father's death so badly, dear boy. Could you believe that he allowed his father's inventions to be patented under other people's names? Or I should perhaps say, he actually preferred it to be that way."

"This must be something very Hungarian, I presume. Is it that once they prove themselves as successful, it's not in their noble blood to enjoy the fame and money that follow?"

"Precisely, Aziz *Bey*. You've met Irén's father-in-law, haven't you? Monsieur Patrik Merse. He's the forerunner of the Impressionists in Hungary. Can you imagine such a great artist not touching his brushes for fifteen years? It's quite incredible, isn't it?"

Aziz rang the little porcelain bell on the table. Asiye *Hanım* ran into the dining room. He asked her to refresh their tea. "Don't forget to make Madame de Kurzón's tea lighter than ours." He then took two slices of salami and gave one each to Pepa and Goya, who had been waiting patiently at his feet. Portakal, slightly raising her proud head from the sofa in the drawing room where she was lazing away, stared disapprovingly at her gluttonous friends. A few minutes later, however, no longer able to resist the temptation, she came to the feet of her mistress and gobbled down the piece of cheddar she gave her. Alex, recalling how the habit of feeding the pets off the table annoyed her mother, most delightedly gave Portakal another piece of cheese. This was her house; Portakal, Pepa and

Goya were her pets; and only she and Aziz dictated the rules here.

Aziz was talking to Gizella. "We shall be going hunting in Thrace the weekend before Christmas and shall stay at İskender's hunting lodge. We could go all together if you wish. It might be an occasion for you to see a different aspect of our lifestyle." He paused as if he had just remembered something. "I'm so sorry, it had slipped my mind that you didn't really approve of hunting."

"I don't take pleasure in what you call hunting nowadays." Gizella fell silent for a second before she continued, "or rather, in what your generation takes to be hunting, I should say. Like everything else, hunting was different during peace time."

"What Mother means by peace time is the period before 1914. She thinks that peace ended at the outbreak of the Great War."

"We'll definitely find things to divert you here. Now if you'll excuse me, I have to go. The Electrical Works expect me."

After seeing Aziz off, Alex and Gizella sat at the table for a while longer, chatting.

"Aziz is not happy with his job at all, Mother. What he earns is a pittance. We wouldn't make it if he didn't have the income from his real estate investments. However, the main problem is not his salary. He carries something very heavy on his shoulders, the heritage of a family that comes from one of the prominent prime ministers of the Ottoman Empire, a family that occupied the most honourable positions in the country's diplomatic, political and military forces. He looks down upon commerce and can't tolerate being a civil servant. Worse still, he says he can't bear taking orders from people with no manners, no background and no roots."

"I understand him perfectly well. He's absolutely right." Gizella's face lightened with a sweet smile.

Alex thought how much she needed to see her mother smile. She reached for her hand. "I miss you all so very much, *Anyukám*. I miss Magda. I miss *Öcsi*. It's been more than a year since I last saw them. This separation has taught me so much. I now realise much better how difficult it is to be away from Magda and how much I love *Öcsi*." She looked at her mother in the eye and, with the passion of a child who wants to listen to the same fairy tale over and over again, begged her. "Please, tell me again. Please tell me what Magda is doing. I want to hear even the tiniest detail again and again."

"I've already told you everything, sweetheart."

"Tell me again, would you please?"

"They work like crazy, Miklós and Magda. Their life revolves around their ceramics. Thanks to her new last name, your sister is becoming more famous by the day. She now has a strong signature: Nerády."

"Don't be so unfair, Mother. Everyone except you agrees that Magda is very talented indeed. She's a great artist in her own right."

"I know, but ... Well, anyway. There is no way I can understand the art of Magda or of Károly."

"You can't understand anything about Károly," Alex thought. "Does Károly write to you often?" she asked instead. "It seems to me that he intends to settle down in Paris for good. What do you think?"

"I do hope he has no such absurd intention. Even if he did, he'd hardly make it there. What is he going to live on? Shall I keep sending him money forever and ever?"

"It's not so easy to make it out there. It's not for everyone to survive in Paris as an artist, but Károly will do it. He will."

"My, my! I thought you wanted your brother to return to Budapest."

"Of course I do, but not because he could not make it in Paris. I just hope he chooses to return."

"How is that going to happen, if I may ask? It's obvious what Károly would choose as long as Ada insists on staying there."

"Let us leave it at that, shall we?" Alex was angry at her mother for the way she treated Károly and Ada. It was her who had driven *Öcsi* away by putting too much pressure on him. Magda was the only one of them who could manage to live only a few kilometres away from Mother. She was strong, resilient. Magda ... How much she needed her sister to be here with her now.

"Why didn't she come, A*nyukám?*" she asked.

"Whom do you mean, sweetheart?"

"Magda. Why didn't she come?"

As a matter of fact, she was not waiting for an answer since it would not be satisfactory whatever it was. There could be no justification for Magda not coming, given that even their mother could make it. "Have we drifted so far apart?" she pleaded. "Why?" Could her mother say something to console her? She wished she could. "The pain of not having her with me is far greater than losing my baby, you know."

"Don't exaggerate, Alex."

"Do you know how I feel sometimes? I feel as lonely as a little girl left all alone in the dark, a little girl who was playing happily in the garden and, in the heat of the game, forgot about everything, ran out into the street, strayed away from her home and when the darkness fell could not find her way back." She held her mother's hand. "You must show me the way home, Mother. I need to know that my home and my family are still there and that I still can reach them." She could not help the trembling in her voice. "I feel so utterly lonely, *Anyukám*," she mumbled.

"It was your choice to be away from your loved ones and from everything else. You didn't listen to me. And now you have to shoulder the consequences."

"I didn't choose, *Anyukám*. I was chosen. I was pushed to choose. Can you understand that?"

"Nobody forced you to go to Istanbul. You were very happy when you left. Besides, you have a much better life here than I guessed or feared. You're blowing everything out of proportion." She stroked Alex's hair. "You're going through a very difficult time, sweetheart," she said tenderly. "It'll pass. It'll all pass. You have the perfect husband. Appreciate it. You took an uncalculated risk and were unexpectedly very lucky, so to speak. Last night at the reception, I talked to Aziz *Bey*. He's madly in love with you and very proud. He praised you all evening as if I didn't know you. He says he truly appreciates how quickly you learned Turkish and how well you've adapted yourself to your new environment."

"Do you know how much I've given up to do that?"

"And, as far as I can see, he knows very well how to handle you. You're not an easy woman, Alex. You never were. You were a difficult child and a difficult young girl. Your ups and downs and, most significantly, your rebellious nature might drive a man crazy. You're extremely lucky to have found a husband who could put up with it all."

"What else, Mother? What other vices do I have? Any other faults you can think of? Do you have any idea how hard I try to keep my self-confidence on its feet?" Alex felt her breath shortening.

"I'm only saying these things to make you appreciate your husband, dear."

Alex did not want to listen to her anymore. As she had guessed, her presence served only one purpose, and that was to make her more depressed. She stubbed out her cigarette firmly on the ashtray a few times, stood up, took the plate where a few slices of tomatoes and cucumbers lay almost shrivelled up, and went to the kitchen.

"Why didn't you call me, madam? It's not your place to do these things," said Asiye *Hanım* as she rushed towards the dining room.

Alex followed Asiye *Hanım*, piled up a few plates and walked back to the kitchen with angry steps. Her mother was behind her.

"Why do you run about, for God's sake? You've practically become a maid here."

How was she going to put up with her for another three weeks? As they moved into the drawing room, she asked Asiye *Hanım* to prepare them Turkish coffee, before sitting down on the sofa next to Portakal. Her orange tabby cat, quite chubby for her one-year of age, settled cosily on her lap, while Gizella sat in the armchair across her.

"Thanks to you, Mother, it's the first time that I've been invited to a shoot. He goes hunting every single weekend and so far has never even once asked me to join him. Not that I would enjoy seeing animals get killed, but this is the only way I can be with my husband on the weekends. He doesn't give up hunting even when we're so close to Christmas. He would have gone to the Balkans and missed Christmas altogether if I hadn't insisted otherwise."

"Why doesn't he want you to go with him?"

"Women are not welcome to go hunting in Turkey. It's not in their tradition. My mother-in-law almost had a heart attack when she heard that I wanted to go."

"How are you getting along with her?"

"Ours is a bitter-sweet relationship. She's been rather distant ever since the miscarriage. I guess she blames me for having killed the child of her beloved eldest son, although she doesn't say it to my face." She lit a cigarette with trembling hands. Her eyes burned. She bit her lips to stop herself from crying, but tears slid down her cheeks. She took a deep puff from her cigarette.

"Please, sweetheart. Please don't cry."

"She's right. It's all my fault. I was smoking too much. I stopped too late." She watched her tears dropping on Portakal's soft fur.

"It has nothing to do with cigarettes, my dear. Ectopic pregnancy is caused by your physical makeup."

"They say the chance of another miscarriage is only ten per cent," she said looking at her mother, hoping for some words of confirmation.

"Of course, dear. Please don't worry so much." She came over and sat beside her, pulling Alex's head against her chest. "Next time," she said as she stroked her hair, "as soon as you get pregnant, you should come to Budapest; there you would be much more comfortable and much better looked after."

Asiye *Hanım* came in with their coffee.

"Please give the one with more froth to my mother," she said, sobbing.

Seeing Alex cry, Asiye *Hanım*, almost in tears herself, said, "It's the evil eye, madam. I beg you to take my advice. Let's have some lead poured for you. That'll straighten everything up. Trust me."

Alex turned to her mother and, not quite sure whether it was her wish to lighten the conversation or her desire to become a mother that made her want to try anything, eagerly said, "Asiye *Hanım* insists that I have the evil eye on me and that we should have lead poured for me."

"What does that mean?"

Alex wiped away her tears. "I don't exactly know, but they stretch a bed sheet over your head and circle a pot of melted lead above it. Prayers, and all that ... Asiye *Hanım* thinks that what has happened to me is because of an evil eye set upon me by someone who is jealous of me."

Her mother seemed to be devastated as she listened to Alex. "Do these Turks always blame others for their misfortunes? And the remedies they devise seem prone to worse kinds of misfortunes. Now you listen to me, Alex. Don't you go and do something stupid."

"I'm ready to try everything, *Anyukám*. Anything! I must have a baby."

39

The second Christmas Alex celebrated away from her country was more felicitous than the first, despite her mother meddling in everything, determined to ensure that all the exigencies of their centuries-old traditions were duly carried out, even if they were in a foreign country.

"You're to buy presents for those in your service – for the people who earn their living under your roof – even if, God forbid, you find yourself in a situation where you can't do so for your own family. Christmas might not be a feast for them, but a festivity is taking place in this household, which is theirs as well. Do please ask Asiye *Hanım*, the concierge Recep and the driver Erol to come here with all their close relatives on Christmas Day, no matter how many of them there might be. *Noblesse oblige*, Alex. You owe it to the blood that runs through your veins to carry out your obligations."

As she saw her mother off at the Sirkeci Train Station a few days after New Year's Eve, Alex cried more than she could have ever imagined. Her mother, although pertinaciously inflexible and insupportably harsh upon Alex at times, had always been there to shore her up had she shown any sign of sinking. She was the indestructible pillar of strength in her life, who, on her own, had managed not to droop her shoulders no matter what happened, never losing the respect of others and, most importantly, her self-respect. She was the mainstay of their home in Rózsadomb and had kept it intact through and through. It was slowly dawning upon Alex how much effort she must have put in to keep herself on her feet all her life. Now she could see how lonely she must have been all those years.

Her mother's visit had stirred her feelings of nostalgia, and soon an acute yearning for Budapest budded in her. She wrote Magda several letters and sent her telegrams one after another, insisting that she come to Istanbul, which she finally did in May. At long last, she was once again with her sister, her other half, her heart and soul. They had not drifted apart; they never would. The thousands of kilometres between them were not enough to change the fact that they were the two halves of a whole.

The two weeks they spent together heightened Alex's spirits, and, under the spell of springtime turning the city into a visual feast of colours, her depressive mood completely disappeared. Seeing his wife happy and jovial, Aziz's good mood, sense of humour and, most importantly for Alex, sexual drive made a strong comeback. Alex could feel that very soon she would become pregnant again.

That morning Alex and Magda were feeling rather tired after having roamed the city for two weeks in line with Alex's hectic and head-spinning schedule, and decided to spend a peaceful day on Büyükada, the largest of the Prince's Islands on the Sea of Marmara. As they sat on the rear deck of the boat that was to take them to the island, nobody but the boy who brought their over-brewed black tea saw Alex's bare legs, which, being "the property of her husband," were reserved exclusively for his eyes, but which Alex nevertheless exposed to the sun, pulling up the highly fashionable loose trousers Magda had brought her from Budapest. Neither did anybody feast his eyes on Magda's shoulders and low neckline, which she bravely displayed, stretching down her blouse in the hope of getting an early tan. The sesame rolls they had bought before embarking tasted different that day, as did the vanilla ice-cream and the lemon sorbet they bought from a street-vendor on the island, despite Magda's doubts about the hygienic reliability of the old vendor's services. They toured the island on a phaeton, saluting the trees, Magda as Károly IV, the King of Hungary, and Alex as Zita, the Queen.

"The maritime pines here, don't they remind you of our childhood in Albisola?"

They each lit a candle in the church up on the top of the hill, making a wish. Knowing very well that they were supposed to keep their wishes secret, but not considering themselves as separate individuals, they simultaneously whispered the same words into each other's ears.

"I want to have a baby."

"I want to have a baby."

They hugged each other, giggling. Alex noticed a sudden shadow of sorrow flit across Magda's face.

"I can't convince Miklós. He's been refusing to have a child ever since your miscarriage."

"So does Aziz, but I'm not going to listen to him."

Having their inner strength kindled by each other's presence as well as by the candles they had burned, they left the church feeling excited and much more determined than before. Alex took off her orange espadrilles, which Magda had brought, for she wanted to walk barefoot and feel the earth under her feet. Magda followed suit. They sauntered down the hill arm in arm, watching the glittering rays of sunlight dance on the Sea of Marmara.

"It's so hard to be away from you, Magda."

"You are, after all, happy here, aren't you? I can see it in your eyes that you are." She was gazing straight into Alex's eyes. "You *are* happy, aren't you?" she asked again, holding her hand.

"It's rather difficult to give you a straight answer. I think marriage is about two people trying to get accustomed to each other. Aziz has a heart of gold, but sometimes when he loses his temper, his reactions can be terrifying. Mind you, he never raises his hand against me as he considers such an act of violence way beneath his dignity. He does shout, though. He roars at the top of his lungs, although he doesn't consider it shouting. Sometimes he shouts at the dogs, and I know that he's actually angry with me. However, his fury is very short-lived. A couple of hours later or the next day at the most, he does everything he can to make me forgive him. As I've already said, we're trying to get accustomed to each other. What I find difficult to get used to is the lifestyle here. I miss my freedom so much."

"Aziz is head over heels in love with you. It's so obvious in everything he does. You've made the right decision, Alex."

Her sister's words brought Rudi to her mind, a thought she had managed to keep at bay for quite a while now, an image that seemed to have blurred in the distant past. "What's he up to nowadays?" she asked without much thought.

Magda, of course, understood whom she was talking about. "We don't get to see each other much. He's far too busy, travelling all the time. They say he's now one of the most prominent financiers in the country, in addition to being the most well-known lawyer. He's still very much into his tennis, of course, with very high aspirations – the Olympics. He's incredibly ambitious. No girlfriends, or rather no one he has introduced to us as his girlfriend so far. You know how he is, very secretive in these matters. To be honest, I think he's become even more ruthless in his relationships with women than ever before. He'd never settle down. You've been very clever in your decision, Alex. His lifestyle is intolerable."

Unwilling to listen to his stories anymore, she abruptly changed the subject. "The view is breathtaking here, isn't it? Shall we paint?"

They spotted a pine tree to lean on with a trunk large enough to accommodate them both. They spread their blanket on the ground, took out their painting materials and started to paint while nibbling from the picnic basket Asiye *Hanım* had filled with the food she had insisted was good for them. They savoured the spinach pies and the slices of bread generously spread with liver pâté, concluding their make-shift feast with the extra-sweet syrupy Turkish dessert, apparently not so good for them but claimed by many to be a must at the end of any meal. A short while later Alex, having lost interest in the view, began drawing her sister. Her hair was longer now like Alex's, reaching down to her shoulders, which made her remember one of her mother's sardonic remarks: "Both of you might eventually look like a proper woman if you managed to let your hair grow a little bit longer." Alex smiled as she realised that she even missed her mother's surliness.

"I want to buy a *fez*, Alex. There's a craze for it at the moment. It would be great to wear an original."

"We might go to the Grand Bazaar again tomorrow, if you wish."

"I need to buy some presents as well. Éva ..." She leaned over and touched Alex's arm with a slightly mocking smile. "You wouldn't believe it, but she asked me to get her a belly-dancer's outfit with a lot of sequins. Can we find one?"

"Éva, you said?" They giggled. "How is Teodor, by the way? Whom does he look like?"

"He's the spitting image of Józsi. He's only eighteen months old, but already a little count."

They talked about what Károly wrote in his letters, although they had already shared his news a couple of times. They regretted that he could not come and see them, and talked about Ada, though not as lovingly as about their brother. Magda said they should stop being jealous of her; Alex strongly objected. "She has no right to keep him away from his family for such a long time. It's been more than two years, Magda," she grumbled. She made her sister tell her again and again all the gossip in Budapest, although she had already listened to it several times in detail. She avidly listened even to János's successful and rapid rise in the National Railways, and to his secret activities in the illegal Hungarian Communist Party. She was sorry to hear that János and Margit had split up before Christmas, but rejoiced over hearing that they were closer than before as two old friends. She could not help but hope that perhaps Margit might finally respond to Sándor's love for her, then thought Magda was right in saying that Sándor did not stand a chance, for little Margit needed someone strong like János who could protect and guide her. Magda recounted how madly in love she still was with her husband Miklós, and how they spent every minute of the day together. She talked about the ceramics they made at the workshop in their garden, about the exhibitions they had opened and about how adorable her in-laws were. Magda was lucky, truly lucky. Mother was right, thought Alex. I couldn't take her as an example. I couldn't find someone like Miklós. I couldn't fall in love with a man who could be my husband.

The sun was about to set when they returned home.

40

"Four Hearts."

Was it the right bid? Perhaps she should have declared Three No Trumps. Well, never mind, she thought. She was craving for a cigarette. Her baby moved inside her as if she had read her mind and were trying to help her overcome her urge to smoke. She touched her belly and stroked it through the pleats of her loose dress. She was four-and-a-half months pregnant. This time she had kept her baby. She had felt that she was pregnant the moment she had conceived it, and, from the very beginning, she protected it with all her might, trying not let it go anywhere. It was rapidly growing inside her.

Throughout November, she had done everything to convince Aziz to take her with him to the hunting party in Italy, insisting that his Italian friends were taking their wives along and that İskender's wife Feyha wanted to join them as well. She used every seduction technique she knew and eventually made him take her to Italy, where she succeeded in getting pregnant although Aziz was away shooting all day and was very tired in the evenings, ready to fall asleep as soon as he touched the pillow. Her pregnancy was like the exceptionally bright sun unexpectedly showing through the clouds after a drearily lonesome grey autumn. She had hidden her pregnancy from Aziz, for she dreaded that he might ask her to have an abortion – to kill her baby! At the moment, she no longer ran the risk of an ectopic pregnancy, but could not bring herself to break the news to him since she was scared of his reaction to her having kept it a secret for so long.

It was Aziz's turn to make a bid. Alex looked at him. His eyes had moved away from the cards in his hands and were fixed on Alex's fingers moving among the pleats of her dress. Had he noticed? She sat up on her chair, pulled away her hand from her belly and placed it on the edge of the table. "Come on, Aziz. It's your turn."

"Three No Trumps."

"Aziz? What are you doing? You can't bid Three No Trumps."

"I'm sorry. What was your declaration, Alex?"

"Four Hearts."

"Four Spades, then."

Everybody passed. İskender made his opening. Aziz placed his cards on the table. Alex always found it difficult to concentrate when it was her turn to play the contract, and this time she had completely lost it. She was staring blankly at the cards fanned out in her hand. She played with difficulty and went down by two tricks. Aziz flared up like a dry leaf.

"You really needed to try very hard to go down with such a hand, Alex!" He jumped to his feet, bringing his hands firmly down on the table. "Are you going to pull yourself together or shall we play Chase the Ace?"

"Give me a break, Aziz. Please."

"Come on, now. It's just a game," interrupted Feyha as she stood up. "Come along Alex. Let's bring in the fruit."

* * *

As soon as the guests left, all hell broke loose. Aziz was furious and started shouting like mad.

"You'll get rid of it, first thing tomorrow morning! I'm not going to sacrifice you for a child."

"Nobody can touch my baby. Nobody!" Alex was repeating the same thing over and over again through her sobs, sitting on the sofa with her arms clasped around her belly and her knees drawn closer to her body. "You'll have to kill me first," she burst out, suddenly jumping to her feet. She ran out of the drawing room and into Aziz's study. She could still hear him shouting. Opening the gun cabinet, she grabbed the double-barrelled rifle and returned to the drawing room. "Do you want to kill my baby?" she cried out, pressing the rifle onto his chest. "Then you'll have to kill me first. Do you understand? You'll have to shoot me first!"

Aziz snatched the rifle from her hands and seized her arm. "This is not a game, Alex. Don't you realise what a great risk you're taking?"

"There's no risk any more. It's been four and a half months now!"

"I truly can't believe that you've taken such a decision single-handedly. How could you do such a thing to me?"

"I haven't decided on my own. We've done it together."

"You've taken a fatal risk, Alex, all on your own without even letting me – your husband – know about it! You've been lying to me for months. What else is there that you hide from me, eh? My God, you could have died. You'll drive me to my grave, Alex, if you continue like this. God, please help me. Grow up, Alex! Grow up, for God's sake!"

All of a sudden, Alex stopped crying. She fell dead silent. I'm not scared of anything, she thought. I have no fear. Nothing, neither Aziz nor death nor anything else can deter me from having this baby. She turned around and walked towards their bedroom, calm in her firm determination, murmuring to herself with her arms still tightly clasped around her belly. "I won't let anyone kill my baby. Nobody can touch her. Nobody!"

Next morning she stayed in bed until she heard Aziz shut the door behind him as he left the flat. The doorbell rang when she was having her morning coffee. The boy from the florist was standing at the door, holding forty-one yellow roses with a delicate coral tint around their petals. She opened the card Aziz had placed on the wrapping.

I beg forgiveness from the world's most beautiful mother-to-be

First, the edges of her sulking lips curved slightly upwards, then she embraced the roses in bursts of laughter, planting kisses on Aziz's card, not minding the thorns scratching her arms. She pirouetted along the corridor with the bouquet held close to her chest and glided into the kitchen to give Asiye *Hanım* a hug.

"I'm going to be a mother, Asiye *Hanım!* I'm going to be a mother! A mother!" she sang before dashing out of the kitchen and into her bedroom. She put some decent clothes on, grabbed her purse and ran back into the corridor. "I'm going to the post office." She had to send a telegram to Magda and Károly to let them know of this great piece of news.

Aziz came home early from work that evening. He asked Alex to forgive him, begging her to try to understand his reaction while he placed a topaz pendant around her neck.

"For me, there's nothing in the world more precious than you, Alex. I'm unbearably scared of losing you."

They celebrated her pregnancy with tears in their eyes; Aziz showered her with kisses throughout the evening. He said that they should talk to her gynaecologist tomorrow and that she should go to Budapest if he allowed her to travel. He wanted Alex to spend the rest of her pregnancy with her mother and stay there until after the birth of their child. Alex's feet were practically off the ground with happiness. She thought she should send another telegram to Magda and *Öcsi* first thing in the morning and another one to her mother. She would be going to Budapest. She felt the urge to share the emotions she would not be able to express in a telegram and took out her writing papers.

Istanbul, 3rd April 1935

My darling Magda,

You will have received my good news by the time this letter reaches you, but I wanted to write to you in any case. I have two pieces of great news for you. The first one is that Aziz has finally learned that I'm pregnant. Initially, he created havoc but eventually calmed down. Now I can enjoy my pregnancy to my heart's content. The second piece of good news is that I'm coming to Budapest. Yes! Your pregnant sister is coming to Budapest! I'll be staying there until after the birth. I will certainly need to stay a bit longer after that as well. I can't put into words how excited I am. We'll be together, Magda. We'll be together during the delivery. I want you to take my baby into your arms as soon as it is born and say something into its little ears. I want it to smell you and to hear your voice because anything I do without you seems incomplete. It's going to be our baby, Magda. It'll start its life in our arms. I'm so utterly happy that I'm scared I might be dreaming it all. I won't be able to write anymore for I'm too excited to even hold my pen straight.

    With much longing and love as always, I send you my warmest kisses.
    Your other half,
    Alex

That night, for the first time since her marriage, Alex fell asleep with a sense of joy in her heart that was beyond description and slept like a baby through the night without a dream to remember.

41

The blue wagons of the Orient Express started to pull out of Sirkeci Train Station in Istanbul at precisely ten o'clock. Alex leaned out the window to wave goodbye to Haldun, Necla, Ayla and her baby daughter Yasemin, who gradually shrank in size as the train rumbled out of the station. She was going to Budapest, to her beloved city, after three long years. It had taken her days to pack. They were travelling with three large trunks, but she was still unsure if she had taken everything she would need. Had she taken her orange dress? Well, it was not so important since she could buy anything she needed in Budapest. She was going home. She was going to see Andrássy Boulevard. The Danube. The lilac trees. Would they be in blossom by now? It was May, so they should be. The violet flowers of her beloved lilac trees, a sight for sore eyes, coyly swaying against the heart-shaped dark green leaves accentuating their beauty. And the wisteria, its magical perfume permeating through the whole city – it must be flowering too. A great sense of joy invaded her. I'm pregnant, and I'm going to Budapest. What else could I wish for? When her gynaecologist İbrahim Osman at the Teşvikiye Clinic in Istanbul had told her that she could travel, she had showered him with kisses, unable to believe her luck. "I'm going to Budapest with my baby inside me," she said almost inaudibly, as if trying to make herself believe it. Life was so beautiful. She nestled her head against her husband's chest. She was so happy, so very happy.

It proved to be a very long trip for her despite all the comforts of the wood-panelled compartment of the wagon-lit. Aziz used all his talent to entertain her and they played several good games of bridge with the couple from Ankara travelling in the next compartment. Finally when the train's long whistle told them that they were approaching the Keleti Train Station in Budapest, her baby started to move, as though it had felt what was going on from the thundering heart of its mother. She smiled. She would be in Rózsadomb in a couple of hours. Rózsadomb ... Magda ... her mother ... Károly. Her cruel brother was still in Paris, but he might come to see her, she hoped. She would be seeing her friends, Margit, János, Éva, Józsi, their son Teodor ... Teodor was two and a half years old now. How sweet he must be. And Rudi? Would she see him as well? Would they run into each other somewhere – him probably with his arm around his wife? She quickly shook her head to send away the truculently dispiriting thought and asked Aziz to lower the window. She wanted to smell Budapest. The train was slowly entering the station. Was it Magda standing there on the platform? Yes, yes it was her. Then she saw her mother behind Magda and could no longer hold back her tears.

They got into their raven-black car, impeccably lustrous, to the envy of many. She had missed it all so very much, the red velvet seats, the mahogany panelling daily polished to perfection by their driver Ádám, the tassels dangling from the two tiny lampshades and even the minibar, details that now meant a lot to her, details that meant home. All the way to Rózsadomb, sitting between her mother and Magda, she did not let go of their hands except for when she wanted to hug Magda, which was almost every two seconds. She breathed in the long-missed perfume of the roses of Rózsadomb, the welcoming fragrance of her lilac trees longingly waiting for her at the garden gate, and the sweet odours of her childhood impregnated in the walls of their house. She wished she could put all these smells into a bottle and take them with her to Istanbul to use sparingly as an exquisite perfume on her skin, to smell whenever she yearned for home and to spread on her wounds as a healer from her childhood. Hand in hand with Magda, she strolled around the salons, the rooms, the bathrooms, the basement, the attic and every little corner of the garden. She engraved each tiny detail into her mind to make sure that she did not and would not forget them. She noticed how her mother, despite her fifty years, had not changed a bit, how Aunt Irén was, as always, well-groomed and in excellent spirits, and how Aunt Etel looked so old next to them. In fact, Aunt Etel had always looked aged, but now she really was, perhaps because of the excess weight she had put on, or perhaps because of the darkness that had captured her soul after the death of Uncle Kelemen. Her brown hair, which used to make her pale complexion look whiter than it already was, had gone white, with a particularly snow-white patch extending from her right temple, making her skin look dark to match her spirit in tone. She looked not fifty-seven but easily seventy-seven winters old.

After the excitement of the first few days subsided, Alex felt as if she had never left Budapest. A soothing silk cloth seemed to be spread over her frayed nerves. She was as light as a feather, a bird out of a cage. A week later Aziz went back to Istanbul, happy to have left his wife in safe hands.

In June, despite Gizella's insistence, they did not move to Balatonfüred for the summer. Alex wanted to be close to Magda as well as to their friends, for she had not yet quenched her nostalgia for life in Budapest. Throughout summer, Magda came to Budapest from Verőce almost every day. On some weekends Miklós joined her, and they stayed overnight in Rózsadomb. Alex and Magda spent hours together, traipsing around the city day in and day out, making up for the time they had spent away from each other, so much so that at one point Miklós had to admit that he was beginning to be jealous of their intimacy. Alex was greatly inspired and produced a series of paintings glowing with joyful vitality, contrary to those melancholic aquarelles she had been painting during the last two years much to the dismay of everyone around her who found them impossibly bleak. She called all her friends, inviting them over or going out with them to lunches and dinners. She wanted the whole world to know that she was pregnant. She took advice from Éva on motherhood, and they dreamt about the future of their children. She listened to what Margit had been learning at the nursing school, her new venture, which – God only knows why – she had taken up with great enthusiasm. She was happy to see her friend take such immense pleasure out of helping others, but sad to notice how she tried to hide her undying love for János behind a veil of friendship. She was bored to tears as János, even darker and more serious than he had ever been with his new unruly beard covering almost all his face, talked about politics in escalating doses. She learned how Hitler's Germany was discarding the Versailles Treaty article by article, how some Hungarians, hoping that their country would get back some of the territories it had lost by the Treaty of Trianon, admired Hitler just for that reason, and how János thought that communism was the only way out for their country. She smiled at Fábián's monologues, which she actually found abominable but nevertheless tolerated, for they, being exclusively made up of love, sex and infidelity, lightened up the gloominess of János, while she could not help but be amazed at how Rózsi could pretend that she knew nothing about the continual short-term extramarital relationships of her husband.

Károly did not come from Paris but only sent several letters. Despite the worldwide mania for travelling, he said, he could not move an inch, since he was working very hard designing advertisement posters. He had enclosed a photograph of the poster he had recently created for the ocean liner *Normandie* – an impressive modern design giving the onlooker a feeling of being squashed underneath the gargantuan ship. He also wrote about the latest news, rumours and gossip about a lot of artists, the most shocking of them all being the marriage between Raoul Kuffner, the owner of the manor house neighbouring their estate in Eger, to Tamara de Lempicka. Paris did in fact keep Károly busy.

At the end of August Aziz came back to Budapest. And on the second day of September, after a fairly swift and easy labour, Alex gave birth to Nilüfer – or Nili as she preferred to call her – who literally flew out in the blink of an eye, causing her mother virtually no pain. Alex felt that she was at a turning point in her life. She had finally made it. This time, she had not lost someone she deeply loved. Not listening to her mother's advice, she categorically refused to hire a nanny, since she wanted to look after her baby herself. Aziz kept saying that he now had two people in his life who were most precious to him and was quite unwilling to separate from them when the time came for him to leave for Istanbul a week after the delivery. Alex, having convinced Aziz that it would be much better for Nili not to travel until she was at least a few months old, as they had been advised by her doctor, remained in Budapest. The autumn and the winter that followed proved to be the happiest time of her life. Unable to part from her daughter, she took her everywhere, even on the bone-chilling days of winter. They went to Kengyel to pay a visit to Sándor. She showed her the playroom, the lake, the horses, the deer, the pheasants, the acacia-lined road, the hunting lodge, the dogs, everything. They breathed in the smell of the earth, of the trees, of Kengyel. They went to Verőce and stayed over at Magda's, who welcomed Nili as if she were her own, admitting that her desire to become a mother had intensified a thousand-fold ever since the arrival of her little niece. They made ceramics together that carried Nili's tiny fingerprints. And finally when Aziz came back for Christmas, the pieces of the puzzle were complete. That Christmas was almost as merry as the Christmases of her childhood, for she had all her loved ones with her except for Károly.

Right after New Year's Eve, she returned to Istanbul with her four-month-old baby.

"Welcome home, little Nili."

Alex found her home shipshape and ready to embrace the new member of their family. During the eight months of her absence, Asiye *Hanım*, considering it her duty to keep their home running smoothly, had continued to cook a hot meal for the man of the house every single day, although Aziz had spent most of his time with his mother at Haldun Pasha Mansion. Alex lovingly placed the little clothes she had brought from Budapest into the drawers in Nili's bedroom. Despite her mother's and Magda's insistence, she had persevered in her refusal to bring a nanny with her to Istanbul. She was not only unwilling to entrust Nili to the care of a stranger, but also hungrily desirous of enjoying every instant of her daughter's existence. Aziz continually nagged her, saying that she had lost too much weight, especially because she had to wake up several times during the night to check on Nili, and told her to stop being so stubborn about not letting him hire a governess. Alex, however, could not care less if she was tired, frail or skinny. Once, in the middle of a very crucial moment during their lovemaking, Alex heard Nili cry and jumped out of bed to run to her daughter, leaving Aziz midway. She had fallen asleep in Nili's bedroom, an unfortunate incident that had not provoked a very pleasant reaction in Aziz, who, in the morning, firmly declared that they had to put a stop to this nonsense, grumbling that he would not allow a small creature to ruin their lives. She could not believe Aziz being so selfish. Was he jealous even of her attention for their daughter? He should learn how to sacrifice his pleasures for a while. She was not going to leave her baby in anybody's care, not after having ached for her for so long.

In February, Aziz's family decided to erect a five-storey apartment building in one section of the garden of the mansion. Alex could not understand the motive behind Aziz's desire to move there along with the rest of his family when it was finished, claiming that it would mean the end of all their problems. Did they have a problem? Was Nili a problem? What did he think – that she would leave Nili with Mehpare *Hanım* at night just to let Aziz enjoy a more comfortable sex life? He must have gone mad! Alex started to brood darkly over how to make Aziz change his mind about moving to the new apartment building. She would surely find a way.

42

Everything had a new meaning with her baby – or rather everything finally had a meaning. Spring swished by before she even realised it had arrived, and, with the onset of the balmy days of early summer, the nine-month-old Nili, who had been a rather fragile baby so far, finally showed signs of plumping up. Alex took her out every day for some fresh air. On some days, which was at least three times a week, she let her take her nap in her pushchair by the tennis court in their back garden while she played tennis with Lucienne, a French lady who, with her husband Abdülhak Hamit *Bey*, had moved to the flat downstairs a couple of months ago.

They had done the same thing this morning, and after the game Alex had invited Lucienne upstairs for a chat. They had changed into their swimming costumes and were now basking in the sun on the balcony, sipping their lemonades. Alex was thinking how she had never before loved being in Istanbul so much.

"Has Aziz decided on a surname yet?" asked Lucienne. A law had been issued back in 1934 requiring every Turkish citizen to take a surname and register it no later than within two years.

"Yes, he did. It'll be Giritli. What about you?"

"We've decided on Tarhan."

Alex felt very close to Lucienne, who was a very sweet lady and, although four years older than Alex's mother, was like a friend to her, being incredibly young at heart.

She took a sip from her lemonade, relaxed on her chair and turned her face to the sun. Life was so beautiful.

"I'm really sorry that the Hungarian tennis team was beaten in the second round. I truly wish somebody had defeated the Nazis." Lucienne was talking about the match played two weeks ago at the International Lawn Tennis Challenge.

"So do I," said Alex. "A friend of mine was on the team – Rudolf Takács. I know him rather well." She felt a wave of heat rising towards her neck. After taking another sip from her lemonade, she stood up and moved to a chair in the shade of the umbrella. "It's awfully hot today, isn't it?"

With the experience of her fifty-three years, Lucienne seemed to have understood why Alex was feeling so hot, probably better than Alex herself did. "Was he your boyfriend?" she asked, smiling softly.

Alex hesitated for a second, not quite knowing what to say. This was a subject strictly forbidden in this household. "He was my fiancé," she replied, somewhat timidly.

"How is your brother? And your sister?" asked Lucienne, changing the subject; the expression on Alex's face must have told her that she should ask no further questions about Rudolf Takács.

"Károly has had enough of being short of money. They're considering moving back to Budapest, but he can't seem to make up his mind. Magda, on the other hand, is very happy. I can't tell you how much I miss her. I'm trying to convince her to come to Istanbul this summer. It's only been a short while since we've seen each other but the more I see her, the more I want to be with her. You'd love her, I'm sure."

They heard the doorbell ring. It was Necla. "Why on earth did she have to come now at this hour?" Alex thought, cringing at the unasked-for surprise. She made to stand up but then gave up the idea and waited until Necla approached the French windows opening on to the balcony. "Hello?" she said in a tone that sounded more like, "Why are you here?" "Why didn't you bring Osman?" she enquired, her dull voice betraying a strong note of indifference. She gestured to Asiye *Hanım* to bring another glass of lemonade for their new guest.

"He's running a fever. I shan't stay long. I just wanted to see Nilüfer." She turned to Lucienne. "We don't get to see her much, you know."

These reproachful remarks drove Alex mad. Wasn't it enough that she took her daughter to the family mansion every single day? Was she supposed to carry her to Necla's as well? They had much better things to do together, mother and daughter.

Trying to stay away from the sun, Necla sat in the armchair Asiye *Hanım* had moved closer to the balcony, drank her lemonade, showed some care and attention to Nili and left as fast as she had come. Lucienne, on the other hand, heartily urged by Alex, stayed for lunch and afternoon tea as well. They chatted about Istanbul, about Paris and about Budapest. Alex related how in February one of her other sisters-in-law, Sema, had been elected from her constituency in Adana to become one of first female deputies in the Turkish Grand National Assembly.

When Aziz came home from work in the evening, Lucienne had long gone, but Alex was still on the balcony, busy with the painting she had started that afternoon. She had been painting sunsets lately. The orange skies had a strange effect on her.

"Hello," she said without getting up.

"And hello to you too, Madame Gauguin."

She could not quite figure out whether Aziz was paying her a compliment or just being sarcastic. Her style had nothing to do with Gauguin's, but she was reading books on his life lately, and that was probably why Aziz had rechristened her with this new nickname.

"How was your day, Aziz?"

"Splendid."

She did not quite like the inflexion of his voice, knowing too well that he assumed this ironic tone only when he was extremely furious but tried to suppress his rage. His eyes were as dark as a sky prone to an imminent thunderstorm. This was one of those moments when she needed to get out of his sight. "I'll get Asiye *Hanım* to set the table right away," she said before excusing herself to go and check on Nili.

Her daughter was sleeping deeply. How very beautiful she was. Alex heard the sound of the wardrobe in their bedroom shut. Aziz must be changing. She leaned over Nili's cot and, taking care not to wake her up, silently breathed in the sweet smell of her skin, that unequalled perfume which was priceless for her. I don't care about anything as long as I have you, my darling. Not a single thing.

Hoping that whatever had upset Aziz had lost its effect, she returned to the drawing room. He had prepared two glasses of *rakı* and was already sitting in his place at the head of the table. His eyes were still abysmally dark. God help me, she thought, as she perched on her chair on Aziz's right. In tense silence, they watched Asiye *Hanım* serve the mincemeat-stuffed eggplants with pilaff rice.

"You may leave now, Asiye *Hanım*," said Aziz. "We'll manage the rest, thank you."

They ate without uttering a single word. When they were about to finish the food on their plates, they heard Asiye *Hanım* go out by the service door.

"I'll bring the olive oil dish. We have butter beans," muttered Alex as she made to stand up, only to collapse back onto her chair when she heard Aziz roar her name.

"Alex! Do you want to make my family the ridicule of all Istanbul, for God's sake?"

She could not raise her eyes from the remains of the eggplant shrivelled up on one side of her empty plate.

"Ever since you came back from Budapest, you seem to have forgotten where you're living. Isn't it enough that you run around Nişantaşı after Goya and Pepa with your low necklines as if you were ..." He turned his blazing eyes up to the ceiling, then brought his fist down on the table with all the force of his body. The knives and forks rattled as Alex's heart skipped a beat. "It apparently isn't enough since you sunbathe on the balcony in a swimming costume. I can't believe it! You're impossible, Alex! You're crazy! Out of your mind! Why on earth don't you go to our mansion in Baltalimanı? You have everything there, the garden, the sun, whatever you want. What else do you want? To drive me insane?"

Alex had had enough of his jealousies. She tore her eyes away from her plate and, with all the courage she could muster, looked at Aziz in the face, if not in the eye, before she blurted out, "I'm sick and tired of you and of your family being so conservative. Doesn't Necla have anything better to do than gossip? I don't want her to come to this house again."

"Hold it there, young lady!" roared Aziz, jumping to his feet. "You listen to me now and listen very well!" he roared again. "You seem to be forgetting whose house this is. My family can come and go as and when they wish to do so." He was tapping the tip of his finger on the table as if to show where he meant they could come. "I don't want to hear any more such remarks from you ever again. Is that clear?"

Alex saw flashes of madness in his eyes. "They have no right to interfere with our private life, Aziz," she mumbled meekly.

"Of course, they do. And if you don't like it, you'll have to go back where you've come from." His finger sticking out of his fist was directed towards the door now.

Alex had a few more things in her mind that she meant to say, but Aziz's last words drove them all out. Did he really think that way? No! He must have said it in a fury. He did say it though. "What do you mean, Aziz?" she asked, her voice begging for an apology. "You must have had too much to drink."

"You heard what I said. You ought to mind your manners."

Her heart was sinking deeper and deeper. She took another sip from her *rakı* and then another one. Aziz was still shouting, but she wasn't hearing any of it. Why was she still sitting there? Why didn't she just leave the table and go to her room? Actually, it didn't really matter anymore. He no longer scared her but only broke her heart, hurt her a little bit more each time he shouted like that. She took another sip. Her jaws tightened as tears clouded her eyes. She should not cry. She tried not to listen, not to hear. Think of something else, Alex. Listen to the music. It's so beautiful. Listen to it.

Aziz was holding her arm. How long had it been? A couple of hours? She could not tell. They were still at the table. The empty plates had gone. She had a new plate in front of her, full of butter beans soaked in olive oil.

"I'm so sorry, Alex. I'm really terribly sorry. I don't know what I'm saying. Please forgive me. You know that I can't do without you. I love you. I love you so very much."

"You're hurting me," she said dryly, trying to wrench her arm free from his grip. She wanted to get up and go to her room, but Aziz would not let go of her. "Leave me alone!" she demanded as she brusquely turned her head away from him.

Aziz slowly released her arm, but Alex could not stand up. She picked up her fork and started to fidget with the beans on her plate. She took one into her mouth. It tasted of nothing. "What am I doing?" she asked herself. Her mother's words hurried into her mind. Had she really jumped out of the frying pan into the fire? To think that I could spend all my life with Aziz just because he loves me. What naivety! What ignorance! Besides, how much does he really love me? What kind of love is it? Is it possible to hurt a loved one so much? This was love of the most ghastly kind. It strangled her. She was suffocating. Her soul was swiftly falling down into a dark well of desolation. This city depressed her. What was she doing here all alone, away from everyone? It was all Rudi's fault. She was here because of him. He was the one who had driven her into this solitary existence. She wondered what he might be doing right now. Perhaps he was married. Perhaps he had a pregnant wife. Her pride did not let her ask anyone anything about him, and no one told her anything anymore.

June 2004
Istanbul

Rüya reluctantly nibbled at her food. After a few forkfuls, she gave up trying to swallow whatever she had in her mouth, which seemed to have doubled in size, and excused herself from the table. Her already unhealthy appetite had disappeared altogether. The knot that had grasped her stomach when she had left the hospital earlier on had grown into a huge web. With her mind benumbed to blankness in self-preservation, she went straight into Mami's bedroom, sat on her bed and, taking out her nightgown from under her pillow, pressed it to her nose to breathe in her heart-warming smell. A strong pain spread from her chin towards her temples. Her eyes burned. What shall I do without her, she thought with a strong sense of panic? What shall I do without her love? How can I survive without her? She buried her face in the nightgown, her whole body convulsing with sobs. You can't leave us. You can't leave me. This is unfair. "Unfair!" she repeated again and again among her sobs as her fists clenching the nightgown hit her knees, giving expression to her helpless agony.

I think of how much I've missed my sister as I watch her lying in the deckchair under the shielding tranquillity of the veranda.

"Happiness is neither in the past nor in the future," she says in her unruffled voice. "Yesterday is history, and tomorrow is only speculation. Neither of them is real but a veil that prevents you from realising your dreams. You can only be happy if you live the moment, if you can see the reality of this very instant as it actually is."

I'm somewhat confused. "What does it mean to see the reality of this very instant as it actually is?" I ask. "I see everything, don't I?"

"Think again." She sits up and takes the glass of lemonade. "Lemonade. It might be a refreshing and sweetly lemon-flavoured drink for you, but for me it's too sour and too cold. It might as well be far too sweet for someone else. Life, of course, is not like lemonade. It is, however, very similar. Everyone

perceives life differently because everyone lives through a different life and carries different scars that trigger different fears. To be able to understand the true taste of lemonade, we need to face our scars from the past and our fears about the future."

Why is that important, I ask myself? It serves no purpose but to torture myself, to grind dirt into my cut, to accept that I'm doomed to be alone, to be abandoned, to lose all my loved ones ...

"It's important," she says, reading my thoughts, "because if you ignore your scars, the nightmares you try to bury in your subconscious creep out and haunt you at the most unexpected moment. The fears these scars spread into your heart close all doors. It's only when you face your fears and let the reasons behind them surface that you begin to get to know yourself."

I think I know myself pretty well.

"Do you? Do you really know yourself or do you just think you do?" she asks as she rises to her feet. "Come with me," she says, holding out her hand. Her movements are as light as a feather floating in the air.

We walk down the steps of the veranda, glide along the garden and reach the shore. I feel the warmth of the white sand underneath my feet. As we tread along the wet sand where the waves lick the shore, our feet are covered with sand, which the waves soon wash away.

Rüya's sobbing had stopped, but her silent tears kept on rolling down her cheeks. Her blank gaze was fixed on the slightly open door of the lilac wardrobe. She stood up with a spontaneous sense of curiosity – the instinctive nosiness that used to seize her as a small child. A strong sob shook her body like an aftershock. She was rather timid about peeping into the wardrobe. Quietly and tentatively she pulled its door open and burst out crying in racking spasms as soon as she saw the packets of dried apricots piled on top of each other. She rushed back to the bed and sank her head in the pillow. Weeping, she breathed in Mami's smell. Eventually, her wailing turned into a persistent cough. She needed to drink some water. She stood up. The door of the wardrobe was still open. As she cast another look at the dried apricots, she caught a glimpse of the lower shelves. They were packed with notebooks she had never seen before. They ought to be Mami's sketchbooks, although they looked different from the simple notebooks she used. Some had leather covers, tattered and worn out, mostly faded.

She knelt down. Her coughing had stopped. Timidly she took the notebook on the very top. It said 1955-56 on it. She flipped through its pages. It was Mami's handwriting. Was it her diary? She reached out for the other notebooks. 1932 ... 1919 ... There was a black one, really worn out, larger than the rest. She opened it. On the first page, was written, "Budapest, 1944." The handwriting was not Mami's. Most of the pages bore brief notes and pencil drawings. Underneath one of them, was scribbled, "Károly de Kurzón." She quickly put them all back and hurriedly shut the wardrobe before storming out of the room and into the kitchen. She opened the fridge, took out a bottle of water and poured herself a glass with trembling hands. A second later she was putting the glass back on the counter without knowing if she had drunk the water in it or not. Her mind was at the lilac wardrobe.

Suddenly she noticed her mother Aslı standing by the other end of the kitchen. Her vacant eyes were ranging over the empty water bottles neatly lined up on the counter. She moved one bottle an inch back and another an inch forward, checking if they were properly aligned, then sliding each bottle slightly to the right or to the left as if she wanted all of them to be at exactly the same distance from one another. Her actions seemed automatic, for her mind was apparently somewhere else. Warm tears were falling down onto the cold marble countertop. Rüya went behind her and embraced her drooping shoulders, resting her cheek on her head.

"I no longer want to be strong, Rüya," she mumbled, finally leaving the bottles alone. "When you're strong, you have to shoulder everyone's burden," she continued, her fingers wiping away the teardrops on the marble, "you have to keep on standing on your feet. You have to hide your suffering and look happy. You have no right to be sad. Nobody helps the strong. I want to be weak, fragile ... I want to deserve others' compassion. I want to be helped out. I don't want to shoulder anything anymore. I want to be pitied rather than condemned." Sobs choked her words.

They heard Daphné crying upstairs in her room.

"Go and take a look, Rüya, would you? See what's wrong with her."

Rüya hesitated for a moment before she left the kitchen and slowly walked across the hall. Then, with gradually increasing strides, she quickly climbed the stairs, went into the room she shared with Daphné and sat on the little girl's bed.

"Hush baby, hush. It was just a dream," she whispered, stroking her silky blond hair and giving her a kiss. She then snuggled down by her and, hugging her tightly, closed her own eyes. "It was nothing but a bad dream."

A Hungarian Rhapsody
A Novel in Three Acts
Act One, Tableau Two
1936 - 1939

43

During the long eight months Alex had stayed in Budapest, she had found it rather hard to believe that Károly could not find the time or the money to come to Budapest to see her, not even for one brief stay, but she had accepted it. She had been offended but had tried to understand. This time, however, she was truly hurt. She did not know how she could ever forgive him for this. The cold and dry telegram he had sent in July, informing her that he and Ada had returned to Budapest, was curtly followed by another in early August, breaking her heart irreparably.

We married STOP

In her letter, Magda said that they had married without letting anyone know. Her mother wrote that she would never forgive Ada, bitterly concluding, "I wouldn't have expected anything better from that girl anyway." *Anyuká* was right. For the first time, she was right. Why did he do it? Was it his way of declaring his independence? No! It had nothing to do with independence or freedom. He had simply ignored his family. This treacherous behaviour from her brother was far worse, much more excruciatingly painful, than having been apart from him for four long years. She felt betrayed and found it unbearable that he did not want to share the happiest day of his life with Alex and with his family.

At long last, his letter arrived; he must have finally thought that he should at least have the courtesy to scribble a few lines.

Budapest, 17th August 1936

My little Alex,
I knew that you'd be furious, but we thought it would be better if we tied the knot without letting anyone know ...

It would be much better, my dearest *Öcsi,* if you had said, "Ada thought," wouldn't it? She could not even imagine the shock and pain her mother must have felt. How on earth had he found it in his heart to deprive them from celebrating such an event?

... When this letter finds you, your little pumpkin – *our* little pumpkin – will probably be celebrating her first birthday. I wish our little one a healthy and lucky life. I'm also a family man now, Alex, but we're rather far away from the idea of having any children yet. First, we should sort out our own lives and settle down. I'll be starting a special course on advertising and window dressing at the Budapest Academy of Commerce. Your brother will be a student again, a thirty-year-old mature novice. I do continue painting, of course. Finally, I surrendered my soul to my true love: Surrealism. It has permeated through my whole being and invaded my soul. I'm just letting myself drift in its irresistibly tempting embrace. I'm so excited, so full of energy. We're planning to rent a studio in Szentendre. Endré (Bálint) and Lajos (I don't remember if you've met Lajos Vajda) live there. We spend most of our time with them. I wish you could see my paintings. Surreal creatures floating behind a brume ... A poet friend christened my last painting: *Monsters of the Orange Mist.*

I know that you're not interested in politics at all, but I can't help put in a few lines. First and foremost, my most insincere congratulations for the "Nazi Olympics," with special thanks to those friends who had the heart and the mind to refuse to participate. János says, "Shame on those who participated and lost." I, on the other hand, simply feel sorry for them. What do you think of the Nazis over there? How does it all sound to you? Here, they have a terrifying resonance. We all know that our Right Honourable Prime Minister Gömbös's intention is to have a Nazi government sooner than later. I hope the best for us all. It makes me sick to see politics trodden down by the likes of him.

The phone was ringing. It was Mehpare *Hanım*.

"Was it you who called a while ago? I couldn't answer it," said Alex flatly.

"What were you doing? Were you taking a bath?"

What is it to you, she wanted to say. "No," she said instead. Did she have to give an explanation for everything she did?

"Well anyway," Mehpare *Hanım* said after a disturbing pause. "We wanted to drop by this afternoon with Ayla. I meant to ask if that would be all right with you."

At long last, they had learned not to come over without calling first.

"Of course, it is. I'd be very happy indeed." She was lying. As usual, she was truly delighted that Ayla would be coming. Mehpare *Hanım*'s presence, however, did nothing but fill her with consternation and alarm. Besides, they would stay until very late and, once Aziz was back from work, would never leave. Have they chosen this very day on purpose or were they still unable to remember that August 28 was their wedding anniversary – a special day to be celebrated in private? They probably did not *want* to remember. The last thing she wanted on such a day was their company, but she had no choice. She could no longer complain to Aziz about his family's comings and goings or, for that matter, about anything else concerning them, fearing his reactions. His insults opened up deep wounds in her heart, widening the distance between them as husband and wife, while his excuses did not suffice to heal her bruised feelings. As a matter of fact, she had to think twice before opening her mouth whatever it was she wanted to talk about, and choose her words most carefully after having calculated what would annoy him or what would win his approval. Such insincerity really upset her, for she believed that she should be able to talk to her husband openly and fearlessly about what she had in mind – be herself, so to speak. That was, of course, if they were fighting on the same front against life. Sometimes she felt as if they were fighting on opposing fronts.

Mehpare *Hanım* and Ayla came late in the afternoon and, as Alex had guessed, stayed until Aziz came back from work. He, just as she expected, insisted that they stay a bit longer, which, of course, they did. Around nine o'clock, Ayla finally excused herself, saying that she had to go back home to her husband and to her dear daughters Yasemin and Azra. Mehpare *Hanım* surprisingly followed suit, saying, "Oh, my Goodness! How could I have forgotten that it was your wedding anniversary today!" She must have decided to be more understanding than her son and grant Alex and Aziz a late night tête-à-tête.

Next day and throughout the autumn and winter months that followed, Aziz went hunting almost every weekend, and when he did not, they spent their time with Mehpare *Hanım* and Aziz's sisters. They hardly saw any of their friends. As a matter of fact, they practically did nothing together. Alex was feeling lonelier and lonelier day by day. She eventually decided that it might be better if she had another baby. Nili ought to have a sister or a brother or both, she mused in reminiscence of Magda and Károly. She ought to taste the love of a sibling.

In February, the construction of the Giritli apartment building was completed. Haldun insisted, and the whole family agreed, on pulling down the mansion to erect another apartment building in its stead, as soon as the rainy season came to an end in April. Alex was devastated at the idea, finding it unbelievably atrocious. How could they even consider demolishing that most attractive house to build yet another horrific edifice of concrete? Why did the exigencies of modernity demand the uprooting of the old and replacing it with monstrosities of a very primitive character – if one could say they had character at all? Why did they have to put up those ghastly structures that served no better purpose than to erase the past from people's memories? Would it not be better to look after the aesthetics of the old, protect them, refashion them so that they could be adapted to the novelties of the times? Apparently it would not, for otherwise the city would not be turning into a concrete monster. Necla and her husband Nezih vacated their flat in Şakayık Street and moved to the first floor of the new apartment building with their son Osman and their little baby girl Selma. The second floor was allocated to Haldun, who was extremely excited about the freedom it would give him in his endeavours as a bachelor, while Ayla and her husband Cevat moved to the third floor with their daughters Yasemin and Azra. The fourth floor, which belonged to Sema, who was busy shuttling between Ankara and Adana, was rented out despite objections from the rest of the family. Aziz, much to Alex's surprise and contentment, agreed to continue living in the Maçka Apartments, and, therefore, his flat on the fifth floor was allotted to the use of Mehpare *Hanım* – a solution that pleased Haldun more than anybody else since otherwise he would have had to share his flat with his mother.

Slowly Alex was getting to the bottom of the intricacies of Aziz's character, discovering ways and means of not making life harder for herself. His jealousy and his consequent violent reactions were not in any way fewer, but Alex had somehow got used to them, or rather no longer cared. Neither his thunderous fits of rage and ruthless bellowing, followed by his pleadings for forgiveness the next morning, if not within a few hours, nor his most fiery expressions of how much he loved her, carried any meaning for her anymore. The time they spent together was so scarce that their life was going round in a mediocre circle, flawlessly gyrated by Alex's efforts to "manage" her husband – a method she detested. Once in a while, her old self woke up from her forced torpor and created havoc. In April, for instance, when their landlord Monsieur Caivano asked the freshly-widowed Lucienne to leave her flat, Alex went berserk. "I can't believe it, Aziz. Neighbours complained about her sunbathing on the balcony half-naked. Half-naked! What is this, for God's sake? Are we living in the Middle Ages or what? Besides, the poor woman still has her mourning clothes on, let alone wearing a swimming costume.

They're being too impertinent. I'll talk to Monsieur Caivano. He might listen to reason for the sake of Uncle Kelemen's memory, if not for anything else." She could not talk to him since Aziz did not let her, nor did he himself have a word with him. Alex and Lucienne, however, continued to wear their swimming costumes and sunbathe throughout the summer months, perhaps not on their balconies, but either in the garden of the Giritli Mansion in Baltalimanı or in Izabella's garden, against the splendid view of the Bosphorus.

Following a heated marathon of lovemaking on the night following Nili's second birthday, Alex whispered, rather apprehensively, in her much-satiated husband's ear that she was three months pregnant. Overcome by a sudden tinge of misgiving upon seeing Aziz express his happiness about this good piece of news without any objections, Alex questioned if he still loved her as much as he used to. The very next morning, however, she was reassured that she was still very precious to him when he said that he would talk to her doctor, and, if required, she should immediately have an abortion.

The doctor said that there was no problem and that she could keep her baby. That evening they had a family dinner on the fifth floor of the Giritli apartment building to celebrate her pregnancy. Alex immediately began planning her trip to Budapest, to which she desperately looked forward as she would be seeing Károly, who had returned home. Aziz, however, refused to let her go. "I can't stay away from you for months, my darling. The doctor says that there is no risk. This time, why don't we invite your mother over here?" Offended, like a child deprived of her favourite toy, she did not talk to Aziz for days. She did everything she could, using all her sexual attraction to make him change his mind, but Aziz persevered. "I'll think about it," he kept saying, although it was obvious that he intended to spend Christmas at home with his wife and his daughter.

Alex wrote to Magda and Károly, begging for their help in the matter.

Istanbul, 9th October 1937

My dearest Magda,

I was hoping that we'd be celebrating our twenty-seventh birthday together. Unfortunately, Aziz deems it unnecessary for me to go to Budapest this time. I can't make him change his mind. He won't give in no matter what I say or do. I'm at my wits' end. I can't even enjoy my pregnancy. Please, I beseech you to write to Aziz right away. Beg him. Devise a white lie. Tell him Mother is ill. Please. You'd know what to say. I miss you all so very much, and you most of all. Whenever I look in the mirror, I imagine that I'm looking at you and start talking to my reflection to ease my longing heart. They would take me for a fool if they saw me.

Aziz listened to no one, and Alex remained in Istanbul. Christmas came and went by, evoking mixed feelings in her, for she was extremely happy to have Nili – now at the sweetest age of two – and exulted at the idea that her second baby was rapidly growing inside her, but at the same time she could not get used to the idea of being away from her sister and brother. Why could they not be together like Aziz and his siblings were? He was so lucky to have his whole family with him. The only person he probably missed was his sister Sema, who was not too far away anyway. No wonder he could not understand her yearning to see her family. The more she mused over these thoughts, the more frustrated she became. In time, her frustration turned into indignation with a strong sense of chagrin simmering underneath it, which often brought Rudi to her mind. She tormented herself thinking that she could have been married to him, living the perfect life in Budapest in her own familiar surroundings, close to her family and to her friends.

44

The new year brought nothing new. Alex, very much pregnant now, was still in Istanbul because Aziz, who kept saying, "I'll think about it," apparently thought about it and decided not to let her go to Budapest. He, on the other hand, did not hesitate to go hunting every weekend, leaving her all alone. Scared of being on her own in the cold and dark winter nights, Alex was happily kept company by her most loyal friend Anastasia, who not only stayed with her throughout her pregnancy but also proved to be an excellent help for Alex in looking after Nili, as if she were her own flesh and blood. She was the only one with whom Alex could entrust Nili since, despite having no children, she was as experienced as a mother of ten. At times Alex had the feeling that even she was not as tender as Anastasia was with Nili. She would make an excellent mother, Alex often thought, regretting that she was still unmarried. She had been turning down all her suitors, making up a myriad of excuses. "He's twenty years my senior! I have no intention of looking after a husband on a deathbed while I'm still young." "They say he's a compulsive gambler." "Too handsome. Not a good asset in a husband." "I can't believe they thought him suitable for me. He's practically a midget, hardly reaching my shoulders." There was one thing in her mind: her career. She was working day and night, waking up at four in the morning to prepare work for the nine girls who worked for her in her dressmaker's studio. Nothing but Nili could divert her attention from her work.

Alex sent letters to her mother entreating her to come to Istanbul, but failed to convince her to do so before mid-February. Gizella arrived a month before Alex was expected to give birth and, only three weeks after her arrival, started to show signs of impatience. "Hurry up, Alex. This child seems to have no intention of coming into this world." She implied her desire to go back to Budapest as soon as possible, since she had been feeling uneasy after Hitler's Third Reich Army had annexed Austria.

Károly, in his last letter, was talking about the black clouds hovering above Budapest. Although not interested in politics at all, Alex was nevertheless distressed at what her brother had written in his most perturbed letter, expressing his apprehensions about having the Nazis so close to Budapest now and his misgivings at Hungary's obligation to be friends with Germany. Aziz, on the other hand, said that a new Germany would be an alternative to capitalism and communism, claiming that this new development offered an opportunity for some, because Germany's rebirth from its ashes would mean the end of the burden that had been weighing heavily on nations defeated at the Great War following the destruction of the whole continent.

A few days later Alex gave birth to her second daughter, and thus ended all her concerns about the dark clouds over Europe, the Nazis and the worries of Károly. They called the little girl Leyla, since a name like Lilac would not be acceptable to Aziz's family although Alex, intentionally or otherwise, mispronounced it and from the first day onwards called her Lila.

Gizella returned to Budapest a week after Lila's birth. A few weeks after her departure, the Orient Express, which had taken Gizella away, brought in Terézia, whom Magda had diligently chosen from among dozens of candidates. Nanny Teréz, who had been a primary school teacher in Verőce, not only proved to be the perfect caretaker for Nili and Lila but also brought a strong and permanent fresh breath of air from Hungary to the Maçka Apartments. Alex, despite her monotonous and almost lustreless relationship with Aziz, spent one of the best springs of her life, completely rejuvenated with the zest and verve her daughters instilled in her. Feeling as sprightly as she used to be in her younger days, she most willingly embraced all her responsibilities, intent on raising her children to the best of her ability.

It was a bright Sunday in June, promising a delightful summer ahead – one of those rare occasions when Aziz was not away from home for the weekend. They were walking on Teşvikiye Avenue towards Mehpare *Hanım*'s for lunch. Alex had put on her white trouser suit which her mother had brought from Budapest, definitely not chosen by her but by Magda, being such a modern outfit. She felt good in it despite Aziz's sarcastic remarks: "Where are we sailing, Captain Alex?" "I can't understand why you want to hide that beautiful waistline of yours." She did not care since everybody they passed by in the street was looking at her with envious admiration.

"Would you please slow down, Mademoiselle Teréz," said Aziz to Teréz, who was walking ahead of them with Lila's pushchair.

As always, Aziz was very smartly dressed and very well groomed. He walked proudly with his head held high, alongside his daughters whom he adored and his wife whom he loved. Alex knew that he was still madly in love with her although he broke her heart at times and left her alone quite often. But why could she not say that she loved him back? She did love him, but he was not the love of her life; he was simply the father of her children. It was more like she loved the way he loved her so much. She loved the way he doted on her daughters so passionately. But she was not in love with him. What was love anyway? Did she want to be in love? Love meant suffering, for it had pain in its nature. Aziz also suffered from time to time. It was his pain that he sought to conquer when he shouted. Was it worth living a life without love? A life like an empty canvas – colourless, square and meaningless.

"Will Yasemin and Azra be there as well, Daddy?"

"Certainly, my love. You'll see all your cousins – Yasemin, Azra, Osman, Selma. The whole family will be there."

Nili started jumping up and down, hanging on to her parents' hands. She seemed so happy. It is such a bliss being a child, thought Alex.

They walked through the heavy iron door of the Giritli apartment building into the white marble-floored hall and went up in the elevator. Mehpare *Hanım* was at the door. She must have been waiting for them at the window and had seen them arrive. Knowing Aziz's punctuality about mealtimes, she showed everyone to the table at exactly half past twelve. Nili, Yasemin, Azra and Osman were also given a place at the table, provided that they proved their table manners to be good enough to allow them to eat with the grown-ups. They perched on their chairs, raised by pillows. Hüseyin, the butler, entered the dining room carrying a large service plate lined with steaming fillets of sea bass.

"Our fishmonger Nejat in Eminönü insisted on sending these over. I couldn't say no although, according to Aziz, fish are not to be eaten in months without an 'r' in their names." Mehpare *Hanım,* sitting at the head of the table, was, of course, referring to the names of the months not in Turkish but in French. They usually spoke Turkish among themselves since Alex's Turkish was almost perfect now, but Mehpare *Hanım*'s sentences were always full of French expressions.

"Mami, should I be using this flat knife for the fish?" whispered Nili, her eyes moving anxiously between her mother and the deboned fillets of fish in front of her as she tried to remember which of the knives and forks lined up on both sides of her plate she needed to use for each dish with the disquietude of a schoolgirl preparing for a tough exam.

"Yes, *tatlım*, the flat knife is for the fish."

"You must keep quiet, Nilüfer," intervened Aziz.

Mehpare *Hanım*, seeing the children struggling with the silver cutlery too heavy for their tiny hands, announced that they could continue using only their forks, an announcement made with the haughty air of a headmistress confirming that her students had passed their exam.

"How is your mother, Alex? And Magda? Károly?" asked Ayla, apparently exclusively curious about how Károly was.

"Magda is very happy. Károly, on the other hand, will soon be moving back to Paris, if you ask me. He obviously won't be staying in Budapest much longer. Lately his letters are brimming with his nostalgia for Paris. He seems not to have learned his lesson. It's as if he enjoyed suffering."

Should she talk about the International Exposition of Surrealism in Paris Károly had mentioned in his last letter, complaining bitterly about not having been there? She secretly revelled in the thought of Aziz's and Mehpare *Hanım*'s shock and fury if they heard the details of the exhibition, where a series of mannequins arranged like prostitutes lined the streets of Paris. She suddenly recalled another detail of Károly's letter, a detail that was most disturbing. "Károly mentions a law that was passed last month, limiting the rights of the Jewish population. He says that Ada's father wouldn't be affected, but I'm still worried."

"He's written to me about it as well. I don't think it's of any consequence," said Aziz, turning to Haldun sitting at the other end of the table as if he were the only one who would understand what he was going to talk about. "According to this new law, certain liberal professions can only be practiced by those who are members of the relevant professional chambers or association. And they limited the number of Jews to be accepted to any such association by twenty per cent of the total number of its members – a quota specified on the basis of the percentage of the population of the minorities to the total population of the country. The same restriction is to be applied to all other minorities as well." He paused before he continued, raising an eyebrow as he looked at Alex. "In brief, they'll be limiting the rights of the Jewish people to do business."

Were lawyers subject to this restriction? What would happen to Rudi and his father? Alex hid the remains of the fish on her plate under the vegetables piled up next to it. She would not be able to finish it. They always put far too much food on her plate. Luckily, Hüseyin appeared to take away the empty plates. Did they still have their law office? She suddenly realised that she had not thought of Rudi for a long time. How long had it been – a month, two months? God, no! Hüseyin was serving *suböreği* now, a most filling cheese turnover, for which Alex had no appetite left whatsoever.

"I wonder what will happen to János's father," she said.

"How should I know?" burst out Aziz. "I haven't read the law, have I?" He then turned to Mehpare *Hanım* and, abruptly changing the subject, said, "Your turnovers are most delicious, Mother. As always, you're spoiling us all."

What did it all mean? She must openly ask Károly. Rudi was an old friend of hers before anything else. Was it reasonable to worry about Ada and János and not even think about Rudi? There was nothing wrong in asking.

Like Nili and Azra, Alex finished her *suböreği* with great difficulty, pushing mouthfuls of it from left to right in her mouth before she gulped it down with water, and almost fainted with nausea upon the arrival of the *imambayıldı*, the eggplant dish bathed in olive oil with an intolerable amount of onions. Children, although exempt from the olive oil dishes served after the main course, had long ago learned that they would have to remain seated at the table until dinner was over. Finally, following the syrup-soaked Turkish dessert *tulumba tatlısı*, the children went to the back to join Lila and Selma for their afternoon naps while the grown-ups moved on to the drawing room where coffee would be served. Aziz presently started to snooze in one of the armchairs, leaving Alex alone with the others. Fortunately, Necla, the chatterbox of the family, took the reins of the conversation and, despite her husband Nezih's polite interventions, did not stop talking until it was time for them to leave, which was well after teatime.

Upon their return home, Alex impatiently waited for Aziz to go to bed, for she wanted to be alone to write to Károly, asking after Rudi. As luck would have it, Aziz, who usually went to bed very early, seemed to have been struck by insomnia. At long last, towards midnight, he rose from his armchair where he had been scrutinising the newspaper for the last two hours.

"Aren't you going to bed?" he asked.

"I'll write to Magda and *Öcsi*."

"At this hour?"

"I'm not sleepy at all."

"I'm turning in. Goodnight," said Aziz, kissing her on the forehead.

Alex watched him leave the drawing room. He was really happy, not in the least aware of how drab their relationship had become. As a matter of fact he wanted it to be like that, flat as a calm lake. He did not want any breeze or any ripples that might disturb the peace and the quiet.

Alex, on the other hand, was suffocating.

Istanbul, 19th June 1938

Öcsi bácsi!

You'd better get used to this new form of address that Nili invented as she heard me call you *Öcsi* on the phone. Now for her – and for the rest of us – you're not Károly *bácsi* but *Öcsi bácsi*.

What was she going to ask? Should she write, "Do you know anything about Rudi's business affairs?" or should she just say, "How is he doing?" This was ridiculous. She was blowing everything out of proportion. Neither Rudi nor the well-experienced György Takács was stupid. They most likely knew very well how to organise their affairs. Why couldn't she admit that what she really wondered was what Rudi was doing? Was it because she was ashamed of herself for not being able to forget the person who had made her suffer so much? Had she no pride left? She put her pen aside. She did not want to write anymore. She lit a cigarette and went out on the balcony. She knew that she would not be able to sleep tonight. Think about your daughters, Alex. You're not alone. Think about your sweet Nili. Think about your sweet Lila.

229

45

Budapest. She was finally back in her beloved city after another three tediously long years. Ultimately Aziz had taken pity on her and let her spend this Christmas in Budapest, along with her daughters. She had been here for almost a month now but still could not get enough of it. Quite the reverse, the more she saw the places where she had spent her childhood and youth, the more her yearning intensified. Winter, in all its freezing splendour, had impounded the capital, but Alex felt as free as a snowflake drifting in the air. Despite the large chunks of ice floating on the Danube, exaggerating the gelid sensation one already had, she somehow felt much warmer than she had in a very long time. She hugged her silver fox coat, not because she was cold, but out of an all-encompassing sense of joy that had captivated her whole being. She took a deep breath, just for the joy of sucking in the liberating air of her hometown. Even her hair blew differently in the wind, each of its strands declaring its independence at the magical touch of a gust. Andrássy Boulevard was alive with people. Nothing kept the well-dressed and sophisticated gentlemen away from this boulevard, where they could savour the marvellous sight offered by the beautiful ladies strolling along in their fashionable fur coats.

Arriving at the Japán Kávéház where she was to meet her friends, she saw through the windows that László and Anna had already arrived and were sitting at what was known as the Artists' Table, by the large window overlooking the boulevard. Like in the old days when they were students at the Academy, László was keeping an eye on the pretty girls passing by. "I'm observing," he used to say, "I'm observing life."

Once in the café, she paused briefly to admire the walls covered with majolica tiles painted over with bamboos, chrysanthemums, vases and dreamlike birds. She already knew them by heart, but looked at them attentively once again to make sure that they remained in her memory forever. She inhaled the warm aroma of coffee. This is home, she thought, this city, this smell is where I belong.

"Alex! We're over here," she heard László call out, waving his hand.

The café was packed with people. She squeezed through the tables buried under a heavy cloud of smoke, trying to make her way towards her friends. She had missed it all so very much, even being in a place where everyone spoke Hungarian. "Hello, everyone," she beamed before taking her coat off and hanging it on one of the hooks on the wall. A waiter was already standing next to her, ready to take her order.

"Might I have apple *rétes* and coffee, please? *Presszó*."

In a few minutes, her coffee and favourite dessert were on the table. She took a large dollop of whipped cream from the bowl standing on the marble table-top and stirred it into her coffee. A sudden feeling of melancholy struck her as she thought of Károly, who had moved back to Paris in August with Ada. "I wish Károly were here with us," she said stirring her coffee, her wistful eyes momentarily lost in the tiny eddies in her cup. "Do you know how long it's been since I last saw him? More than six years! And only a very brief encounter in Paris – a short dinner – when I was there for my honeymoon. We seem to have been playing hide and seek ever since."

"Hasn't he been to Istanbul at all?"

"Paris," Alex said and fell silent in hesitation before she went on, "and Ada apparently make him forget about anything and everything."

"Paris is like a mistress," said László, lost in a reverie, his eyes still observing the life outside flowing by the boulevard. "It embraces you with a warm and open heart but, at the same time, makes you feel absolutely free, never asking any questions. Once you have a taste of the life it offers, you can't get it out of your mind. Ever! Nothing else matters anymore."

"How is Magda, Alex?" asked Anna, cutting her husband short. "We haven't seen her for weeks. I heard that she's pregnant. We're truly happy for her."

"Me too. Our family is growing, Annuska. I'm more excited than she is, I think. I don't want to go back to Istanbul. I'd love to stay with her at least until after the birth. However, I can't convince my husband."

She did not want to leave Magda alone, for she could hardly get her own pregnancy – the first one – out of her mind. She was very scared for her sister. Magda, on the other hand, seemed to care about nothing; she was far too happy for having talked Miklós into having a baby after all these years.

"Well, hello beautiful."

She winced at the sudden frisson as a cold cheek pressed against hers. János had arrived unnoticed and clasped his arms around her shoulders.

"Jancsi!" she exclaimed. "You're cold."

János seemed determined to cover up for Károly's absence when it came to teasing Alex. "What can I do? I have no one to warm my heart," he said, playing the unfortunate. He kissed Alex on both cheeks and forced a smile at Anna and

László before he sat on the chair next to Alex.

"You have, Jancsi, but you don't let her into your heart. Poor girl is bound to become a spinster because of you."

Everyone, including János, knew that Alex was talking about Margit. The two ex-lovers had been the best of friends for the last six years, and János claimed that they were too friendly to be lovers again. It was not so clear if their close amity was a source of torment or happiness for Margit.

János reproached Alex for depriving Budapest of her beauty for so long, expressed his fury at those who had failed to make her happy, thus causing her to run away in agony, and softly whispered in her ear that the loyal city of Budapest would never give up waiting for her.

"How is life around here?" asked Alex, in an effort to change the subject and received a reply typical of János.

"Sub-Carpathian Ruthenia is in turmoil."

To her surprise, she realised that she had even missed János's depressing political monologues.

"Despite the regained territories, millions of our compatriots are still living outside Hungary – Hungarians without a country."

"How much more can we afford to sacrifice for the lost territories? That's the question we should be asking." László seemed to be more willing to sort out Hungary's problems than János was.

Alex's interest gradually drifted away from their conversation, and she started to check out the crowd in the café. "That's Ernő Szép over there, isn't it?" she asked below her breath, leaning over to Anna.

"Yes, it's him. He's been famous as a playwright rather than a poet since his *Purple Wisteria* was made into a film in '34."

"He was one of the fifty-nine people who undersigned the letter of protest last year while the Parliament was discussing the Fifteen." János was incredibly skilful at shifting any subject – even poetry – to politics. "To no avail, mind you. The bill won the support of the Catholic, Lutheran and Calvinist churches."

"What is the Fifteen?" Alex asked indifferently, giving up her efforts to steer away from boring topics, since in János's presence she had no choice but to feign interest in politics.

"The law they issued in May last year, limiting the Jewish ..."

"Oh, yes. Yes, I know," she cut him short. All of a sudden, she was truly interested in the subject. "What about your father, Jancsi?"

"For the moment, we're fine. They had the courtesy to consider the fact that my father was decorated as a hero in the Great War. They've decided that it would be unfair to impose such limitations on those who risked their lives for their countries. And, luckily for us, they took pity on their families as well. Surprisingly considerate, don't you think?" His voice was gradually assuming a dark and solemn tone. "Just before Christmas, however, they proposed a new bill to Parliament. It definitely isn't very promising." He raised his coffee cup and finished its content in one angry movement. "Germans were not being Samaritans when they gave the south of Slovakia and of Sub-Carpathian Ruthenia to Horthy in November."

"Where is all this going to end? I hate politics. Why don't they leave people alone? What do they want? What's going on?"

"Let's begin from the beginning, dear Alex, if you wish. Actually, I should be saying the beginning of the end. In March last year, the balance of power in Central Europe changed entirely when Hitler annexed Austria, and the Nazis became our immediate neighbour. And Hungary had to set aside its efforts to regain the territories it lost in 1920 and start worrying about the preservation of its existing borders and of its independence. However, our beloved country refuses to give up hope at all costs. Finally in May last year they issued the anti-Jewish Fifteen, a seriously 'illegal' law, to prove to Hitler how well-intentioned Hungary is or rather – please excuse the expression – how good our country is in licking Nazi asses."

"Those with an optimistic streak," intervened László, "see this law as a step taken by the right wing to cool down the extreme rightists and thus provide some protection for the Jews."

"They don't see anything. They don't *want* to see anything. They persistently turn a blind eye to all that's going on. To protect the Jews, my foot!" János scoffed before he turned to Alex. "I don't know how much of this news is covered in Turkey, but the situation has become dreadfully grave in the last six, seven months, Alex."

"We all heard Hitler's speeches. I read *Mein Kampf* like everybody else did," said Anna, with a tint of embarrassment in her voice. "It seemed ... I don't know ... like the fantasy-like novels of Jules Verne. It never occurred to me that he really meant what he wrote. When I listened to his speeches, he sounded more like an actor putting on an act to entertain people than a real menace. What he said never seemed real. He sounded too surreal, too fantastic, too ridiculous, too extremist."

"The Night of the Broken Glass changed everything," said László. He was referring to the atrocities committed against the Jews in Germany on November 10. "Rumour has it that similar things are going on in Hungarian villages. They talk about Jews being beaten up, synagogues and cemeteries being defaced. Thank God, we witness no such misery in Budapest. Here, they're quite assimilated."

Suddenly Alex felt a hand on her shoulder.

"You shouldn't be smoking, Magda. You have a baby to think about now."

It was his voice! It was him! No, Alex. No. It's the exceptional ingenuity of your mind creating yet another illusion. Her heart skipped a beat. She froze for a brief moment before a wave of heat emanating from the hand on her shoulder kindled her heart. An acute sense of alarm gripped her. Millions of butterflies started fluttering in her stomach. Don't turn around, Alex. Don't look. Her head, refusing to listen to her plea, tentatively turned. She first saw his fingers, powerful and domineering, firmly holding her shoulder; then she slowly raised her head. An intense pang of longing seized her as she looked at his eyes, his deep blue eyes still tender in resistance to the sharp expression on his face. A quiver of desire thrilled through her. She could not utter a sound.

"Alex?"

Was it a shadow of excitement that had just flitted across his surprised eyes? Had he momentarily tightened his grip on her shoulder? His touch sent shivers down her spine. In panic, she averted her eyes. Control yourself, Alex. With all the courage she could muster, she looked up again. "You've grown a beard," she said, the words streaming out of her mouth of their own accord. What on earth was she saying? Couldn't she find anything better to say after all these years? "Will you join us for a cup of coffee?" she asked in an effort to efface what she had just said. Rudi slightly raised his hand to show the cup he was holding. Alex was so entrapped by his eyes that she had not even noticed it. He had come with his coffee. He obviously meant to stay. Letting go of Alex's shoulder, he smiled at the others, pulled up a chair from another table and sat next to Alex.

She had to say something to lighten an atmosphere that was suddenly laden with a pregnant silence, but could not think of anything. Tongue-tied, she just sat there, scared that a comment, albeit seemingly insignificant, might turn into a blast of provocation, triggering an unwanted avalanche of harsh words. He might readily say something that would hurt her or make a fool of her in front of her friends. Apprehensively she looked around, mutely begging for help from the others around the table. Eventually, stealing a furtive glance at Rudi, she realised how unnecessary her trepidation was, for he looked as relaxed as he would have been if he had just come across a friend he had seen the day before. After making a few sarcastic remarks on some triviality and paying a series of compliments to Anna, he politely asked how everyone was. Finally, he turned his penetrating gaze to Alex and, caressing her up and down with his eyes, aroused a tremor of excitement in her by saying that she had not changed a bit and that she was still exceptionally ravishing. After a meaningful pause, he reiterated, whispering softly, that she, in fact, had changed and was even more beautiful than before, more radiant in a captivatingly mature way.

Alex was spellbound, quietly watching her friends like a silent movie rolling before her eyes. Not knowing what to do with her hands, she fidgeted with, and then took a sip from, her empty coffee cup. Her senses were so busy with other emotions that she was completely put off her dessert, which she had been waiting to indulge herself in for the last three years. For an instant, she thought she smelled the unmistakably seductive scent of Rudi's skin. Did she really or was it a figment of her overheated imagination? Yes, of course she did. It was the unforgettable ambrosia of her past. Alex! Stop this nonsense! Come to your senses!

Rudi carried on talking, and she listened to him with a blank ear; she could hardly concentrate on what he actually was saying. A licentious desire possessed her to touch his aquiline nose, which, as it had always done, sent a surge, a thrill through her whole body. She wanted to caress his bony cheeks, still visible through his well-trimmed short beard. Enough of it, Alex! You're being ridiculous. What's wrong with you, for Heaven's sake? Have you lost your mind? She dragged her eyes away from him and fixed them on her own hands. She noticed that she had been fidgeting with her wedding ring. Waving her hand in front of her eyes to shoo away her thoughts, she blurted out, "How is business?" Her question dropped like an untimely bomb on the table. Without realising, she had interrupted János. "I'm sorry, Jancsi. I didn't mean to barge in."

János held Alex's hand, which was now playing with the fork. "It's perfectly all right, gorgeous. It has slipped my mind that you're not very keen on politics. Time has this tendency, you know, to make one forget things. Yes. Let's talk about something that you're interested in, shall we? Tennis, for instance. Or law."

Alex did not like the tone of János's voice at all. He clearly did not enjoy Rudi's company. Has he now taken on the role of being the guardian angel of little

Alex? Did he take himself as Károly's proxy? "Please do go on, Jancsi. Finish what you were saying."

As soon as János ended his boring lecture on the bill presented to the Parliament before Christmas, Alex turned to Rudi and repeated her question. Rudi went on to describe the changes he had made in his company and the novelties he planned to bring to the business world in Budapest in great detail, which, under normal circumstances, would push Alex's patience over the edge but now, under the current situation, proved to be rather interesting for her. He talked about his ever-increasing business trips, the deals he had made with his partners in England and the peculiar business mentality of the British. Eventually, he stopped, as he had probably noticed Alex's lack of genuine interest and, with enthusiasm that was more feigned than felt, changed the subject to their day-to-day diversions. He moved from one topic to another, talking about the tennis match he had had with József that morning, about the reception he had attended in Vienna the week before, about what had happened at the last New Year's Eve party he had thrown, and furnished Alex with the news about their mutual friends. He talked breathlessly, as though he too were afraid that silence or a wrong remark would lead to an eruption of unwanted emotions.

The more Rudi talked, the more Alex relaxed. There was nothing to be afraid of, nothing to worry about, she told herself. Thanks to János, she had felt uneasy for no reason. She did not need to protect herself from Rudi. "I'm still beautiful. I'm married to a man who loves me. And I have two adorable daughters. Nobody can hurt me," she reassured herself. As she relaxed, she started to burst out laughing at László's jokes although they did, at times, prove to be rather out of place. The more she laughed, the more Rudi fell silent, watching Alex with his head slightly tilted to one side and, as Alex delightedly noticed, with an almost imperceptible hint of adoration in his eyes. Alex talked and talked – about her daughters, about her tennis, about the bridge games and about Istanbul. She recounted the amusing aspects of her life as well as its less agreeable features, which she nevertheless tried to present as delightful. She went on and on about her friends, her dogs and her cat. Despite János's interventions, Rudi's compliments had put her in great spirits. She herself was surprised at her own good mood. There was only one person who did not enjoy himself at the table, and that was János. He stayed a bit longer without uttering a single word and finally, excusing himself on some business, he left. It was much better that he did, for his absence lightened the atmosphere and improved the mood of the table.

June 2004
Istanbul

Rüya woke up the next morning long before the alarm of her mobile phone went off. She had no intention of waiting for anyone; she wanted to get to the hospital as soon as possible. Not taking a shower, she only washed her face and hurriedly brushed her teeth. Although her reflection in the mirror looked ghastly, she did not want to lose any time making up her face. She threw on some clothes and ran downstairs. Her grandmother Nili and Lila *néni* were on the veranda, while her mother was in the kitchen, telling Hatice, who was preparing breakfast, what she must already know by heart.

"I'm off. See you all at the hospital," said Rüya to no one in particular as she walked into the kitchen.

"It's too early. Why don't you have breakfast with us, dear?"

"I'll grab something at the hospital."

"*Un café?*" asked André from where he was standing by the coffee machine.

"*Non, merci.*"

Rüya planted a kiss on her mother's cheek, dashed out of the kitchen into the garden, got into her car and headed for the hospital. At Akıntıburnu, a boat was struggling upstream against the infamously dire current at that point on the Bosphorus. She felt her heart sinking. Her mobile phone started ringing. It said Sinan on the screen.

"Yes?"

"Good morning."

"I'm driving at the moment. Shall we talk later?"

"I meant to talk to you about our dinner date this evening. I ..."

"You really are something, you know. Mami is fighting for her life and all you can think of is our dinner date."

"If you would let me finish, I'd be telling you that I've cancelled our booking for this evening. I also meant to ask if it would be appropriate for me to come to the hospital."

"Don't! She's in intensive care. They only let us – the family – in and only one at a time."

"I just wanted to come to be with you, Rüya."

"Never mind me. Don't come. I'll give you a ring later on. I need to be on my own for a while anyway."

"As you wish, my love."

"This is what I wish. Goodbye."

She hung up before Sinan could say anything else. Her heart sank a bit deeper.

In the afternoon, they took Mami out of intensive care. The room Aslı had finally chosen was really spacious and most comfortable.

"Mami dear, look! You even have a sea view," said Lila, never leaving Mami's side and continually caressing her forehead, as though she wanted to make up for all the time she had been away from her.

"There's a little bay on the island where you live, Lila," said Mami weakly. "And there, right below the large rocks, there's a tiny white cottage with blue shutters, three olive trees in the garden and four goats, each a different colour." She turned her tired eyes to her daughter and, with a serene smile on her face, continued, "I want my ashes to be buried there." She closed her eyes as her voice sank into a whisper. "Next to him," she sighed.

"What did she say?" asked Nili.

"I think she's talking in her sleep."

A jolly and clamorous melody rose from one of the handbags in the room. It was Aslı's mobile phone.

"It's Nur."

Rüya's aunt Nur had been living in New York for the last fourteen years, the selfish Aunt Nur who, being so busy earning money and pursuing a career, had no time either for the family she had left behind or for getting herself a husband. As usual she was incapable of sparing more than a few minutes on the phone, even at a time like this when Mami – her grandmother, for Heaven's sake! – was on her deathbed. She ended the call after a brief exchange of information that lasted no more than ten minutes.

"What's she saying?" asked Nili.

"Nothing. She was asking after Mami."

"She can't be bothered to come, can she?" fumed Rüya.

"Why should she?" snapped Nili, protecting her daughter. "She can't be rushing to Istanbul all the way from New York for every soul who catches a cold, can she now?"

Rüya found it unbearably annoying how her grandmother could be so openly nonchalant. "You're incredible. All of you! She's fighting for her life, if you hadn't noticed."

"Be quiet. Nothing is wrong with Mami. She'll be fine, just fine."

Mami whispered something under her breath. Rüya sprang to her feet and ran to her bedside.

"Did you say something, Mami?"

"Everything changes, Nili. Everything *has to* change. You can't live in the past, darling. If you do, there's no way you can be free of pain."

"Poor soul. She's completely lost it. She thought you were me," said Nili, addressing Rüya.

"No, Nili, I'm talking to you, sweetheart," whispered Mami, almost to herself, before she turned her head towards the door. Her tired eyes suddenly brightened when she saw her friend enter the room. "Hello, Anastasia," she beamed.

Anastasia had arrived on the arm of Bedri, the driver. She was an old friend of Mami's, more like a sister to her now after decades of friendship. Mami managed to talk to her only for a few minutes, after which she was exhausted and fell asleep. Nili and Aslı went downstairs to fetch some tea and something to eat; Lila went out, dying for a cigarette.

"She sleeps so peacefully, doesn't she?" said Rüya softly, without taking her eyes off Mami.

Anastasia was gazing apprehensively at her friend; Mami looked so small and so fragile. "You know, dear," she said, "those who didn't know her past very well could not really understand the reason behind her profound melancholia. They either blamed it on her artistic disposition or thought she was too spoiled, being so beautiful and so excessively loved. Now she no longer has that melancholy but only a certain degree of calmness, or rather serenity, I might say. Over the years, her exceptional beauty has gradually transformed itself into something more peaceful, something much purer. Looking at her, one wonders where all the scars left by her sufferings are gone. Her skin is unblemished; she has almost no wrinkles as though she had never once frowned in her entire life."

"What makes you say that *Thicha* Anastasia – Aunt Anastasia? She didn't suffer much, did she? She had a husband who adored her and spoiled her rotten. Apparently, he was madly in love with her all his life, until the very day he died. He gave her the perfect life to live. She had children, grandchildren, great-grandchildren. We all loved her dearly and still do. She was never alone; we were always by her side. Surely she was happy and led a rather comfortable life."

"Listen dearest," Anastasia said, holding Rüya's hand. "Do you know anything about water lilies – the flower? A beautiful water lily in full blossom floats so gracefully and so peacefully on the surface of calm waters that, looking at her, one is fooled into believing that she has an easy and carefree life. However, she has to nourish herself from the mud where her roots are deeply embedded, grow in murky waters, and eventually break through the surface to see the sunlight before she can bloom so sublimely."

Rüya stood up. She suddenly realised how little she knew about Mami's past. Neither her mother nor her grandmother ever talked about the past. It was as though Mami had no history. For Rüya, she was simply the mainstay of their home, a perfect great-grandmother, a perfect grandmother, a perfect mother and once, undoubtedly, a perfect wife.

"As a matter of fact," Anastasia went on, "what consumed her was not her suffering so much as her failure to heal the wounds those sufferings had opened in her heart. She lived with an acute sense of nostalgia for a long-lost past. Getting stuck in the past is an awful feeling; its unbearable weight crushes you. Your Mami lived in the past, Rüya – practically all her life. She kept saying that she felt as if she were stuck in the mud, unable to move just like a slave. The waters were always murky for her. She had many regrets, which gradually turned into bitterness and then into anger. Eventually, all of those emotions gave way to an incurable feeling of melancholy."

Rüya was pacing up and down the room, trying to assimilate what Anastasia had just told her. Suddenly the hospital room felt suffocating. She stopped in front of the window to look at the sky for some relief.

"It's rather curious, Rüya, that someone who is so observant in her art can be so blind to what's going on around her. She didn't see. She didn't even *try* to see. She was completely unaware of how much better it would have been both for her and for those around her if she had opened her eyes. She lived in profound desolation, dreaming about a future when she would be able to see the sun, be able to bloom and relive her wasted past. At long last, she realised where happiness lay and how easy it actually was to grab it, but it did take rather a long time. After losing her last connection with her past, it was the love she had for you that saved her from falling into an abyss."

"When did you meet Mami?"

"A long time ago, my dear girl, a very long time ago." She raised her eyebrows and pursed her lips, moving her head up and down. Apparently, she was finding it hard to remember exactly how long. Then letting out a deep sigh, she said, "We met in October 1932, a few days after her twenty-second birthday. I was nineteen then. Our friendship goes back seventy-two years."

"Please, please tell me more."

"There's so much to tell, dear. Why don't you come and visit me one day, and I can tell you everything in detail." She reached for her walking stick. "I'd better be going now."

"Let me accompany you downstairs," said Rüya broken-heartedly, reluctant to let go of her. "The driver should be waiting for you. You will make sure he takes you all the way up to your flat, won't you?"

After seeing Anastasia off, Rüya returned to the room and sat in the armchair next to Mami. Looking closely at her face, which seemed to have shrunk lately, she thought she caught a glimpse of the melancholy hidden, somewhere deep under the surprisingly few wrinkles.

"Did Anastasia upset you, *tatlım?*" murmured Mami, opening her eyes a little and, with great effort, raising her hand to stroke Rüya's cheek. Although her Turkish was impeccable, she still could not pronounce the Turkish "ı" and said *tatlim*.

"No, not at all."

"My darling Rüya, do you know when the knot gets untied? When you realise that the past, be it bitter or sweet, is not real, when you stop dreaming about the time when your lost ones will return." She spoke with great difficulty but went on. "What you lost in the past never comes back. You must see the scars your losses have left behind. You must accept them. You must make peace with them. What you've lost is replaced by other loved ones. You must see them before you lose them as well. You must live the day. You must enjoy life." She was exhausted.

"You're tiring yourself. You ought to rest now," said Rüya, apprehensively. "Please close your eyes." She pulled her armchair closer to the bed and put her arms around Mami. She nestled her cheek in Mami's hand where it rested limpidly on the bed and breathed in her warm smell.

> *"Why is it important to know yourself?" I ask.*
>
> *"So that you can forget about the past and the future, and live in the moment ... so that you can realise your dreams ... so that you turn your dreams*

about the future into the reality of today."

I'm even more confused. "What has knowing yourself got to do with realising your dreams?" I ask.

"It has a lot to do with it because unless you know yourself, you'll have no tolerance towards yourself, in which case you'll never be tolerant towards others. Unless you can forgive yourself, you can never forgive others; unless you're free yourself, you can never give others their freedom; and, most importantly, unless you love yourself, you can never love anybody. When you're unable to love, when you're unable to open your heart, you'll never be able to overcome your fears because you'll never have a chance to see how unfounded they are. And your fears will, unfortunately, prevent you from realising your dreams."

The sun's rays glittering on the water look like shiny stars scintillating in the dark of the night. They brighten up the soul. I smell the salt emanating from the sea. It gives hints of freedom. I think of how much I love myself. I think of my loneliness, of my fears, of my dreams which I know won't come true, and of the pain this knowledge inflicts upon me. I hug my sister tightly. How much I've missed her smell. Do I remember how she smelled or is it her smell that reminds me of the past? I don't know, and I don't want to know. Everything feels so light ... so weightless.

"Wake up, Rüya. You'll get a cramp, dear."

Rüya woke up at the sound of her mother's voice.

"I must have fallen asleep. What time is it?" She raised her head. Her back ached slightly. Sitting up, she stretched and looked at Mami, who seemed to be sound asleep. "Is she all right?"

"She should be. You'd better go home now, Rüya."

Mami opened her eyes and reached for Rüya's hand. "Are you leaving?"

"Yes, Mami. Mum will stay with you tonight. I'll be here early in the morning. Tomorrow night, I'll be staying with you."

"How long are they going to keep me here?"

"Not for too long. You need to get some rest, that's all." Rüya stood up and took her handbag from the wardrobe. "See you tomorrow morning," she said to her mother, who was tidying the newspapers and magazines scattered around the room. She took a final look at Mami, who had closed her eyes again. She approached the bed, leaned over and gave her a kiss on the cheek.

"When you go home, Rüya, open my lilac wardrobe," whispered Mami without opening her eyes, as though she were talking in her sleep. "Take whatever you fancy. Dried apricots are delicious. So are the dried figs. However, you won't be able to finish them all, so don't rush. Consume them slowly, dear, or else you'll have a severe case of indigestion. Do you understand what I mean, *tatlım?*"

A Hungarian Rhapsody
A Novel in Three Acts
Act One, Tableau Three
1939

Tableau Three

46

Alex unlatched the heavy iron garden gate, which slowly gave way with a groan. Her dream of the previous afternoon carried on. Rudi was waiting for her, leaning on his white Mercedes parked in front of the gate on the snow-covered street. He opened the door to his car, and his face opened into a smile.

"Good morning," he said, planting a rushed but nevertheless warm kiss on Alex's cheek.

Once in the car, she panicked, lost for words to start a conversation. She felt oddly like a total stranger next to Rudi – to the man who was once her fiancé. They drove down Rózsadomb, the engine of the car barely disturbing the peace and quiet of the Sunday morning on the hill of roses.

"What would you like to do?" he asked softly.

"Actually, I'd like to walk the whole length of Andrássy Boulevard."

They crossed over to the Pest side, uttering a few phrases of trivia in an effort to break the silence accentuated by the peaceful lulling of the snow that had folded the city in its arms like a soft white blanket. There was not a cloud in the sky. It was freezing cold, although the sun's heart-warming reflection on the snow somehow mellowed the iciness in the air. They parked the car on Deák Ferenc Square. Walking along the imposing Neo-Renaissance and Neo-Baroque style buildings of Andrássy Boulevard, a myriad of questions started buzzing in Alex's head. Was it a clever move to walk two-and-a-half kilometres in this cold? More crucially, was there any sense in having a stroll on the most crowded boulevard in Budapest with Rudi at her side, parading past the cafés bustling with life? Come off it, Alex. There is no need to be so timorous. Live the moment while it lasts.

"Do you still live in this apartment?" she asked as they walked past number twenty-three.

"Yes, I do."

She stopped and took a long look at the Opera House across the boulevard, enjoying its magnificent façade. The sixteen impeccable stone sculptures of the greatest of composers stood erect even under the heavy weight of the snow piled upon their shoulders. Beethoven, Mozart, Liszt ... She looked at the people passing by. They all seemed to have smiles on their faces despite the breath-catching cold. Suddenly she was struck by a desire to hop along the pavement as she used to do when she was a child, freely, carelessly. A thrilling sense of joy lifted her soul. She could not recall the last time she had felt such exhilaration. She was smiling, her whole being was smiling. She wanted to breathe in the whole city, the air, the cold, the people, everything. She spread her arms wide apart and took a deep breath.

"I presume that in Budapest there are no rules against a lady taking the arm of a gentleman, Mademoiselle de Kurzón," said Rudi, extending his arm as he slightly bent it at the elbow.

"Madame Giritli Azizné," she corrected him before timidly taking his arm. "Is it all right to walk like this?" she thought only a second later. All her senses were concentrated on the spot where her hand touched Rudi's arm. Come on, Alex. You've become a true Oriental. Aziz's jealousies have turned your values upside down. People are more civilised here, have you forgotten? She breathed in the Budapest air once again. Almost feeling the warmth of Rudi's skin through his coat, she felt an uncontrollable urge to stroke his arm.

"How is marriage going?" he asked.

Neither she nor Rudi had mentioned the name of Aziz since their encounter yesterday – not even once – acting as though Alex did not have a husband.

"Fine. What about you? I don't see any ring on your finger."

"I have a girlfriend," he said and, pursing his lips, added, "No one important. In other words, no one I wouldn't give up if I met someone better, if you catch my drift."

What was that supposed to mean? Was he accusing her? Why on earth did he say that now, right out of the blue? Regretting she ever asked such a question, she looked at him in search of a warm smile, something in his face that might help disperse the sudden uneasiness squeezing her heart. All she saw, however, was his freezing stare emerging from underneath his eyelids half draped over his pupils, and his tightened lips faking a smile. She averted her eyes and looked down at the snow-covered pavement stones. His words had hit her like a sharp slap on the face and caught her unawares, just at the moment when she had gladly thought that they had overcome all that had happened between them. He was about to act the way she – fearfully – had expected him to. He would hurt her, ruthlessly seeking revenge by showering her with unbearably pungent verbal attacks. I cannot let him insult me, she thought, quickening her steps as if they would help her move away from this perilous subject. She made to pull her arm away, but Rudi held her hand and firmly pressed it on his arm. Then, stroking her cheek with the back of his finger, he gave her a smile, a thawed smile that immediately melted her heart and miraculously soothed her turbulent mind. She could not understand him. She could not make heads or tails of what he wanted to do. Clumsily, she started talking about Istanbul, recounting the many beauties of the Bosphorus.

"Wouldn't you ever consider coming to Istanbul for a visit?"

"Is this a joke?"

It would be better if she did not speak at all. Silence was golden and definitely less belligerent than heedless small talk. The more she talked, the worse it would become. They crossed over to the other side of the boulevard at Oktogon Square or, to use the new name that nobody could get used to, at Benito Mussolini Square. Alex was now walking on Rudi's right, nearer to the roadside. He removed her hand from his arm and, stroking the back of her waist, danced around her to the other side, held her other hand and slid their interlaced hands into the pocket of his coat. Alex tried to go on talking as though nothing had happened but had completely forgotten what they were talking about. She felt her hand yielding to Rudi's strong grip. Her whole body surrendered. Her soul melted down. She forced herself to think of something to say. Catching sight of the blue flag of the Budapest Skating Club, she pointed a finger at her saviour, "The ice on the lake in Város Park is apparently thick enough for skating. It must be full of skaters now."

Rudi did not say anything. He was stroking her hand in his pocket. Alex did not object. Why, Alex? Why can't you say no to him? She didn't want to say no. What do you think you're doing? What was she doing, really? She was a married woman walking hand in hand with a man, a man who was not her husband. What did it all mean? Was she being unfaithful to her husband? Was she having an extramarital affair with a man who had made her suffer terribly and who was giving all the signs of a strong possibility that he might do the same thing again? She had to be crazy. Rudi was squeezing her hand even more tightly now, almost hurting her. "Rudi!" she said trying to free her hand from his harrowing grip.

"I'm so sorry," he said, letting go of her hand. His expression had suddenly darkened. He was looking at the building they were passing by with anger in his eyes, hatred more likely, even a hint of repugnance. "The infamous Number Sixty," he spat between his clenched teeth. "The headquarters of the Arrow Cross. They've been busy ruining our lives from here for the last two years."

A chill ran through Alex's body. A freezing cold wind brushed her fur. She took a deep breath and tucked her hands in her pockets. She heard the jingles of the skates in the hands of a group of young girls walking by, one of the merry songs of Budapest winters, a welcoming tune from her past. She smiled bitterly.

They walked along the last section of the long Andrássy Boulevard, past Rudi's parents' mansion, and reached Hősök Square. At the sight of the giant sculptures of the great founders of Hungary in the centre of the square, Alex's mind involuntarily drifted to her mother. She winced at the memory of her endless sermonic lectures about the obligations of the nobility throughout their childhood and adolescence, of her ambition to find her children spouses suitable for their noble blood, and of her obdurate refusal to accept Rudi. She blamed her mother a lot for all that had happened to her. If she had given her a little bit more support in difficult times, if she had given her a little bit of strength, this man walking next to her could have been her husband. She reminisced about the engagement party given in the mansion, which she had not ventured to look at a few minutes ago.

"Are you tired? Shall we go back?"

"No, no. I want to go to the lake."

They entered Város Park. The lake by the castle was frozen. The young and the old were skating, despite the numbing cold. They bought *perec* from a stall. God, she had missed these salty pretzels! They ambled towards the Szécsenyi Baths, Alex making every effort to steer away from delicate subjects, and Rudi taking every opportunity to tease Alex with some offensive remark, only to win her heart back the next instant. She watched people sprinting through the snow and throwing themselves into the steaming open-air swimming pool, something that inexplicably evoked a warm sensation in her. How much she now appreciated the things she had once taken for granted.

"It's been almost seven years since I last saw Károly," she complained.

"I know, Alex. Károly always talks about how much he misses you."

Rudi gave a detailed account of how much fun they had had at the farewell party before Károly and Ada's departure for Paris and of how happy Károly had been. Listening to Rudi, a question lingered in Alex's mind: did Rudi and Károly still see each other? Károly never wrote anything about Rudi in his letters, not even making a short mention of him.

"It's Károly's birthday the day after tomorrow. We must drink a toast to him, Alex."

Were they so close that they celebrated each other's birthdays? Should she be angry or pleased? "I understand that you two see each other quite often," she blurted out without thinking.

"I'm not so childish as to lose a friend just because his sister made a grave mistake," he said, with an exaggerated expression of feigned surprise.

Alex thought, yet again, that it would be much better if she kept mum.

On the way back they took the underground railway that ran beneath Andrássy Boulevard and got off at the terminal near the square where they had parked the car.

"Shall we walk to the embankment?" proposed Rudi.

"Yes, why don't we?"

They sauntered towards the riverbank.

"There's something I meant to ask you years ago, Alex, but I could never bring myself to do it."

She knew what that question would be and wished he would never ask. She had managed to talk about things of no consequence so far and did not, in the least, want to probe into the past now.

"Why Alex? Why couldn't you wait? Why did you do it?"

"Why did I do *what?*" she asked, knowing exactly what he was talking about. A memory of a few seconds that she had buried into the depths of her consciousness stirred in trepidation. She ought to suppress it. She must not allow it to surface. She did not want to remember.

He seemed not to have heard her question. "You really hurt me, you know," he said, sounding suddenly vulnerable.

Who hurt who, for goodness' sake? Wasn't he aware of what he had done? "Rudi, as I told you then, I may have been the one to break up our engagement, but it was you who ruined our relationship. You had already left me long before then. You had left me all alone."

"No, Alex. I'm not asking you why you broke up the engagement. I'm talking about something else, about another time when you put an end to everything between us. I'm asking you why you were unfaithful to me."

"What on earth are you talking about?" she spluttered, her voice quavering.

The curtain that hid everything was suddenly drawn aside, ruthlessly exposing those few seconds entombed in the depths of the past, that brief instant of no importance, that ephemeral lapse of strength she had hoped Rudi had not seen, that fleeting slip into weakness she had made herself believe that he had not witnessed.

"I'm asking you why you kissed him!"

Rudi's frozen voice mingled with the roaring sound of the icy Danube, curdling Alex's blood. She could not raise her eyes from the pavement, her gaze fixed on Rudi's feet striding across the stones. She felt his warm breath hit her cheek.

"Remember Italy, Alex? Remember the day you kissed him in the woods? You should have broken up with me before you decided to kiss another man."

Alex felt a pang in her chest. She could not breathe. What was she supposed to say? What should she say? What did he want her to say? "I didn't want to kiss him, Rudi. It just happened. He kissed me, just like that. I couldn't have stopped him."

"Well, he doesn't seem to be an idiot with no manners. He wouldn't have attacked you just like that. Are you sure you didn't lead him on?"

She wished this conversation could end there and then. "I don't know. I really don't know. It's been more than six years."

"Seven years and two and a half months, to be precise."

"Well, perhaps," she started and then fell silent. She wanted to be pitied, not accused. "Perhaps," she carried on with difficulty, "perhaps he gave me something you hadn't been giving for a long time ... such as some attention ... some love. I don't know." As soon as she said it, she knew that she had made a mistake.

"Now then," he said in a wickedly delighted tone, "ought I to take it that now I might be offering you something Aziz has not been giving you for a long time?"

Alex made as if to speak, then stopped. There was no point in going on with this treacherous duel. She wanted to forget about all that had happened. Now was not the time to remember the past; now was the time to live the moment.

"I trusted you, Alex. I trusted you like I trusted no one."

"Right!" exclaimed Alex, suddenly furious. "So much so that you thought no matter what you did, no matter how unfairly you treated me, I'd be there for you forever and ever. I was too nice and therefore too easy, too boring, too unchallenging for you. I was a wild bird already hunted down, obediently waiting in her cage for her master."

"I did nothing that would hurt your pride, Alex. I was never unfaithful to you. I was going through a very difficult time. I was setting up a new life. I was trying to cope with the difficulties of leaving a life that I was used to, that I loved, and of stepping into a brand new, different world: marriage." He paused briefly. "I was scared, Alex," he went on. "And you ... you couldn't see what was actually going on. You blew everything out of proportion. You were living in a reality of your own creation. You couldn't wait, and in the end it was *you* who hurt *my* pride. On that day in Italy I realised that I could never trust you again. Never!"

Alex felt her eyes brimming with tears. She did not want to lose him again. "Why didn't you break up with me there and then?" she asked helplessly.

They had arrived at the Lánc Bridge – the Chain Bridge. The snow that had settled on the stone manes of the lions guarding its entrance deceptively softened their fearsome appearance.

"I didn't want to. I couldn't." He fell silent momentarily before carrying on in a subdued tone, almost a whisper, "I loved you."

"Well, your behaviour in the following months proved quite the reverse. You acted as though you hated me."

"You had been unfaithful to me, Alex. Remember?"

"That's not true, Rudi," she mumbled. "It was just a few unplanned seconds of no significance. I don't know what you want to hear. There's nothing I can say now other than to ask your forgiveness. Please ... please forgive me. All that is history now. Let's leave them there. Please. Let's forget it all."

"I don't think I can ever forgive you, Alex."

With an impossible knot in her throat, she looked at him in desperation, silently pleading for some understanding. His eyes were fixed on the rushing waters of the Danube down below. He was gone. He was gone far far away.

Next morning, as she sipped her coffee in bed, she was thinking about Rudi and the fact that he would probably never want to see her again. She had had a terrible night. After much struggling, she had fallen into a restless sleep, with tears in her eyes triggered by self-pity more than anything else. She woke up several times during the course of that turbulent night with the peculiar sense of being thrown off course by some celestial force. She could not change the past. That was impossible. She took another sip from her coffee and reluctantly got up. It was ten o'clock. She ought to find a way to keep her mind busy. Slipping into a dress, she walked out of her room. She heard Nili's voice from the room that used to be their playroom, then their study and nowadays served as the library no one used anymore.

"Good morning, *tatlım*," she said as she went in.

Nili was playing with the dollhouse. When she saw Alex, she jumped to her feet and rushed to hug her. "Mami! Mami! *Anyukám* bought us a lot of prezzies."

Alex leaned over and kissed her. She then took Lila in her arms and went to sit next to Gizella on the sofa in front of the window.

"I took Nili shopping on Saturday. For the last two days, however, we haven't had a chance to show you the things we have bought, Madame Giritli. Aren't you tired of going out?"

"I can't get enough of this city, Mother."

Nili pulled out a dress from among the numerous presents spread on the sofa and held it up. "Look Mami. This one is my favourite. Look at the flowers. They're so colourful." She began showing each of her presents with great excitement. "These are Lila's. We got some things for her as well, although she's only a baby and doesn't understand anything. Look! Look Mami! Look at my shoes! They're so shiny. They are ... What are they called, *Anyukám?* I can't remember."

"They are patent shoes, my little pumpkin."

"Nili, sweetheart, make sure you break them in while we're here, all right?"

"What does that mean?"

"Wear them a little bit so that they lose their brand new look."

"Why?"

"Because I say so." Alex turned to Gizella. "Otherwise, they would confiscate them at customs in Turkey."

"Mami! Have you seen my pushchair? It's even nicer than the one *Anyukám* brought when she came to Istanbul. That one was for Ayşe Doll and this is going to be for Ilka Doll. She was really jealous of Ayşe, you know."

The head butler, Álmos, appeared at the door. He announced that Rudolf Takács was waiting in the Blue Salon. Alex's depressed spirit instantly lifted. She jumped to her feet and handed Lila over to Teréz, under the scrutiny of Gizella's worried and fuming eyes.

"Teréz, would you please dress them and take them out to the garden for some fresh air?"

"Do you have any idea how cold it is outside? They're not going anywhere." Gizella's tone of voice was impossibly intimidating, but Alex refused to be cowed into a bad mood by her mother's dispiriting remarks.

"All right, all right. You can leave now, Teréz. Leave Lila here as well. Let them play a little."

"Don't you worry, Alex. We shall not let them miss you during your absence," said Gizella, agitated, and, after a brief pause to make sure that Teréz had left, continued in a hushed tone. "Since when have you started to talk to your servants in the familiar 'you,' if I may ask? You have no distance left between you and her, for God's sake!"

"Please Mother. Please stop interfering with my life."

Nili, having guessed that her mother was about to leave, rushed to her grandmother. "*Anyukám*, would you please tell me again the story of my heroic grandfather?" she implored, hugging her. "And the story of his heroic grandfathers?"

"Mother. Please. She's only four and half, far too young for all that family saga. She can't understand a thing you're telling her."

"She loves to listen to it. Not everybody is like you, Alex." She took Nili by the arms and seated her next to her. "Now, my darling girl," she began. "Don't you ever forget who you are and where you come from."

Alex dashed out of the room and rushed down the stairs. She went into the Blue Salon. Rudi was standing by the window with his back to the door, looking out at the front garden that gave on to Vérhalom Street.

"Hello, Rudi. I wasn't expecting you. Aren't you working today?"

"I couldn't have wasted such a lovely day locked up in the office, could I? It's very cold, but the sky is crystal clear. I was thinking of going to Szentendre for the day. What do you say?"

Alex was unable to hide her elation at the idea. "Great! Give me five minutes to change into something respectable."

"You're always respectable."

His sense of humour reassured her that everything was all right.

On the way to Szentendre, they were mostly silent, uttering a phrase or two now and then or engaging in brief snatches of conversation. This time, however, silence did not make Alex feel uncomfortable, and she did not force herself to break it.

"Did you hear what Hitler told the Czech foreign minister? He said, 'We're going to destroy the Jews.' The situation doesn't look very bright."

"Do you still have your law office?"

"Yes, we do."

"The law they issued last year didn't affect you, then?"

"No, it didn't. Those who were baptised before August 1919 are not considered Jewish. I've always admired my father's foresight." It was a question mark whether György Takács's motive for their conversion was his foresight or his desire to do business with the state more easily, but it was obvious that it had been a clever move. "However, this doesn't mean that we will definitely be safe in the future. One shouldn't bet all his money on one horse."

"How do you mean?"

"I mean one has to keep the exit doors open."

At Szentendre, a small village that always reminded Alex of her childhood when they used to live on the northern shores of Italy, she wanted to walk through its winding narrow streets down to the embankment along the Danube. On one of the streets, she saw a little girl holding her mother's hand, chewing on a liquorice stick, something that immediately took her back to the time when they used to come over from Italy for their summer holidays and go to their estate in Eger. She reminisced how, while waiting for the horses to be prepared, they used to chew on the liquorice sticks the stableman gave them. A warm sensation enveloped her heart. This was one of the rare memories she had of what she used to do with her father, one of the brief episodes of utter happiness she vaguely remembered – or thought she did. She could not recall when she had last been there.

They stopped on the crooked old footbridge and leaned on the stone railings to silently watch the raucous stream flowing by in its way to join the Danube further down.

"You blew it, Alex," said Rudi, finally breaking the silence. "You blew everything for us. We could have had a completely different life. We could have had children ... You couldn't wait."

A withered branch passed by underneath, tossing and turning as the waves kept slapping it. "I'll repeat something I said years ago, something you most probably misunderstood. Infidelity, Alex, infidelity is very hard to swallow. Once you face it, you can't but burn with an impossible desire to seek vengeance. After that incident in Italy, I wanted to take revenge on you. I wanted you to hurt as much as you had hurt me. I was desperately trying to make peace with myself and regain my self-respect."

Was it a simple kiss that had so enflamed Rudi's blood, provoking him to torture her so mercilessly for months? Was it that chance meeting of lips that had compelled him to insult her so relentlessly? And all those insults, for which Alex could find no justification, or perhaps preferred not to find one, were they because of an accidental peck on the lips? Of course they were, Alex. Of course, it was a simple kiss behind all his intolerable conduct. It was not something Rudi could take. How could she have been so daft! So blind!

"Unfortunately, my vanity and pride blinded me to the fact that I had exaggerated and pushed your patience far beyond its limits." He clasped his hands as they rested on the stone railings and was now firmly squeezing his fingers. "The truth hit me in the face like a heavy blow the moment you took off your engagement ring and left it on my desk, the truth that I had left you without love so much so that you were ready to kiss another man ... the truth that I had failed to take care of you. It was the biggest blow of my life, Alex. Right there and then, I made up my mind." His gaze was fixed on the branches of the trees upstream, stooping down towards the water. "Do you remember the day when we went to Lukács Cukraszda after I had returned from the tournament in Vienna? It was the last time we saw each other, the day you told me that Aziz had proposed to you, the day you interrupted me. I recall every single detail as though it had happened yesterday. I remember saying, 'I realised that I want to spend the ...' when you interrupted me. What I was going to say was, 'I realised that I want to spend the rest of my life with no one but you, Alex.'" He paused looking resolutely into Alex's eyes. "I don't want to spend the rest of my life with anyone but you, Alex."

She could not take her eyes off the water rumbling by down below, not daring to look Rudi in the eye. "Forgive me. Please forgive me," was all she could manage to say.

He held her by the shoulders and slowly turned her towards him. Holding her hand, he took it to his lips and planted a long kiss without taking her glove off. Then with both his hands, he pressed her hand on his chest. "I don't think I'll be able to do that, Alex. I'll never forgive you for what you did." His eyes were in hers. "But that doesn't mean I'm not in love with you."

A tangled knot weighed heavily in her throat, slowly sinking towards her heart. She averted her eyes as she whispered, "I'm so sorry for all that happened."

His lips gently touched her cheek, almost on the edge of her lips. Her heart trembled.

"There's something I would have given you a long time ago," he said as he slowly removed the glove on her right hand, "at our wedding," he whispered, putting on her empty ring finger an antique amber ring with a six-pointed star trapped inside it. "This ring," he said, "has been in our family for generations. For

255

me, it is priceless."

Her tears were wetting his hand, her own fingers, the ring ... Rudi was right. She had ruined everything. She could not wait. And now it was too late. Too late for everything! The life she had lost would never come back. With an onerous sense of responsibility, she unwillingly took off the ring and put it in his palm. "I can't wear it, Rudi. Not now. And I would ask you to keep it for me until I can."

Would she ever be able to wear it? She wanted to believe that she would. She wanted to believe that she would be, once again, with the man she loved, and that they would start all over again from where they had left off.

In the evening she hardly waited for her mother to retire to her room so that she could talk to Magda, who had come to stay with them in Rózsadomb for a few days.

"I still can't believe you're pregnant, Magda. I'm so happy. You're going to have a baby. A baby! Or perhaps twins! Just like us." She could not stand still. She grabbed her sister's hands. "I don't want to go back to Istanbul. I can't tell you how excited I am."

"Alex, I have seven-and-a-half months to go before the delivery," said Magda, holding Alex's chin, trying to catch her eyes. She knew Alex well enough to see that the reason behind her excitement was not only her pregnancy. "Please be careful, dear. Please don't make a mistake."

There was no point in Alex trying to hide her feelings any longer. "He seems to have changed so much, Magda," she blurted out. "You wouldn't believe it."

"Haven't *you?* We've all changed, Alex."

"You might be right, but ... well, I never felt ... he's never made me feel this way even when we were engaged – or perhaps I should say *especially* when we were engaged."

"Alex! Forget about him. Budapest seems to have blurred your judgement. Think about Istanbul. Think about your family."

"Magda, I can't live without love. I need to know that I'm loved, and, more importantly, I need to love. I need to fall in love. I desperately need love. I'm going crazy thinking if Aziz was the right choice. I'm totally confused. And my heart is ... in turmoil."

"Please Alex. Please don't let your mind or your heart get confused. You are loved. Perhaps even too much. You have two daughters who love you and a husband who adores you. Don't you ever forget that. And you have a dear friend whom you love: Rudi. Keep it that way. Don't complicate your life more than it already is."

"Quite the reverse, I think my life would be much less complicated."

"Aziz will be here tomorrow. You ought to pull yourself together, Alex."

47

Alex was in the music room by the Crimson Salon at the end of the North Wing, staring out the window. Disregarding the black patches where the snow had melted, her eyes lingered on the captivating last rays of sunlight dancing on the white areas. The sun had shone with astonishing strength throughout the day, and the sky was crystal clear now. It would be full of stars later on. At night, in the stillness of the *Puszta*, one often had the sensation that the sky was round and understood much better the meaning of celestial sphere.

"It's good that the snow has thawed a little bit. The dogs can't smell well through the snow," said Aziz as he approached Alex, holding a glass of wine. He was in excellent spirits, repeatedly expressing how delighted he was to be here, for it was to be the first time he would be going hunting in the estate of Erzsébet Manor. He had arrived in Budapest the other day, and yesterday they had all moved on to Kengyel.

As the sun slowly disappeared behind the horizon, they went back to the Crimson Salon to join the others.

"Will the children be dining with you this evening, my Lady?" asked Terézia, who had changed her mode of speech shortly after their arrival in Budapest under Gizella's deadly cold stare, putting an artificial slave-master distance between her and Alex, much to the vexation of the latter.

"Dearest Teréz," she replied in an exaggeratedly casual tone, looking not at Terézia but straight into Gizella's eyes. "As we shall be dining rather early this evening, Nili can certainly join us, and you can feed Lila."

Nili and Teodor were waiting behind Terézia, their small faces eagerly radiant. Nili, just like her mother used to do when she was a child, was bouncing up and down on her knees, betraying her excitement. Teodor, on the other hand, acting far too maturely for his seven years of age – as would be expected from József's offspring, was trying hard to hide his feelings, but the sparkle in his eyes and the slight smile on the edges of his lips betrayed his enthusiasm. He seemed keen to show that he was much older than his age and did not need to wait for another two years for his first shoot.

"I'll have Nili seated on my right and Teodor on my left," said Giuseppe, as the children were sent to the playroom until dinnertime.

Maria and Giuseppe had arrived from Italy, bringing in a fresh breath of warm air from the shores of Liguria. Alex said that she had organised this shooting party primarily to convince Giuseppe to come to Hungary, so that she could spend some time with her dear old friend Maria, whom she had not seen for years. After Kengyel, they would be staying in Budapest for a few days, an occasion that Alex looked forward to with great delight. József, Éva and their son Teodor had joined them this morning. Since Christmas, they had been staying in Martfü, a village about ten kilometres south of Kengyel, at Almás Manor, which was not far away from the Kurzón's hunting lodge, being located in the northern edge of their rather small estate of four hundred hectares which lay adjacent to the southern border of the estate of Erzsébet Manor.

Alex settled next to Magda on one of the sofas next to the fireplace, close to the warm light of the flames that promised to overpower the imminent darkness of the approaching night. She placed her hand on her sister's belly. It was as though a new life were being created in her too. They were to have another baby in the family, a cousin for Nili and Lila, maybe even two. She was so happy. They all were.

Given the smells wafting out of the kitchen downstairs, the legs of the boar Sándor had hunted last week should almost be done. A few minutes later the head butler Csaba came to announce that dinner was ready to be served. Miklós, fussing over Magda, whose pregnancy was not even noticeable yet, offered his arm to help his wife get up. Magda accepted his help, albeit quite unnecessarily, and slowly rose to her feet, enjoying every moment of her husband's unending attention, which had become more intense than ever before. Gizella, sitting on the sofa opposite, stood up and took János's arm, either because she considered it extremely rude to refuse the arm of a gentleman or because lately the iron door between them seemed to have opened a crack. Although trying not to show it, she had obviously started to nurture a slight admiration for János, who had always been most respectful towards her, and, as importantly, had become the talk of the elite circles in Budapest as a wise, ambitious and hardworking man on a rapid rise in the State Railways towards a successful career.

They all ambled into the dining room. Sándor sat at the head of the table, and Etel, who followed her son everywhere, took her place next to him, leaving Gizella the honour of occupying the seat across from Sándor at the other end of the table. Alex was transfixed by Aunt Etel's chin, now adorned with folds due to the excessive weight she had recently put on, and by how it undulated as she laughed. Her already short neck had disappeared altogether, leaving almost no distance between her chin and her shoulders. Her thin lips, almost invisible between her fat cheeks, had been in a constant upward curve as she had never stopped smiling since their arrival at Kengyel. Her hands, which used to look too plump for her body when she was younger, now seemed to have too little flesh on them.

Sándor rose from his chair, raising his glass for a toast. "I'd like to drink to the health of my dearest cousin, who is not with us right now and whom I think of every single day. I wish him all the best in honour of his thirty-third birthday, albeit belated by three days. Happy birthday, dear Károly."

"Happy birthday, *Öcsi.*"

"Happy birthday, *Öcsi.*"

"Happy birthday, son."

Everyone else at the table joined in, expressing their good wishes. Gizella made no effort to hide either the tears that welled up in her eyes or the sobs that followed. She proposed another toast when she finally managed to restrain her emotions. "I do hope that he will come to his senses," she murmured.

"I wish we would be all together again," said Alex, raising her glass.

As the steaming *potage aux legumes* was served, Giuseppe was already into a heated recount of the last shoot he had attended, moving his hands and arms considerably more than Gizella would approve. Alex could not hear the dialogue between her mother and Éva, but was certain that they were exchanging the latest gossip in Budapest. Éva was Gizella's favourite among Alex's friends, such favouritism being undeniably – and strongly – influenced by the fact that she was the daughter of Baron and Baroness Orbánstein. Alex's mind shifted to Orbánstein's villa on Andrássy Boulevard, then to their neighbours Monsieur and Madame Takács, and finally to her engagement party.

"Look Mami! I've finished my soup. It was yummy." Budapest had kindled Nili's appetite, and she had finally put on some of that very much required weight.

Alex stroked her daughter's hair.

"*Brava!*" said Giuseppe, encouraging little Nili, whom he thought was far too skinny. "*Sei una brava bambina.*"

"I want to speak Italian."

Aziz, sitting on the other side of Alex, leaned over to tell Nili to be quiet.

Sándor, retired behind his usual expression, which conveyed nothing but an Arcadian staidness, had long been immersed in the depths of his soup. He seemed to live in a world of dreams. When they were children, Alex used to think that he was extremely timid. It was only years later that she had realised that what she used to take as timidity in her cousin was actually an extremely high level of amour-propre, mixed with condescension towards everybody around him. At times he looked at people with such haughtiness that nobody dared approach him. She wondered if he would have been any different if he had married Margit.

Sándor had finished his soup. He let his eyes swiftly skim around the table to make sure that others had finished as well. Then with a slight movement of his pupils and a barely visible lift of his thin eyebrows, he looked at Csaba waiting in one corner of the dining room, clad in his black tailcoat and bow-tie, watching the table with eagle eyes, ready to catch even the slightest movement in his master's face. Used to interpreting the instructions Sándor conveyed with hardly noticeable gestures of an eye, a finger or the head, as though unwilling to waste his breath, Csaba reiterated the same instructions in similar silent gestures to the servants waiting on both sides of the dining room door. The serving staff stood at a distance far enough not to hear any whispered conversation but close enough to leap to the table at the lowering of an eyelid. This distance between masters and servants had been carefully calculated generations ago. The empty plates were removed from the table in absolute silence. A few minutes later the well-roasted legs of boar made their glorious entrance through the service door, their mouth-watering smell preceding them. Sándor, who readily tired of long discussions and did not believe in having any conversation whatsoever during dinner, suddenly broke his silence, obviously uncontrollably excited at the sight of such a sumptuous feast, a sight that left everyone else tongue-tied.

"I'm rather astonished at how some people might find country life monotonous, empty and depressive. They seem to be oblivious to the fact that it's only in the provinces one can be rid of the inanities of life and understand the true meaning of existence."

The honour of carving was bestowed upon József. Sándor went on talking about Kengyel and how pleasant his life here was. In no more than fifteen minutes everyone, including the children, had wolfed down everything on their plates. Alex, despite her long-lost appetite, had no difficulty in finishing the thin slice that

József, who knew Alex's gastronomic limits quite well, had mercifully carved for her. Leaning back on her chair to relax her nevertheless overfilled stomach, she tried to decide which one of the various voices rising from the table she wanted to listen to. Cheese was being served. The children had long ago finished their desserts and, after bidding goodnight, had unwillingly followed Nanny Teréz to withdraw to their rooms for the night.

"Hungary does you good, Alex," said Aziz in a soft tone of voice as he stroked her cheek. He then turned to Miklós sitting opposite them. "Even her paintings are different, full of light, don't you think?" Finally addressing Gizella at the other end of the table, he said, "I should send Alex here more often."

Gizella looked at Alex with fuming eyes, emptied of their customary glacial acerbity. "She surely will be coming here much often from now on," she said, before pausing briefly to accentuate the weight of what she was to say. "To see us!"

Alex thought how unnerving her mother's sardonic expression was. She looked at Magda, beseeching her help.

"You've neglected us for too long," Magda jumped in. "Three years! You stayed away for three years. I do hope you'll come more often, at least to see your nephew or niece," she continued, caressing her belly.

Alex felt her spirits collapsing. She had no intention of letting her mother upset her with her bitter remarks. She wanted to leave the table there and then but waited, albeit with much uneasiness, until they finished their desserts. Fortunately, Sándor, with his aversion to staying at the table longer than necessary once the dinner was over, placed his napkin on the table as soon as he swallowed the last sip of his coffee, thanked everyone, pushed his chair back and stood up. In some respects, he looked so much like his father – only in some respects though.

Alex jumped to her feet before everyone else and, although she knew that neither her mother nor Aziz would approve of her going to bed before the guests did, she excused herself, saying that she wished to retire for the night, mumbling something along the lines of, "You all know how much I hate waking up early." "Six-thirty is an unearthly hour for me to start the day." "I'd be unbearable in the morning if I slept less than eight hours," before she concluded, "Goodnight, everyone," and went out of the dining room. She needed to be in good fettle tomorrow.

It was freezing in her bedroom. The fireplace was lit, but apparently the fire was not enough to warm up the large room. To maximise sleeping time and minimise dressing-up time when she woke up the next morning, she stacked the clothes she would be wearing the next day in the order she would be putting them on and placed them on the armchair before going to the bathroom to brush her teeth and take off her already faded makeup. Looking at herself in the mirror, she suddenly pulled the toothbrush out of her mouth. "What are you doing, Alex?" she whispered below her breath. "What on earth are you doing?" she hissed. Come to your senses! The bathroom was even colder than the bedroom. She hurriedly rinsed her mouth, rushed back to her room and climbed into the bed, shivering. Shortly she would be warming up under the eiderdown. She turned off the light and closed her eyes, hoping to sleep sooner than later so that morning came faster. Unfortunately, she was not in the least bit sleepy. "It's going to be a long night," she thought with a weary sigh. She turned the light back on and waited until her eyes got used to the brightness. Taking her book from the bedside table, she pulled the eiderdown up to her nose and started reading.

She read for about an hour before she decided that she had better try to sleep. She lay on her right, then on her left and finally on her back, noticing, for the first time in all these years, how uncomfortable her bed was. Her mind, as restless as her body, refused to go to sleep. The more she thought, the more confused she got, and the more difficult it became for sleep to come. She should not think. She needed to be fresh in the morning and look her best, not like a zombie. When she heard Aziz enter the room, she thought that was it; he would immediately go to sleep and start snoring, which would be the end of any hope for the solace she sought in the arms of Morpheus, since she still found it very hard to ignore the sound of his sporadically thunderous snore. I have to sleep before he does, she thought in panic and closed her eyes tightly, pretending to be fast asleep.

Someone was stroking her hair. She opened her eyes. Aziz was sitting on the bed, watching her.

"Good morning, *ma petite*."

"What's the time?"

"Six thirty."

He had already dressed and was ready to go. She jumped out of bed and rushed towards the bathroom.

"My! My! Aren't we fast this morning?" said Aziz, surprised.

She did not answer. It was so cold that she would not even think about taking a bath. She had no time for it anyway. Shivering, she washed her face and brushed her teeth in a jiffy. Her face in the mirror resembled that of a ghost. Unwillingly she took off her peignoir and nightgown to quickly wash her underarms. God, she was freezing! She threw her peignoir back on and, after putting some blush on her cheeks and brushing her hair, returned to her room. Aziz had already gone. She dressed in a rush, dashed out of the room, almost ran through the corridor and the hall and went into the dining room. They had finished their breakfast and were having coffee in the Crimson Salon. "Good morning everyone," she sang.

Aziz came over with a cup of steaming hot white coffee and put his arm around Alex's waist. "I can't tell you how uplifting it is to see you in such good spirits at this hour, *ma petite*," he said, kissing her temple. "Good morning, yet again." He handed her the coffee cup.

Alex took a Danish pastry from the breakfast table before going into the salon.

"I've taken your wellies to the truck," said Aziz. "Don't forget your gloves and hat. Will that sweater be warm enough? Have you put on your woollen vest?"

"Stop worrying, Aziz. I'll be all right."

"Let's make a move, shall we? It's almost seven," said Sándor as he made for the door.

They all put on their coats and furs in the hall.

It was freezing outside. Sándor had already mounted his horse and was waiting impatiently. János would also be riding with him to the lodge. The others climbed onto the pickup trucks. Teodor, utterly excited, wanted to go with his mother in the truck Giuseppe was to drive. In the other truck, Alex sat between József and Aziz. Despite the cold, she lowered the back window and stuck out her hand to stroke József's dogs Hó – Snow, who had been born under heavy snow, and Nap – Sun, who had come on a sunny day. They stopped jumping up and down and began licking Alex's hand. Nap was waggling his bushy eyebrows to express the feelings he was unable to articulate.

"He really talks with his eyes, this one," said Alex lovingly.

"Nap is a newly bred wirehaired Vizsla. He's the grandson of Zsuzsi, a Magyar Vizsla, and Astor von Potat, a German wirehaired pointer," said József, with visible pride in his voice.

"How is his nose?" asked Aziz.

"It's only his second hunt, but we definitely have a champion here. He's very promising. He learned how to stand dead still very quickly, though he still needs to stay put a bit longer. I don't want to teach him how to retrieve yet. Its Hó's job."

Upon hearing his name, the English Springer Spaniel started jumping about excitedly.

They set off on the acacia-lined road towards the hunting lodge at the south end of the estate. The day was slowly breaking. The houses of Kengyel came into view, stifled under their snow-covered roofs, their wooden shutters peeping through the white vista, surrounded by an army of white trees with their trunks resembling burnt matchsticks. The sky was crystal clear again. The earth, sequestered under a blanket of snow, was waiting for the imminent sunrise, ready to declare its freedom, if only in patches, the moment the sun's rays touched it. Alex smelled the earth – a scent from her childhood. Did she really smell it or was it her imagination that brought about this familiar smell? They rumbled along the road for about a quarter of an hour before they arrived at the hunting lodge. There were a number of trucks already parked there. The huntsmen were on the patio in front of the lodge, some putting on their boots, some sipping their coffee and all of them bragging about their previous shoots. The dogs knew where they were and why they were there and, all hopped up, were already in a frenzy of excitement, running to and fro frantically with all their feet off the ground, eagerly waiting for their masters to get going.

"How many are we?" asked Alex.

"More than twenty. There'll be fifteen guns, I imagine."

József parked their truck next to the others. Alex changed into her rubber boots. A few minutes later Sándor and János arrived on their horses. They all walked towards the dogs' sheds next to the lodge. Seeing Sándor, their master, the Vizslas, the English Setters and the Pointers started barking in an unruly chorus.

"Which ones will you be taking today, Sanyi?" asked Alex.

"Öröm and Fürge."

"The famous Fürge!" exclaimed Aziz. "Is it true that he sets twenty birds in four hours?"

"Easily. Even more, I should say."

The Gordon Setters must have heard the trucks arriving and the sound of the other dogs, for they were excitedly running around their huts in their little garden surrounded by a wired fence. At the sight of Sándor, the mature Fürge and the nine-month-old Öröm knew that they were the chosen ones and started barking even more loudly, practically clambering up the wire fence. As soon as the gate opened, they ran to Sándor to show their gratitude by jumping onto him and licking his hands, before they hurriedly moved on to smell the others and finally dashed towards the other dogs.

"Shall we have some coffee?" offered Sándor.

The sun showed up over the horizon like a misty ball of lemon. They walked towards the patio where the other huntsmen were having their coffee. Suddenly Alex felt Aziz firmly grab her arm. He was hurting her.

"Aziz? What are you doing? You're hurting me!"

"Did you know he'd be here?"

"What are you talking about?"

Squeezing Alex's arm even harder, obviously in the sudden grip of a surge of fury, he brusquely raised his chin, slightly moving his head towards the huntsmen sitting around the patio. His eyes were blazing. Alex threw an apprehensive glance towards the patio, knowing what she would see. Rudi was sitting on one of the chairs, putting on his boots. This was what she had been secretly longing for, but now that her wish had come true she felt not a sense of joy but sheer panic. "Let go of me," she hissed, trying to break her arm free.

"Did you?"

"Did I what?"

"Did you know Rudolf would be coming?"

"How could I have known that, Aziz?"

"Well, well, well! Look who's here! What an honour to have you here, old chap," hollered Endré as he moved away from the crowd towards Aziz with his arms spread wide apart.

"The honour is mine to be here with you," said Aziz politely.

They shook hands and patted each other on the shoulder to express the strong rapport between them.

Alex could not take her eyes off Rudi. When he finished putting on his boots and raised his head, their eyes met. Although he tried to hide his emotions at seeing Alex by stifling a smile, his eyes betrayed his feelings. Alex gave a hesitant, almost unnoticeable, smile before she turned towards Aziz and saw him staring intently at her. He fixed his squinted dark eyes on Alex's as he moved closer to her. Barely moving his pupils towards the patio, he thundered through his clenched teeth, "What the hell is he doing here?"

She felt crushed under his voice, which had a threatening rather than an inquisitive tone.

"You knew, Alex. It's not the first time you've seen each other after seven years."

"Please. Please stop being so ridiculously jealous."

He took her by the arm and dragged her towards where Rudi was standing.

"Hello, Monsieur Takács."

"Hello, Monsieur Giritli," said Rudi, extending his hand.

They shook hands as if they wanted to break each other's bones.

"Madame Giritli."

Alex could only manage a slight movement of her head in greeting.

"What a pleasant surprise after all these years. Good hunting," sneered Aziz.

"To you too."

Following this short exchange of pleasantries filled with hatred, anger and frustration but draped with a feigned politeness heavy with irony, they moved away from Rudi as fast as they had approached him.

"Yes, Giritli Azizné de Kurzón Alexandra," growled Aziz, his voice enflamed with repressed fury. When he addressed her in Hungarian like this, he was as frightening as a sky burdened by dark clouds announcing an imminent storm. "The last time we saw Rudolf, we didn't have Giritli as our surname. I was still Halimzade Aziz *Bey* then."

"Aziz, you know better than I do that in Budapest people have nothing better to do than to gossip. We don't need to see each other for him to know that our last name is now Giritli. Besides, what if we did see each other?"

"I'll answer that question later. Now let's go and hunt some game."

Alex felt her legs almost give way. I shouldn't have come, she was thinking. I shouldn't have. This is pure torture, nothing but self-torture. I'm crazy. Completely nuts!

The group of huntsmen slowly set off on the dirt track, flanked with bushes that looked like white balls of wool scattered on one side and endless frozen fields extending into the horizon on the other. The dogs were running wildly in all directions with their noses never leaving the ground, where patches of earth peeped through the melting snow. As they went in and out of the bushes, sending the snow on their branches flying about, the white balls of wool transformed into intertwined strands of withered spaghetti. After a while, the huntsmen left the dirt track and moved ahead into the field. A few minutes later Hector, the veteran German Braque, suddenly froze in front of a bush. His master Giuseppe, or *Il Capo* – The Boss – as everyone called him, raised his gun. Although extremely excited and eager to set the prey, Hector knew he had to wait until his master gave his order before making a move. He waited proudly, though impatiently, and, as soon as he heard Giuseppe's voice, set the bird. The guns went off. The pheasant, after a tiny summersault, came down elegantly. Hector dashed towards the hunted bird, took it gently between his jaws, careful not to hurt its already dead body, rushed back to deliver it to the hands of Giuseppe and stormed away in search of new scents.

Desperately trying to take her mind off Rudi and Aziz, Alex tried to concentrate on the shooting, or rather on the dogs. Anyone who was not fond of dogs should go hunting with them, she thought, to understand that they can be more human than human beings. "These lead shots, would they kill a human being?" she asked Sándor.

"They might. It depends on how close you are to your target."

The hunt continued. Inexperienced as she might be, Öröm set a bird as well, although she was still unable to stand put long enough. Apparently finding it very difficult to get her mind off her catch, she kept jumping up and down behind Tamás, the gamekeeper, to play with the dead birds dangling over his shoulder – not the best behaviour for a hunting dog, frequently eliciting a good scolding from Sándor, whose harsh voice sent her dashing away towards another bush, sniffing the ground with great enthusiasm. Alex, feeling sorry for her, wanted to stroke her for some consolation, but knew that she should never intervene in the relationship between a dog and its master.

After three and a half hours the dogs, having been in and out of the stream, were drenched, muddy, tired and exceedingly happy. The huntsmen seemed happy and delightfully satisfied as well, if not as tired as the dogs. A group, including Rudi, was moving along the other side of the stream, sporadically disappearing behind the bushes lining both sides of the waterway. Wise and attentive as his name suggested, Fürge picked up a new scent and froze in front of a bush, holding one of his front legs up in the air and fixing his unwavering stare on something in the depths of the entangled branches. As soon as he heard Sándor's order, he set the bird. The huntsmen raised their rifles. Alex saw Aziz turning his rifle towards the other side of the stream, with its barrel directly aimed at Rudi.

"Aziz!" she exclaimed in panic and pushed Aziz's arm up. The rifle fired.

"What do you think you're doing, Alex? Have you gone mad?"

"*You* must have gone mad!"

"Go away! Stay away from me!" he shouted as he pushed Alex aside, slightly pressing his hand against her chest.

Éva rushed over to Alex and took her by the arm. "Come with me, dear. Let's go to the other side." They walked over a tree trunk to cross over the stream.

"I've got to sit down, Éva." Alex's heart was pounding.

"Are you all right? You must be very tired," said Éva apprehensively, the compassionate expression on her face somewhat soothing Alex's strained nerves. "We'll be going back soon, anyway. You just rest now."

When they were back at the hunting lodge, Alex joined others to go and look at the dead birds hung from their necks on an iron rack next to the dogs' shed, waiting to be distributed among the huntsmen. Suddenly feeling sick to her stomach, she moved away from the ghastly sight and went to the truck to get her shoes. Back on the patio, she changed into her shoes and went to the sink in the back garden to wash the mud off her boots.

"Let me do that for you, my Lady," said Tamás, the gamekeeper, as he made to take the boots from her.

Wanting to stay away from both Aziz and Rudi, she sought refuge inside the hunting lodge. The grizzly bear lying on the floor in front of the fireplace gazed at her with offended eyes for having been neglected for so long. Her heart sank, as it usually did, when she looked at the stuffed birds lined up on the walls surrounding the rustic dining table and along the wooden stairs leading upstairs. The other walls were decorated with a variety of Austrian guns and English daggers, basically anything related to hunting that her mother preferred not to have at the manor house. Alex thought she smelled her father in here. She turned around abruptly and went out.

The dogs were still running about. True to her name, the cheerful Öröm started circling around her. She extended her hand to stroke the friendly Gordon Setter.

"Alex! Don't touch her!" Sándor hollered.

Both Alex and Öröm froze. Apparently, Öröm had just attacked a dead bird and bit into it. Sándor took her to the back of the truck to have a one-to-one talk. Alex could hardly keep herself from showing some compassion to the poor dog, but she knew too well that it might be disastrous if a hunting dog in training tasted blood and that it would be wrong to touch the offender, let alone show her affection. Like many a hunting dog, Öröm was learning; like many a huntsman, Sándor was teaching.

When Sándor finished upbraiding his dog, Alex went to the truck without bidding farewell to anyone. On the way back, she was thinking that the best part of hunting was watching the dogs – up to a certain point that was. The rest was all too violent for her taste.

* * *

Back at the manor house she went straight to her room, practically running away from Aziz. The fireplace had been lit. She put on her bathrobe and went to the bathroom, locked the door and turned on the tap. As she undressed, she inhaled the steam rising from the water and went in before the tub was full. Sitting, she poured some water over her breasts, neck and arms. A chill ran through her. She slid down and waited for the water level to come up to her neck. Then, taking a deep breath, she submerged first her chin, then her lips, then her cheeks, nose and finally her ears. She closed her eyes and completely went under. The water penetrated the roots of her hair, alleviating her soul, cleansing her mind. She ran out of breath but stayed motionless for a few seconds longer. And then a few seconds more ... A pain grabbed her chest. Her temples throbbed. Her heart was beating in her brain. Slowly she surfaced. Her eyes were still closed to the outside world. She was listening to her heart.

48

Everyone had dressed for lunch and sat waiting for it like famished wolves. Exhausted, they were lounging on the sofas around the fireplace in the Yellow Salon and sipping their wine, some enjoying a great sense of fulfilment after the shooting. The snow had just started to fall heavily again after a long break of several weeks.

"Did you enjoy the hunt, Alex?" asked Miklós.

"I don't believe women can really enjoy hunting. The hunting instinct is exclusive to men, I should think."

Aziz was poking the wood in the fireplace to kindle the flames. "Women also have that instinct," he joined in with a sarcastic tone in his voice, "but their hunting ground, as well as the game they hunt, is rather different."

"The instinct you're talking about is the instinct of procreation, my dear Aziz, not of hunting," interjected Magda. "It simply is a search for the cleverest, the strongest and the healthiest partner who would help them procreate in the best possible way. Their search – or their hunting instinct as you put it – is satisfied when a new life is born. The male hunting instinct, on the other hand, is only satisfied when a life is spent, and that is basically death."

Alex looked at her sister with gratitude. As always, she was protecting her.

"Thank you so much, my dearest," she whispered mutely.

"We hunt so that life can be sustained, so that we can bring food to our families," said János, laughing at his own remark before anyone else did. The men in the room joined him.

"Yes, sure," Alex barged in. "You must be living in the Stone Age, Jancsi. There are many other ways to feed ourselves, don't you think? You have no grounds that could justify why you hunt other than your killing instinct." Her voice was tensing.

"Alex, you do realise that you exaggerate, don't you?" interrupted Sándor, apparently keen on closing the subject. "You shouldn't be eating chicken meat then or veal or those pork chops that you adore. They might not be hunted down but, one way or another, they get killed. This is the law of nature, dear cousin. Some need to eat other living beings to survive."

"I hope you won't say that you're killing to survive. Well, perhaps you should try and hunt a wild boar without a gun, my dear Sanyi. Doesn't the law of nature dictate that as well?"

"It's quite incredible how she married a huntsman like me," said Aziz, his voice heavy with cynicism.

"I hate hunting," said Alex faintly, frowning.

"Why did you join us then?" inquired József.

"Because I was curious. I was curious about the things I listen to day in and day out. And let's say that I joined you because I was hoping to understand the male species a little bit better." She could not, of course, say that she hoped to see Rudi one more time. She was uncomfortable about admitting it even to herself.

"You said it yourself, Alex," put in Maria, sweetly smiling as if trying to cover up for the bitterness of what she was about to say. "The hunting instinct of men is really strong. If they don't go shooting, they're bound to seek different prey to quench their thirst. Therefore, we should let them hunt game. We should in fact let them go for the difficult shoot because they won't be satisfied with easy ones." She put her arm around Alex's shoulders.

"I guess you're right, Maria," said Alex as she pressed her temple against her friend's cheek, her eyes unintentionally travelling towards Aziz, who was staring at her with an unbearably frightening glint in his eyes.

Lunch started and ended late at around four o'clock, leaving everyone very sleepy. They all went to their rooms for a nap. Alex, neither daring to face Aziz in the privacy of their room nor willing to be left on her own, convinced Maria to stay with her in the drawing room to make up for the time they had spent apart.

She delayed dinnertime as much as she could, claiming that nobody could possibly be hungry and, after the light supper they had, dawdled over cups of coffee and glasses of cognac, detaining Maria and Éva for a chat by the fireplace until long after everyone retired for the night. Eventually, she had to let go of her slumberous friends and go to sleep herself. When she entered her bedroom, Aziz was sitting in an armchair, waiting for her. She knew exactly what to expect. He would shout at her; he would shout even if it meant waking up the children sleeping in the playroom next door. She hoped that he would not do so at the top of his lungs out of respect for Gizella, whose room was not far from theirs. Losing no time, he began scolding her in a tone of voice worse than shouting, worse than spitting in her face. He rebuked her for having no pride, since it was inconceivable how else she could still keep in touch with someone who had once treated her so deplorably. He went on, telling her that she should be ashamed of herself and that she should at least have the decency to think of her daughters and how embarrassed they would be of their mother. He grunted that from now on he would never trust her and would never let her go anywhere on her own. In the end, frustrated for not having shouted as much as he wished, he crushed the full brandy glass between his fingers and carried on with his insults as blood dripped from his hand.

Alex could no longer take it. "Enough!" she yelled, probably waking up everyone. "Enough. I'm sick and tired of your insults. Leave me alone."

Aziz lunged across the room towards her and pressed his bloody hand on her lips, grabbing her neck with his other hand. Alex could not breathe. Then suddenly he let her go. In panic, he took his handkerchief out and began to wipe the blood off her lips and cheeks. He kept apologising. Alex froze for a few seconds and then pushed away his hands. "Don't touch me," she said in a lifelessly flat voice. She did not even want to look at him. She went into the bathroom and cleaned her face, trying to avoid her reflection in the mirror. When she returned to the room, Aziz was still standing at the same spot.

"I'm so sorry, Alex."

She no longer feared his assaults nor took his excuses seriously. She did not care anymore because she finally had something in her life that added colour to it, something that warmed her forlorn heart, giving her the strength and desire to carry on. She longingly embraced her thoughts as she undressed and put on her nightgown. She went to the window and opened the curtains. The snow was falling heavily. The stars, which had filled the sky the night before, were now invisible. Like *Puszta*, they had surrendered to the snow. A deer that must have come out of the woods was standing dead still by the frozen lake. Suddenly it turned its head towards the house. Alex smiled. Could it see her? She put her hand on the glass. The deer slowly turned around and walked back into the woods.

Aziz was still talking when Alex went to bed. She did not want to hear his voice. She pulled the eiderdown up to her ears. She thought of Japán Kávéház ... about Szentendre ... She was about to have a sweet dream.

49

It had been two weeks since they had returned from Kengyel to Budapest. Aziz had finished his business at the Ganz Factory the day before yesterday, and tomorrow they would be going back to Istanbul. After Kengyel, Aziz had been behaving as if nothing had happened. What had happened anyway? She was not the first woman to show some interest in a man other than her husband, was she? Was it a crime to feel for someone who was not her husband – a husband who always left her alone, insulted her, hurt her and suffocated her with his jealousies? If she had ever committed a crime, it was her readiness to surrender to Aziz and her failure to set up a family with Rudi. She ought to admit this at least to herself, as difficult as it might be.

She had not seen Rudi since that day in Kengyel. Once, she had called him on the phone, only to hang up without saying anything. But now she had to talk him as soon as she could, for she was extremely worried about him. Yesterday a hand grenade had been thrown among the people leaving the synagogue on Dohány Street. Nothing could have happened to Rudi or to his family since they had converted to Christianity and obviously were not going to the synagogue, but Alex was scared of what this incident might lead to. Her mother and Aziz continuously talked about it throughout breakfast, as though they wanted to torture her.

She waited for the long morning hours to pass, lunch to end and Aziz to retire for his afternoon nap before she called Rudi. She asked his forgiveness for Aziz's strange behaviour and for having left so abruptly after the shoot without even saying goodbye. She expressed her worries about the incident at the synagogue, asking if anything had happened to anybody he knew. Rudi said that he was really upset about the atrocities committed against the Jewish people in Germany and, like everyone else, was shocked at yesterday's events, although that was something they all feared would happen sooner or later. He was saying that it was time to take action. In the end, he asked when she would be coming to Budapest again.

"I hope I'll be here for Magda's delivery."

There was silence on the other side. Had the line gone? "Hello?"

"I'll miss you, Alex. Very much."

Another moment of silence. She dared not say, me too.

"I accepted Sándor's invitation to the shoot in Kengyel because I wanted to see – I had to see – your relationship. I had to see Aziz as your husband. I had to see what he – the man for whom you left me – looked like after all these years."

She wondered if he also thought, "I had to see the man whom you will soon be leaving for me."

"Seeing you with him stirred up memories, painful memories of the greatest loss of my life."

Was he determined to win back what he had lost? His voice betrayed unflinching resolve. Alex quailed at his unrelenting self-confidence. Rudi had never been good at accepting defeat. But at the moment it was not him who was losing.

"I'd like you to give me your address, Alex."

"You shouldn't write to me. I beg you not to."

Eventually, she gave in to his pleas and next morning left her address, her heart and her mind in Budapest before setting off for Istanbul with her husband and daughters.

50

When she saw Rudi's handwriting on one of the envelopes the postman handed over, her heart started to beat thunderously, more out of fear than joy. After having returned to Istanbul, nothing had remained of the courage she had gathered in Budapest. She dreaded to think what Aziz would do if he found these love letters, which, although unsigned, were obviously written by Rudi. This was going to be the fourth letter she would leave unanswered. After reading it over and over again, she wet its pages in the sink until all the ink was rinsed away and the words disappeared. She then shredded them to pieces and threw them in the dustbin. This was sheer madness. She should tell him never to write to her again. He would not bring colour to her life but only wash out its existing hues. But then there was no hue in her life, nothing meaningful except for these letters. And she did not want to deprive herself of them. Struggling with her vacillating mood, she barely waited for the evening to come and, after dinner, sat down to write to him.

Istanbul, 20th March 1939

Dearest Rudi,

I've received all four letters you sent although I could not respond to any of them. Please rest assured that every word in your letters adds meaning to my life, but I'm terrified of Aziz's reaction if he were to find out about our correspondence. I would, therefore, implore you not to write to me, at least not until after I talk to Izabella about our situation and ask her if you could post your letters to her address.

This time, returning to Istanbul proved to be painfully difficult. I don't think I could have survived here, even for a day, if it were not for Nili and Lila. I'm terribly lonely. Aziz has gone hunting as usual, now to the east of Turkey. And he instructed his sisters to keep me entertained. It doesn't occur to him that I can't stand any of them. Loneliness amid a crowd is an unbearable burden. The solitude of the soul consumes you.

Looking back, I can't believe it was me who did all those cheerful paintings in Budapest. Nowadays I do force myself to paint in an effort to avoid a headlong plunge into the lethargy that I'm prone to suffer from, but what comes out of my desolate soul is awfully depressing. They are so insipid, so boringly monochromatic and so sad ... I really don't know why I'm writing these things to you. There is practically no one here with whom I can talk about my art. Aziz doesn't understand my work. He does like them, but only because he loves me. In fact we have almost no common interests in that the books we read, the music we listen to and anything else we enjoy doing are totally different.

"Mami? Are you writing to Magda *néni?*" Nili was standing in front of her in her pyjamas.

"Yes, my love."

"I wrote this with Nanny Teréz. Would you please post it?"

"Of course I shall, *tatlım.*"

"Don't read it though."

"All right, I won't. You go to bed now. It's really rather late."

As Nili ran back to her bedroom, Alex unfolded her letter.

Istanbul, 20th March 1939

Dearest Magda *néni*,

I already miss you and Miklós *bácsi* so much. Has the baby arrived yet? We'll come over when it does. We're all much happier there. Mami has been so sad and so nervous ever since we came back from Budapest. She always argues with my aunts. She sometimes paints and often lets me watch her. She gives me some colouring pencils to draw as well, but I can never draw as beautifully as she can.

We go to Aunt Izabella's a lot. They have a lovely garden where I play with Évike. We'll go and visit them when you come to Istanbul. When will you come?

Lila is fine. She never gets sick. Sometimes she cries at night, and I take care of her.

Lots of love from me and from my sister to you and to *Anyukám*, to Etel *néni* and Sanyi *bácsi*, and also to my great aunt and uncle, and a lot of kisses to Miklós *bácsi*.

Your loving pumpkin,
Nili

Alex folded the letter. God only knew when she would be able to go to Budapest again. Would Aziz let her go for Magda's delivery? Hungary was in turmoil. The army, with Germany's permission, had occupied Sub-Carpathian Ruthenia up to the Polish border. Her heart sank. She took herself out onto the balcony and lit a cigarette. As she blew its smoke towards the sky, she saw a shooting star. "*Maradj velem*," she whispered in haste.

51

"Madam! Madam, wake up!"

Alex started at Teréz's voice. She jumped out of bed. "What happened? What's wrong?"

Teréz was holding a telegram in her trembling hand.

Aziz? Something must have happened to Aziz. Or is it my mother? Magda! Is it Magda? Something happened to Magda! She snatched the telegram from Teréz, unable to control the sudden shivering in her body.

Magda had a haemorrhage STOP Is in hospital STOP Not to worry STOP Miklós

An icy hand grabbed her heart and started squeezing the life out of it. Her knees gave in, and she collapsed onto her bed. She had to go right away. She had to be with her. Why did she leave her in the first place? The same thing had happened to her. It would pass. It would certainly pass. It shouldn't be anything important. Magda is strong. Nothing will ever happen to her. I had a haemorrhage as well. I had the same thing. She'll be fine. She'll get pregnant again, just like I did. She'll be able to bear children, just like I did. We're the two halves of a whole. We're exactly the same. She will have children, just like I did. She tried to stop her hands from shaking. I have to leave right away. Right now! I must go to her. She must be suffering so badly. I have to reach Aziz. He should come back straight away. No, no, I can't wait for him. I'll call Haldun. It's too early to call. I don't give a damn!

She stood up, throwing the crumpled telegram onto the floor, and rushed through the corridor almost unconsciously, with her mind fixed on her target: she needed to call Haldun. He would take care of everything, send a telegram to Aziz and buy the train tickets. She had to leave as soon as possible. When would the next train be? She shot into Aziz's study and, with a trembling finger, dialled her brother-in-law's number.

The day was breaking.

52

She pushed aside Álmos, the head butler who had opened the door, and stormed into the entrance hall, dragging Nili behind her. She stopped at the foot of the stairs. "Where is she? Magda! Where is Magda?" she shouted impatiently. "Why doesn't anyone know anything? Where is my sister? Isn't she back from the hospital yet? Where is Mother?"

"She's in her room, my Lady. I'll let her know that you're here."

"Don't bother," she said as she let go of Nili's hand. Taking her fur coat off, she threw it over the railings and rushed up the stairs. "Please give the children their bath," she called out to Teréz, who was standing with Lila in her arms, lost for what to do.

Once upstairs, she dashed through the Gallery and ran up the stairs to the next floor. She darted through the crystal corridor, knocked on her mother's bedroom door and, without waiting for her reply, flounced into the room. Gizella was sitting in one of the armchairs by the window with her eyes fixed somewhere out in the garden. She had not heard Alex enter.

"Where's Magda? How is she? Isn't she back from the hospital yet?"

Gizella slowly turned her head, her bloodshot eyes looking blankly right through Alex.

"Is she all right? She is, isn't she? Answer me, *Anyukám!* Answer me! Please answer me!" she begged as she ran to her mother. Grabbing her shoulders, she started shaking her with all her might. Gizella's spent body shook like an empty sack between Alex's hands. Without uttering a word, she turned her eyes back to the garden.

"No!" screamed Alex. "No!" she cried out helplessly. "No ..." she rebelled almost inaudibly as her energy suddenly drained away. Her legs could no longer carry her weight. Her knees buckled and she crumpled to the floor. Her desperate pleas and muted weeping gradually turned into hysterical cries of agony, only to die down again into lifeless whimpers suffocated under her throbbing sobs. "No!" she wailed uncontrollably. She was holding her mother's hands and hitting them against her thighs. "Tell me. Tell me that she's fine. Talk to me, why don't you!" she beseeched her. Then she clasped her mother in her arms as tightly as her enervated body allowed her. "No, Magda! No!" she shrieked. "You can't leave me! You can't!" Desolately she buried her head on her mother's lap. She wished she could drown among the pleats of her skirt. Nothing meant anything anymore. Nothing! Everything, all the values she had been taught throughout her life, had lost their meaning. Young dying first ... It was unfair. It was against nature. Against the natural order of things. Time out of joint. The world turning upside down. All that she had believed in since she was a little girl had been destroyed. The good was supposed to be rewarded, or was it all a big lie? From now on she would never believe in the innocence of anything. She shuddered at the onslaught of an impossible feeling of mistrust, threatening to capture her whole being.

"Please don't cry, my love."

Károly! It was Károly. Upon hearing her brother's voice, her sobs once again turned into wailing. She feebly raised her head. Károly squatted beside her and held her arms. She embraced him with longing. A sharp dagger was turning in her heart. "She's gone, hasn't she? She's left us, hasn't she? I couldn't make it. I shouldn't have gone away in the first place. I should have known better. I knew it. I knew it, *Öcsi.* The same thing happened to me. Exactly the same thing. She was just like me. We were exactly the same, the two halves of a whole. Why did I leave her? Why didn't I warn her?" She was crying out loud and, with each cry, was hitting her fists hard on Károly's chest, his shoulders, his arms.

"Calm down, my baby. Please calm down."

Her body, exhausted under the strain of her violent sobs, seemed to have bled itself of energy. She felt her soul numbing. Pulling herself away from her brother's protective arms, she dragged herself up to her feet. After a brief moment of hesitation, she left the room with a decisive and fast tread. Her sobbing stopped as she passed the crystal corridor. She could hear Károly calling after her, but her senses were closed to the outer world. She had gone to another time, to another place. As if hypnotised, she slid down the stairs, walked through the door opening into the Gallery and went downstairs, accelerating her determined pace with each step. "I want to be alone," she hollered as she dashed through the entrance hall with Károly running after her. She steamed out the main door into the freezing cold. Her lips started quivering uncontrollably again and a fresh torrent of tears flooded down her already moist cheeks as she faltered towards the garden gate. She struggled to open the heavy gate, shrugging her shoulders to free herself of the fur coat Károly had draped over her shoulders, and finally threw herself into the street.

Death! What a meaningless word. Meaningless until you lose your other half, until you feel, somewhere deep inside you, what death really means, until you lose someone you thought you would never lose. Her heart ached. She wanted to scream, to shout at the top of her voice until her throat tore apart. "Magda!" she wailed. Her mouth had opened, but only a muted cry had escaped. "Why?" she uttered in a loud, long, piercing cry. Why you? Don't think, Alex. Don't! Just count your steps. One, two, three ... Why? Why? There is no answer to that. Don't think! Just count. Twenty-one, twenty-two ... Faster! Faster! Faster! Even faster! Forty-two, forty-three. She was running now. She let herself stumble down the hill of roses. Run Alex! Run as fast as you can. Run until you have daggers in your stomach. Run!

She stopped out of breath when she reached the Margit Bridge and leaned on the railings. The Danube. Flowing by in all its vigour. Surrender yourself to its turbulent waters. Let it carry you far away, wherever it decides to take you. Don't think! She held her head between her hands. "Magda! Magda! Magda!" she repeated over and over again as if in a dream, hitting her head with her clenched fists. She wanted to disappear. She ought to disappear just like she did. She ought to go away with her. "Magda!" she screamed between her sobs.

"Alex!"

Károly was behind her, embracing her tightly in his arms. "Come, my love. Come on now."

She yielded to her brother's arms, nestling her head in his chest, shaking like a leaf in a storm.

"Please, baby. Please don't cry. You've got to be strong. We all have to be strong. Please think of your daughters. Please." He was showering Alex's hair with kisses.

Alex turned around and hugged her brother with all her might. "I'm scared, *Öcsi*. I'm so scared. Please don't leave me. I beg you, please. I don't want to lose you as well. Please. Please don't let me go to Istanbul. Let me come to Paris with you. I beg you, please."

"You're not alone, my darling. You have me. You have Aziz. You have your daughters. There is *Anyukám*. You're not alone."

"No! No, *Öcsi!* I'm all alone now. She's gone. My Magda, my everything, my other half has gone. She just left me. She abandoned me. I'm all alone now. I shouldn't have left. I knew that something like this would happen. We were exactly the same. I knew that she was at risk of a miscarriage, just like I was. I could have saved her life. I could have warned her more. I could have been with her. It's all my fault. She died because of me. She died because I couldn't take care of her as I should have." She was bouncing up and down on her knees in an agony of regret. "We always did everything together, *Öcsi*. We were always together. We were born together. We grew up together. And we should have died together. I should have been with her. I should have been by her side."

"Alex, my love, you couldn't have done anything. Please don't blame yourself. If we were to think like this, then everybody is to blame. Miklós is to blame because he met her, because he married her, because he let her get pregnant. Mother is to blame because she brought her into this world. Magda herself is to blame because she ... simply lived. Should we think like this? No, my love, it's nobody's fault. This is how life is, my precious."

"Hush. Please hush. I don't want to hear any of it!"

June 2004
Istanbul

Dinner had already been set out on the veranda when Rüya arrived home.

"God only knows why we have to eat so early," she murmured irritably, almost to herself.

"You've forgotten to turn on your mobile phone. Sinan called. He's worried about you."

"I'll call him later, Grandma. I have no energy for him right now."

"Dinner will be ready in a minute."

"I'm not hungry."

She went straight into Mami's bedroom and stood in front of the lilac wardrobe; she had been thinking about it constantly since last night. The phone started ringing. She picked up the cordless handset on the bedside table and checked the number on its screen. It was Sinan. After dithering about it for a moment, she pressed the green button.

"Hello?"

"Rüya? Where have you been? I was truly worried about you."

"You shouldn't have been. I was at the hospital, you know that."

She went back to the wardrobe and squatted in front of it.

"How is Mami?" said the voice at the other end of the line.

He had no right to call her Mami. She found it extremely annoying that he took the liberty of considering himself so close to her family. "What do you expect? She's pretty bad."

Her eyes were fixed on the diaries stacked up in the wardrobe.

Sinan was still talking. "... tomorrow. What do you say?"

"I'm sorry, what was that?" she snapped, losing her patience.

"Tomorrow, I was saying ..."

"Sinan, I'm terribly tired now. I have no energy to fix a date with you. Please let me breathe a little. Don't call me for a while, all right? I'll call *you*."

She hung up before he could say anything else and put the handset down on the floor. I've broken his heart again, she thought. Why am I so cross with him all the time? He hasn't done anything wrong, has he? He does suffocate me though. "Well," she said to herself, shrugging her shoulders, "now is not a good time to brood over him." Timorously extending her hand towards the wardrobe, she started taking out the diaries. She was picking one up with utmost care and placing it on the floor before reaching for the next one, her movements ever so gentle, as if she were scared that they might perish between her fingers if she handled them too harshly. She remembered the conversation she had had with her mother the other night at the gazebo. "I wish we all had a life like hers," she had started saying, when Aslı had cut her short: "I don't think you would want that, Rüya." What had happened in Mami's life, a life that seemed so perfectly long, that made Aslı insinuate that it was not a life to be envied? Anastasia had said that Mami had suffered too much. What was it that had made her suffer? "Everybody suffers in life," she thought. But then why am I so curious about what happened to Mami? Is it a simple surge of inquisitiveness triggered by an absolute lack of information, because nobody has told me anything about her life so far? Or is it that I secretly hope to alleviate my own pain by proving to myself that I am not the only one in our family to have suffered? Why did Mami imply that she wanted me to read her diaries? Did she have a premonition of her life approaching its end? Did she want to leave her memories in safe hands? No! No! She vigorously shook her head in objection to her thoughts. No! Don't even think about it. Mami is not going to die. She can't and that's that!

We're walking along the shore. My sister bends down and picks up a piece of broken glass. She holds it up against the sun. I see the light break. A rainbow in all its colours appears in the sky. She extends her hand, grabs the rainbow and pulls away the red strip. A sudden twilight embraces everything, dull and depressive.

"Why did you do that?" I ask in panic.

She opens her hand and places the red strip back where it belongs. "To show you that light needs all its colours," she says. "If you want your dreams to come true, you must try and understand the other colours that are different than yours. To understand others, however, you need to understand yourself first; you have to face the fears gripping your heart and see the reasons why you can't open your heart."

She picks up a stone and throws it into the sea. It creates a tiny ripple where it falls, which spreads wide in little waves that gradually become bigger and bigger.

"Do you see the waves? Nothing happens out of nothing. Everything that happens or does not happen initiates a relationship, continuously creating a change. Everything is connected to everything else in a cause-and-effect relationship."

"Why?" I think. "Why?"

"Unfortunately, sometimes it's not so easy to see this cause-and-effect relationship," she carries on.

I feel the sand slip away from underneath my feet. I lose my balance and hold on to my sister's arm.

"Never give up in the face of hardships. Open your heart. Try to understand. Only you can help yourself."

Rüya noticed a diary, a much more tattered one compared to the others she had spread out on the parquetry floor. On its faded red leather cover, there was an inscription in Hungarian written in golden calligraphy. *To dearest Alex, 10 October 1914.* She gently opened it.

Albisola, Italy, 11th October 1914

My name is Alexandra. It was my fourth birthday yesterday. This notebook is a present from Nanny Ildikó. It's a diary. In it, I'll write what I do, what I think and what I feel. I write beautifully, but for now I speak, and Nanny Ildikó writes. I do check if she writes correctly though.

She gave one to my sister too because it was her birthday as well. It wasn't my brother Károly's birthday, but she gave him one too so that he doesn't feel left out. He, however, only makes drawings in his.

So far nothing has happened today, so I'll write what happened yesterday. It was our birthday yesterday. Magda and I, we received plenty of presents. Our mother invited all our friends. I was mostly happy that my best friend Maria could come. It was very cold, but Mother said we could go out in the garden if we dressed up warmly. After cutting our birthday cake, we played in the garden. Sanyi and Károly were very naughty and teased all the girls. Sanyi, or Sándor, is Uncle Kelemen's son. He's not really naughty. It's always Károly who pushes him to do naughty things. Well anyways, everything went very well. We had lots of prezzies, but my favourite was Snow White, which was Magda's present for me. She's really beautiful with her soft blonde hair. We put her to sleep in her wooden cottage with the Seven Dwarfs to protect her. The cottage is a present from Mother for both of us. And the Seven Dwarfs are my present for Magda. They're all so very beautiful. We will go and play with them in a moment. If Károly lets us alone, that is.

I lav may diary. Tanks Ildikó. I rote this line.

Tears started to trickle down Rüya's eyes. For the first time in her life, it was dawning upon her that Mami, just like everyone else, had been a little girl once. An unexpected, dolefully compassionate, feeling embraced her. Her beloved Mami, the stout mainstay of their home, the perfect woman, she was also a child once, a fragile little girl, vulnerable and hungry for love, who eventually grew up to be a young woman. What was she like in her youth? What did she do? What did she miss in life? Her life could not have been as two-dimensional as it was in the old photographs or as static for that matter. All the faces in those photographs had had a name, which Rüya did not know and her grandmother Nili could not, or pretended not to, remember. Each face had had a life and a place in Mami's life. They might not have been as happy as they looked in those photographs. What they lived through might not have allowed them to be happy. Lives, thought Rüya, especially Mami's life, should not be sequestered in a few faded photographs, condemned to be forgotten for all eternity. Her life may have been insipid, monotonous or ordinary, but even if that had been the case, her memory ought to live. Rüya's children – if she were to have any, of course – ought to know about her, about her loving personality. They ought to know this beautiful person. Most importantly perhaps, it was Rüya, more than anybody else, who needed to know her better. She had to make her grandmother Nili tell her everything she knew. She had to make her remember what she did not. And anything she preferred not to tell, she should learn from Anastasia.

Rüya did not sleep at all that night, reading some of Mami's diaries, all written in her cryptic handwriting, which at times proved to be extremely difficult to decipher.

A Hungarian Rhapsody
A Novel in Three Acts
Act One, Tableau Three
1939

53

Alex snapped open her eyes. Where was she? What was this strange place? What had happened? Her conscious mind refused to take over. It seemed to have locked itself up to forget what had happened, to entomb its agony in the depths of the subconscious, never to allow its passage to the surface again. The pain, however, found a way to crawl up to the surface as her consciousness unlocked itself. Reality began to impose itself, ruthlessly crushing her under its unbearable weight.

She was in her bedroom in Rózsadomb. It was morning. She had had a terrible night, tossing and turning, half asleep, half awake, but in both cases a night full of nightmares. She was lying down on her bed now with her eyes fixed on the ceiling. She slowly closed them. "Magda is lying down like this now," she thought. Motionless. Lifeless. Cold. Her body is there, but she isn't. It's only her outer shell that lies there. Where is *she?*

She did not want to get out of bed; she did not want to wake up; she did not want to talk to anyone or see anyone. Thoughts nibbled at her brain. Her head was splitting. She was really offended that Aziz was not here with her now. He had sent a telegram saying that he would be in Budapest on Friday. What was it today? It must be Wednesday. I should listen to the birds, she said to herself, to suppress the sound of my thoughts. She got up, opened the window and drew in the fresh air. Would cold numb her soul? Would it ease her pain? She went back to bed and closed her eyes again. Birdsong. Listen to their singing, Alex. Their chirping was drilling a hole in her brain. She would not survive this. She wanted to leave everything and go. She wanted to run away from it all, from this pain, from everything.

There was a knock on the door. She opened her eyes. Had she fallen asleep? She guessed she must have. It was freezing cold in the room.

"The Takácses are here, my Lady. Your mother asked me to let you know."

"What time is it?"

"It's half-past four, my Lady. I was told not to disturb you for lunch. You were sleeping."

She had been in bed for almost twenty-four hours. She should get up and make herself presentable. She could not let anyone, especially Rudi, see her in this condition.

She went to the bathroom and washed her face. As she reached for the towel, her gaze stopped at her reflection in the mirror. Magda! Magda was standing right there in front of her. She held her left ear and stroked the upper part where a little piece was missing. She stroked it and stroked it. It was the right ear of her reflection, but it lacked the extra bit of flesh that Magda had. Magda did not exist anymore. She pulled her ear as if she wanted to tear it away. In impotent fury, she pressed her hands over her reflection in the mirror. She could not stand it. She could not stand looking at her own face, especially at her own face. She hurried out of the bathroom. She ought to dress and go down.

When she entered the drawing room, Nili ran to her and hugged her legs. "Mami, Mami, won't I ever see Magda *néni* again? Is heaven too far? Can't we go and visit her there?"

"Nili, leave your mother alone, sweetheart," said Gizella almost inaudibly. "Mademoiselle Terézia, would you please take the children out into the garden?"

Everybody was there, sitting on the sofas and in the armchairs in absolute silence. Károly stood up and came over to Alex. He clasped his arms around her. The lifeless gaze of Ada sitting on the sofa, the bloodshot eyes of Sándor slumped next to her, the dark circles around Aunt Etel's big eyes, darker than ever, and the sullen lips of Rudi sitting in the armchair opposite them ... Rudi!

Alex could no longer repress the sobs lined up in her throat, waiting to erupt. She could not breathe. "Please excuse me," she whispered, trying to control her trembling voice. "I need some fresh air." She pulled herself away from Károly's arms and rushed out onto the veranda. Leaning on the railings, she took a deep breath. Tears were coursing down her face as her gaze riveted itself on the lawn and then hung on the branches of the trees. She stood there, motionless. Frozen. Benumbed. Her soul ached. The shadows in the garden were becoming longer and longer. It would be dark soon. You must not think about the past, her inner voice kept telling her. The more she thought, the more sobs welled up from her chest; the more she sobbed, the more her tears gushed out. Magda was no more. No more! She had abandoned her. She had abandoned them all. She had abandoned life. She had abandoned everything. She could not believe that she was no more. But why? Why? This question would eventually drive her mad.

"Come along, Alex. You'll catch cold."

Rudi had taken her by the arm and was ushering her towards the conservatory. She had no strength left; she was about to collapse. A strong urge to surrender her body to the comforting force of gravity seized her. Rudi must have sensed this, for he grabbed her firmly by the waist.

"You must be strong, my precious. Come on now, lean on me."

She succumbed to Rudi's strong embrace. They went into the conservatory and sat down on one of the sofas. She no longer had any control over what was happening, listlessly witnessing it all as if it were happening to someone else, as if she were having a nightmare that she knew she would presently wake up from. Rudi was extending his cigarette case towards her. She took a cigarette and watched him take out his lighter. A flame. A deep puff. The smoke. Her eyes followed the smoke, a dense grey slowly thinning out as it floated about in the air to finally disappear into nothingness. It was no more. It had become one with non-being. Emptiness. Nothingness.

"Don't cry, Alex," said Rudi, holding Alex's lifeless hand resting on her lap. "Please don't torture yourself."

Her weeping turned into a cough. She angrily pressed her cigarette into the ashtray, only to snatch another one from Rudi's cigarette case a second later. She stared with empty eyes at the flame of his lighter. "I should have warned her more. I should have known better. She didn't know. She couldn't have. She said she had no pain. But I should have been by her side in any case." Her gaze moved to the garden and stopped at her daughters scampering around. The sun had disappeared behind the house, leaving the garden in the shade. It must be getting really cold now. The children should come back in before darkness fell. Nili might catch cold. She waved at Teréz to beckon them to come inside.

"Don't be unfair to yourself, my love."

This time it was Alex who held Rudi's hand. I feel so lonely, Rudi, she said to herself. I'm all alone now. "I'm all alone," she mumbled beneath her breath. Please help me, begged her heart. Please help me out.

Rudi had pulled away his hand. Alex reached out in panic. Don't leave me! I don't want to be alone. She watched him loosen his tie and start unbuttoning his shirt. She watched his hands, his fingers. He was so strong. Don't leave me, please.

He was holding the amber ring dangling at the end of a chain on his neck. "I want you to wear this, Alex. I want you to be able to wear it."

She stood up, ignoring what he had just said, dropped her cigarette in the ashtray and walked to the gramophone. Beethoven! She had to listen to Beethoven. *Appassionata.*

"I'm scared, Rudi. I'm so scared."

"What are you scared of?" he said softly, extending his arms towards her. "There's nothing to be scared of. You should stay here with me. You shouldn't go back to Istanbul."

"That's impossible."

He leaned over, held Alex's hand and made her sit down again. "Marry me, Alex."

These words she had waited for all those years, that utterance which was supposed to make her forget her pain somehow hurt her even more, reminding her, yet again, of her impuissance. "I'm already married, Rudi," she mumbled feebly.

"Divorce him. Take your daughters and come here. Very soon I'll be transferring my business to London. It won't be long before it will become impossible to live in this country. I'll take care of everything. We can start again from where we left off. We can go on with our lives in another country."

"What you're saying is only a dream, Rudi," she interrupted him, "an impossible dream."

"Anything is possible. You just tell me that you'll come."

She was so utterly weak and crippled in her desolation that she could not find the strength to make such a decision, a decision to set up a new life. She felt deeply offended that Aziz – the man who supposedly loved her so – was out hunting some birds instead of being here with her at a time like this. What kind of love was it anyway? Should he not be the one who was by her side now? Or perhaps the man sitting next to her should have been her husband. She was feeling so frail, unable to think straight about what she should do. She looked at Rudi's compassionate eyes and silently thanked him for being here. "I wish I were a little girl again," she said. "I wish I could start everything from the beginning."

His fingers were caressing her cheek. "We can begin again, Alex. We really can."

"The Nerádys have arrived, my Lady," announced the head butler from the door opening to the drawing room.

They both started. Alex jumped to her feet and dashed inside, running towards

Miklós, who was kissing Gizella's hand. They embraced as two victims tortured by the pain of their common loss. Alex uttered a prolonged and mournful cry. Miklós kept stroking her hair.

"We must be strong, Alex, very strong."

"Why did she leave us? Why? Why?"

Miklós moved away his arms and took out a small red velvet box and an envelope from his pocket. "She asked me to give this to you."

Wiping away her tears, Alex opened the box. There was a single emerald earring inside. Her knees buckled; she collapsed onto the floor. Her sobbing had stopped, but tears were pouring out of her eyes uncontrollably, her heart sinking deeper and deeper. She recalled the day before she had left for her honeymoon when she had given Magda one of the emerald earrings her mother had given her as a wedding present. "So that we'll remember each other every time we put them on," she had said. Gently putting the box on her lap, she took the envelope and opened it with trembling hands. There was a note with a single line written on it.

From now on, I shall always be with you, my beloved Alex.

She was benumbed. All her senses had cut themselves off from the external world. She did not hear any of the voices around her. She did not want to. She put the earring on her right ear, stood up and left the drawing room. Her feet dragged her up the stairs and into her bedroom. Her hands took out the other emerald earring from her dressing table and put it on her left ear. Finally, her debilitated body threw itself on her bed. "She was a part of me," she murmured to herself. Her soul, her whole being was being ripped apart. Her body, unable to survive this internal rupture, was also tearing itself in two. The pain was unbearable. She would not be able to survive it. We came into this world together, Magda, and were supposed to leave it together. It was not meant to be like this. A part of me is dead now, gone, finished, disappeared. Is this possible? No! No, it is not! It is not possible. I want to sleep. I want to sleep very deeply. An endless sleep ... till eternity. I want to be at peace, at peace alongside my beloved Magda.

54

Springtime. Scents. The Bosphorus. The Judas trees painting the hills. Spring meant nothing this year. There was nothing but sorrow in Alex's heart. They were sitting on the veranda of Izabella's house on the grounds of the Istanbul American College for Girls on the Arnavutköy hill overlooking the Bosphorus. She had been coming here with her daughters almost every day since she had returned from Budapest in April. She could breathe here, so to speak, although she could not, in her heart of hearts, enjoy the wonderful panorama. Even the rebirth of nature filled her with grief as she kept reminding herself that Magda would not be able to see any of this anymore. For her, nature would never be reborn. Alex was angry, furious at all the beauties of this world, at the Judas trees announcing the approaching summer, at her incapacity to change things. She wished she could tear up and throw away everything she had lived so far, just like she could tear up and throw away an aquarelle she did not like, and paint a new life for herself. Her helplessness infuriated her. She wished she could leave everything. Just leave. Abandon. Her thoughts scattered at the touch of Izabella's hand on hers. She had left an envelope on her lap. Holding it tightly between her hands, she turned her gaze onto the Bosphorus again.

"I miss her so very much, you know. I can't get used to the idea that I won't see her ever again. I'm all alone now, Izabella. It feels as though they have ripped apart half of my body, of my soul, of my whole being. I'm half dead and shall never be a whole again. The pain such mutilation inflicts upon you is so terrible that it crushes your soul, so much so that your body can't handle the loss, the terrible destruction. You can't do anything. You can't even think. Everything gets blurred. Then there comes a point when you can't even rebel against all that has happened. A deep sorrow takes over. Eventually, that too dies away. You become numb. You don't feel anything anymore. You feel as though it wouldn't matter if you died."

"I don't know what to say, Alex. Nothing could ease such pain. But life must go on, dear. Think about your daughters. They'll make you forget everything. They're the best healers. Believe me."

Alex looked at her daughters playing in the garden. Nili was capering about with Évike; Lila was toddling on the lawn. She suddenly fell down, grabbed a handful of grass and attempted to stuff it into her mouth. Seeing her nanny Teréz coming towards her, she scurried away from her on all fours. Alex realised that she had been smiling as she watched them. She lowered her eyes to the envelope in her hands. I must tell Izabella, she thought. She desperately needed to share her secret with someone, and there was no one else she could open her heart to. Izabella must already be guessing who the originator of these letters was and might give her a much-needed piece of advice. She was utterly confused and did not know what she wanted anymore.

"I'll bring the tea. It should be ready by now. I brewed a very dark Turkish style tea for you, my dear – as dark as a hare's blood, as the Turks put it. And guess what else I made for you?"

She must have baked *rétes*. Izabella was a true friend. She did everything she could to make her feel better. Her eyes suddenly filled with tears. She reached for her handbag and took out her cigarette case. "I cry so readily nowadays," she said, her voice trembling.

"Everything will be all right, dear. You'll see, everything will be all right," said Izabella, hugging her.

Alex wanted to believe that. She wished everything would be over, and all this suffering would end. Whatever was going to happen should happen sooner than later. She had lost Magda. What could be worse than that? She watched Izabella go inside and disappear from sight. She looked at her daughters to make sure that they were still playing and, calmly, without thinking, opened the envelope.

Budapest, 8th May 1939

My precious darling,

I thought I should write to you without waiting for your reply to my last letter, since it must be rather difficult for you to write to me. I can't wait for the day when you'll be telling me that you're coming here with your daughters. I beseech you to talk to your husband. There is nothing to be afraid of. Everything will be much better, believe me. I repeat, yet again, that a brand new life is awaiting us.

My beloved, I'll be sending this letter by hand as well. No one really knows what risks the current situation actually entails or what will happen in the near future. A few days ago, the Parliament ratified a bill after months of discussions. This new law imposes some further limitations on the Jewish people's rights to do business. This is certainly not very good news. We could call it a coup d'état, a blow to wipe out the Jews from social and economic life. This time, my family and I, we're likely to be affected as well, although we surely will find a way out of it.

Despite your strong disinclination for politics, I can't but write about it, for, trust me, we do nothing but try to deal with the consequences of political developments.

Things have taken a rather unfortunate turn lately, but I entreat you not to worry about it since I have everything under control and meticulously planned. All I need is for you to be here. Please my love, please tell him you want a divorce without further ado.

Izabella was back, carrying a tray with glasses of steaming hot tea and delicious-looking *rétes*. As always, the warm smell of cinnamon and apple took Alex back to her childhood, somewhat sharpening her appetite, which had been almost completely lost recently. She reluctantly put Rudi's letter back in its envelope. Izabella placed the tray on the table, cut rather a thick slice of *rétes* and put it on the little side table by Alex, along with her glass of tea. After a brief moment of hesitation, Alex darted another quick look at her daughters and seized Izabella's hand.

"There's something I meant to tell you."

Izabella's eyes said that she already knew what Alex was about to say. "You don't have to tell me anything."

"I want to go back to Budapest."

Izabella cut herself a slice, took her plate and glass of tea and sat down. Still unable to hold the glass in a way that would save her fingers from burning, she transferred it from one hand to the other before taking a cautious sip. "Is he someone worthy of breaking up your marriage?" she asked without taking her eyes off her glass as she put it back on the table.

"I don't know. I can no longer reason. I'm sure you'll take me for a fool when you hear who he is." She paused briefly, then in a tone of voice that implored her friend's support, said, "Rudi wants to marry me."

"Alex. Oh, Alex ... my dear, emotional friend Alex. You love to complicate your life, don't you? You're playing with fire, dear. Please do be careful. And please don't do anything silly. You're going through a very critical period. Please give yourself some time before making a move. Please."

This was not the answer Alex was hoping to hear. She had expected her friend to say something to support her, to encourage her. She would not be able to leave everything and go without a little help from her friends.

55

She could not write. It had been weeks now and she had not been able to write a single line to Rudi. She did not know what to write. She did not know what she wanted. What was she waiting for? She did not know the answer to that question either. She wished she could go back in time. This was all she had been thinking of these last few days: to wind the clock back, erase everything that she had lived so far and draw another life for herself.

The phone was ringing. She went into Aziz's study.

"Hello?"

"Alex?"

She could not believe her ears. It was Rudi! "Are you out of your mind? Aziz could have been at home. He would have killed me!"

"Why don't you answer my letters?"

"I can't talk right now, Rudi. I shall write. I promise."

"You must tell him that you want a divorce. You must, Alex. Will you?"

"Yes," she said. When she was in Budapest, she had told him that she would do all she could and try to open the subject as soon as the timing was right. But now, she had no courage left to do that. Her eyes, burdened with the weight of her penitential thoughts, were fixed on the gun cabinet across the desk. "Well, I'll try," she mumbled. "When you were next to me, I was thinking that I definitely would get a divorce. But now ... I don't know ... he's so ..."

"He's so, what? I can't understand what you're waiting for."

"I'm scared, Rudi. He'll kill us both. He frightens me. Sometimes he's terribly menacing." She closed her eyes to tear them away from the gun cabinet and turned around to look out the window.

"There's no need to be scared. I'm sure you are exaggerating everything. You do have a wild imagination after all."

"He almost killed you in Kengyel at the shoot. It's so easy for him to pull the trigger, to shoot at a living soul. Killing comes naturally to him."

"Come, come, Alex. Killing a human being isn't so easy. It's not the same as shooting birds."

"I dare not say it. I just can't say I want a divorce."

"If you won't, I will!"

"No, no, please. I'll talk to him. But please do be patient. I beg you. For the moment, I can't. It's impossible. Just impossible."

56

Alex raised her head up from the writing paper in front of her. Her gaze rolled down the carpet-like lawn and came to a halt at the tiled roof of the hut at the bottom of the hill. Since their telephone conversation at the beginning of summer, Rudi had written her four letters. Alex, on the other hand, had started to write but left unfinished maybe fifty. She ripped apart the last one she had commenced and took a new sheet. "Polonezköy, 20th August 1939," she began. She did not even know how she should be addressing him. My darling? My love? She decided to write, "Dear Rudi." She should write about Polonezköy, her paintings, her daughters and about this and that. She lit a cigarette and continued.

> ... I had an awful summer. I could not draw a single line despite knowing that painting was my only way out. Why, I ask myself? Why do I suppress my artistic streak? Is it an effort to silence the voice of my subconscious? Please do forgive me, for I'm simply blabbering. Well, after months of idleness I finally took my brushes out of their box today. We're in a heavenly place in a small village in the countryside around Istanbul, staying at a pension run by a Polish immigrant. The serene atmosphere here is very likely to resuscitate my creativity. It does me a world of good to be away from home and from Aziz. Nili and Lila are also happy to be here. They stay outdoors practically from dawn till dusk, prancing about in the fields and rolling down the hills. Poor Teréz is exhausted running after them, but I presume it does her good as well.
>
> I love being on my own as I no longer have any patience for anyone. Can you believe that someone like me – someone who wouldn't be happy with less than dozens of friends around her – would be unable to tolerate the presence of even one single person? I see only Izabella and Anastasia, and that's about all, for only they can understand me.
>
> Do you see János? How is he? I find it unbelievable that such a bright mind could be laid off just because he is Jewish, and forced to work as a blacksmith at his father's smithy. He could move here, you know. They would just grab him. What would János say? Would he want to? Aziz will help him out. I'll write to him about this.

What kind of a letter was this? A letter to a brother rather than to a lover. She might as well send it to Károly. She nevertheless carried on.

> ... How is business? Izabella told me that some Jewish lawyers, to avoid losing their businesses, were transferring their companies, though only on paper, to Christians whom they refer to as their "mercenaries." Do you also have such a mercenary? How are you getting along?

This was utter rubbish! Moreover, it probably was not a good idea to put all this in writing; all correspondence was checked by the Hungarian authorities. She did not know what to write. In fact she was not sure if she wanted to write at all. Things might have been much easier if Rudi had not entered her life and complicated everything. She should not write. She should tear him away from her life, from her heart and from her mind, for she was falling down deeper and deeper into a dark abyss. She ripped the letter to pieces.

Spring had gone by and a long summer had followed, but she had not been able to bring herself to talk to Aziz. Why was that? What was she afraid of? What did she really want? Did she know what she wanted? Izabella had told her that she would not be able to take her daughters out of Turkey. Was this true? Whom could she ask if it was? As things stood, she apparently would not be able to go anywhere. Rudi was simply daydreaming.

On the dirt road below, an old woman clad in black despite the scorching summer heat was trying to keep a gaggle of geese together, poking them with the thin stick she held in her emaciated hand. Time and again, a free-spirited goose among the flock covering the road like a white cloud flapped its wings and broke away from the rest, only to join its flock again when she felt the old woman's stick on its back. They passed by like a cloud. The dirt road returned to its isolation.

"Mami, I wish we could stay here forever."

"You like it here, don't you?"

"Yes, but what I like is that you always smile when we're here."

"Don't I smile at other times, *tatlım?*"

"You do ... when we're at Aunt Izabella's."

There was a knock on the door. Terézia came in carrying Lila, who had just woken up from her afternoon nap. "I ordered the tea. They'll bring some Danish pastries as well. I asked them to prepare pork chops for dinner and some of their homemade smoked ham to take away. You said we should take some to Istanbul, right?"

"Mami, can I ask you something?"

"Yes my love, you can."

"Are Évike's parents poor?"

"What makes you say that?"

"They sleep in the same room, in the same bed. Don't they have enough money to buy two beds like you and Daddy?"

Alex hugged her daughter. "You ask too many questions. Now why don't you set up a nice game while I paint?"

"All right, Mami." Nili started to talk with her dolls in a subdued voice so as not to disturb her mother. "Now you behave yourselves. No funny tricks! We mustn't upset our mother. You do exactly as I tell you."

57

It had been a week since Alex had come back from Polonezköy. She was still in the throes of an excruciating dilemma. She desperately wanted to get a divorce, but the thought of Aziz's reaction terrified her. She was also uncomfortable about how shattered he would be, were she to leave him. He loved her to distraction, and it would be the ruin of him. No. No, that was not true. He would be furious at first, but gradually would get used to the idea. He had much more important things in his life than Alex. He would go shooting with a clear conscience and spend as much time as he liked with his family. He would even marry a proper and obedient Turkish girl who would not drive his mother mad. And they would all live happily ever after. She should talk to Aziz. There was nothing to be afraid of. Her hands were sweating. She hated herself for being so scared of him and loathed Aziz for instilling that fear in her. She should gather all her strength and face him with firm determination. She ought to keep calm and cool-headed no matter how much he shouted. She did not want to hurt him, but what could she do? She simply loved someone else, and it was better to tell the truth than live a lie. She would definitely talk to him. But she had to choose her words very carefully. A wrong word, a badly timed utterance might readily blow everything out of proportion. She did not love Aziz anymore, but she could not possibly tell him that, let alone admit that she loved another man. She felt so weak ...

She heard the key turn in the lock of the main door. It had to be Aziz.

She was trying very hard to control her trembling hands, but to no avail. The ice cubes in her *rakı* rattled as she put her glass back on the table. It was not like she could say she was cold; it was August and unbearably hot. Control yourself, Alex. Talk to him. How on earth was she going to open the subject? Don't think. Don't! You'll think of something when the time comes. The time had come. She would not be able to put up with this torturous wait any longer.

"Did you like the *pasta asciutta*?"

"Absolutely delicious. Exceptional as always."

She had to think of something to say, but nothing came to her mind. "I hope Nili won't start crying in the middle of the night to come home," she finally managed to say.

Aziz did not say anything.

She had sent her daughters and Terézia away to Ayla's for the night. For days, Nili had been complaining about how much she had missed her cousins, Yasemin and Azra. If hell were to break loose, it would have to be tonight while they were away. Tonight was the night to talk to Aziz.

"How is your mother?" she asked.

"She's fine."

Throughout dinner, she talked about everything and nothing, meaningless utterances of no import just to break the silence. "I'll tell him after Asiye *Hanım* leaves," she thought. Dinner had gone on for too long. She had gathered all her courage. She was ready.

At long last, Aziz finished his dessert, taking the last mouthful of the generous serving of the syrupy *şekerpare* on his plate.

"Asiye *Hanım*, you may clear the table."

"I have to work, Alex. Too much to do these days."

"Could you prepare me another glass of *rakı* please?"

Alex picked up her cat Portakal, who was circling around the table, and went out onto the balcony. A few minutes later Aziz brought her drink.

"It's really nice out here. Why don't you sit with me for a while?"

"I'll join you later."

She would be open with him. He would not kill her, would he? He would shout, he would insult her, but none of that mattered anymore. She could not possibly suffer more than she already did. Perhaps it would be best if she took her daughters and just left without saying anything to him. Could she do that? There had to be a way. What if she went away, never to see him again? What if she left no trace of where she went? She took a sip from her *rakı*. What are you saying, Alex? What on earth are you saying! You must be out of your mind. Are you that cruel? How can you do such a thing to Aziz? And to your daughters! How can you deprive them of their father? You're being monstrous.

Asiye *Hanım* was saying something, standing at the door to the balcony.

"Excuse me, Asiye *Hanım?* I didn't hear what you said."

"Aziz *Bey* is calling you, madam. I'm done for today. Can I go now?"

"Yes. Yes, sure."

She put Portakal on the floor as she stood up. Going inside, she set her glass on the side table and walked to the study. Aziz was not at his desk. She heard Asiye *Hanım* close the main door as she left.

"Alex!" shouted Aziz in a thunderous roar. His voice was coming from the back of the house. She walked along the corridor and entered her bedroom. He was standing in the middle of the room with his hands clasped behind him. He fixed his gaze on Alex over his reading glasses, his eyes blazing like hot charcoal. This was bad news. She noticed her handbag lying on its side, wide open. It suddenly dawned upon her that, after having returned from Izabella's, she had forgotten to take Rudi's letter out of her bag to destroy it. A sudden wave of panic grabbed her. How could she have been so stupid, so careless? She could feel her pulse throbbing in her heart. "Have you been going through my bag?" she said, with a slight quiver in her voice.

"At this moment in time, Alexandra, it should be me who is asking the questions, not you!" he growled furiously, hurling his glasses onto the dressing table.

She quietly perched on the edge of the armchair next to the wardrobe. He had started pacing the room, scrunching Rudi's crumpled letter in his hands.

"Very odd," he said, as he came up closer to her, his eyebrows raised in simulated confusion. "Don't you think it's rather strange?"

"What are you saying?" she mumbled, with her eyes glued to the ground.

He started to pound up and down the room again. What was written in the letter, she tried to recall? Her mind had come to a standstill. Was it obvious that it was from Rudi? How had he signed it? Had he signed it at all? God, she could not get her thoughts together. She noticed that she was digging her nails into her palms. Trying to relax her hands, she interlaced her fingers on her lap. Aziz was standing right in front of her now.

"This letter, Madame Giritli, is not addressed to you. The envelope has Izabella's name and address on it. Rudolf is having an affair with Izabella, and his opened love letters happen to be in your handbag. Very strange indeed." He sharply clacked his heels together and bent over towards Alex, waving the letter in front of her face. "What are you up to, little Alexandra?" he hissed, giving the papers a firm shake. They slapped against Alex's cheek. "Precious darling! Are *you* his precious darling?" he shouted menacingly. "Tell me! Are you?" His fury echoed on the walls, growing out of proportion.

"Don't shout. The neighbours will hear."

"I will shout! Let them hear! Let everyone hear. Are *you* his precious darling? Answer me!"

She did not know what to say. If she were to say yes, he would kill her. He would kill her and he would kill Rudi. If she were to say no, how was she to explain it all? I must deny it at all costs, she thought. I have to. She opened her mouth, moved her lips, but no sound came out. If she were to deny it, where would she be putting her dear friend Izabella?

"Of course, you are! Because in the letter, he talks about your daughters, not Izabella's. Izabella doesn't have daughters; she only has one."

It was all over. An iron hand clutched at her heart. "I want a divorce," she blurted out unexpectedly, just like that, letting the words roll out of her mouth. Her eyes riveted on the floor, she recoiled, waiting for a blow. Nothing happened. She timorously raised her eyes.

Aziz was frozen still, staring at the letter in his hand. He let out a mocking roar of laughter. Then another ... and a few more. He stumbled back a few steps and collapsed onto the bed like an empty sack. "Have I heard you right?"

"Yes," she faintly mumbled under her breath. "Yes, you've heard me right."

"Why, Alex? Why?" he hissed through his clenched teeth, shaking his head in objection to what he had just heard. "Why?"

"You need to ask yourself why," she managed to say hesitantly.

"What have I done to deserve something like this? Tell me! What have I done?" He obviously was trying very hard to control his anger. "Speak to me! Why?"

"I'm so very lonely, Aziz," she replied, barely above a whisper. "So utterly lonely."

He fiercely pounded his chest with his fist, squeezing the letter in it as though he wanted to make it disappear. "Alex, I desperately love you. You have a husband who is in love with you. You're not alone." He pointed his finger towards the children's bedroom. "You have your children."

Was there a tinge of supplication in his voice?

"I feel like an object, Aziz, an object much desired, much admired initially but, once taken possession of, left in a corner to be forgotten, to be condemned to wait for an occasional show of affection. Your love is so selfishly yours to enjoy that it means nothing to me."

"What do you want, for Heaven's sake? What do you want me to do?" He jumped to his feet and, in one big strong step, came over to stand before her again. "I can't believe you want a divorce!" he raged, throwing the crumpled letter at the wall. "Why, Alex? Why?" He was continually squeezing and relaxing his fists in an effort to control his fury. "You want a divorce because of someone who was so cruel to you? You want to divorce me for that bastard who treated you like a piece of rag?" His voice was gradually rising in a crescendo to its former strength. "You want to divorce me for that son of a bitch who broke his promise, who went back on his word?" he finally roared at the top of his voice.

"Don't curse, Aziz. You're being terribly rude."

"Don't talk to me about rudeness. Don't you shamelessly talk to me about it! You're the one who is rude. You're the one who is without any morals."

I have to get out of here, she thought. He was becoming dangerous. She could see the veins in his throat swollen to the point of bursting. She stood up, but it was too late. Aziz had grabbed her arms and was shaking her.

"Let me go, Aziz," she said sharply.

He gave another roar of laughter, this time with a tone more threatening than mocking. "I'll let you go. I will. You'll go to your lover. However, don't you forget that you'll never, ever, be able to see your daughters again. I'll shoot them first, and then I'll shoot myself. Do you understand me?" He was shaking her. "First our daughters, then myself!" he growled, abruptly letting go of her arms. She stumbled, hit the bed and fell down. She could not bring herself to get back on her feet. She was crying in gulping sobs. She was trapped. She was caged. She felt as though she was falling down an endlessly deep well. It was pitch dark. How could he say something like that? He was a monster, for only a monster could have thought of such an atrocity. She was trembling as if in a fever. What was she to do? She must take her daughters and run away. She must get away from this place. Could she? She wiped away her tears and dried her hands on her skirt. She had to think of something. She had to find something to say, something to calm him down. Her vacant stare wandered around the curly patterns on her skirt, her finger nervously retracing them in search of a magical hint as to what to say. She dared not look up, hearing Aziz's heavy tread up and down the room. A debilitating sense of hollowness filled her. Aziz was now standing before her. With an empty gaze, she watched him kneel down and gently hold her chin.

"Alex. You're beside yourself. You don't know what you're doing."

He was holding her arms, trying to embrace her. She shook him off in panic. She could not bear him touching her. He pulled her towards him. She tried to free herself from his grip, pressing her hands against his chest, pushing him away. He was too strong.

"You're completely distraught after the loss of Magda. And I know that I've left you alone too much. Please, let's forget about all of this, all that we've talked about."

He was holding her face between his hands in an attempt to kiss her lips.

"Let me go, Aziz! Let me go!" her inner voice screamed in silence as she pulled her head back in alarm. He was hurting her. She held his wrists and tried to free her head from his clutch. "Let me go!" she finally cried out.

"I can't, Alex. You're my wife. You're my love. You're my one and only love. I can't let you go anywhere."

He was forcing a kiss on her lips. He did not understand her. He did not understand that she did not want him. Her cheeks were crushed between his unyielding hands. She pushed against his chest again with all her might. He would not move an inch. Next thing she knew was that she was lying flat on her back on the floor with Aziz impatiently trying to unbutton her blouse. Finally, he rapaciously ripped it apart. What on earth was he doing? He must have gone mad.

"Aziz! Have you lost your mind? What are you doing?"

"Aren't you still my wife? I want to remind you that you are in case you've forgotten. You are mine." He slid her skirt up.

"Leave me alone! You're being absurd. Pull yourself together, for God's sake!"

She pushed him as hard as she could, no longer able to recognise her husband who seemed like a total stranger now. He was between her legs, firmly pressing his knees on her thighs to keep them spread apart. She attempted to kick him but was unable to move; he had practically nailed her to the floor with a force that she had never witnessed before. He had clutched her wrists with one hand, holding them pressed against the floor above her head while opening his zipper with his other hand. Finally, he thrust himself upon her like a wild animal. It's no use, she thought. I can't stop him. Where can I go? She looked at his eyes. They were the eyes of a madman. Was this man the gentleman who had once conquered her heart? All of a sudden, she decided to let it go, to surrender, to give in and lie like a piece of meat. Give up, Alex. Just give in. What difference would it make? Think about something else. She realised how much this man on top of her disgusted her. She closed her eyes tightly, tried to seal off her sense of smell, blocked her ears, her skin, her mind, everything. And she waited. It was bound to end sooner or later.

At long last, it did. Aziz was lying on the floor beside her, panting like an exhausted beast. Alex's eyes were screwed onto a tiny spot of stain on the ceiling.

"I'm sorry, Alex. I'm so sorry. Please forgive me. I didn't mean to hurt you. I don't. I know that you're still very much upset. It'll pass, *ma petite*. It'll all pass. Please pull yourself together and don't do anything foolish. Please," he said breathlessly, lying on his back with his eyes closed as if talking to himself. "I love you so very much. I'm head over heels in love with you, you know that. You can't leave me. You can't leave us. You can't abandon your children."

This was the end. She felt like a caged wild bird, unable to fly anymore. She listlessly pulled her ripped blouse together without thinking about what she was doing, as if she were obediently following the orders of some unseen force in a dream. She straightened up her skirt and stood up. A bath. She needed a bath. The water would cleanse everything. She slowly walked to the bathroom, turned the hot water on, undressed and got into the tub. She began scrubbing her whole body vigorously, with all her might, incessantly, until her skin was patched with red blotches, until all her energy drained out. She wanted to get away from it all ... from everything ... from everybody!

She threw on her bathrobe and went out of the bathroom. Going into the kitchen, she poured herself a glass of water. Aziz was on the balcony, leaning on the railings. He was standing dead still. She drifted to her bedroom, opened the drawer of her dressing table and took out a sleeping pill. As she swallowed it, a thought struck her. Freedom! A way out! She looked at her reflection in the mirror. I'm coming to you, Magda. I'll soon join you. It was so easy. Years ago, when she had lost her baby, she had chosen to live, to continue living this wretched life. What she needed to do now was to choose death, to take the voyage she had been yearning for, to get away from all this suffering, to go to where Magda was waiting for her, to where there was peace, to where there was happiness. This misery had to end. I must go. I must leave everything. She emptied all the pills in the box onto her palm. I should crush them, dissolve them in water and drink it all. All at once! In one single shot! I want to leave right away. Right now. Without any further delay. She pulled open the drawer again, looking for something to crush the pills. The handle of her hairbrush? The hand mirror? No! She had no time to lose. Aziz might come in any minute. She started to swallow the pills one after the other. A huge sip of water. Another pill. And another ... She finished all the pills in the box.

Her lifeless steps took her over to the gramophone. Liszt. *Hungarian Rhapsody, Number Thirteen.* Lying down on her bed, she took out her diary from the drawer of her bedside table and opened a new page. She could hardly hold her pen in her trembling hand. "Farewell," she began to write. "Farewell all my loves. Farewell all my sufferings. Farewell." Her eyes shifted to the poem on the previous page, the poem that she had written this morning.

> *Les arbres glacés d'une forêt noire*
> *Rêverent d'une prairie lointaine et calme*
> *Où le vent tranquil murmure les mots légers*
> *Au dessous d'un ciel bleu et tendre*
>
> *Les arbres tranquils de la prairie ennuyeuse*
> *Rêverent d'une forêt d'une nuit foncée*
> *Où on danse avec les étoiles amoureuses*
> *Qui scintillent dans un ciel noir d'obscurité.*
>
> Stamboul, le 27 Août 1939

She put her diary on the bed and slid under the white sheets. "The frozen trees of a dark forest," she mumbled in a subdued voice, hardly audible even to herself, "dream of a serene plain faraway where tranquil breezes whisper light words under a tender blue sky." Her eyes were getting heavier, her mind slowly drifting off. "While the tranquil trees of the boring plain, dream of a forest in an endless night where they could dance with the amorous stars twinkling in a mysteriously black sky." Everything felt so light now. Peace ... peace at long last.

- CURTAIN -

June 2004
Istanbul

It took Rüya ten days to read all of Mami's diaries and make up her mind. Intending to talk about her decision to Anastasia before anyone else, convinced that she would be her most valuable source of information, she had invited her to tea. They were sitting at the gazebo in the front garden.

"Are you really going to write this book, Rüya?"

"Yes, I will. I've already started my researches. Next week I'll be going to Italy, to a town by the name of Vado Ligure – to a factory once called Westinghouse, which of course, has a new name and new owners now. From there, I'll be moving on to Albisola."

"Will you go to Villa Marchese Gavotti?"

"Yes, I certainly shall."

"They say it has become a venue for receptions and that sort of thing. How very sad, isn't it? Won't it be heart-rending for you, my dear girl?"

"It'll be emotionally taxing, I know, but I've been doing a lot of thinking these last five days – since we've lost Mami. It will be an exceptionally poignant experience. On the other hand, writing this book will make me live Mami's life, so to speak. It might actually be the best way to get used to her absence."

"Do you have a title for your book yet?"

"*A Hungarian Rhapsody, A Novel in Three Acts*."

"A novel in three acts? What do you mean by that? Will you be writing for the theatre?"

"Think of the world as a stage and us as the spectators, *Thicha* Anastasia. There certainly may be times when we ourselves take the stage as well. Sometimes we mistakenly perceive what happens on stage – all that's being lived or has been lived on the stage of the world, so to speak, be it poisonous or nourishing – as being different than our own reality. It's a bit like considering a theatrical performance to have a different reality than real life. Don't you think that those plays are only reflections of real life and that the roles played by the actors are a part of their lives? Isn't everything – the actors, their roles, the script, the music – included within life itself? Aren't these plays part of the whole, just like everything else is? Similarly, aren't dreams, where real and unreal mingle, an integral part of our lives?"

"It's all Greek to me, sweetheart. However, what you just said reminds me of your Mami. There was something she often repeated. 'In Hungary,' she used to say, 'it's difficult to understand what is theatre and what is real life.' Well, anyway." She leaned over to stroke Rüya's hair. "It's not important at all if *I* understand it or not. I'm sure you'll write something good. Now, let's hear what you have to ask me."

"I'd like to hear everything you know about Mami, every little detail, everything she told you about her life in Hungary before she came to Istanbul and what happened afterwards."

"Everything?"

"Yes, *Thicha* Anastasia, everything. I've read ..." She paused as she felt a pang of shame for having read Mami's diaries. The idea of disclosing the secret life, the disguised emotions of someone she adored, disturbed her, but it was Mami herself who had implied that she wanted her to read them. There was nothing to be ashamed of, really. "I've read all her diaries," she finally blurted out, trying to overcome her feeling of remorse. "Everything. Rudi ..."

"Then I'm sure you know more about her life than I do."

"There must be something you can tell me, surely, a phrase, an emotion, a brief anecdote, something."

"Your most important source is Károly, my dear. Rudi was a very close friend of his."

"I've read a few of Károly's diaries and the notes he took in his sketchbooks, those I found in Mami's wardrobe. He mostly talks about his love for Ada." Rüya had no doubt that Anastasia, who had been Mami's friend for seventy-two years, knew everything about Rudi. "About Rudi," she insisted, but Anastasia cut her short.

"You should talk to Károly's daughter, my dear child – to Juli. Your great uncle was bound to have other diaries. Now! Let's talk about your boyfriend, shall we? What was his name? Sinan, was it?"

"There's nothing to talk about, *Thicha* Anastasia."

Act Two

Friss, the second part of the rhapsody, marches in like an army.
It roars. It is destructive. It ruthlessly burns everything down.

A Hungarian Rhapsody
A Novel in Three Acts
Act Two, Tableau Four
1939 - 1942

Tableau Four

58

On September 1, 1939 Hitler's Nazi Germany invaded Poland with a new and devastating tactic known as the *Blitzkrieg* – the lightning war. Two days later those who were tuned in to the BBC radio to listen to a speech delivered by the British premier Neville Chamberlain in a tired and strained voice at 11:15 am, following a programme on tinned-food recipes, learned that Britain was at war with Germany. The same day at 5pm, France followed suit, declaring war against Germany as well.

Alex had been out of the hospital for almost a week now, but had not been out of bed since she came home, for she had been feeling exhausted. Finally this morning she had dragged herself out of bed and managed to put on something decent, although she still felt utterly worn out. She was lying down on one of the sofas in the drawing room, gazing out through the French windows opening on to the balcony. She saw a bronze-coloured leaf fall, hesitantly at first, then melancholically floating about in the slight breeze, trembling every now and then. She watched another do the same. Their descent was dolefully beautiful in the pale light of the autumn sun, shining a little jadedly after a very hot summer. Were they aware of the imminent death awaiting them? Death ... war ... How could anyone kill another human being? How could people hate each other so much as to take each other's lives? How could they be fighting in the midst of such beauty, of the serenity the world offers?

"Mami? Would you please help me write to Évike?" asked Nili from where she was playing with her dolls on the floor next to Alex.

"They left only yesterday, darling. They should still be on the train. There's quite a while before they reach Budapest."

"It doesn't matter. I want to write now."

"All right, then. Go and ask Nanny Teréz for some writing paper and a pen."

Nili scurried towards the corridor and disappeared from sight, to return a few minutes later, holding a pen and a few sheets of paper. She leaned on the sofa next to her mother and clasped her hands, with a donnish expression on her face.

"My dearest best friend Évike," she began, curiously watching her mother's hand holding the pen over the paper. "Are you writing?"

"Yes, dear."

Istanbul, 5th September 1939

My dearest best friend Évike,

I already miss you a lot. Nanny Teréz will be leaving tomorrow as well. I'll miss her a lot too. Everyone is moving to Budapest. I want to move there as well.

"Mami? Why don't we move to Budapest?"

Neither she nor her daughters would be able to go anywhere now. They had become prisoners in this country.

"Your father can't leave, darling. He works here. We can't leave Istanbul. Well, what else shall we write, then?"

"Last week my mother got very sick. She was deranged. But she's getting well now."

"Where on earth did you hear that word – deranged?"

"When you were running a fever last week and Daddy took you to the hospital, I asked Aunt Necla what was wrong with you. She told me that you were deranged."

What were they telling her? She would talk to them – each one of them. She hated his whole family.

The doorbell rang. Asiye *Hanım* came out of the kitchen, walked unhurriedly to the door and opened it. It was Anastasia.

"Shall we continue later, *tatlım?* We have a guest now."

Nili sprinted towards Anastasia and jumped into her arms, whooping for joy, although it was only the night before that she had seen her.

Alex told Asiye *Hanım* to put the kettle on and then turned to Nili. "You should get some fresh air, darling. Please go and ask Nanny Teréz to take you to the park."

Unwilling to part from Anastasia, Nili initially refused to go, but eventually the park proved to be too irresistible. A few minutes later Asiye *Hanım* came in with the tea tray, bringing in the cheese turnovers she had baked "with her own loving hands," as she put it, and the apple strudel from Kıyık Patisserie, which Anastasia had brought. After setting them on the coffee table, she went back to the kitchen.

"I feel the whole world caving in on me, Anastasia."

"It's not easy, I know. The unbearable pain of losing a sibling is very hard to get over. You should be strong though. Think of your children. You ought to survive for their sake." She was squeezing Alex's hands as if she wanted to give her the strength she needed. "This wretched war is not helping either. You have every reason to be unhappy, dear. We all have a very difficult time lying ahead of us. We must hold on, Alex."

"He wants me to marry him," she said with unexpected abandon and, unable to look into Anastasia's quizzical eyes, quickly averted her gaze. She had not yet told her anything about him; just that she had once been engaged to someone called Rudi. She had somehow been ashamed to do so, not quite knowing why. Perhaps it was the discomfort of betraying Anastasia's respect for Aziz, she reasoned. However, she could no longer hold it back from her, especially having no one left to share her secret with after Izabella's departure for Budapest. She did not have the strength to shoulder such a load all by herself.

"What are you talking about, dear?"

"Rudi ... He wants me to take my daughters and move to Budapest."

Anastasia let go of Alex's hands and took a long sip from her tea before asking, "How long has this been going on?"

"How long?" Alex asked herself. Was it since January when they had come across each other in Japán Kávéház? Or was it since the moment he had held her hand the following day? Had it all begun the next day when he had asked her to wear the amber ring, or was it after she had received the first love letter from him in February? Had he become her lover in March when he had asked her to marry him as they sat in the conservatory after the loss of Magda?

"He asked for my hand after Magda's death. We have a longer history, but ... let's say it's been going on since January. It's been nine months."

Anastasia reached for her plate on the coffee table and placed it on the linen napkin she had carefully spread over her lap. She started fidgeting with the raisins in the rich apple filling between the paper-thin layers of the thick slice of strudel on her plate, apparently trying to find the right words to express her thoughts.

"You're still feeling the shock of Magda's death, dear," she finally said, without taking her eyes off the pastry. Then she slowly put her plate and napkin back on the table to hold Alex's hands again. "Your pain might affect your judgement. Please give yourself some time before you do anything, Alex," she said entreatingly. "It's impossible for you to make the right decision at a time like this. I wouldn't want you to do something that you might regret for the rest of your life."

"I already told Aziz that I wanted a divorce."

Anastasia's eyebrows suddenly twisted into a frown, and her lips tightened in apprehension. Her eyes said, "What have you done, Alex?" as she let go of her hands and stood up. Her furrowed eyebrows and her interlaced fingers with her thumbs rubbing against each other in front of her chest revealed her anxiety over what Alex had said and her urgent effort to think of what could be done. She then placed her hands on both sides of her waist and walked towards the French windows, her gaze following her steps. "What was his reaction?" she finally asked, as she raised her head and looked outside, her eyes chasing the falling leaves.

"He said that he would first shoot our daughters, then himself," Alex replied, her voice trembling like a leaf in a storm. "I'm facing a terrible dilemma, Anastasia. I can no longer put up with this life. I want to leave. I want to get away from it all, but ... I'm too scared."

"You know perfectly well that Aziz would never do such a thing. Are you sure that it's his fury that is behind your fear?" said Anastasia, now standing in front of Alex, holding her shoulders and looking straight into her eyes.

Of course, she was sure. What else could she be scared of?

"It might not be so easy to take your daughters away with you, dear. It's actually impossible if Aziz doesn't give his consent. Bear this in mind, would you? You would lose them."

"Rudi says he'd take care of it all."

"How much do you trust this man?"

She trusted him. She wanted to trust him. "He won't go back on his word," she mumbled. He would, sooner or later, keep his promise, she hoped.

"Alex. Emotionally, you're going through a very difficult period. Please, I beseech you, don't break up your marriage. Aziz is an exceptional man. He's madly in love with you. Do try to understand him even if it might be hard for you. You could at least wait until you find the strength in you to try to understand."

Why did *she* have to understand him? Why didn't Aziz try to understand her? "It's almost impossible for me to find that strength, especially after all that has happened recently." She took a quick sip from her tea, almost burning her lips. She was dubious about telling Anastasia what had happened before she tried to kill herself. She somehow ought to though, so that her friend would better understand her state of mind. She opened her mouth but could not say anything, lost for the right words.

"Everything will be all right, Alex. Life has to go on."

Yes, but some things do leave a mark, she thought. "Aziz's attitude towards me doesn't help either. Lately he's been behaving very differently than the man I've known to be my husband. He doesn't get cross; he doesn't shout. He is, in fact, cold and distant as never before. He hardly speaks to me. He has uttered no more than a dozen words since I've been back from the hospital."

"Sometimes, dear, when you fear talking about a trauma, you can't get yourself to talk about anything else either. You dread the possibility of anything you say finally leading up to that incident that hurt you so badly."

"There could be only one reason why he leaves me all alone at a time when I need his help the most: he wants to punish me. This is his way to do that. All I've been hearing from him lately is that I humiliated him in the eyes of his family ... that I trampled over his honour."

"Don't say that, Alex. Aziz adores you, and you know that. I'm sure he's devastated and scared to death at the thought of losing you. It must be quite hard for a man to swallow the fact that the woman he desperately loves is so unhappy as to attempt to kill herself."

After seeing Anastasia off that evening, Alex gave Terézia a handful of letters to be posted when she arrived in Budapest, including the one she had written to Rudi after a long period of hesitation. In her letter, she had said that she had finally told Aziz of her desire to get a divorce; and that he had taken it very badly, threatening to kill their daughters and himself. She had told him that she could not possibly divorce him under these circumstances, refraining from any mention of what Aziz had done to her or how she had tried to kill herself. She had concluded by asking him to send his letters, if he absolutely had to, to Anastasia's address, since Izabella had returned to Budapest.

59

Alex's dark mood went on for months. They had not let her kill her body, but no one could prevent her soul from dying. She felt the braid of her life unravelling. A sense of total disintegration was slowly shrouding her whole being. She withdrew from life more and more as her consciousness, in an effort to ease the pain, tried to break away from reality and gradually moved towards a coma. With each passing day she drew nearer to the tranquillity she strove for. Initially, she lost interest in food, becoming oblivious to what she ate or how much she ate. She did not even notice whether she was hungry or not; she could have died of hunger for all she cared. What was the point of nourishing a body that was to perish? Eventually, she cut herself off from the conversations around her, not caring to hear what others had to say. Words began to lose their meanings; they became subdued, as if coming from the depths of a dark well. She alienated herself from her daughters, from Aziz, from her dogs, from her cat, from everyone and everything. She no longer had any inclination to appreciate the setting sun or the rising moon.

As Christmas drew closer, Aziz kept saying that he had had enough and that she should stop sulking and pull herself together; that she had no right to neglect her daughters and her home. "You're burying yourself into a ridiculously foolish nightmare of your own creation. It's about time you woke up," he said, accusingly. No! No, she did not want to wake up, because this realm where she sought refuge was not a nightmare but a sweet dream that alleviated her incubus, a reverie where her memories warmed her soul, a daydream that carried her to the day when the war would be over and she would be free to leave. To cheer herself up at least a little bit during the approaching cold and dark festive season, she had no choice but to reminisce about her past or simply imagine what had happened where her memory failed her. Some anecdotes were told and retold so many times that she no longer knew whether she actually recalled them.

She remembered things being different at Christmas time before her father had gone to war – the time when they used to live in Italy but went to Budapest for the festivities. It was with acute nostalgia that she recollected the crowded Christmas dinners when their extended family used to come together, how she and Magda used to be the centre of attention as everybody kissed and embraced them, how spoiled she was with all that love she received, and how, unaware that she might not always be loved that way, she was fed up with all the attention. It gave her a sense of utter desolation when she thought of all the presents piled up under the huge Christmas tree that seemed to reach up to the high ceiling of the drawing room, gloriously sparkling and generously decorated with golden stars, tiny silver angels, glittery baubles and cotton wool meant to represent snow fallen on its branches. She vividly recalled how the warm light emanating from the hundreds of candles lit in different places of the house reflected from the cascades of the crystal chandeliers, specially cleaned and polished for the occasion. And more than any of this, she reminisced about how, on Christmas Eve, they were allowed to fall asleep in the strong and loving arms of her father in front of the fireplace.

Her father was no longer there to celebrate Christmas after they had moved to Budapest. In an effort to compensate for his absence, everyone gave them a myriad of presents, despite the difficulties of wartime. She used to sit with Magda and Károly on one of the uncomfortable sofas in the Blue Salon in Rózsadomb, eagerly anticipating their turn to receive their presents. Their mother sat in her majestic armchair, placed near the Christmas tree, to distribute presents to the servants and their families. They used to wait at the entrance hall with their spouses, children, parents and close relatives in a line until Álmos, the head butler, with a slight movement of his head from where he stood behind Gizella, motioned them to enter the drawing room in the order specified beforehand. As they silently walked on the slippery parquetry floor in timid steps, their eyes revealed how proud they were to be there for this unique occasion, when they were allowed to kiss their mistress's hand, and how excited they were about the presents they were about to receive.

Alex remembered it all very clearly, how they waited impatiently as they watched the servants curtsying and bowing, her mother saying a few words of endearment while her hand was kissed, Álmos handing out the presents lined up on the tables extending from the Christmas tree to the music room, and the servants hurrying out of the drawing room after taking their presents with trembling hands. Their presents were usually pretty boring things such as sweaters, jumpers, dresses, coats or boots. Hours used to go by before the long line ended and it was time for Alex, Magda and Károly to receive their gifts. A few days later the same ceremony would be repeated in the Crimson Salon at Erzsébet Manor in Kengyel, except that they, of course, would not be receiving any presents.

All of this was long gone by. They were all dispersed now, far apart. She wondered how Károly would celebrate this Christmas. Tête-à-tête with Ada, away from his family. In his letter, he mentioned that they would be celebrating New Year's Eve at La Coupole again. The war had not yet shown its ugly face in the City of Lights, he said, and their life, unlike what they had feared, had not changed at all except for a few minor details. "Our life in our beehive home at La Ruche continues as before. All we do differently is to stock food. We still go to La Coupole and Les Deux Magots to have our coffee or drink Pernod with friends, and discuss art, philosophy and politics," he had written. Ada, who scribbled a few lines at the end of Károly's letters, wanted to return to Budapest, as she was extremely worried about her parents. "Home is the best place to be at such times," she wrote. "Hungary is neutral at the moment and might manage to stay out of the war altogether. Besides, I don't want our first baby to be born in a foreign country, which is at war. I'm not pregnant yet but, sooner or later, I want to start a family."

I don't want to. *I* want to. First person singular. What does *Károly* want? Wasn't it important what he did and did not want? Ada's inconsiderate attitude irritated Alex. It was much safer for Károly to stay in Paris at the moment. What if Hungary entered the war? He would be drafted then, wouldn't he? Madame Ada de Kurzón was apparently incapable of figuring out when to be in Paris and when to be in Budapest. Well, it was not her who would be going to the front, was it? Fortunately, Károly thought that it would be better if they did not rush things, and waited to see what was going to happen before making a decision. He was really worried, and so was Alex, especially after having read János's letter. Good old Jancsi hardly wrote, but, when he did, he certainly drew a very bleak picture. This time, however, he had every right to be so pessimistic. Soon after the outbreak of the war, they had classified iron and other metals as war materials and confiscated his father's smithy, upon which János opened a small ironmonger's shop. It must have been awfully difficult for him to stomach it all. Many of his friends had been conscripted into the army, and he expected to be drafted any minute now, despite being thirty-three years old. Conversely, Gizella's letters provided some relief for Alex's aching heart. She had written saying that nothing much had changed in their daily lives; the gentlemen continued to go to their offices and the ladies went on gossiping and frequenting the beauty parlours.

The doorbell rang. She was not expecting anyone. She ran to the door before Asiye *Hanım* had a chance to make a move. It was Anastasia.

"*Votre postillon d'amour, madam.* The humble servant of your secret emotions."

"Do come in, please. I was about to put the kettle on."

"I shan't be staying long, Alex. I have a few errands to run, but I thought I'd better give this to you first."

Alex snatched the envelope from her friend's hand and tucked it away in her pocket. "Anastasia, I can't possibly thank you enough. No one would do what you do."

"I hope I'm doing the right thing and not getting you into trouble."

"Don't worry. All you do is give me some strength to hang on to this life." She hugged her friend tightly.

"May God protect you, Alex."

She impatiently watched Anastasia hurry down the stairs and disappear from sight before she shut the door, took her packet of cigarettes and matches from the drawing room, ran to the bathroom and locked herself in, fearing that Aziz might unexpectedly turn up or Asiye *Hanım* might see the letter and inadvertently make an uncalled for comment in the presence of Aziz. She closed the toilet seat and sat on it. As she read Rudi's letter, her whole world lightened up. I shall not give up on you, he said. I shall never give up on you. I won't let you stay there. You must come to Budapest before the war comes to Istanbul. Right away! With your daughters! You must come whatever the cost. Don't you worry about your daughters, for there surely is a way to take them out of Turkey. I'll be taking care of it all, he said. You only need to tell me that you're ready to leave. All you have to do is take your daughters and go to the British Consulate in Istanbul, he assured her. She read it once again, lit a cigarette and read it again. When she finished her cigarette, she read it again until she memorised it, until she had engraved every single word in her mind. He wrote that he had used all his contacts to avoid conscription into the army and obtained a report saying that he had had tuberculosis, a report that had solved the problem. He had meant to obtain the same report for János, but their stubborn and patriotic friend had categorically refused the idea. He was asking Alex to write to János and try to talk him into it.

She lit another cigarette and read the letter once again from beginning to end, after which she walked to the sink and reluctantly held her cigarette to a corner of the letter. She watched it burn to ashes and then go down the drain. She ran out of the bathroom and into her bedroom, sat at her writing desk and took out her writing paper, all in a rush as if she were scared to forget what she had just read. "My one and only love," she began to write.

... I can't possibly put into words how much I rejoiced in your excellent news. Learning that you won't be conscripted was the best thing that could have happened to me amidst all this misery, a source of sheer bliss that shed some light onto the approaching dark Christmas. I see that, reading my last letter, you've already gathered the state of mind I was thrown into by the mere thought of losing another loved one to the war after my father.

She stopped writing. She could not bring herself to say that she was ready to leave. Now with the war, she could not go anywhere, even if she risked it all. How could she drag her daughters to the heart of a war, throw them into a burning inferno? She had become nothing but a slave in the clutches of her husband. Recently, since the outbreak of the war, Aziz's eyes had sparkled cruelly, betraying his secret delight; it seemed as if he was taking it as his victory. How would she survive this acute sense of yearning? "You must persevere, Alex," she whispered vehemently to herself. The war would end sooner or later. You must be patient. Please Rudi, I beg you, please tell me over and over again that you will never give up on me, that this war will not go on for long, and soon, very soon, our misery will end and we will start a brand new life together. Tell me over and over again about the life that awaits us in London. Tell me that again and again, in each and every letter. Make me believe that our dreams will soon come true, please I beg you. You're the only light of hope in my forlorn existence. Please don't give up on me.

"Passion has hopelessness in its nature. Otherwise, it becomes calculated expectation." Why did she think of this now? She tried to remember where she had read it. She could not.

60

Hungary had finally entered the war, after having stayed out of it for more than a year. Ever since she had heard the news, Alex had been constantly listening to the radio with a heavy heart, trying to keep up with the latest developments.

Pastoral was playing on the radio. She found Beethoven so relaxing. Lying down on the sofa, she started reading Károly's last letter, hoping to find some consolation in it. Her brother, who had returned to Budapest in June, wrote that the

Jews were in relative safety in Hungary despite all that had been going on. Aunt Irén and Uncle Filip had moved in with them to the house in Rózsadomb, making their house a much livelier place despite the war. He talked about the difficulties of the war and the cold dark winter. Ada's pregnancy was well advanced and she was expected to give birth towards the end of January – something which Károly said he was very excited about. "However, I'm really worried about you, my darling sister," he had written. "You might need to come here. Please keep your suitcases ready. It might not be so clear where we are going as a country, but you would at least be in your homeland."

To go to Budapest! It was nothing but a dream. The war was spreading like an incurable plague. She felt as if she were sequestered in a dark room with no walls to lean on, an open prison where she was frozen stiff with an unbearable helplessness, unable to move a finger, not knowing when she might be stepping into an abyss.

Pastoral was still playing. Music was her saviour. She listened to it with her heart and soul, her lips joining the orchestra in involuntary little wriggles, nature coming alive before her mind's eyes. She forgot where she was, finding herself wherever she wanted to be, next to whomever she longed for. It felt like violating all those stringent rules, rising against the existing system and overriding all boundaries. The much-admired Strauss's waltzes, for instance, which sweetened life or made it more cheerful, meant nothing to her. They were, as far as she was concerned, misleadingly colourful pieces of music that took you away from your inner world and incarcerated you within the four walls of a ballroom. Beethoven, on the other hand, was so wonderful, so magical ... Beethoven! The genius who placed a mirror in front of you and let you dwell on the depths of your heart and soul. As she listened to his music, her inner world surfaced and revealed its most intimate recesses.

"Madame Beethoven! Lost in the wonderland again, are we? We have guests for dinner, have you forgotten?"

Aziz was back early for lunch. How quickly the time passed. She stood up half-heartedly, reluctant to do anything. A slight sense of relief embraced her as she saw that Asiye *Hanım* had already set the table. She could hardly wait for lunch to finish and Aziz to go back to work, for she meant to write to Rudi in the afternoon to ask him if there was any risk of his conscription after Hungary's entry into the war.

At dinner that evening, Alex was feeling completely worn out, not physically but more with a sense of spiritual weariness. Aziz had invited his whole family again in honour of Sema and Zeki, who had arrived from Adana the day before. When they came, they came in packs. She had spent all afternoon cooking, something that she found frustrating, since food shortages made it exasperatingly difficult to come up with an acceptable menu. She wished they would all leave, and she could go to sleep, so that morning would come and she could write to Rudi, for she had had no time to write anything this afternoon.

They talked about nothing but war and politics. She was so sick and tired of it all. She was choked to death; she wanted to hear no more of it. Aziz kept on telling them what was happening to the Jews in Europe, going into every detail, as if he wanted to torture her.

"It was a wrong move on Hungary's part. According to our British friends, the first two years of the war will see Germany going from victory to victory, but eventually, just like in the Great War, they will be defeated. Hungary is no longer part of the Austro-Hungarian Empire and is free to act independently. Her choice should have been neutrality, which was her only way out of this mess. She has committed a grave mistake. If the British win the war, Hungary will lose; if the Germans win, they will be destroyed."

"Should I just say I have a terrible headache and withdraw to my room?" thought Alex. She would do just that as soon as dinner was over. She could not take it anymore. She would rather have Aziz's male friends over, because then he usually asked her to stay in her room – something which suited her perfectly. She much preferred to be on her own, daydreaming and listening to music, than to serve these people.

"It would have been nice if Alex were here as well," said Aziz with heavy sarcasm.

"I'm so sorry, but I feel rather tired today."

"You must be exhausted after all that cooking, my child."

Don't push it, Mehpare *Hanım*. Don't push it. Her mother-in-law was worse than her mother when it came to driving her mad; and she could say nothing to her but smile obligingly.

"How is the new Pointer?" asked Haldun, coming to her rescue as usual. He had no keen interest in hunting but knew very well how to cheer up Aziz. "What was her name, did you say?"

"Elka! She's impossibly headstrong but she doesn't stand a chance. She will, sooner or later, learn to obey my orders. She's a pedigree, and like all pedigrees it's in her blood to yield to what she's told. I shan't give up; I have much hope in her."

"I must be elected to the national assembly again in the seventh legislative term," interjected Sema, fidgeting in her seat on Alex's right, as her stentorian voice stifled Aziz's. In the 1935 elections, not only she had been one of the seventeen women to become the first female deputies in the Turkish Grand National Assembly, but she had also been branded as the most "talkative" female deputy during her four years in office. Last year she had not been elected, but she was still into politics wholeheartedly and talked about nothing else. Alex was convinced that Aziz had seated Sema next to her so as to make sure she was bored to tears. Sema was now talking to Cevat Bey, telling him about her efforts towards opening youth detention centres and establishing juvenile courts. "I'm unequivocally against putting handcuffs on children."

Alex tried to listen to Ayla, who was chatting with Necla about painting. Her attention was interrupted by a question from Zeki Bey.

"How is your family? The news from Hungary is rather unsettling." His expression, exaggeratedly melodramatic in its pity for Alex, was unnerving. "The other day a colleague of mine, a lawyer, was talking about the dire situation of the Jewish businessmen in Budapest. Apparently, they were left with no choice but to sell their companies. I do hope that your friends are all right."

"They're trying their best. Some of them are transferring their companies, though only on paper, to Christians, whom they refer to as their mercenaries."

"How do you know about these things? Is it Károly?" Aziz interjected, obviously listening to everything she said, even though he was sitting at the other end of the table.

"Of course, it is, Aziz. Who else would write about all that?" she grumbled.

At long last, the morning came. The moment Aziz walked out the door, Alex dashed to the window and watched him walk away. Lately, after they had prohibited the use of private cars, he had been taking a taxi, if he could find one, or otherwise using the tram to go to the office. He categorically refused to use the new system of *dolmuş*, which was basically a system of shared taxis. Alex waited for a few seconds before sitting down at her writing desk. It took her only a few minutes to finish her letter.

Her daughters were still asleep. She told Asiye *Hanım* that she would be going out and asked her to keep an eye on them. She put on her fur coat, tucked the letter in her pocket and ran down the stairs. It was freezing cold outside. She started walking towards the post office in the silence of the early morning. "What are you doing, Alex?" asked her inner voice as she ran her fingers over the letter she was holding firmly in her pocket. What was she doing? What was she hoping for? Had she not suffered enough? Was this life not good enough for her? What purpose did her infatuation for Rudi serve except for making her life more miserable, throwing her into an abysmal state of loneliness? Was she not pushed further down this abyss the more she tried to hang on to her love? I have to forget him. I have to. I ought to be content with what I have. In panic, she shook her head as if to dispel her thoughts. No! No, I can't give up on him. Without him, I'd be completely desolate. I need him even if he is only a daydream. One day it will all come true. I know it will. A little bit of patience, that is all I need.

She entered the post office and handed the letter to the clerk.

61

Alex crumpled the empty cigarette packet and threw it on the floor. She was dying for a cigarette. She ferreted in the drawers of her dressing table in her bedroom, but to no avail. She searched the drawer of the bedside table. Nothing! She dashed to the kitchen, convinced that she would definitely find one there, and rummaged through it. How could there be not even one single cigarette in the whole house? Aziz was throwing them away – of that she was certain. "You smoke too much," he kept nagging her lately. "How can you smoke so much – even when you're cooking? A pinch of ashes for us all!" he grunted. She went into Aziz's study and went through the drawers. At long last! Of course, it was him who hid them. You rascal! She grabbed the packet, pulled out a cigarette and drew in the smell of tobacco. Lighter? Matches. She hunted through the other drawers. Her eyes alighted on a box of matches on the desk. The sound of an igniting match. The first puff. What a relief. She took another deep puff.

Gleefully she relaxed back in Aziz's revolving chair. The letters in one of the drawers caught her eye. Several opened envelopes were stacked on top of each other. She immediately recognised the handwriting on the one at the very top. It was from Károly and addressed to Aziz. Wondering if she had read it, she took the letter out of its envelope. It was dated September 21, 1941. It must have just arrived. With much joy, she started reading it, hoping to raise her spirits by learning the news about her sweet niece Juli. "We're sinking deeper and deeper into a nightmare, Aziz," he had written. "We have bitterly realised, yet again, that the war is not going to end but is only just starting. We, as Germany's supporters, not only declared war against the Soviets, but also agreed to send forty thousand soldiers to the Eastern Front. I don't write about these things to Alex, for she's really disturbed by such news, and I would ask you not to tell her any of this either," she read, her hands shaking. "The anti-Jewish press is talking about a 'Final Solution to the Jewish Question,' but no one really knows exactly what that means. They issue a new law every day. Someone who is not considered Jewish today might be classified as one tomorrow and lose all his or her rights. Recently they passed a law, which is nothing but a race protection law ..."

She flinched in pain. Her cigarette had fallen off her fingers onto her leg. She picked it up with trembling fingers, put it into the ashtray on the desk and pressed it hard until it came apart. None of this was true. Couldn't be! Shouldn't be! She grabbed the ashtray and hurled it onto the floor with all her might. The bronze ashtray tumbled over the parquetry; the ashes scattered around. She was squeezing the crumpled papers in her fist. "I must write to Rudi," she mumbled. No, she should call him – straight away. She would ask him to tell her everything without hiding anything from her. Not knowing drove her insane. She reached for the telephone on the desk, only to stop the next instant. What would happen if Aziz came home while they were talking? She changed her mind and ran to her bedroom, took out her pen and writing papers. "Istanbul, 15th October 1941," she started to write, and finished her letter in a flash. She had to post it right away. Now! Without losing another second! She hurried into some proper clothes and rushed out of the house.

A long wait pursued, lasting for months. Her spirits sunk further seeing Nili, who had started school this year, often bedridden with a fever, suffering from chronic bronchitis. An abnormally cold winter, coupled with worsened economic conditions, brought the coal shortage to a critical level and drained the gas stocks, sparking gas supply restrictions. Alex felt trapped as the shortages did not allow them to use their car and the curfew banned them from going out at night. The long dreary winter nights, unbearably bleak because of the blackouts, left her increasingly more depressed. She had no tolerance for anyone anymore; she even shouted at her daughters and could hardly put up with the caprices of Goya, her favourite dog, or those of Hera, the new arrival after Pepa's death. To make things worse, Aziz continued to go hunting and left her all alone with her daughters for days, making it more difficult for her to survive the darkness of lugubrious winter months. There was not a single soul to take care of her. The cold war between her and Aziz persevered in all its grimness. He did not shout. He did not even argue with her, but drove her insane with his sarcastic and scornful attitude. Nothing in this miserably desolate life, however, devastated her more than the lack of any news from Rudi, especially when the news from Hungary was starting to become increasingly more worrisome. According to Aziz, the situation had taken a frightening turn lately. In January the Hungarian government had issued a decree abolishing the legal status of Judaism, defining it as a tolerated rather than a recognised religion, and thus ripped apart the delicate membrane over an irremediable wound, which started festering and exuding its most repugnant pus. Shortly after that, they received another piece of news that ground dirt into the cut: Germany, having difficulties fighting against the Soviets, had decided that it was time Hungary paid its debt and demanded that Horthy increase military aid. Rumour spread that all males between nineteen and thirty years of age were to be drafted for the army and all able-bodied male Jews, irrespective of their age, were to be "invited" to join the forced labour battalions.

Finally in mid-January, following a painfully long period of despondency, Rudi's letter arrived.

Budapest, 10th December 1941

My precious darling,

Today, I received your letter dated 15 October. Haven't they taught you not to read other people's letters? There is nothing to worry about. Please don't take seriously any of what Károly has written to Aziz; you know what he is like – always exaggerating things, being such a highly charged soul. You shouldn't worry about what is going on in Poland. Such atrocities could never happen in our country – will never happen. Put aside all those questions that prey on your mind and think of the new life we shall soon start together, my love. We must be patient and resilient.

In the last few weeks, there have been a lot of changes in my life. We sold everything we owned, including number twenty-three Andrássy Boulevard. From now on, I'm a tenant in my own property. The reason is, of course, not that we had any financial difficulties, but that we thought this was the most logical solution. Cash is movable, so to speak, something you can move from one country to another. The other day, we finalised the formalities for the sale of our mansion on Andrássy Boulevard as well, whereupon my parents moved in with me. Our butler Vilmos is still with us. His unwillingness to leave really touched our hearts.

Another change is about my business. Do you remember Lajos, my old friend who had a wine estate in Csopak, the one you thought looked like an English lord? A couple of days ago, he introduced me to a friend of his, a certain Dutchman by the name of Gerhard. He seems a patsy, a rather weird sort but was very useful, I must admit. He said that they needed a legal advisor at Tungsram and that he would be very happy if I accepted the post. (Tungsram, a subsidiary of a Dutch company called Philips, produces electronic parts.) Considering that I can run my "mercenary" remotely, I thought this was a good offer at a time like this and accepted. I'll be starting next Monday. As you can see, I'm not only a tenant but also an employee – a white-collar worker. War does alter everything, doesn't it?

Please, I implore you not to let anyone upset you. Very soon everything will be like it was before, even better. This war, which has ruined all our plans, is bound to end sooner or later. I do have my worries, however, and, although I don't want to push you too hard, I cannot but insist that you think again and think well. These recent developments – the United States entering the war and Britain having declared war on Hungary – have pushed the situation to a new level. I do hope that Turkey doesn't enter the war, and, in case it does, I do hope to have you out of there beforehand. Please rest assured that the instant you say yes, I will take you and your daughters out. All I need is your photographs. I will come and get you out of that country within a week. Please trust me. War teaches you a lot of things, Alex. There is a way out of everything, believe me, and there are many countries other than Hungary and Turkey where we can live in safety until this war is over.

Please, my one and only love, don't ever forget that I love you so very much, that I have always loved you and that I will always love you.

She wanted to believe that everything was all right and that Károly was exaggerating the gravity of the situation. A month later, however, the *Struma* tragedy made her realise in great agony that she should believe what Károly had written to Aziz, that people were openly sent to their deaths and that what was happening in Europe was not hearsay.

In December, the *SS Struma*, a ship carrying Jewish refugees from Romania to Palestine under the British flag, had had a faulty engine and broke down as it sailed through the Bosphorus, after which it was towed to Sarayburnu in Istanbul, where it remained at anchor for weeks, waiting for its engine to be repaired, while its passengers were kept in quarantine and were not allowed to disembark. Soon, hunger broke out, as no one was allowed to board the ship. Aziz, knowing how badly this would affect Alex, tried to hide this incident from her, but Alex eventually heard about it, since the ship's engine was being repaired at a shipyard in the Golden Horn that belonged to a friend of Anastasia's brother Hristo. The very next day Alex went to the promenade in Sarayburnu with Anastasia, without letting Aziz know, and watched the ship for hours, practically torturing herself. "Could there be someone I know on board, a friend who had escaped to Romania and then boarded this ship?" Do something, Alex, she angrily told herself. These people need help. Come on. Prove yourself. She could do nothing but feel like a useless and incompetent insect.

Finally, unable to take it any longer, she talked to Aziz, albeit with much apprehension. "Can't you use your contacts? Isn't there anything we can do, Aziz?" She persisted for days. "You have so many influential friends in Ankara. İskender has so many contacts. You have to do something. These people have been imprisoned in that ship for two months now with no food, no water, no hygiene. What in God's name is their crime?"

"This is something beyond the power of common people like ourselves," Aziz said, ignoring Alex's worries. "The British government has put a quota on the number of Jewish immigrants into Palestine. The ship's engine has long been repaired, but the British are putting pressure on our government to prevent the ship from sailing onwards. It has become an international issue now."

"Why don't they let anybody out?"

"They're in quarantine, Alex."

"But they say that some passengers have already disembarked. Apparently, someone has used his contacts."

"It isn't as easy as you think."

Alex continued watching *Struma* with a heavy feeling of defeat. Finally, towards the end of February, they heard that the ship had been towed to the Black Sea to be disinfected and, following an explosion, had sunk with all its passengers. For Alex, *Struma* was the proof of her nightmares being real and of the life she led in Istanbul being nothing but a dream.

After this incident, she turned completely inward. As far as she was concerned, nothing, neither Istanbul nor the events that went on around her, nor the worries of the people here, had any importance. She did not want to see or to talk to anyone. She had no interest in others' problems as her mind was riveted on one single question: when would her loved ones be free?

April came, and nature, ignoring the bleak picture the war had created, slowly resurrected from its winter torpor. Alex, however, needed a lot more than spring to raise her spirits. She had not received a single line from Rudi for months. She had not burned his last letter, which she had received back in January. She could not.

She took it out from where she had hidden it in the depths of her lilac wardrobe and kissed the sheets of paper, which were wrinkled from having been read time and time again.

"Is it from *Öcsi bácsi*, Mami?"

"Why did you get out of bed, Nili? Your fever will rise again."

"I'm so bored, Mami. Could we write to *Anyukám?*"

"Of course, we can, sweetheart." Alex affectionately placed Rudi's letter between her chemise and her skin.

Nili handed over the writing paper and Alex's fountain pen, which she had brought along. "Dearest *Anyukám*," she said, raising her eyes that looked so much like Aziz's, and fixed them on Alex for a moment before focusing on the pen in Alex's hand.

> ... Two weeks ago, we celebrated my sister's fourth birthday. She didn't get too many prezzies. Daddy says we shouldn't spend too much money because there is a war going on. War is an awful thing. They don't buy us that many toys anymore.
>
> At school, I have very good grades although I often get sick and miss school. However, that's something I don't mind at all because I get to stay home with Mami and with my sister, which I enjoy very much.
>
> Our new cat Duman (which means Smoky) is not as clever as Portakal, but she's much cuter. She's so tiny. She looks like *Öcsi bácsi*'s Füst – his cat in Paris. I can't see Füst's colour in the photographs, but I think his fur is exactly like Duman's, a light grey ...

"How old is Füst now?" Nili asked, looking at Alex.

Alex paused for a second. "Ten. He must be ten years old now."

"Do you think he's still alive?"

"Of course he is, *tatlım*."

Sometimes animals are luckier than human beings, thought Alex. Füst must still be living a relaxed life at La Ruche.

"Go on, Mami."

"All right then, tell me what else we should be writing."

> ... Duman sleeps in my bed. I miss Portakal a lot, but I know that she's in heaven now. Mami says she's very happy with the angels. Goya will soon join her there because he's very sick. He can't even move now.
>
> I'm so glad that spring is here because we're all much happier in spring. We go out more. I wish it were always springtime. I wish everything remained as it is now.

Alex stroked her daughter's hair. How happy she was, despite all this misery around her, how extraordinary it was that she could find joy and happiness in the trivial details of life. She wished she were a small child again. Why could she not be like her? Why could she not be content with what she had? She ought to learn to do that. The colour of the blossoming Judas trees, a few words of love in a letter, a few lines of hope, a paragraph of a dream ... They should be sufficient to make her happy. They had to be enough to give her joy. They had to.

"Are you writing Mami?"

Of course, she was writing. That was, in fact, the only thing she had been doing: writing letters and waiting for letters, isolating herself from the outside world so as not to allow her hopes to be shattered by the events going on around her, detaching herself from reality and living in a dream, like a sleepwalker, day in and day out, her life perforated by moments, sometimes by hours, of total detachment from reality. A long summer wasted away in expectation, another dreary autumn bringing in nothing but melancholy and, following the feigned warmth of the Indian summer, the month of November funereally announcing the imminent arrival of yet another dark winter. Károly becoming the father of a second baby girl shed some light upon her dark days, only to be followed precipitously by a surge of grief for not being with him to share his happiness. Then came along another bitterly meaningless Christmas.

A new year was to begin in two days' time. Would it be another year of longing? The war had been going on relentlessly, for more than three years. Alex had almost no hope left that it would ever be over. It would last longer than the Great War, she thought with a sinking heart. The Great War. She could not bear even the thought of it.

That afternoon she had taken her daughters and gone to Beyoğlu to meet Anastasia and her brother Hristo at the Marquise Patisserie. Anastasia was in a terrible state of mind because she, like many other members of the non-Muslim minorities, had been plunged into turmoil by the cruelly insensitive speech given by İsmet İnönü, the National Chief as he was known, at the Ankara Hippodrome during the Republic Day celebrations, where he had made referral to some "degenerates," not explicitly describing whom he meant by the term. Soon after that speech, in November, a tax law had been passed under the name of Capital Tax, the aim of which was claimed to be the levying of a tax on the high profits made under the war conditions – something, they claimed, that would serve to fill the state treasury against a possible German or Russian invasion. A short while later they had announced the lists prepared by the tax assessment board. All Turkish citizens were subject to this law, but rumour had it that much higher tariffs were generally imposed on the non-Muslim citizens. Neither Aziz nor anyone in his family appeared on these lists. Anastasia and Hristo, on the other hand, were, and they were obliged to pay their dues within fifteen days. In case of default, a receiving order would be issued and their assets would be sold, and the proceeds used to pay their debts. Had the proceeds failed to suffice, they would be sent to a labour camp. The day before, they had sold their shop and flat for an amount much less than their worth, and this morning had fulfilled their obligations as loyal citizens. Both Anastasia and Hristo were in a worryingly strange mood. They were heartbroken and offended. "We feel betrayed," they kept saying.

August 2005
Istanbul

Rüya was visiting Anastasia in her flat, which resembled a flying deck perched on the top floor of a twelve-storey apartment building in Çiftehavuzlar on the Asian side of Istanbul. Initially, she had avoided Rüya's questions with brief and vague explanations, but eventually she had given in, becoming Rüya's most helpful source of information during her research. It was time for Rüya to dig into her memories again.

"Madam will be with you in a moment. Please make yourself comfortable," said Meşhure *Hanım*, ushering her into the drawing room.

Refusing to sit on the spacious sofa she was shown to, Rüya settled in one of the velvet armchairs with intricately carved woodwork placed in front of the bay windows, which opened onto a balcony that seemed to extend far into the sea.

"How would you like your coffee?"

"Turkish coffee, please. Without sugar."

Anastasia, after her brother Hristo's death, had married at the ripe old age of sixty-three and moved to this flat, only to be left on her own six years later when her husband had passed away. To many of her friends, who had been telling her to move out of this apartment saying that it would not survive another earthquake, her response had always been the same: "I shall never leave my home of thirty years. We've been through so many earthquakes and survived them all. We shall surely survive them in the future." Neither earthquakes nor any other type of shocks or upheavals had been enough to frighten Anastasia, who was brave at heart. Rüya could understand why she was so adamant about not leaving this flat, which offered a spectacular vista of the Sea of Marmara extending from Sarayburnu in the west to the Prince's Islands on the east, and even to Yalova in the south, when the sky was clear enough.

The sun was shining brightly in a crystal clear blue sky. The white shutters were lowered, for Anastasia had obviously had her share of the sun. Rüya, on the other hand, could never have enough of sunlight, which was something of an obsession that had initiated in sunless England, where she had spent eleven years of her childhood and adolescence.

"Shoo! Shoo, you rascal!" shouted Anastasia, tapping the window with the back of her finger in an effort to scare off a well-fed crow that was getting ready to attack her flower-beds. The black raider shot a terse glance at the sound that disrupted its mission and took flight.

Rüya stood up and hugged Anastasia. "How are you? Are you well?"

"Let's say I'm fine, then I'll be fine, my dear girl."

They settled down in the armchairs facing each other.

"Shall we raise the shutters a little bit more?"

"Go on, do as you please."

Meşhure *Hanım* came in with a silver tray carrying two cups of Turkish coffee, which she always prepared diligently so as to make it really frothy; but however hard she tried she could never make it to the level of perfection that would win Anastasia's approval. She left the cups, accompanied by two small glasses of water, on the coffee table standing between the armchairs and went back to the kitchen.

Anastasia was ninety-two years old with surprisingly smooth cheeks that denied her age and led those who did not know her well to think that she had been blessed with plastic surgery, although nothing even close to a surgical knife had ever touched those cheeks. Not even any of those expensive creams, she claimed, had ever been part of her cosmetic artillery, which consisted of nothing but the simple Cream Pertev, Dr. Renaud Paris or the good old Nivea in its dark blue metal container. The peelings from the chopped cucumbers she added to watery yogurt to make the garlic-laden *cacık,* and the skin of the bananas she sliced and lined on the milk pudding *muhallebi,* along with many other vegetal cosmetics – which she jealously refrained from disclosing – had to spend a while on Anastasia's face before they were thrown into the bin. She often preached to Rüya the importance of "ironing" her face with a finger massage for five minutes twice daily.

"Well? What are you going to tell me today?"

"As you know, all I do is write, write and write."

"Isn't it finished yet, your book? How long have you been working on it?"

"It's been more than a year now. I've finished the First Act, and for the last couple of months I've been writing the Second Act. There are a couple of details in that act that raise a few questions in my mind, details I can't seem to figure out.

I guess I'll have to go to Budapest again and maybe to Paris too. There are also a few things I'd like to ask you."

"What was the title of your book? Rhapsody something, isn't it?"

"*A Hungarian Rhapsody, A Novel in Three Acts.*"

"Yes, yes, I remember now. Like a play."

"As a matter of fact, Mami's rhapsody is a broken one. You know that rhapsodies consist of three parts, but Mami's life didn't have a *Csárdás*, the third part where emotions reach their climax. It's as if she was stuck in the second act all her life. However, I did imagine a *Csárdás* for her. If I can pull it off, I'll write a happy ending for her – the end that she very much deserved but could not have."

"Do please help yourself," said Anastasia, the edge of her lips curling in a strange smile as she pointed at the lacy crystal bowl filled with a selection of mint, lemon, pistachio and rose-flavoured Turkish delights. "The rose-flavoured ones are truly delicious."

Rüya loved the smell of roses, but only when they came from the roses in the garden or in a vase. The heavy perfume of rosewater added to desserts reminded her of the vague scent left on her grandmother's cheeks after she cleaned her makeup with it instead of using facial tonic; and every time she was offered a rose-flavoured dessert she felt as though she was about to take a bite out of her grandmother's cheek. "I prefer the minty ones," she mumbled, taking one that seemed greenish, as far as she could figure out through the thick coat of icing sugar sprinkled on it.

"Rüya darling, you're missing the earring on your right ear."

"No, I'm not. I haven't put any on that ear."

"Why is that? Is it the latest fashion?"

"I don't know. I just felt like it."

"As a matter of fact, you could have transferred a few of those on your left ear to the right one. Well, whatever. Let's not lose track of what we're here to talk about, shall we? What was it you wanted to ask me, dear?"

Rüya took a sip from her coffee, more relaxed now that the conversation about her earrings was over. "No one tells me anything substantial about Károly. Grandma only talked about how Mami and *Öcsi* could not see each other for years, and how terribly she used to miss him. That is about all that she tells me. Juli *néni*, on the other hand, said that she didn't get to know her father Károly very much and recounted only a few anecdotes she had heard from her mother Ada. When I visited her in London, she gave me a few diaries that *Öcsi* had kept. There's really nothing in them other than his passionate love for Ada." Rüya was determined to push Anastasia into telling her what she knew – if she did know something. "When did you two meet?" she asked.

"Do you mean when I met Károly?" said Anastasia, turning her eyes to the restless waters of the Sea of Marmara sparkling under the sun. "Too late, my dear child. Unfortunately, too late." The strong light of the sun had made her eyes water. "But I had known him long before we met. Your Mami continually talked about him, about their childhood, their youth, his dreams, his problems, his free spirit, his love, everything."

Rüya knew these things; what she wanted to delve into was something else. "Didn't she talk about what he did during the war?" she cut in. "And what he did during the revolution later on?"

"Would you like another Turkish delight, sweetheart?"

A Hungarian Rhapsody
A Novel in Three Acts
Act Two, Tableau Four
1943 - 1944

62

Alex woke up, drenched in sweat. "Where am I?" she thought, looking around her in panic. Thank God, I'm in my room! It was all a bad dream. A nightmare! She dragged herself out of bed. Zeus opened his eyes from where he was snoozing next to Alex's feet, to check if his mistress would be going farther away than he would have liked her to. Zeus was the new puppy, a Gordon Setter, who had arrived last week to replace Goya, who had passed away a few months ago, on the eve of the new year.

Alex lit a cigarette and walked to the window. The moon was about to set; dawn would soon break. The nightmare was gradually withdrawing from her mind. She remembered drinking wine, red wine. They were at a wine estate. She recalled hearing a voice. "If you attend this meeting," he said, "you will become part of a much larger network. You must know that the dangers you would be encountering would also be much greater. Even the slightest mistake would result in death." He was someone she knew in the dream, but now she realised that his face was not familiar at all. She recalled a feeling of horror as she noticed that it was not red wine but blood in her glass. Squeezing her hand, she had broken the glass, spilling blood all over the place. Her hands and arms were covered in blood. Her hands, however, were not her hands. What a weird nightmare it was. She should not listen to what others said. The other evening, she had been thoroughly demoralised at the cocktail party at the British Consulate. Listening to Sir Owen O'Malley, a former ambassador in Budapest, and to his wife Lady Mary O'Malley, she had realised how very desperate the situation in Hungary was. Christine, a young lady İskender had introduced that evening, and the stories of her valour had been bitter reminders of how very cowardly she had acted by staying in Istanbul.

Christine, like her boyfriend Andrew, was of Polish origin. They were, in fact, Krystyna and Andrzej. Christine was a countess who had escaped to Hungary with

Andrew after Germany invaded Poland, joined the Hungarian resistance against the Nazis and in 1941 had to escape from there as well. "Thanks to Owen, our British passports were ready within a week," she had said, rekindling the painful sense of remorse in Alex. If she had said yes to Rudi, she could have been in Hungary now with her loved ones. The former ambassador, who called Christine by her childhood nickname, had said, "Vesperale is the bravest female I've ever met. I don't know any other woman who so adamantly yearns for danger."

"I wonder if you met my brother when you were in Budapest," Alex had asked her eagerly, "Károly de Kurzón?"

"I didn't, although I've heard a lot about him from János. The Young Jewish Resistance Fighters was very new when I was there. We heard more about his exploits as time went on. You have a very valiant brother, Madame Giritli. You ought to be proud of him."

She looked at her watch. It was a quarter past four. Aziz was snoring heavily in his room. There was no way she could go back to sleep now. Károly was playing with fire. He did not say much in his letters, but she could guess what her rebellious brother might be up to. Would this war end before he got himself into trouble? And what about János? In his last letter, Károly was complaining that they had not heard from him since he had been transferred to the Eastern Front the previous August. "We're extremely worried," he had written. "We have the most alarming news from the Eastern Front. Upon the Soviet counter-offensive about a month ago, the German divisions started to withdraw without informing the Hungarian troops at the front. It is rumoured that our soldiers are fleeing westwards from the shores of the River Don in a fatally chaotic retreat. We keep our hopes up, praying that Jancsi will be able to make it back," he concluded. Poor Jancsi. He probably was back already. She could not get herself to think otherwise.

Károly's letter was dated February 18, 1943. That was almost two months ago – it was the seventeenth of April today. April 17: Rudi's name day. *Boldog névnapot kívánok.* Happy name day, Rudi. Would he be celebrating it? He must be in bed right now, she thought, closing her eyes. He must be lying face down on his bed. She imagined his wide shoulders and the muscles on his back left bare by the white sheet, which came up only to his waist. His hair was dishevelled, his face buried in the pillow. She would have given so much to be next to him now, if only for a few hours, even for a few moments. Her heart sank. She was a prisoner of her daydreams, unable to survive without them. She put out her cigarette and lay on the bed. She closed her eyes. She had to carry on daydreaming, for there was no other way out for her.

63

"János is back! He's back and he's not injured. Aziz! Aziz!"

Alex ran through the corridor, waving Károly's letter in her hand. The door to Aziz's study was shut. He had been in there with İskender for hours. She hated him when he spent those rare weekends, which he had not gone hunting, with his friends. She stormed into the room.

They were sitting comfortably in the leather armchairs in front of the window, smoking their cigars, which they said was their greatest luxury in wartime, and, as far as Alex could tell from the tone of their voices, were talking about serious things.

"The Photographer was in Istanbul again to call on the Special Operations' liaison office as a representative of the Hungarian Front," İskender was saying.

Nili and Lila, exulted by their mother's joy, dashed delightedly into the room, following Alex.

"They secured a promise from the British to help organise the resistance against a possible German occupation," İskender carried on. "It's been said that they want to hand their country over to the British and to the Americans before the communists take over. Kállay is playing an undoubtedly dangerous game that might presently provoke Hitler."

"Daddy! Daddy! Jancsi is back!" screamed Nili and Lila, announcing János's safe return from the front, happy at this great piece of news for someone whom their mother said, "He's like an uncle to you."

"Aziz! Jancsi is back! He's back safe and sound."

"Thank Heavens for that."

"I'm so happy for you and for him, Alex."

Alex hugged and kissed Aziz, then İskender and finally her daughters, after which she started reading a passage from the letter she was trying to hold tightly between her fidgety fingers.

"He says that János was very lucky. They had sent fifty thousand Jews to the front to work in the labour battalions. Only a handful made it back, he says. In

August he crossed the Hungarian border and, after being disinfected, was dismissed from the labour battalion." Alex turned around and dashed to the door. "I must write to Margit," she said, excited beyond description. "She must be so happy. Oh, God! He's back. He's back safe and sound."

She was filled with hope. There were those who made it back from the front. War did not necessarily mean death. It would end. They would survive it. They would all survive it.

Ten days later, returning from her stroll with Hera and Zeus, she came across the postman who gave her a bunch of letters including one from János.

Budapest, 4th November 1943

Hi there, beautiful!

I guess I'm a tough nut to crack after all. I have survived this as well although you wouldn't want to know how. I can tell you one thing, however: I learned that hell might also be freezing cold. I can't possibly describe it, Alex. Even your thoughts freeze; your soul becomes frostbitten. You want to die since it means freedom – freedom from pain. The desire to die strengthens each day, and you yearn for the moment when you will fall into a sweetly warm sleep.

What was more difficult than the cold, however, or than being forced to work like an animal instead of fighting like an honourable soldier, was the loneliness, Alex ... being all alone amidst an army of people. You're alone because you don't want to get attached to anyone, scared that he might soon die and you would lose another loved one. The solitude intensifies, driving you mad. Months go by before you receive a letter. Not knowing how your family is, how your friends are or what is happening in your country poisons your soul, killing it at a painfully slow pace. You rarely receive a letter because they destroy them; you can't write a single line to your family or friends because, for the Jews serving their country in labour battalions, the punishment for writing a letter is execution by the firing squad.

Alex put the letter on her lap in anguish. Why was he telling her all these things? To torture her? To dig deeper into her wounds that never healed? Or was it a simple selfish desire to be pitied finding expression in a thoughtlessly and insensitively scribbled letter?

... Finally in mid-January, we received our orders to retreat. We were defeated but could not care less if we had won or lost. The single thing on our minds at that moment was that we were alive and that we had survived. A fatal march commenced. We walked, sometimes thirty, forty kilometres a day in deep snow, on ice and through snowstorms. Our clothes were in tatters. We saw dead horses, tanks stuck in the snow, soldiers frozen in an ice storm, so far as one could understand from the unusual shapes their bodies had taken. Once, there was a corpse standing up, leaning on a pile of snow with his eyes open as if he were waiting for someone. We dug into the backpacks of dead soldiers hoping to find something to eat. We dug into the snow and the earth in the fields searching for edible roots, sometimes finding carrots or potatoes if we were extremely lucky. We picked undigested grains in frozen animal faeces.

"Mami dearest, why are you crying? Has something happened to *Öcsi bácsi?* Or is it their new baby? Is she sick?"

Alex hurriedly dried her eyes. "No, *tatlım. Öcsi bácsi* is fine. So is their new baby Dóra. The letter is from Jancsi. He talks about how awful the war is, how much he suffered, but he's all right now."

"Why are you sad then? Shouldn't you be happy if he's all right now?"

Nili's attention wandered as Zeus jumped onto her lap. They ran out of the room.

Alex could not get herself to read the rest of the letter. Don't tell me these things, Jancsi. Don't! Why did you have to write me all that? Was it to remind me of my father, who had probably been through the same misery or perhaps even worse? She was crying hysterically. These wars would wipe them all out. They would all die. It was only a dream to hope that Rudi would survive this massacre. It was an illusion. She would lose him as well and maybe *Öcsi* too. These thoughts were driving her mad. God, please help me. Help them! Aziz! Where are you, Aziz? Where on earth are you?

"Mami, please don't cry. Jancsi is fine. Don't be so upset. Please, stop crying." Nili and Lila had come over and were trying to hug her.

She enfolded them both in her arms. They were all she had left. Suddenly a fierce sense of panic grabbed her as she was possessed by the fear that she might lose them as well. She pressed them tighter to her chest.

"Mami, stop. You're hurting me."

"Me too, Mami. Don't squeeze so much."

She would not let them go. She would not let them out of her sight, ever!

64

Alex's hands fell lifelessly on her lap, no longer able to hold the newspaper she had crumpled up. She was staring blankly at the headline.

German military forces occupy Budapest

Not being able to do anything, she thought, not being able to wake up knowing that you are having a nightmare, not being able to move, waiting for that moment when someone would wake you up. She threw the paper on the floor in disgust. She ought to do something. This nightmare had to end. There had to be a way to bring her family over here, to bring Rudi over. She should talk to Aziz. They had to help them.

Tosca was playing. Caruso was singing *E Lucevan le stelle*. She turned up the volume to its maximum.

> *Svani per sempre il sogno mio d'amore.*
> *L'ora è fuggita*
> *e muoio disperato!*
> *E non ho amato mai tanto la vita!*
>
> *My dreams of love disappeared forever.*
> *The moment has gone by*
> *and I'm dying in desperation!*
> *And I have never before loved life so much!*

She sat at her desk and took out her writing papers. Her trembling hands could hardly hold her pen straight. She lit a cigarette. She had to write to Károly and tell him everything about her relationship with Rudi. *Öcsi* would understand; he would help Rudi; he would protect him and save him. He was strong. He now worked at the Swedish Legation and definitely had good connections. He would find a way. Perhaps they would all come over, flee from that inferno. "Istanbul, 20th March 1944," she started to write.

"Perhaps," she hoped, "perhaps, at long last, they would all be together again, even if not in their own country." She suddenly thought how disturbingly bizarre it was that such a tragedy had evoked a light of hope in her, even if it was such a feeble one.

With the occupation of Budapest, Alex practically locked herself up at home and refused to go out. For weeks she did nothing but listen to music all day long, forcing herself to cook something for her family. What kind of a life was this? Was it a life at all? Nothing meant anything anymore. Wake up in the morning, smoke a cigarette, listen to music so that your soul sinks even deeper, smoke another cigarette, think! Think some more! Let your mood collapse into an abyss, falling further down with every passing hour. Smoke yet another cigarette, cook, try to look happy to your daughters, cook some more, make small talk with Aziz, read without understanding a word of what you're reading. Aziz kept telling her to paint. He had to be joking. What was she supposed to paint? Was she to paint trees while people in her country were being massacred? Was she to paint the armchairs, the curtains, the vases in her drawing room while her friends, her neighbours were being thrown out of their houses and sent into exile? She could not even tolerate the sight of the things around her, let alone paint them.

The time did not pass. It would not. A day went by, and then another. Nights, endless nights. She had suspended her life and was waiting. Waiting and thinking, thinking of Rudi, thinking of another life. Whatever she did, it was the same thing she saw in her mind's eye. Whenever a star fell, whenever she thought of Budapest, whenever she walked along a street or wore her silver fox fur coat, when she bid goodbye to Aziz as she saw him off to hunting, when she stroked her dogs – whatever she did, she always thought of Rudi. Everything carried her to him. She did not want to open her eyes in the morning, for an unbearably melancholic sensation draped over her the moment she did. She had no tolerance for the lucid lights of spring leaking through the curtains, or for the promising warmth of the morning sun, which was supposed to cheer her up. She did not even wish to open the curtains; she had recently come to hate the sky, the colour of which had changed into a ferociously metallic grey. The moment she raised her eyes, she saw planes hovering above, dropping bombs and killing her loved ones.

That morning she woke up in the same mood. She closed her eyes tightly as she had been doing for the last four weeks since the occupation of Budapest. She should not wake up. She wished she could sleep deeply for a long time until it was time to open her eyes into a different world, into a world where everything had changed, into a world where the war was over, a world where she would start a brand new life. Would that be possible? She so wished it could be, just like in the fairy tales. To go back in time to the days when she was seventeen ... to Balatonfüred ... to the picnic. Putting her arms around Rudi on the motorcycle ... Rudi's warmth in her hands ... his shirt billowing in the wind and touching her lips. And the Márkus Restaurant ... lighting the candle. *Csárdás.*

She struggled out of bed. She had to listen to Liszt. A rhapsody. *Csárdás.* She put on her dressing gown, took her cigarettes and matches from the bedside table and went out into the corridor. Nili and Lila were playing in their room. Last night she had scolded them terribly and unjustifiably so. She had repented for what she did and slept by their side until daybreak.

She went into the drawing room. *Hungarian Rhapsody Number Eight.* "*Capriccio,*" she whispered. She spread the green baize on the dining table, took out her solitaire cards and sank down on one of the chairs. Her cat, Duman, jumped onto her lap; Hera and Zeus settled down on the floor by her feet. She lit a cigarette. Asiye *Hanım* was standing next to her with a highly diluted cup of coffee and a plate of biscuits baked with almost no sugar.

"Cigarettes won't nourish you, madam. Please try to finish these biscuits."

She had no appetite whatsoever and was continuously losing weight. She was not even thirty-four, but she knew that she looked much older; her face had shrunk as she became thinner and thinner. She sucked in a puff from her cigarette.

"Did the girls have their breakfast? Did they eat well?"

"They did. I took them to the park after breakfast. It's beautiful outside. You should also get out a little bit, take some air. You don't even take the dogs out anymore."

"Ask the concierge Recep *Efendi* to take them out, please. And would you prepare their lunch, if you don't mind? I have no energy left."

She started to line up the cards on the table. One card face up, six cards face down ...

Ada, who usually scribbled a few lines at the end of Károly's letters, had decided to furnish Alex with a separate letter this time, which successfully darkened Alex's mood even further. The things she had written were etched in her mind; every word had been echoing in her brain for days. She had started her letter with a cruelly blunt recount of the difficulties encountered by János, who had been drafted for forced labour at a camp right after the occupation and continued with a detailed description of how they had put guards in every train station in Budapest and on every street corner, carrying out identity checks before they let anyone leave the city and arresting those that looked Jewish without even looking at their identity cards. "Police stations and prison cells are overcrowded," she wrote. What else, Ada? What other atrocities would you like to tell me? Would you, one day, say, "They've taken Rudi away!" Would you say that as well? Her letter went on in the most sombre tone, causing Alex's heart to sink even deeper. "Ever since the occupation, the Nazis are showering the Jewish Council with orders," she had written.

> A regulation was put in place, obliging all the Jews older than six years of age to wear a yellow Star of David on the left side of their outer garments. Those who fail to obey this order are immediately deported, so is anyone who is unemployed and is wearing a star. Jews are not allowed to work. They are forbidden to visit public places, even to use public telephones. Those carrying a yellow star on their chests are prohibited from using any transportation other than the trams. The final blow came the other day when they ordered all Jews to hand in their jewellery, precious stones, gold, silver and foreign currencies to the authorities in "custody" on the claim that the state needed financial resources during wartime. As yet, they haven't passed any orders regarding the synagogues. Apparently, they prefer to leave religious issues alone – at least for the moment – since they must be thinking it a good idea to lull the people who are in pain.
>
> I don't like to upset you with all this horrific news, but, although these events sound quite unreal, that is what we're living through. Mind you, we do have nice things in our life as well. Juli and Dóra make us forget all the misery around us. Dóra is not even one, but she's about to start walking. She's giving her sister a very hard time. Károly adores them. The other day ...

"What is this, madam? Are you into fortune-telling?"

"This is patience, Asiye *Hanım*. Solitaire with cards."

"What does that mean?"

"Patience and loneliness."

"Does it teach you to be patient then?"

"You could say that."

"Have you ever been to a fortune teller?"

"Yes, once. And that was the last time."

Once in Budapest, a Gypsy woman had read her palm. She did not believe in such things and had forgotten all that she had said with one exception, which remained in her memory until to this very day. "I see something with four wheels," she had said, "carrying death." Was it Alex's death she had seen? Or was it the death of someone Alex loved? Don't think, Alex. Don't think about death. Don't!

"I could do without you reminding me of that, Asiye *Hanım*."

She put out her cigarette, stood up and, taking her cat Duman in her arms, went to her bedroom. She should dress, but she had neither the desire nor the energy to do that. What was the point of dressing up anyway? For Asiye *Hanım?* For her daughters? Yes, perhaps for them. She did not want them to remember their mother like this, always in a dressing gown, without any makeup and with her hair tousled. But she did not feel up to grooming herself. She opened the curtains an inch to let in some light, walked to her lilac wardrobe and took out Rudi's letter, which Anastasia had brought the previous day. Compared to what Károly had written to Aziz in his letters, especially with the last death song he had composed, Rudi's letters seemed to be coming from another city, from another country, giving her hope – a tiny light of hope.

Taking her writing papers and fountain pen, she sat on her bed, taking a few pillows to lean on. She reached for Thomas Mann's *Buddenbrooks* from the bedside table to use as a support. Nowadays she read only the books banned by Hitler; it was the sole act of resistance she could manage, trying as she might in her pathetic paralysis.

She lit a cigarette and started to write.

Istanbul, 26th April 1944

My one and only love,

This morning I received your letter dated April 1. I've read it so many times that it's already worn out; I've smelled you on it so often that I'm scared there will soon be none of you left. Longing is an unbearable feeling. There comes a moment when I feel I can take it no longer. Right there and then, all I want to do is to run away from it all, to be free and come to you. Then I tell myself to be patient. I think of the things you say in your letters. My hopes rise as I remind myself that you're waiting for me out there somewhere and that I shall soon be with you. I daydream. I feel you by my side while I sleep. I'm with you while I'm awake. You're there right beside me while I read, while I eat or play with my daughters. I tell myself that we don't need to hear each other's voices or look into each other's eyes or touch, smell, taste each other. Then comes a moment when dreams are no longer enough, my love, and helplessness drives me insane.

Asiye *Hanım* was standing at the door. "You haven't finished your biscuits, madam."

"Put them here, would you please? I'll eat them later. Shall we cook some pasta for lunch? I won't be able to cook today."

Leave me alone! Leave me alone in my own world. Leave me alone where I can survive even if it is only a dream. I want to belong to another realm. I belong to another realm, a realm thousands of kilometres away from here. I belong to my country, to my loved ones. This is not where I'm supposed to be. Let me be there, at least in my dreams.

December 2005
Budapest

It was already dark when Rüya left Number 60, that once infamous building on Andrássy Boulevard. She decided to walk, hoping that the breathtaking cold would resuscitate her mind, which felt as if it had drowned under a torrent of ghastly new information. She followed her steps, not knowing where she was heading.

She had arrived in Budapest the previous night. This was her third visit to the capital. She had come across a small detail in the documents she had gathered during her research the last time she had been here, and she wanted to pursue it without knowing exactly where it would be taking her. She had been unable to learn anything worthwhile about what Károly or Rudi did during the war. There was almost nothing in Mami's diaries. Most likely, her brother did not write to her about what he was really up to so as not to upset her. Neither had Anastasia been much of a help other than telling Rüya a few anecdotes she had heard from Mami about their youth – their happy cheerful, buoyant and passionate youth.

Early this morning she had had a meeting with the manager of the museum at Number 60, which used to be the headquarters of the fascist Arrow Cross Party. The manager, whom she had called several times before coming to Budapest, had been discouragingly serious, making it very difficult for her to get an appointment. Not sounding very helpful at first, he had finally delved into the depths of the archive with surprising ardour, showing and telling Rüya things that were far more atrocious than anything she had seen at the museum before or had read so far. When she had put together what she learned and what she already knew, several windows had opened up in front of her.

Her thoughts dispersed at the sound of a train blowing its whistle. She had not even noticed that she had arrived at the station, which was swarming with people. The voice of the museum manager echoed in her ears as her mind's eyes went back in time, watching the people in the station – old and young, women and children ...

Towards midnight, they arrived at the station. Stretching out their right arms and shouting the Nazi greeting, they saluted the guards lined up at its entrance and wished Szálasi a long and healthy life. The most difficult part of this masquerade was to act like the Arrow Cross thugs they detested. They entered the station without a problem. On one of the platforms stood a train of covered wagons that were used to carry animals in normal times, with padlocks on their sliding doors and barbed wire on their small windows. The first and the last of the wagons had open tops and were full of armed Hungarian soldiers. He heard people locked inside the wagons shouting, moaning, asking for water, begging for a doctor. A cleaner approached one of the windows and, through the barbed wire, squeezed in a cup of water. He was lucky; the guards had not seen what he had done. He then bent over and picked up the pieces of paper thrown out by the people locked inside, shoved them in his pocket and carried on sweeping the platform. He would deliver these messages to their intended addresses once he was finished here. He would do it in the name of humanity. He would do it risking death. He would do it hoping to be of some help.

Usually, it was the gendarmes' duty to collect the Jews and put them on these trains. Today, however, there were Hungarian soldiers and a couple of German soldiers as well, helping to squeeze more people into the wagons, which had arrived at the station already overcrowded with the Jews collected from the countryside. The young man and his friend approached one of the German soldiers keeping guard next to the train that was ready to take off.

"Heil Hitler!"

"Heil Hitler!"

The young man handed over the false papers. The Nazi soldier, used to obeying orders blindly, was apparently impressed by the documents containing a myriad of stamps and signatures, some of them quite out of place, and released, with surprising docility, all those whose names were on the list. They accomplished their mission smoothly, without even having to resort to bribery.

Rüya darted out of the station. There was not a single taxi in sight. She started scurrying along the pavement. She wondered if she could make it to the hotel on foot. By now, she had got to know every street in Budapest by heart, so she decided to take the shortcuts. She needed to hurry so that she could organise her notes as soon as possible, without skipping any details. She was racing from one street to another. Soon she ran out of breath and slowed down. She thought she heard someone running after her. She turned around. The street was deserted. She was sure she had heard footsteps behind her. Was someone following her? "Don't be ridiculous, Rüya!" she told herself as she hastened towards the hotel. Lately she had been having difficulty distinguishing dreams from reality.

A Hungarian Rhapsody
A Novel in Three Acts
Act Two, Tableau Four
1944

65

Aziz had gone hunting again. Even war could not keep him away from chasing after his game. He had been away in Thrace for two weeks since the beginning of June and had neither called her nor even sent her a telegram. She would not know if he died. It was beyond rhyme or reason that he could be so passionate about shooting. He was in love with his guns and dogs, not with Alex.

"Mami, would you please tell the story of these earrings again? I've forgotten what this green stone is called. Emerald, is it?"

"Yes, *tatlım*, emerald. These earrings are part of a set; there is also a necklace to go with them. Your grandfather Gusztáv gave this set to *Anyukám* when she gave birth to me and your Magda *néni*. When I got married to your father, *Anyukám* gave me the earrings as a wedding present; and she gave the necklace to Magda when she got married to your uncle Miklós."

"Stop it, Zeus!" said Nili cheekily, pushing away the devoted Gordon Setter busy licking her toes. Zeus hardly left Nili alone, whining after her when she went to school. He was, therefore, in great spirits since the schools were closed for the summer.

"That means when I get married, this necklace will be mine," sang Nili, who knew the story of almost every piece of jewellery her mother had. She was looking straight into Alex's eyes while holding the necklace Aziz had given Alex after Nili's birth.

"Of course, my love."

Alex could not see the Lacloche Frères necklace and earrings, which were Aziz's wedding present. It had been so long since she had last worn them. She did not feel like wearing jewellery at a time like this. Could it be in the safe in Aziz's study? It ought to be. She should ask him when he came back.

"What about all the others?"

"They will all be yours and Lila's, *tatlım*."

"Mami? You've never told me the story of this angel. I think this is the most beautiful piece of jewellery you have," said Nili, looking at Alex with beseeching eyes.

Alex watched her daughter's tiny fingers around the box that held the brooch Rudi had given her at their engagement party. "It doesn't have a story, dear. I've already told you that I bought it myself for no particular occasion."

"It doesn't matter. Tell me where you bought it? When did you buy it? Does the angel have a name?"

"I shall, some other time. That should be enough for today. You have a lot of homework to do this summer, don't you, darling? And I have a letter to write to *Öcsi bácsi*."

They put the jewellery back in their places, and Nili reluctantly went to her room. Alex lay down on her bed to read Károly's last letter once again. It was dated May 12 and, unlike his other letters, was laden with anger. "Our patriotic friend finally came to his senses," he wrote and continued using allegories to inform Alex of János's escape from the labour camp and of the bitter realities of war, painfully talking about a new decree that required Jews to be collected in areas called ghettos. "I finish my letter with the hope that Eichmann," he concluded in apparent disgust, "soon finds himself drowning in the quagmire he is creating as he moves ahead in his determined quest to solve the Jewish Question."

On the other hand, Rudi said nothing that would upset Alex in his letter, which she had received this morning – nothing about the ghetto or about any of the atrocities. He mentioned how Tungsram had appointed him to work in Switzerland for a month, imploring Alex to be patient, repeating that they should hold on a little bit more and assuring her that they would survive this war, while drawing a very optimistic picture of the life they would soon be having together. Lately all his renderings seemed nothing more than a colourful painting to Alex, and she knew that the dreams depicted in paintings came alive only in fairy tales. Despite the Nazi occupation, he wrote, life in Budapest carried on as before, and he beseeched her not to worry since he was in no danger, saying that they were doing everything they could, for they were determined not to surrender Hungary into the hands of the fascists. Alex could see how teed off he was and, knowing perfectly well what he was capable of doing when he was filled with indignation, dared not think what risks he might take. She ought to write to him immediately and beg him again and again to keep away from harm's way. Please, I implore you to live in obscurity, she would say. I know you, Rudi. I know that you fearlessly plunge headfirst into danger, but this is not an adventure. Please try to stay out of it. Disappear. Be invisible. Please, I beg you. I'm so scared of losing you.

66

The large envelopes bearing her brother's handwriting filled Alex with joy like an unseasonal Christmas present, and the postman delivering them seemed as blessed as an out-of-place Santa Claus. Károly sometimes put several letters together and sent them in the diplomatic pouch. His last letter of June had been accompanied by letters from Gizella, Sanyi, Ada, Margit, Éva and János, all of which she had read again and again throughout the summer months.

Margit had written that she was now working as a nurse at the hospital on Bethlen Square, taking care of helpless people – emotionally needy, whiny and inept Margit helping others. Alex was so happy for her. She had also written about how very much in love she still was with János, and how their friendship had reached a new dimension where they were almost always together, claiming that such a relationship was perhaps even better than marriage and concluding that she was attached to him more than ever before after all the calamities and losses he had suffered. For her, it was worth the whole world to know that she would be with the man she loved all her life, even if only as a friend. Good old optimistic Margit.

Letters from János, on the other hand, filled Alex with grief. He hardly wrote anything, only sending his love through Károly, but when he did write – which was once in a blue moon – his letters overflowed with the most tragic news. His last letter was just another one that resembled a newspaper column rather than a letter to a friend. Alex, however, looked forward to hearing even from him, for she needed to hear all she could, even the worst news, from home. Éva and Józsi, who had moved to Martfü a while ago, were now back in Budapest, as the Russians were about to cross the Hungarian border. Éva's letters were no less pessimistic than those from János. She complained about almost everything, telling her how hard it was for Józsi to cope with the difficulties of war and how he was making their already miserable life even more unbearably lugubrious.

She had received nothing, not even a single line, from Rudi in the last six weeks. He still refrained from signing his letters and, on the rare occasions when he did, he signed them as Robi. Alex was supposed to call him by that name as well and address her letters to Róbert Tímár. He had insisted that she did, without any exception. Alex felt it strange to call him Robi. There were so many better ways to address him such as "my precious," "my love," "my one and only love." "My one and only love," she started writing. She would be filling her letter with questions again, with suffocating sentences that expressed her worries. There was not a single piece of good news to write to him, or rather there was not a single piece of news to write, since she was not in the least interested in what was going on around her in this city. Perhaps I shouldn't write at all, she thought, perhaps I should wait for his reply to the letters I wrote to him in July and August. Taking a new sheet of paper, she wrote, "Istanbul, September 1st, 1944," and continued, "Dear Öcsi." She had not received anything from her brother either for almost two months now except for two dry telegrams. Didn't they have the time to scribble even a few lines? Or was it that something bad had happened to one of them and they could not write to her?

She looked at the ceramic book holders on the bookshelf next to her – a boy and a girl in folkloric Hungarian clothes, trying to hold the books together with all their might. On the pleats of the little girl's dark green skirt, she could see Magda's fingers shaping the clay. She caressed the tiny hat of the boy before taking him in her hands. The books fell to one side. She felt Magda's hands between her fingers. Tears started wetting her face. You were spared, my beloved Magda, she thought. You were spared from this misery, from witnessing all this suffering, from the shame and pain of Hungary, of our Budapest.

"Why are you crying, Mami?"

"I'm not crying, Lila. I must have something in my eye that made it water."

Lila moved her little fingers on the book holder Alex was holding. "Shall we give them a name? They should have names like my doll Fatoş."

"They should, my love."

"What will it be then?"

"This one should be Jancsi," said Alex without thinking. "And the other one, Margit."

"Is he her brother?"

"He's not, my darling, but he loves her like a sister." She stroked the blond hair of the little ceramic girl still holding the other end of the books. "And she loves him more than as a brother," she whispered softly.

"But they're always apart. Do they always have to have books between them?

Can't we put them together?"

"Of course, we can, but this is what they're here for – to hold the books together."

67

Alex had celebrated her thirty-fourth birthday five days earlier, a most abominable birthday that she would not want to remember for the rest of her life. Aziz had gone hunting again. Anastasia and her brother Hristo, determined not to leave her on her own, had come over with their presents and an abundance of appetisers. However, neither her friends nor their thoughtful presents nor Hristo trying very hard to make her smile with his jokes, had been enough to make her forget her loneliness. After having drunk a drink too many, Alex had convinced them to stay for the night. Sending Hristo to bed in Aziz's room, Alex and Anastasia had stayed up until the early hours, during which time Alex had continually cried, desperately worried about not having heard from Rudi for so long.

There was still no news of him, not even a single mention in Károly's last letter either. Alex feared that something awful had happened to him and they were all hiding it from her.

Budapest, 9th October 1944

My dearest sister,

Please don't reproach me for writing to you so rarely. We have so much to do and never enough time, for it takes a lot of time to try to save the honour of a nation. I beseech you to keep your composure. Rest assured that we're doing everything in our power to put things back on track.

You ask about the air raids. Yes, they do continue in all their vigour, but we're used to them now, as it were, so much so that we might even feel something missing from our lives when the war is over. We keep our windows open except for short "warming periods" so that the glass doesn't break during the bombings, as sirens occasionally fail to work. They say it will be a very cold winter. It already is quite nippy. Luckily, in our wine cellar – or in our shelter, as it is called nowadays – we have a few more bottles of wine to warm us up and a few more bottles of bubbly to celebrate when the Russians arrive.

These last three months, I've been feeling like another man, my dear Alex. I might even say that I've understood, for the first time in my life, why I came into this world. I was born for a reason, and it was not a simple task such as painting or carrying the blue blood of our ancestors to the next generation. I feel as if I'm sowing a seed, albeit a tiny one, in the name of humanity; I feel I'm watering the seeds already sown, so to speak. In a peculiar way, this tragedy has nourished my desire to live, to survive and to dedicate my life to the happiness of others. I can't think of any other reason for my existence more meaningful than this, Alex.

Now let's forget about all this and talk about beautiful things, shall we? Do you know where you're wrong, my dearest sister? You only paint when you're happy. However, one needs to be overwhelmed with emotions stronger than happiness to be able to produce the most intense, the most meaningful, the most striking works of art. Hatred, for instance, betrayal, unfairness, desertion and doubt. You, on the other hand, try so desperately to bury the feelings that hurt you that even your subconscious forgets about their existence. You let yourself plunge into an artistic coma so as to block their way to the surface even in your paintings. Do not fret, Alex. Don't be scared so much. Let go. Let out all that is buried deep inside you and freely express them in your paintings. You'll burst one day if you don't. Listen to your brother. Our paintings should be the mirror of the moods where there is no longer any conflict between life and death, reality and dreams, past and future. We should use our art to release whatever there is in the natural world of humanity and break down the restrictive rules of civilisation.

Hoping that, one day, we shall again paint together and argue to our hearts' content about our conflicting styles,
  With much longing,
   Your
    Károly

She heard the doorbell ring. It was only ten and too early for her mother-in-law to arrive; she didn't expect her till teatime. As usual, Aziz had told Alex to invite his sisters along with Mehpare *Hanım* to tea, something he had the habit of thinking would be of great entertaining value for Alex during his absences. In fact, he had invited them himself. "Please do come for tea on Sunday so that when I come back from the shoot in the evening, we shall all be together one last time before seeing Sema off to Adana on Monday." Was it on purpose that he always chose Sundays for these occasions so as to make them more torturous for her, it being Asiye *Hanım*'s day off?

It was Anastasia at the door. From the expression on her face, she immediately understood what she had in her handbag. Her heart started thundering. At long last! Thank you, God! Thank you. Finally!

"Apparently, it had arrived on Friday, Alex, but I found it today upon my return from the Prince's Island. I came here right away. I'm so sorry for the delay."

Alex snatched the letter with a trembling hand and ran to the drawing room, forgetting to invite Anastasia in. She impatiently ripped the envelope open and read his long letter in a breath. Overflowing with words of love and yearning, these few pages were the best birthday present she had had, even if belated. Rudi was alive. He was safe and sound. What else could she ask for in life?

She jumped to her feet with enthusiasm. "Would you give me a helping hand in the kitchen?" she asked cheerfully, taking Anastasia's arm.

With a vigour she had not had for a long time, she baked a cake and prepared some savouries for the afternoon tea as lavishly as she could despite the shortage of supplies. She was in excellent spirits and kept Anastasia for lunch, after which she insisted that she stayed a bit longer. They sat down with Nili and Lila to look at the albums. Having finally found the strength to look at the old photographs without being emotionally shattered and crying her heart out, she nevertheless failed to hold back the tears brimming in her eyes.

"What does Churchill mean, Mami?"

"Churchill is the British prime minister, *tatlım*."

"Is she beautiful?"

"What makes you think Churchill is a lady, Lila?"

"Once, you had this fur-collared coat on," said Lila, showing a photograph Aziz had taken that winter, "and the children playing in the street called you Churchill."

She found it sad that Churchill was the first thing that came to the minds of these poor children when they saw a well-dressed foreigner though she was sure that it was much better than what some other people – Aziz's sisters and his mother, for one thing – thought of her. She cringed at the thought of what they might be drilling into the little brains of her daughters. She could actually guess what they said behind her back, and it drove her absolutely mad.

"Mami?"

"Yes, *tatlım*?"

"Is this you?"

"No, that is Magda *néni*. She was the one who loved rowing. I preferred water-skiing." She flipped through the pages of the album. "There you go. This is me."

"You're exactly the same. I wish I were exactly the same as Nili."

"You look like each other more and more with each passing day."

"Perhaps when we grow up, we shall look like each other as much as you and Magda *néni* did."

"I don't think that could be possible, *tatlım*."

"Were you truly identical?"

"At times, even our mother could not see the difference, even our voices being exactly the same. The only difference between us was a tiny curve," she said, holding her left ear, which missed its upper curve. "We often played tricks on our nanny Ildikó."

"What kind of tricks? Please tell us what you did. Please."

"Once, we had climbed a tree and ended up having resin in our hair. Nanny Ildikó got her hands on me first, and it hurt so much while she cleaned it that, to save Magda from the same painful experience, I went to our nanny, pretending to be Magda. "Look Nanny," I said, "I don't have any resin in my hair." She took me for Magda but later on at dinnertime, when Magda appeared with her hair all sticky with resin, everything became clear, and *Anyukám* gave us a good scolding."

"What about Daddy? Could he tell the difference between you two?"

"In the beginning, he used to mix us up too. When he first saw Magda *néni*, he thought she was me." Alex turned to Anastasia, smiling. "We were at a hotel called Villa d'Este by the shores of Lake Como in Italy – the hotel where Aziz proposed to me. You should have seen the expression on his face when he was introduced to Magda. A total shock! 'It can't be possible,' he kept saying. And then for years, whenever he wanted to tease me, he often repeated, 'I must have proposed to the wrong sister.'"

Alex remembered how Miklós used to joke about having fallen in love with Magda and Alex at the same time but eventually had been entrapped by Magda, who was cunning enough to fall in love with the right man. Miklós was right; Magda had lost her heart to the right man.

"Who is this man, Mami?"

"It's János. Your Jancsi *bácsi*."

The photograph Nili was holding had been taken during the picnic in Balatonfüred. How young Jancsi was then. How young they all were, each with a dream, with great expectations from life. And look what happened to them all. And what might have happened. What would happen from now on? She should not give up hope. A lot could still happen. A lot would happen. All this misery

355

would eventually end.

Alex's mood, already brightened by Rudi's letter, cheered up at teatime, which proved to be a much more pleasant occasion than she had feared. She watched Necla's impish son Osman's inexhaustible energy and her chatterbox of a daughter Selma's constant nattering. She admired Ayla's daughter Yasemin, a sight for sore eyes, and younger daughter Azra, who was a coquette at heart, casting a shadow over her sister's beauty. She was truly impressed by Sema's sixteen-year-old son Ekrem, a true gentleman despite his young age, taking care of all his cousins. And she enjoyed seeing Nili and Lila shine with joy at having all their cousins around them, which made her realise with a sinking heart that she should stop being unfair to her daughters and try to socialise more with Aziz's family, even if it bored her to death.

Aziz came home at eight with the most horrid news, which grieved everyone and weighed heavily upon Alex, like a poisonous mist darkening her brightened mood and cheerful day. There had been a coup d'état in Hungary. The fascist Arrow Cross Party had taken over the government. Coup d'état! Dreams shattering. Dreams going down the drain. Alex remembered Gyula Krúdy's words: "Happiness is a moment's interval between desire and sorrow."

January 2006
Budapest

At the end of December, Rüya had gone back to Istanbul for New Year's Eve and three days ago had returned to Budapest to carry on with her research. For the last two days, she had been digging into the documents and photographs in the archives of the Dohány Synagogue and had finally reaped the benefits of her efforts. Leaving the synagogue in a bitterly excited mood, she headed for the Szikla Church, the place that had impressed her the most when she had been here years ago. It had been her first visit to Hungary. She was eleven then and had come here with her mother, grandmother and Mami during the Christmas holidays, a few months after having started the boarding school in England. Her cousin Attila, who had just begun his career as a journalist in those years, was working in Budapest and showed them everything that had to be seen. At the time, she could not quite grasp why Mami – despite her eighty years – had insisted that they walked through each and every street of the city and why, during their promenades, she had often had tears clouding her eyes, sometimes weeping uncontrollably and sometimes carrying a bitter smile on her lips. In that innocent age of youth, Rüya had not yet come across any of the painful surprises life was to offer and had not tasted the excruciating sorrow of losing a loved one. It was three years before the sea accident, before all her dreams were shattered, before her ...

"Forget the past, Rüya!" shouted the voice in her. Think about what you need to do now. You have to shed light onto the past of another life. Yes, the Szikla Church ...

The young man met his friend at the legation building on Gellért Hill before nine. They went over a few last-minute details, after which they walked to the mansion at number ten to prepare themselves for that night's mission. After putting on their frocks, they silently walked out. The young man noticed that he was holding the brown leather case far more tightly than the circumstances required. He forced himself to relax his fingers. The leather case contained a B2, Type 3, Mark II radio transmitter, one of the most reliable and efficient radio transmitters developed by the British. It was the most important communication device between the resistance groups and Allied Headquarters, with coverage of one thousand five hundred kilometres, and could be fitted in a case not larger than one span of the young man's hand in width and two spans in length. The punishment for being caught with this small and seemingly insignificant case was not insignificant at all: death by instant execution or after torture.

It took them less than ten minutes to reach the Szikla Church. They both knew very well what they were supposed to do during the night mass, which they had attended many times before. As soon as they entered the temple, Father Soos met them as usual and accompanied them to the altar, after which he left them. The young man placed the brown leather case under the cloth draped over the altar. They crossed themselves. There was no one around to notice that the young man's friend did not cross himself correctly. A few minutes later a priest appeared in the archway on the left and hurried towards them, taking his place on the other side of the altar. He crossed himself. The young man did not know this new priest, who, with his pale complexion, looked extremely suited to his role. Perhaps he was a real man of God, after all.

"Isn't Legionnaire here?" asked the young man.

"He's inside," said the pale-faced priest, as he slid the small Bible over the altar towards the young man. "This is to be delivered to the Diplomat. The information he needs is in Luke 10:19. Tell him that Uncle sends his kindest regards," he said and, bringing his hands together against his chest, continued, "Luke 10:19 says, 'Behold, I give unto you power to tread on serpents and scorpions, and over all the power of the enemy; and nothing shall by any means hurt you.'"

The sound of their breathing echoed on the uneven walls of the silent cave. After a few minutes another priest, a well-built man, came through the archway. He was the Legionnaire. He hastily crossed himself in front of the statue of a crucified Jesus Christ and moved silently towards Uncle. "Orion is here," he whispered, leaning towards his ear. They took the brown leather suitcase and disappeared behind the archway.

The young man placed the Bible in the inner pocket of his frock, and they left the temple without looking back.

That evening Rüya went to Művész Kávéház to meet the grandson of a cousin of János. Dávid, who was fifty years old but looked at least sixty, did not say much, although the few anecdotes he had heard from his parents matched what Rüya had learned at the synagogue and resembled the script of a spy movie rather than a real life story. Throughout dinner, Rüya could not control her tears, not knowing exactly why she cried so much. Was it because she felt for Mami and pitied her for all that she had lost, imagining how she must have once sat here, in this same coffee house, by this same window, with Magda, Károly, Rudi and her friends, eating the same food as Rüya was eating now? Or were her tears triggered by a deep sense of yearning for all those she herself had lost, as the smell of the delicious duck liver pâté evoked her childhood memories? Or was it simply because she pitied herself?

A Hungarian Rhapsody
A Novel in Three Acts
Act Two, Tableau Four
1944 - 1945

68

"I had another really eerie nightmare. We're at home, right here, having dinner. We're pretty crowded as the whole family is here, cousins and all. Suddenly I see Aziz outside, walking past the French windows, accompanied by İskender and some other men I don't recognise. As a matter of fact, I don't recognise İskender's face either, for it's someone else's face. I notice that the house we're in is not actually this house. We're in a different city, on the second floor of a building, but Aziz is standing out there on the street, leaning over the railings of the balcony, looking at us as if we were on the ground floor. I introduce him to those at the table as if he didn't know them. Then I realise that the man who is watching us is not Aziz. His face is Aziz's, but his name is not Aziz."

"Your mind is very confused, dear. And your dreams are even more confused than your mind. Did you eat too much at dinner?"

"I'm in a terrible state of mind, Anastasia. I can't take it anymore." Alex was playing with the letter Anastasia had brought, turning it around between her fingers. Tears started rolling down her cheeks. "It's Rudi's birthday tomorrow," she mumbled. "November 23. He'll be thirty-nine years old. It's all gone, Anastasia. It's finished. I wasted my life away. I wasted *our* life."

"Please, Alex. Please don't say that."

"It's the end. They're deporting everyone. They're murdering them! The other day, we were at the British Consulate again. I was devastated listening to all that's been going on. We're living in a dream here. Budapest is burning; it's a raging inferno. It's worse than war. There is no front. The front is people's doorsteps, their homes. I'm so frightened. I'm terrified that he might not make it. Do you know what it means to go to bed with this fear each night, wake up with the same fear each morning, wait for a line of good news day in and day out?" She hugged her friend as her sobs tormented her body.

"I'll talk to Aziz. He shouldn't leave you on your own so much."

"He went hunting again yesterday. He said he wouldn't be back before Christmas. A whole month! What sort of hunting is this, for Heaven's sake? If I didn't know him, I might even suspect him of having an affair."

"Vre ke esi, Alex! Don't be ridiculous! Please."

"Mami?" Nili had approached them, holding a book on Goya. "Did you name our Goya after this painter?"

"Yes, my love. And Pepa was Goya's wife, just like our Pepa was Goya's."

"Is Zeus also a painter? And is Hera his wife?"

"Zeus is not a painter, *tatlım*. He's a Greek god. And Hera is his wife and a goddess."

"Do Greeks have more than one god?"

"The Ancient Greeks, Nili. Greek mythology, which is a bit like a fairy tale."

"Please tell me the tale of Zeus. Would you please?"

"Daddy will tell you when he comes back from hunting, *tatlım*."

"Did he choose this name?"

"No, it was Uncle İskender. You know that Zeus is the son of his dog Cronus."

"Let me tell you his story," said Anastasia as she put her arms around Nili. "Why don't you come and sit by me."

Nili, bubbling over with enthusiasm, settled down on the sofa next to Anastasia.

"Zeus was the greatest god of the Ancient Greeks, Nili. When he was born, he was miraculously saved from being swallowed by his father Cronus and hid on the island of Crete until it was time for him to dethrone Cronus and settle on Mount Olympus in mainland Greece. He was a furious god, thunderous like lightning and strong like a storm. His fury, however, was short-lived as he was a Samaritan at heart, protecting people and helping warriors in difficulty towards victory."

"And Hera?"

"Hera was one of the most beautiful goddesses. Zeus was desperately in love with her and did everything he could to marry her. And he did marry her in the end."

"Our Zeus is also very much in love with Hera. But he's not as furious as Zeus, the god. All he does is to bark sweetly."

69

Aziz had been in the drawing room for hours, talking to İskender. He had asked Alex to leave them alone. She was offended that her husband wanted to spend even Christmas Day with his friend and, locking herself in her bedroom, started rereading Rudi's letter, which had arrived the other day. It was dated December 16 and surprisingly had arrived in one week. For quite some time now, she had not been destroying Rudi's letters and, instead, giving them to Anastasia to keep. However, she could not get herself to give this one to her, not caring less if Aziz saw it or not. He could get as furious as he wished. She was not scared of him anymore; now she had worse fears in life than her husband's shouting – the fear of death, for instance, or the fear of losing her loved ones forever.

Rudi, on the other hand, seemed to fear nothing. He only talked about the future as if there were nothing else to write about. He seemed to be living in a world not struck by the war. He went on about the operas he had been to, the dinner parties he had thrown at the Ritz and the tennis matches he had won. It all sounded like a fairy tale, and Alex took none of it to be true, knowing very well that the situation was so extremely critical that even Károly, who always took things lightly, could no longer hide the bitter realities of their life from Alex. Most probably, Rudi was drawing such an optimistic picture to hide his helplessness, his weakness. Alex felt a little seed of pity growing inside her. To feel pity for Rudi ... what a bizarre feeling it was. However, she sort of liked this feeling, a feeling of compassion, which made the violent and rapacious love that nibbled away at her soul gradually give way to a deeply rooted love for him. She now realised much better how very profoundly she loved Rudi.

This time she had kept his photograph as well. He had lost a lot of weight but still was very handsome. She could gaze at his photograph for hours even though she had already memorised every single detail of his face. She had never before noticed how his right eyelid was lower than his left, hiding half of his pupil and giving him a cruel expression. Or had his expression become merciless in recent years? His aquiline nose still stirred her heart. She caressed his face with her fingertips. She missed everything about him so much, the curls in his hair, the hardness of his chin, the depth of his eyes, the way he held his head slightly tilted to one side, everything. She even missed the new scar under his left eyebrow, although she had never touched it.

She heard a knock on the door. "Mami?" she heard Nili call out. Hastily putting the letter back in its envelope, she hid it among the leaves of one of her sketchbooks in the lilac wardrobe and went to open the door.

"Mami? Have I done something wrong? Are you cross with me?" Nili asked, her little voice full of apprehension.

"No, not at all, my love. What makes you say that?"

"You've always been so cheerful at Christmas time, but this year you're not even smiling. Please cheer up. You should be happy now that Daddy is back. Are you upset because he could not hunt a boar this time, not even any birds?"

"He did hunt a boar, darling. They killed a big wild boar but left it in Uncle İskender's hunting lodge. They'll soon be sending us the sausages and the salamis made from it."

Aziz had finally had the decency to return a day before Christmas, remembering, after having left his wife and daughters he adored all alone for exactly four weeks, that he should be home for the festivities.

"Or is it Lila who upset you?"

"Not in the least, *tatlım*. You both are my angels." She kneeled down in front of her daughter and took her head between her hands, gently holding her cheeks. "It's just that I miss *Öcsi bácsi* a little. Wouldn't you miss Lila if you were away from her?"

She could hear Aziz and İskender talking in the drawing room.

"Yesterday they raided the Social Services' building on Bokréta Street. They've taken away Sister Sára Salkaházi along with the Jews who had taken refuge there. Nobody knows where they are now."

"Everybody is going missing."

"Why can't we go and see *Öcsi bácsi* then, Mami?"

"We can't travel, sweetheart. There is a war going on."

"Why can't we?"

"Why?" Alex asked herself. "Because it's dangerous."

"Why is it dangerous?"

"You ask far too many questions, Nili," she said, stroking her daughter's hair. "Now listen to me and listen to me carefully. Don't you ever forget that there are two people in this world I love the most: one of them is you and the other one is your sister."

"What about Daddy? Don't you love *him*?"

Alex hugged her daughter tightly. "I love him, Nili. I love him too."

"Zeus!"

"Why is Daddy shouting at Zeus?"

"You could have at least had the loyalty of your dog's litter, İskender! You can't play with people's fate. What are you? A God? You're despicable! A traitor! This is the deepest hole you could ever fall into!"

Alex could not believe her ears. She had never before heard Aziz shout like this at İskender or at any of his friends for that matter.

"No, my love, he's not shouting at Zeus. Now you go back to your room, close your door and play with your sister." In panic, she led her daughter to her room and shut the door.

"What do you mean 'a star fell,' İskender? What the hell do you mean? How can you commit such a treacherous crime? This is inhuman! How can you be part of something like this? He is our brother, no matter what. Our brother, you remember? Someone we have to help whatever the circumstances are. You seem to have forgotten that you're obliged to hold out a helping hand to the fallen even if he is your enemy. And all you did was to strike the final blow. How could you have done that?"

"For you Aziz. I did it for you."

"Are you totally out of your mind? What do you mean, for me? This is not a game! Can't you see that? I do wish I could believe that you've used your power in ignorance of the horrific consequences your action was to trigger. Otherwise, you're to be damned as the darkest epitome of shame, not only for our friendship and for our brotherhood but for all humanity."

Alex could not make head or tail of it. What on earth was going on? What fury! He was going to shoot him. She darted into the drawing room. Aziz had grabbed İskender by the collar and was howling at the top of his voice.

"You won't be allowed to remain among us. Don't you ever think that I'll keep this a secret. I would never do that. Never!"

"Aziz! Aziz! What are you doing, for God's sake?"

"Get out, Alex! Get the hell out of here!"

Alex ran over to Aziz and grabbed his arm, only to stumble back as he shook her off his sleeve. "You stay out of this!" he roared. "Don't aggravate me more than I already am."

İskender fled to the entrance hall, scrambled into his coat and hastily put on his hat. Aziz was still bellowing after him. "You traitor! You treacherous bastard! I neither want to see you nor hear your voice until you make up for your mistake. I no longer have a friend by the name of İskender."

70

Rudi had engrossed her whole being so much that she could no longer tell how much she missed him. Yearning had become an integral part of her life, permanently nestled down in the most vulnerable part of her heart like a chronically bleeding wound. There were times when she thought it no longer hurt, only to cringe in unbearable pain a second later and start thinking of Rudi again, unable to give her mind a rest for days on end. This morning she had woken up with Rudi on her mind again and for the last couple of hours could concentrate on nothing but Rudi.

"It is Aziz *Bey* on the phone, madam."

It was February 14, and Aziz had forgotten to wish her a happy Valentine's Day before he had left for the office. He ought to be calling to do just that. She went into the study.

"Hello?"

"I have excellent news, *ma petite*. Budapest is liberated! The siege is over. The Russians have thrown out the Nazis."

She could not believe her ears. What was he saying? Did he say what she heard? Were her prayers finally answered? God! Thank God! At long last! "Thank God," she mumbled. "Thank you, God! Thank you," she shouted, bursting into a laugh. "Thank you, Aziz. Thank you." She hung up the phone and ran to the kitchen, laughing. "Asiye *Hanım!* Asiye *Hanım!* We're free. We're all free. Budapest is liberated. Hungary is liberated."

"What happened, madam?"

"The siege is over, Asiye *Hanım*. The siege is over. The Russians threw out the Nazis. My brother is free. *Öcsi* is free." She flung her arms around Asiye *Hanım*. "My mother is free. We're all free. It's all over. No more yearning." Her whole body shook as she cried and laughed by turns. She ran back to Aziz's study. She had to call Anastasia. She had to call Haldun, Ayla, Mehpare *Hanım*, Necla, Sema ... She had to make the whole world hear about her liberation. She was free. They were all free. Slavery was over. She could not believe it. "No more yearning, no more yearning," she kept repeating, as if to make herself believe that all that was happening was not a dream. She would finally, after all these years, see her country, her beloved Budapest. She would see Károly, Rudi, her mother, her home, her lilac trees, the Danube, Balatonfüred ... Balatonfüred! The picnic ... the first time she rode a motorcycle.

> *Rudi had followed her.*
> *"What happened?" he asked, looking somewhat worried.*
> *"I fell down."*
> *"Are you all right?"*
> *"Yes. Yes, I'm all right. But ... you shouldn't have left me."*
> *"I didn't leave you. I'm right here, aren't I?" He pouted, imitating Alex's sulking face. Holding her chin, he pulled her closer. "I'm right here next to you," he repeated most tenderly. Then he took her in his arms as if trying to calm down a frightened little child. Alex felt her heart melt. God, he was so strong. She wished they could stay like that forever, for all eternity.*

It was eighteen years ago, eighteen long years of suffering. Suddenly, with a great sob, she broke into tears. She had wasted all those years; she had wasted her life. "Stop crying, Alex," she scolded herself. "Cry no more. You should smile now. You'll soon reunite with your loved ones. Life is beginning now. You're not yet in the *Csárdás* of your life." She could not believe it. At long last ... at long last, she would see Rudi. She wiped away her tears and smiled. Yes, she could, at long last, smile.

February 2006
Istanbul

It had been nine months since Rüya had started writing the Second Act, which seemed to be going nowhere. It was as if she were trapped within the confines of Mami's inner world where she herself had become a prisoner. Like her, Rüya started to look at the world with blinkers. Surely, this could not be all there was to the Second Act. She should break the walls of Alex's world. She should look into what was happening in Károly's life. Was *Öcsi* only a mutinous painter, a crazy artist whose paintings could not even earn him a living, a free-spirited rebel who had turned his back on his family to be with the love of his life, causing much suffering to his mother? Was his role in Mami's life as limited as this? Was this all the place he deserved to have in this story?

The Second Act is being played elsewhere, Rüya. Wake up, girl! Open your eyes! Perhaps it's not Alex but Károly whose life story is worth telling. Perhaps you should write about him. Perhaps it's him who deserves all this space.

She did not want to believe it, but Mami's rhapsody was incomplete. You're forcing it, Rüya. Give up! Your reader knows what happened in Hungary after the war. There's no hope. There's no hope for Alex. There's no *Csárdás* in her life. There's no liberation for her. No happy ending. Her story ends here.

With a sudden urge, she opened the file named "Third Act," which she had started to write on her computer this morning. She had not gone further than its heading yet.

A HUNGARIAN RHAPSODY
A Novel in Three Acts
Act Three

Csárdás, the third and final part of the rhapsody,
is another realm where emotions soar to their climax.

She deleted it. A novel in three acts that did not have a third act. A broken rhapsody that did not have a *Csárdás*. Was that possible? It had to be. Our lives are not novels, Rüya. Real lives have unhappy endings even though novels might not accept them.

Her index finger was still trembling on the Delete button on the keyboard. This time, she had opened the window she had named "A Hungarian Rhapsody" and selected the file of "Version 12" – everything she had been working on for the last year and a half. Delete them all, Rüya. It is not worth going through all this suffering for a drop of happiness, for some non-existent happiness that has no hope of becoming reality. Why should there be a happy ending anyway, or even the hope of a happy ending, a flash promising the ultimate bliss, a tiny flicker, a reverie, a dream? Delete it all!

Was she to throw away all her work? Yes, she was. Whether you want to believe it or not, Rüya, your Mami had lived a dull life, a life with no lustrous ending, a life that had started brilliantly but lost all its meaning through all that suffering towards an insipidly ordinary finale. As a matter of fact it is very much like *your* life, Rüya. Delete all that you have written so far. It was so easy to erase a novel. Unfortunately, lives could not be erased and rewritten as easily as that.

"I give up writing."

Over the cacophony of voices rising from the group around the table, she heard a comment that sent her blood rushing to her temples:

"I think I've reached a point where I'm old enough to act in a simple love story."

She was treading her way between the chairs and the wall to reach her seat. Without turning her head around, she asked, "So you think it's a simple love story, do you?" As she turned around to sit down and saw the person to whom she had addressed her question, an uneasy feeling grabbed her stomach. No! Please, no. It can't be him. It can't be Paul Brechon. The Paul Brechon she adored. The famous actor who, to her great amazement, had accepted the role of Rudolf Takács.

"Well, it is a love story, is it not?" she heard Paul ask challengingly. "And yes, I do think it's a simple love story."

"Let me introduce you," Michael intervened. " Rüya Nevres, the author of A Hungarian Rhapsody. *And Paul Brechon."*

Rüya suddenly opened her eyes. Was it a dream? It was so real though. She raised her head, which had fallen on the keyboard. She must have fallen asleep in front of her computer. In panic, she tried to turn on the sleeping screen. Did she delete the file? No! Please, no. Please be there. She had to go on writing. She should not give up. She just could not.

About The Author

Neslihan Stamboli is Turkish and Hungarian by birth, Italian by heart and English by formation. Her love of letters was not love at first sight. It took her a degree in finance, a brief career in banking, another degree in French Literature from the University of London and an attempt to study psychology, together with years of translation (and with three marriages and a daughter into the bargain) before she wrote her first book. *White*, portraying a contemporary psychological approach to Samkhya philosophy, was published in 2007. *Rüya*, an epic novel, followed suit in three volumes: *Broken Rhapsody*, *A Retake on War* and *Csardas*.

Made in the USA
Middletown, DE
13 October 2015